Blood on the Beanstalk

The room was one of the High Frontier's finest—luxuriously appointed and quite large by up-Stalk standards. The low, slanted ceiling and one wall were part of the outer hotel dome and were partially made of a curved sheet of transplas rather than titanium steel. That was no digitally projected image of the Earth, impossibly blue and white, suspended in the blackness directly overhead, but the real thing. The Beanstalk was a thread-slender dark scratch across the Earth's face, vanishing into her center.

The room was bathed in Earthlight, ethereal and beautiful. That made what the light revealed, somehow, that much more horrific.

There was blood everywhere, including on the transplas ceiling directly above the large, square bed. The bed itself—which rose only half a meter above the floor and was covered by what looked like violet silk sheets—was crumpled, burned, and soggy with blood, and there was a pool of the stuff on the floor alongside it…

An

Novel

Free Fall

by William H. Keith

Fantasy Flight Publishing, Inc.

To Brea, who took me into the future.

Paperback edition published in 2011.
Printed in the United States of America.

Cover illustration by Remko Troost.

ISBN: 978-1-61661-097-5

Fantasy Flight Publishing, Inc.
1975 West County Road B2
Roseville, MN 55113
USA

FREE FALL

Chapter One

Day 1

I knew where I'd find the damned *gilún* even before I pinged his PAD. His secretary popped up on my PAD with Flint's lopsided grin and said, "Hey, Fish. I'm out of service right now. But you can leave a message…if you want."

I didn't bother. Like I said, I knew where the idiot was going to be.

A thin, warm drizzle was falling through air so humid I felt like I was drowning. I put my PAD away and looked around. Buildings towered like canyon walls on all sides, some alive with animated graphics fifty meters high, most of them lit with neon and holo-ads. It was well past midnight, but even in daytime the sun rarely made it to the streets this deep in the city. Down here, the illumination came from the pulsing LED light displays and animated projections no matter what time it was.

And it was *noisy*. Wall-to-wall people in a bustling, cacophonous mass babbled away in Spanish, Spanglish, English, Chinese, Arabic, Russian, Japanese, and a hundred other languages and dialects. Most of the street front displays were accompanied by their own entrainment frequencies, a throbbing, pounding thunder of noise that you felt more than heard, overlaid by soundtracks promising everything from new bodies to condohabs on the Moon. I dialed up my filters and slogged ahead, tuning most of the racket out. I wasn't here for the shopping.

The city of New Angeles is *big*, almost sixty thousand square kilometers tucked in between the coast and the Andes, from the Guayaquil District to Esmeraldas, and following the Guayllabamba Valley east through the *Andes del Oeste* to the international border at Quito. They say over a billion people live here, and I don't doubt it. It's big, it's sprawling, it's noisy, it's crooked as a politician's view of life, and, unfortunately, it's home. *Some*day I'll retire and ride the Beanstalk one last time up to Heinlein.

Someday can't come soon enough.

A police drone hovered above the street on whining tilt-jets, but the jostling crowds around me ignored it. Tommy Liu's Diner was a hole-in-the-wall just ahead, a seedy little sitsleazy not far from Levy U., tucked between a bioelectronics resale mart and Happy Trick's Recreational Emporium.

I felt the entrance try to deduct an entrance fee from my balance as I stepped through the heavy door into drugged smoke and darkness, but my credaccount blocked it. This visit wasn't exactly line-of-duty, but it wasn't a social call either. The doorsec bouncer was an Adonis G-mod named Fred, a guy who looked like he bench-pressed airbuses for fun. He was slouched in his armored booth, hunched over the backscatter screen. His eyes widened a bit when he saw the hand cannon hidden under my jacket, but then he saw the holo number projected by my badge and the ping-back from my electronic ID and waved me through the next set of doors with an indifferent sneer.

This joint is so cheap the servers are real humans, and there are cubes in the back where they'll serve you other things than crappy sandwiches or hard liquor if your balance can swing it. Nothing wrong with the place, mind you. It's popular with the noir set. You know the look—kids, mostly, shocking their parents by wearing the fashions of a couple of centuries ago. There were lots of shabby trench coats and old-fashioned fringe skirts in the joint. I even saw a couple of *ties*.

At least the hostess was a bioroid, one of the older Giselle models, I thought, judging from the top-heavy carriage and the blank expression.

"Hello there…*Rick*," she said, putting all the sultry come-hitherness into my name her cyberware could manage as she plucked it from my e-ID. "What's your pleasure toni—"

She stopped in mid-sentence, frozen for an uncomfortable moment. Then a new voice, a *man*'s voice, came from those synthetically wet lips. "Captain Harrison," the voice said. "Welcome to Tommy's. Is there a problem?"

"No problem, Tommy," I replied easily, glancing past her shoulder into the crowd beyond. "Just looking for someone."

"Help yourself. But if things get rough, take it outside, will ya? That last little misunderstanding cost me a bundle."

In twelve years on the Force, I'd never actually met Tommy. Hell, he didn't even live in New Angeles, which was why his bioroid hostess was channeling his voice—an apparent personal upgrade to the Giselle model, as it was something I'd never heard a bioroid do before. Tommy's real name was Sydney Rodriguez and his address was in the Vegas Tower, up on the thousandth-and-something floor somewhere. He worked for a franchise run by Shanghaicorp, which meant he was up to here with the tri-mafs, but that wasn't *my* concern.

I slipped past the bioroid, who'd frozen into immobility when Tommy stepped in. She seemed to relax a moment later, shrugging back into character, as it were, but she ignored me, focusing her gynoid interest on a rumpled-looking noir set streetbanger who'd walked in behind me.

Tapping in Flint's number, I used my PAD to pull up a locator. The arrow flashed and pointed *that* way, giving a distance of fifteen point one meters. Picking my way down three steps into the greasy near-darkness, I followed the pointer.

Tommy had a full house this evening. Music throbbed from ceiling and floors—BluDeth, I thought it was, though I wasn't much for classics. You need enhancements to even hear some of that stuff, much less sort it out from raw noise.

I found Flint alone at a table, a half-empty bottle of Moonwalker and a dirty glass in front of him. The guy looked a bit noir himself, with that antique trench coat of his. He didn't even look up as I walked up behind him. "Evening, Fish," he said. The words were slurred a bit, and I could tell I'd probably already lost him. Poor bastard.

"It's morning," I told him. "Mind if I join you?"

A shrug was as much of an answer as I was going to get. I took a seat as a blond waitress wearing green-glowing stilettos and a matching skinsuit and garterpouch that didn't cover a damn thing came to see what I was drinking.

"Ginger ale," I told her. "With lime."

An animated tattoo set off fireworks across her chest, but her bored expression somewhat ruined the effect. She gave me a sour "so what are you doing here?" look, shrugged, which did delightful things to her upper charms, and said, "You're the boss."

As she sashayed off, I reached out and snapped my fingers in front of Flint's nose, pulling his alchie-fuzzed attention away from the waitress's highly mobile glutes and back to my face.

"We have a job for you, Raymond. Hey! Are you in there?"

"Nobody home, Fish," he replied, and he took a deep chug from his glass, draining it. "Get y'self another…another… wossname." He was having trouble focusing.

"Don't call me that," I said.

"Call you what?"

"'Fish.'"

He smirked as he poured himself another glass, filling it almost to the rim. "You're the NAPD's gallant Captain of Detectives, right? That's COD. Cod's a fish, y'know? Cold-water fish. Swims with the pack. Or it *did*, back before the oceans died..."

"Yeah, but you yahoos don't usually call me that to my face. What happened to 'Captain Harrison'?"

"Dunno. Ain't seen him...ain't seen him since the War..."

This wasn't going to get us anywhere.

"So what's the problem, Ray? The memories again?" I'd seen Flint like this before, way too many times, and I was getting damned sick of it.

"Ain't got no memories," he said, taking another drink. "Not now. Tha's why I'm *here*, right? An' not...an' not chasing damned slimeball perps through rathole sewers on the stinkin' ass-side of this damn frag-hole of a mega...a megapo... city..."

Raymond Flint was a burnout. There were enough of them around; ex-soldiers, former Marines, one-time Striker pilots who wondered why they were alive when the others weren't. And then there was the matter of the girl...some old playmate who'd distracted him long enough to get a buddy killed.

I knew because I'd been on Mars with him. I'd known him during the War—been in the same Striker unit, the 308th. We'd chewed a lot of the same ocher sand, and five years later we'd both ended up in the NAPD. We'd been tight. He'd helped me pull my life together after Nina ditched me.

Yeah, sure, Flint had been through hell, but, damn it, who hadn't? He needed to square himself away and focus on the now, stop reliving the nightmare, stop picking at the scab.

"You know, Ray," I told him with measured words, "if you crawl back inside that fragging bottle, we're washed. I swear, I'll scratch you from the roster. I can't use a detective who can't see past his next drink."

"Yes, mother," he replied, and took another swallow.

"I mean it. You're one of the best detectives on my P.I. list. But you're fragging useless to the Force like *this*."

"An' what do I care about the Force?" He turned his head and looked at me through bleary eyes. "Hell, what's the Force to *you*?"

He had me there. For years, now, I'd been planning on quitting the NAPD and setting up on my own—the Harrison Private Detection Agency. Had a nice ring to it, y'know? New Angeles law says that a P.I. has to have police experience to buy his license, and I'd had twelve years on the NAPD so far, and I was sick to death of the damned politics.

The hell with retirement. I was ready to set up on my own.

But then I would look at a freelance loser like Raymond Flint, and I would start thinking that maybe having the job security of the Force wasn't such a bad thing after all.

"The Force," I told him, "is a steady credaccount deposit ticket. And every once in a while, it's a way to feel like you're good for something, that you make a difference. You feel some self-respect and maybe a bit of dignity. More than you're gonna find inside that bottle, anyway."

"Blaine tell you that?"

Frag. Louis Blaine was one of the Department's *wunderkind*, a top-notch Force detective…but he was right there in the trimaf's hip pocket and everyone knew it—the best cop money could buy. Self-respect and dignity. Right…

"We're not talking about him," I said. "We're talking about *you*…and whether or not I'm going to have to pull your license."

"You can't. P.I.'s aren't licensed by the Force. Y'need… you'd need a court order. And show cause."

Even drunk the guy was pretty sharp. I'd thought maybe I could rattle him.

"So? If I don't send any more cases your way, what are you gonna do? Skip traces and deadbeat dads?"

The waitress returned with my drink. I waved my hand over the reader clipped to her wrist, then popped her a fifty percent tip in scrip. She looked a little less bored after that, and gave me a salacious wink as she made the folding stuff vanish into her pouch. "Thanks, Slick," she said. She showed me the tip of her tongue and the fireworks on her chest got a bit more exuberant. "Anything else I can do for you?"

"Don't have time tonight to find out right now, honey." I turned back to Flint as she left. "I'm serious, Ray. This is *it*. I won't cover for you anymore, and I won't send you any more cases, not if you let me down again."

It looked like whatever brain cells he still had alive behind those haunted eyes were choosing up sides. "A new case, huh?" He wiped his mouth with the back of a hand. "So…whatcha got, anyway?"

"Some corp ristie or other got himself fried," I said with a shrug. "Mining laser, sounds like. Helluva mess, and the Feds are going to be interested. I need someone on the crime scene. Someone I can trust."

"Yeah? Where's the scene?"

I hesitated. This was where I could lose him, I knew.

But I wasn't going to lie. "High Frontier Hotel. Challenger Planetoid."

He blinked. The warring brain cells had at it for a few more seconds, and then one side charged the barricades, planted the flag, and declared victory. "On top of the fraggin' *Beanstalk*? No, Fish. Uh-uh."

"Ray—"

"Get yourself another private dick." When I started to protest he held up a hand. "I *mean* it. I 'prish…I 'ppreciate all the stuff you've done for me, Rick. I do. But…but you know what that damned place…does to me. *Every fraggin' time*."

"If that's the way you want it, Ray." I waited, but he didn't reply. I drained my own glass, slammed it on the table, then stood. "Look at you. The hotshot Striker pilot. Suicide by whiskey. I have no patience with burnouts who hide from life in a bottle, Ray. I'm tellin' you, this is it."

"Yah. Nice knowin' ya, Fish."

There wasn't a damned thing I could do for him.

"You're an alcoholic, Flint," I told him. "You need help."

"Alcoholic...workaholic...what's the difference?"

That made me mad. I clenched my fist and, so help me, I was *that* close to putting the poor, sick bastard down, putting him down *hard*. For an angry moment, I was looking into Nina's eyes again as she called me an addict and a workaholic and told me to get out of her life. But he just sat there, staring straight ahead with both hands locked around the glass.

I don't kick puppies, small kids, or burned-out drunks. I like to think I have *some* self-control left. And maybe just a tattered shred or two of self-respect.

So I made myself relax my fists, made myself turn and walk away. Flint was bent over on the table, now, his head in his arms, and in the dim, blue light scattering through the joint, it looked like his shoulders were shaking.

Screw him. I wasn't his mother. *Mother* was not in my job description. I shook my head and left, the door trying again to deduct an entrance fee as I passed the house bouncer.

Outside, the police drone was still there. It rotated, one of its eyes extending as it gave me a closer look. I tipped it a casual, one-fingered salute and it lost interest, drifting away over the crowd. The drizzle had turned to a steady, steaming rain, acid enough to melt the garbage in the street. I let my smartslick unfold to cover my head, back, and shoulders, and splashed back to my car.

A ragged pack of streetbangers squabbled and scrabbled over something in an alley. A couple of noiries who looked like they'd just stepped out of an old-fashioned black-and-white flatfilm haggled with a street vender. Other venders competed with one another with shouted promises. From somewhere overhead, a voice big enough to be the Voice of God summoned the faithful: "*Opportunity! A chance for a new start! A new life! The Martian Colony! Opportunity! A chance...*"

Zero-three-fragging-hundred; didn't this damned city ever sleep?

So Ray Flint was out. Who was I going to send now?

The Department has two kinds of detectives on tap—the badges and the P.I.'s. Badges are cops, police detectives on the Force roster, but every now and then we'll bring in a private eye. The Commissioner liked Flint, said he gave us "an outside view." I was going to have to tell her that our outside view had turned into a close-up of the gutter.

Who else was there on tap? As Captain of Detectives, I had the roster memorized. Floyd and Caprice were both up in Heinlein working a case. Blaine and Chu were on the Moon, too, chasing down megacorp scandals and threats of miners' strikes, and I wondered again what idiot had decided the Quito Accord was a good idea. Gomez...sick leave. Beckman...unavailable, tracking down a bounty in the Eastside Tenements. Donovan... testifying in court, probably for the rest of the week. Byron... Imahara...Hyneman...all of them, badges and P.I.'s both, assigned to other cases or vanished off the radar.

Well, I told myself, *you wanted to get out from behind your desk...*

A quartet of bangers was working over my Wuhan cruiser when I got there, but they scattered at my approach, vanishing into the faceless crowd. Their spray paint wouldn't stick to the mirror-black finish, of course; it was already washing off in the steady rain. The scratches and shiv-gouges would melt out when I put some current through the body, though I was tempted to leave them. They gave the car a homey, lived-in look that made it just a bit less conspicuous, at least in *this* part of town.

My thumbprint opened the gull-wing door and powered up

the engine. I brought up the holoconsole and switched on the takeoff alert, flashing strobes, and warning chirp, and unfolded the tilt-jets. If the crowd was concerned about my jet wash, they didn't show it, so I gunned the throttle and drifted skyward on a shrill whine.

"You are entering flight-control restricted airspace," the Wuhan's sexy voice told me. Well, *duh*. I was in the middle of New Angeles. It was *all* FCRA, even for hoppers and backpack fliers. "Please state your destination and relinquish manual control."

"Back to the barn," I told it. And I leaned back in the seat to catch some shut-eye.

"Engaging City Flight Control," the Wuhan said in honey tones. "Destination: New Angeles Police Department, Rooftop Garage."

City Flight Control gave me a fairly smooth flight. Traffic was thick at low altitudes, as usual, and it was a couple hours before my car woke me up and I saw the five-hundred-story blue-green tower of the NAPD shouldering out of the mist and neon glow ahead. A trio of police security drones gave me a once-over on approach and escorted me to the roof pad. I let the car park itself while I checked in through rooftop security and escalated down to the bullpen.

Fuentes had the desk watch. "*Que pasa*, Cap?" he asked as I thumbed the log-in screen.

"Don't ask," I told him. "One of those days." My PAD gave a sharp and peremptory chirp, and I cocked an eyebrow at him. "See what I mean?"

I didn't bother to unfold the screen. "Harrison," I said.

"I know who it is," a hard voice said. "I saw your ping when you entered the building. Report to my office immediately."

"On my way."

The Commissioner didn't like to be kept waiting.

Her office was on the upper Admin level behind a labyrinth of secretaries and admin assistants. Chen Mai Dawn was drop-dead gorgeous and athletically lean, pretty ordinary in a town where you can buy a sexy new body as easily as a cheap suit, and the DFM in her rooftop parking space suggested she had the credaccount to do it.

I didn't bother asking what she was doing at the office at… God. Almost six in the morning? It was possible she'd been in her office all night. No one in the Department kept sane hours, not in New Angeles, and that extended all the way to the top.

"So, Harrison," she said as I walked into her inner sanctum, "you find Flint?"

"He's…unavailable for the case," I said. Yeah, even now, I was holding back, protecting him. A word from me now and he'd never work for the Department again. I didn't like the role of executioner.

Dawn reached for an open pack of self-lighting licorice-flavored cigarettes on her cluttered desk, pulled one from the package with her lips, and puffed it alight. Definitely the old-fashioned type, despite the G-mod chassis. She had zero tolerance for shiny looks with sub-optimal performance.

"He's drunk, isn't he?" When I didn't answer, she went on. "Who else do you have for the assignment?"

"Me," I replied.

Her G-mod perfect eyebrows went up. "The Department's not paying you for street work, Harrison."

"And I'm not a house mouse, Commissioner."

"You covering for your old military buddy? Comrades-in-arms, call of duty, all that?"

"Nuh-uh. I need to get out from behind the desk, is all. And we're stretched damned thin. Every damned one of my assets is either on a case or OU." Otherwise unavailable.

"We're *always* stretched thin on assets, Harrison." She considered me for a sour moment from within her smoke cloud, then flicked a bit of ash from her 'ret into the desk disposal. "I'm going to approve this, because you're my best forspec.

And I need the best on this one."

"Why? Something forensics-intensive on this one?"

For answer, she touched her keypad and the empty wall behind her turned into a floor-to-ceiling vidscreen, high-def, like looking into another room right next door, except that Dawn's office was eat-off-the-carpet clean; the vid image looked like the inside of a slaughterhouse. There was even blood on the walls and ceiling.

Low-G can do that. The body, about half of it on the blood-saturated bed and the rest scattered around the room, had been taken apart by something big and hot.

"Who is it?" I frowned, then corrected myself. "Who was it?"

"Roger Mayhurst Dow. Lawyer…and political lobbyist."

"Um. For whom?"

"Humanity Labor."

"Frag."

Them again. I could understand now why the Commissioner wanted a good forensics specialist up there. If Humanity Labor was involved, we were going to need to dot every I and cross every T, because they'd slap you with a lawsuit just for looking at them funny. Litigious bastards.

"Looks like it was personal," I said. "Or someone *really* doesn't like lawyers."

She tapped out something on her keyboard, and the image on the screen swung to the right, angled down, and zoomed in on something that looked like a military BFG, but wasn't. Military hardware, even of the Big Fraggin' Gun variety, tends to be a tad more discriminating.

I leaned forward to read the fine print embossed on the murder weapon's muzzle. "Alpha Prospecting," I read aloud. It was as I'd thought. "A mining laser."

"Huong-Zhen regolith beam laser tunneler, Mark V, Mod 2," Dawn told me in clipped, precise tones. "Man-portable,

100-kilowatt throughput. Serial number identifies it as one reported missing from Alpha Prospecting two days ago."

"So we're looking for a disgruntled miner," I said. I frowned. "Or a disgruntled mining *clone*..."

"Maybe. But it took some sophisticated electronics knowledge to bypass Beanstalk security on this one. How the hell did someone smuggle a mining laser up there into an orange-sec zone? Especially if he was a clone?" She tapped the side of her neck. "Tracking tag."

"So the miner had help?"

"Had to be. Someone with some very serious hacking skills."

"Great. That narrows it down to...what? Maybe five, six million jack-hackers in Earthside New Angeles alone? A few thousand more in Heinlein?"

She click-clacked out another combination of characters on her keyboard. "It's making us look very carefully at one in particular..."

The bloody crime scene vanished, replaced by a larger-than-life-sized image of a kid.

I say "kid," but his bio said he was twenty-two. He looked young, though, with the sullen expression and the casual BDSM leatherwear of the self-made anti-authoritarian rebel. Height one-eighty, green hair, a face full of piercings. He wore eyeglasses, but I knew his vision was G-mod perfect, and the glasses were projection screens for some fairly sophisticated personal electronics.

Yeah, I knew Ji Reilly—"Noise," as he preferred to be called. Boy genius, probably the hack behind the Stuckey IT incident a couple of years back, but no one could ever prove it. I'd been on that case—a slick identity theft that had made half a million dollars vanish from a fat business account with no IP trace and no electron trails. The funny thing was that Reilly had owed a bundle to the 14K...and suddenly he was real cozy with them, pulling down an estimated 5k a month as a software consultant. A lot of us saw the connection, but we couldn't find enough to make charges stick.

"We have an APB out to bring him in for questioning," Dawn told me. "He recently took on a year-long contract with Melange Mining and we don't know why. Usually, he's a freelancer, doesn't like the big corps."

"Oh, he doesn't mind the corps," I said. "He just sees them as targets."

"Well, he's working for Melange now," the Commissioner said. "And they have no reason to love anyone who wants to abolish the use of androids."

"They sure as hell won't want to see anti-clone legislation go down in D.C."

"Exactly." She switched off Reilly's image and turned to face me. "Listen hard, Harrison. The Clone Riots last year left everybody on edge, and there were those rumors last month about android conspiracies. The damned city's about ready to explode. The Feds are watching, and they're just itching to invoke the Accord. If Mayor Wells is forced to declare martial law, the Feds are going to be on our tails like sand at the beach. You follow me?"

"Yeah. A little too well."

"I want this kept quiet. If the news-nosies get wind of this, there could be panic and maybe more dead clones, and we definitely don't need that right now. If a nosie hits you, it's strictly 'no comment.' Got it?"

"Yes, ma'am." She didn't say so, but I knew she was thinking about Lily Lockwell in particular. Damn news-nosie.

"Mayor Wells is already riding me about this one. When the mayor's not happy, *I'm* not happy. And when *I'm* not happy—"

"I've got the picture, Commissioner. Silent running it is." I was accessing the Commissioner's evidence files, downloading the vid she'd just shown me.

"Find me a triggerman," she said, "and get me hard evidence, something that'll stand up in court. We don't want Humanity Labor suing the city because we botched the investigation."

"I'm on it." I looked at my wrist, pressing the skin at the base of my palm to make the time visible. "I'll vid you from the crime scene."

"I want a conviction, Harrison. And I do *not* want more dead clones in the streets."

"Got it."

And I headed downstairs to pick up a club.

Chapter Two

Day 1

I wouldn't have to pack anything. All I needed was to check out a club from the gear locker. Officially, it's a standard NAPD-issue thumb-locked evidence kit, but we call it the "club," for CLB—Crime Lab in a Box. I was going to need it at that bloody crime scene.

My black Wuhan took me northeast, climbing for altitude past the domed sprawl of the Blue Sun Stadium and angling north toward the skyward stab of the Bradbury Tower arcologies. The rain had cleared in the past hour, replaced by a weak morning sun filtering through a toxic haze. I could just make out the slate grey expanse of the ocean in the distance far off to the right. The Andes, to the east, were still shrouded in bank upon towering bank of clouds.

New Angeles is, with no question whatsoever, the biggest and most populous megapolis on Earth, with hundreds of millions of citizens packed in ten or twelve thousand to the square kilometer, and God alone knows how many *disenfrancistos*, streetbangers, sewer rats, under-city scavengers, clones, and bioroids. Downtown takes up a quarter of what used to be the sovereign nation of Ecuador, and if not for hoppers and tube-levs, getting around town would take days.

Sometimes even air travel is slow. New Angeles Air Traffic Control was routing me around to the west with an estimated flight time of one hour. At first I tried to catch up on a bit more sleep, but I was already into full-blown Case Mode, going over the information the Commissioner had given me in my head and on my PAD.

I'd fanned open the display on my Palm Access Device and pulled down the history. Human First was arguably the largest of several hundred underground organizations devoted to doing away with clones and bioroids, and that was just here in the New Angeles area. Their front company—Humanity Labor—the workers' centers, the workers' comp, health insurance companies, even a few religious institutions, all felt that life would be a lot better if the vats and the bioroid assembly lines were all shut down.

And that was a real problem, for New Angeles in particular. Our legal jurisdiction extended all the way up-Stalk to Heinlein, and that meant the helium-3 mining consortia. Bioroids—android and gynoid robots—weren't so much of a problem up there, but clones were. The miners' union didn't like them because they replaced real humans in the workforce; the management of big mining corps, like Melange, loved them because it was cheaper to buy a few thousand Jinteki clones and work them to death—sorry, *fully utilize proprietary assets*—than it was to hire humans and pay for their workers' comp.

Me, I can't say I like the way clones are treated—they're *human*, damn it, no matter what their genomic mods and conditioning—but I also know there isn't anything I, personally, can do about it. That ancient adage about not being able to fight city hall went double for the big megacorps like Jinteki, or the congresscritters they bought and sold like commodities on the NYSE.

I didn't much care one way or the other whether they decided to stop production or not, but then my job wasn't being threatened by Jinteki worker clones or the latest in AI-imprinted hardware out of Haas-Bioroid. The human simulants I knew personally were all decent sorts—better behaved than most people of my acquaintance. I tend to be pretty apolitical myself, but so far as I could see, it was the androids—a catch-all term for both robotic bioroids and the so-called clones—that were getting the raw end of the deal, not the other way around.

The Commissioner had been dead right about one thing: the riots last year had been very nasty. Hundreds of clones had been killed, several bioroids had been rather messily disassembled, and a lot of full-humans had been killed or hurt. The mayor had *just* managed to avoid calling in the Feds. If New Angelinos agree on *anything*—which is saying one hell of a lot—it's on the need to keep the Feds the hell out of our business. They don't like it that we have the Beanstalk, and for thirty years they've been looking for any excuse to move in and appropriate it and the golden cash flow cascading down-Stalk.

And now a ristie—the word came from "aristocrat" and referred to any of the ultra-rich denizens on the tops of their klick-high arcologies—had been offed in a spectacularly messy fashion, and *some* of the evidence, at least, pointed to a miner... and *that* almost certainly meant a clone.

Not good.

I needed to get up-Stalk fast.

I'd given some thought to the possibility of dropshipping up-Stalk—it would be a little faster than a beanpod—but decided I didn't want another lecture from the Commissioner about Department budgets and my sacred responsibility to the taxpayers. A beanpod would get me there quickly enough.

First, though, I had to get to The Root.

I parked in the tower garage in Quevedo at the western foot of the mountains, and took the elevator down to the tube-lev

Metro. With my evidence kit in hand, I electronically flashed my badge to avoid baring all for the backscatter screening, and was ushered through to the main concourse, where a couple thousand people wandered through a hall the size of the Blue Sun Stadium, hunting for baggage, dragging along screaming children, occasionally reuniting in enthusiastic hugs, and raising a dull roar of background noise that constantly echoed throughout the vast chamber, despite the sonic suppressors.

I downloaded my ticket into my PAD and followed a holographic yellow light glowing in the air overhead to find my platform. The car was already unpleasantly crowded when I stepped aboard—I'm mildly claustrophobic in crowds, but I can usually ignore it. I felt the little bounce under my foot as the mag-levs adjusted to my weight. The ticket told me I was in seat 20A, and it only took a few moments to convince a drugged-out tourist that he was in my seat, and would he like to move himself or be moved, now?

A few seconds later, a holographic attendant reminded us all to stay in our seats and buckle our seatbelts, as serious injury could result under acceleration if we did not do so, and that the New Angeles Transit Authority could accept no responsibility for personal injuries if we did not follow the rules.

And then another guy as big as me was sitting in my lap… or at least that was the way it felt as we entered the vacuum and accelerated at two gravities.

The two-G acceleration lasted just eight and a half seconds, and then the mag-lev train was hurtling through hard vacuum a kilometer or more beneath the surface at 170 meters per second. There were no windows, of course—there's nothing to see outside in a tube-lev tunnel, after all—and the kilometers passed in utter silence…well, silent except for the squalling baby in 19B, and the loudly arguing couple somewhere in the back. I pulled the morning edition of the *New Angeles Sol* from my seat dispenser. It was a sheet of silk-fine, carbon-weave cloth when

I tugged it free, but it turned rigid in a second or two, the dark surface coming alive with images and print. I thumb-flipped through the first dozen pages or so, looking for news about the Dow murder.

Nothing yet, thank God.

Cardinal Reese, I noticed, had given a thoroughly inflammatory homily last night as a guest speaker at the Church of St. Theresa on the evils of "soulless android simulants" in today's society...and Human First was calling for the elimination of miner clones to reduce the high unemployment rate among *real* people. Same-ol', same-ol'. The page-one vid of Reese showed him gesticulating repeatedly and angrily, his face florid and impassioned. I considered popping in an earpiece to hear the text of his sermon, but thought better of it. I don't know Who's running the universe...but I seriously doubt that Cardinal Reese or the Temple of Sol or any of the rest of them do, either.

I did a search to see if the rag had anything about Roger Dow, but all I came up with was an article on page 121 about how he was due to meet with a delegation of congresscritters at the Carousel Boardrooms tonight, where he would have proposed legislation allowing for the gradual elimination of simulants, starting with the lunar mines.

Judging from what I'd seen on Commissioner Dawn's vid wall, he wasn't going to make that meeting.

I entered a note to myself on my PAD: make sure that those messy remains I'd seen in Dawn's office *were* those of Roger Dow. The first rule of crime scene analysis was to not take anything for granted. A DNA check would prove the victim's identity easily enough, but I'd run that test myself rather than rely on the Space Elevator Authority.

Never assume.

The Dow article, I noticed, carried Lily Lockwell's byline. If she was interested in him, she'd be following up on that planned meeting tonight. I just hoped I could reach the crime scene before she did, and maybe head her off.

After porting the article to my PAD, I dropped the news rag into the recycler pocket, then keyed my PAD's secretary to pull down whatever he could find on one Roger Mayhurst Dow on the Net.

Netpedia had a fairly extensive bio on the guy. Yale Law, class of '21. Married, one wife, one kid. Private law practice out of college, then a Southern California state senator for four years…followed by a stint in the U.S. Senate for six. Lost a bid for re-election, then joined the firm of Marshall, Applewhite, & Dow the following year—one of the big SC lobbying firms. Turned out the "Dow" on the firm letterhead was his father, Roger Mayhurst Dow, Sr., and the family was better than well off. Junior's estimated personal worth was 450 million, mostly in private investments in both commercial spacelines and the Beanstalk. It seemed politics had agreed with him, and the fact that one of Marshall, Applewhite, & Dow's biggest clients was the North American arm of 14K hadn't hurt either.

He'd taken a temporary leave of absence from the firm four months ago in order to go to work for Humanity Labor. That was fairly routine in the lobbying game. Made having private *tête-à-têtes* with senators and representatives seem a bit less rabidly commercial. He was being paid well—*very* well—by Humanity Labor for hobnobbing with government officials and suggesting just how certain laws ought to be worded. He was also the author of a number of passionate Net articles on anti-simulant legislation.

I wondered what he'd really thought. It was anyone's guess whether he actually believed the Humanity Labor party line; give a guy *that* much money and he'll say he believes in Santa Claus and the Tooth Fairy. Hell, he'll swear out an affidavit that he saw both of them consorting with the Easter Bunny.

The tube-lev trip lasted just twenty minutes. A minute before arrival, the translucent attendant reappeared to tell us to stay put and buckled in, and our seats rotated in place so that we were facing back the way we came. Then that invisible, eighty-kilo lummox was sitting in my lap again as we decelerated into the Root. The doors gulled open, and I stepped out into the heart of Cayambe.

Many years ago, the economy of the tiny South American nation of Ecuador was failing. At the same time, the United States government was looking into building a space elevator—the Beanstalk—a structure 70,000 kilometers high including its main facility (the space complex known as Midway) at geo-synchronous orbit, 35,784 kilometers up. They needed a spot smack on the equator to build the thing, and after considering anchoring it to an artificial floating island at sea, they settled on the third-highest mountain in Ecuador, a glacier-clad mountain in exactly the right spot.

The United States purchased 75,000 square kilometers of land from Ecuador for something like a trillion dollars spread over twenty years. That amounted to about one quarter of the country's total area, including most of the coastal plain between the Andes Mountains and the ocean. Quito, two hundred kilo-meters inland, became an international gateway city, still the capital of Ecuador, but also a dwarfed suburb of the sprawling megapolis that had become the city of New Angeles.

The influx of hard credit had saved the country, of course, and created the ground-side link of what eventually became known as the Beanstalk. New Angeles became *the* means of cheap access to space. Cayambe, sixty-four kilometers north-east of Quito, was the Beanstalk's Root.

I rode the elevator up from the tube-lev station, past level upon level of upscale mall boutiques, restaurants, and city ser-vices buried inside the mountain, emerging at last into the brisk, thin openness of the Plaza del Cielo.

As many times as I've gone up-Stalk, the view from the Pla-za never fails to get to me. It's literally breathtaking…though a lot of that is due to the fact that the outside air is so damned thin 4,700 meters above sea level. Older folks have to wear masks when they leave the under-mountain facilities, though it doesn't bother people with Freitas respirocytes in their bloodstreams or the appropriate G-mods to their lungs.

It's the only spot on Earth's equator with a permanent ice cap, though the facility's big helium-3 reactor heats the surrounding air enough to keep the Plaza itself ice-free. North, the main peak of Cayambe rises above the Plaza for another thousand meters, ice-covered and dazzlingly brilliant in the clear, thin air. East, morning sun glints off blue-white ice in a dazzling flare of light; beyond, the ground drops away toward the vast and sprawling Amazonas agroplexes of Sucumbios District and, beyond that, southern Columbia and northern Peru.

I didn't spend much time looking at ice, though. Like any rubbernecking tourist, I tilted my head back and looked...up.

Imagine a tree—with a trunk twenty meters wide and seventy *thousand* kilometers high—planted smack on an equatorial mountaintop at an altitude of 4,700 meters. The Beanstalk had started as a buckyweave strap one meter wide, woven meter by meter by the constructorbots as it was lowered out of the sky all the way down from synchorbit, over 31,000 kilometers overhead.

Nowadays, the structure's main body was as thick as one of its elevator cars was long, with multiple magnetic tracks around the circumference for up- and down-Stalk pods. Dark grey in color, it arrowed from the mountaintop Plaza into an impossibly deep, blue zenith, dwindling up and up and *up* until it vanished from sight.

A beanpod was coming down now, a vertical cigar-shaped vehicle riding a superconducting mag-lev line gently down the Stalk and vanishing into the elaborately domed and tower-proud roof of Earth Station at the center of the Plaza. A moment later, a much larger car descended on a different track—a cargo pod hauling three monster canisters of helium-3.

New Angeles's life blood, all the way down from the Moon.

The sight was...dizzying; the Beanstalk is by far the largest man-made structure ever built, whether measured by height, mass, or volume. At night, even out on the waterfront districts of Manta or Guayaquil, over three hundred kilometers away, you can see the Stalk clearly, a razor-slash of light, laser-beam straight, descending from halfway up the sky to the horizon. New Angelinos are proud of that streak of starlight; we're the only megapolis on Earth to reach all the way up and *really* touch the sky.

The Plaza was crowded today with several hundred people—most of them squeezed together in an angry, gesticulating mass. Several waved crudely lettered signs for the benefit of the media—things like "*NO CLONES,*" "*HUMANS FIRST,*" "*LA TIERRA POR HUMANIDAD,*" and a badly spelled "*CLONS GOT MY JOB.*" The mob appeared to be playing it up for a number of newsies nearby, identifiable by the small, silver monocams each wore over one eye. Several bored-looking yellow jackets—the Beanstalk's security cops—stood off to one side, watching with folded arms and holstered weapons.

Except for the news media and the guards, it didn't look like the demonstration was garnering much attention. Human First pulled this sort of stunt every so often, bringing in a paid mob to make noise and wave signs for the benefit of the next set of newsrag editions. By crowding together that way, the mob looked a lot bigger and more impressive in-vid than it actually was.

Possibly Humanity Labor was trying to set the stage for the planned Congressional summit later. Too bad Dow's death hadn't been announced. It might have saved some of the screaming crowd members sore throats and hoarse voices.

I walked through the high, wide transplas doors of Earth Station's eastern portal. The security gate pinged my badge and let me go through without paying for a ticket...but this time I had to walk through the backscatter arch.

Nobody can avoid getting scanned upon entering the Beanstalk. They checked me out down to the skin with x-rays...then added the ultrasound overlay to make sure I wasn't carrying anything nasty in my stomach or colon.

The New Angeles Transit Authority takes security on Cayambe *very* seriously. Ten years ago, a Martian terrorist managed to get onto a beanpod with three kilos of surgically implanted exotic explosives in his belly. The pod hadn't been damaged—those things are *tough*—but eight passengers had died, and the blast had made a hell of a mess on the first-class pod's dining deck.

I knew. I'd been part of the official response team.

My pod was leaving in thirty minutes. I caught the slidewalk across the Grand Concourse that would take me to the departure platform.

"Rick! Rick Harrison!"

I turned and saw a young woman running toward the slidewalk, elbowing her way through the crowds with consummate and practiced skill. Legs up to here and auburn hair down to there...and as deadly as fifty-eight kilos of antimatter in a leaky containment field.

"Hello, Lily," I said.

Lily Lockwell jumped onto the slidewalk, nearly knocking an elderly Mestizo couple off as she did so.

"Excuse me! Excuse me, please. *¡Perdón!* Rick! What a wonderful surprise! What are *you* doing here?"

She'd been born Lilith Ramón, but taken the alliterative name of Lily Lockwell as a part of her transformation into a high-powered media-star. She was a roving reporter both for the *New Angeles Sol* and for NBN, and her work was syndicated through a dozen satellite network affiliates and twice as many newsrags.

Dawn had warned me about talking with her, warned me to tell her "no comment," but if I told her that, she'd know I was on a case. I decided to give her a little harmless misdirection instead.

"Sightseeing," I replied. "What else?"

"You *never* sightsee, Rick," she told me. "What dug you out from behind your desk?"

"Just checking on a couple of my people," I told her. "We're stretched pretty thin right now."

"So…you going up-Stalk? Or coming down?"

"Up," I admitted.

She brightened. "So am I! We can travel together!"

This I did *not* need. "I don't think so, Lil. Not this time." I patted my PAD hanging in its holster. "I…have some work to catch up on."

"Nonsense! When do we ever have time to see one another? This is perfect!" She took my arm and stepped a little closer. "We could even get a private cabin on a first-class pod. My expense account will stretch that far."

I decided that my safest bet was to go on the offensive. "So why are *you* up-Stalking? Where are you headed?"

She made a face. "Work. What else?"

"That rent-a-mob outside?"

"Nah. There's a big meeting tonight. Carousel Boardrooms. Senator Rivera and Senator Suarez both are coming up with some Angelino bigwigs. Some senators and representatives on the Congressional Oversight Committee on Workers' Issues are subbing in from D.C. Formal dinner, the works."

I grinned. "I think I read something about that."

"I'm touched that you still follow my pieces."

We stepped off the end of the slidewalk. My gate was just ahead.

She brushed a few strands of that glorious auburn hair back from her face. "You know, Rick, I thought by now we could be honest with one another."

"Of *course* we can..."

"Then why are you lying to me?"

"What lying?"

She gestured at the heavy silver case in my hand. "If you're just 'checking up' on a couple of your people, why are you dragging along an NAPD evidence kit?"

Burned. I winced. "They *are* on a case—"

"And have access to NAPD equipment both in Heinlein and on the Stalk. You also have that look."

"Look? What look?"

"The 'I'm on a case' look. Distracted. A million klicks away."

Lily always could read me, damn it. Hell, she can read anybody. It's part of her job description.

But she knew me way too well, both on and off monocam. We'd been lovers for a while—still were, I guess, though finding time to spend together between her career and mine tended to make it a hit-or-miss affair. I'd known her for years—she was one of NBN's brightest crime-reporting stars and we were always running into her during field investigations and at crime scenes. But we'd become close after Nina left me, something to do with that yawning black hole of emptiness I'd been carrying around inside, I suppose. One thing had led to another, and...

Something occurred to me. Reaching down, I pulled my PAD from its thigh holster and thumbed it on. I'd been pinged recently, though I had it set not to alert me. The record was there, though, and included the pinger's ID.

"So," I said easily, "why are *you* lying to *me*?"

"I'm not!"

"Well, not in so many words, no. But that was a very nice act just now, shouting and waving and telling me what a surprise it was to see me."

I showed her my PAD screen. Lily had pinged me thirty-five

minutes ago while I was still on the Metro, then again twenty minutes later while I was out on the Plaza, and, finally, a third time just moments before she'd spotted me on the slidewalk.

"Stalking me?" I asked. "Maybe using a locator app to track me?"

She looked angry…and, believe me, only redheads can put that much pure fury into a glance.

But I didn't let it burn through my armor. "How'd you know I was going to be here, anyway?"

"I checked in with Fuentes at the NAPD front desk, of course. He told me you'd be here. But I wasn't stalking you, for Christ's sake. Don't flatter yourself, Codfish."

"*Don't* call me that." If I ever found out who'd told her about that…

"You're on a case, Rick, and the Commissioner won't give me the time of day."

"And Fuentes isn't supposed to."

"But you *are* on a case, and it's a big one if you're keeping it this quiet. So what's going down? Or up, as the case may be."

"No comment."

"Aw, c'mon, Rick. Off the record?"

"It's not worth my job."

"There's a rumor floating around that the big Congressional summit tonight is going to be called off. Any comment?"

"Nope. Let me know how it turns out."

"Damn you, Rick…"

"I am sorry, babe." I looked into those deep, liquid eyes and decided to relent just a little. "Look, maybe we can talk later."

"You can forget about that private cabin."

"S'okay. It's a short trip. We wouldn't have time to get *real* friendly…"

"Yeah? When did you ever have time for more than a *cuiqui*?" The Andean slang meant what it sounded like.

"You don't have to get nasty."

She turned and fumed off, leaving me by the boarding gate. I admired the rear view for a moment until she was lost again in the crowd, then shrugged and boarded my pod.

She'd get over it. She always did.

A typical passenger pod—the kind without first-class accommodations—is twenty-one meters long and contains three passenger decks, located in the middle and each about five meters wide. Inside the pointed ends, top and bottom, is the environmental gear—air and water tanks, heating and air conditioning units—and the radar for the paraglider ram-chute hidden amidships, just in case something goes wrong. Nothing ever does, of course. Space elevator safety systems are as close to foolproof as it's possible to get.

Each deck held twelve deeply cushioned seats set around the deck's circumference. Opposite the entryway, the wall swelled inward, taking a bite out of the circular deck. That was the deck's restroom, and there was a beverage dispenser located on the outside of the cubicle door.

I found my seat, stowed my evidence kit in a cabin locker, and strapped myself in. Eight of the other seats were occupied—two rather obvious businessmen buried in their PADs, a young noirie couple lost in one another, a soldier in uniform, a mother and her six-year-old child, and a clone in a grey-green Melange Mining uniform jumper. I brought up the time display on my wrist. Not long now.

A few minutes later, another holographic attendant flickered into visibility on the center of the deck, recommending that we stay seated and strapped in whenever possible. The curving, opaque walls all the way around suddenly turned transparent, displaying a three-sixty vid projection relayed from cameras strategically located on the pod's outer hull.

We were already moving up through the open roof of Earth Station and into the brilliant, mountaintop morning light. The broad, circular Plaza del Cielo dropped away rapidly as the feeling of weight slowly increased, until it felt like someone half my weight was sitting in my lap. Seconds later, we were above the highest of Cayambe's ice-shrouded peaks and still accelerating.

We were on our way up-Stalk.

Chapter Three

Day 1

Not everyone can handle heights.

I heard that once, maybe twenty years ago, a beanpod started up-Stalk and they had the deck set to display the view down—nothing but emptiness beneath the passengers' feet—down, down, down all the way to the clouds far below, then the cloud-shadowed mountains below that. One passenger reportedly went into a panic attack, injured two other passengers who tried to help him, then went into cardiac arrest and died. They reversed the pod and brought them back down, of course, but by the time the med-assist personnel arrived, the man was brain dead, beyond the reach of even the best resus-techs.

My fellow passengers seemed to be handling the ascent okay…all, that is, but the soldier. His breath was coming in short, gulping gasps, his eyes were shut tight, and he was gripping the arms of his chair with a white-knuckled ferocity that threatened to peel them back off their mounts.

The wall behind him showed a rapidly deepening blue sky as we punched up through the highest cirrus layers. On the north side of the pod, of course, behind the restroom, the view was blocked by the blur of the Beanstalk itself, but in every other direction you could already see a distinct curvature to the horizon, and sunlight blasted the pod's interior with brilliant intensity.

The kid was whining to his mother about being heavy. It promised to be a long hour.

The soldier, strapped in on the other side of the deck, was a private second class, and the rank chevrons on his black uniform looked so new they squeaked. He couldn't have been over eighteen, and I figured he'd probably just gotten out of Basic. Maybe he was visiting someone up-Stalk, a relative or a girl or someone, while he was on boot leave. I pinged him and his e-ID identified him as Kaminsky, Raul, PV2, and gave a long serial number and no other information. He was breathing so hard, I thought he was going to hyperventilate.

All soldiers have their blood infused with respirocytes during Basic; it turns them into super-soldiers and vastly improves their endurance and physical performance. Even with the technical assist, though, it's still possible to blow off too much carbon dioxide, raise the alkalinity of the blood, and start shutting down blood flow to the brain. Hyperventilation isn't caused by too much oxygen in the blood; it's brought on by too little CO_2.

His eyes were starting to glaze.

"Private Kaminsky!" I snapped, putting my best parade-ground rasp into the name.

I swear, the kid tried to stand at attention while strapped to his seat. "Sir, yes, sir!"

"Are you panicking?"

Another gulp of air. "Sir, no, sir!" But his eyes were open now, and haunted.

"You'd better not panic, soldier. Your buddies are counting on you."

"Sir, yes, sir!"

God *damn* the military, and the way they turn human beings

into robots nowadays. Used to be, a soldier—a *good* soldier—was trained to think for himself. Since Mars, though, the emphasis had been on hammering out every bit of individuality and creating a brain-dead automaton that obeyed orders very well indeed, but who had precious little personal initiative.

"Unstrap your upper seat harness!"

"Sir, yes, *sir*!"

"Lean forward, elbows on your knees!"

"Sir, yes, *sir*!"

"Cup your hands over your nose and mouth…and breathe!"

"Sir, yes, *sir*!" This last was muffled by his hands. His eyes were a little less glassy and unfocused now, though he still looked terrified.

"Where are you going, soldier?"

"Uh…Heinlein, sir."

"That your new duty station?"

"Yes, sir."

The Quito Accord declares both the Beanstalk and the Moon's Heinlein Station to be a part of New Angeles, and over the years some trillions of dollars have flowed down the Stalk and into the city's coffers—not to mention those of the Weyland Consortium and the invisible host of organizations behind *them*: triads, mafias, banks, and investment cartels from all over the world. Even so, the Feds keep a small U.S. garrison there. Memories of the Lunar Insurrection are still raw.

"Coming off boot leave?"

"Yes, sir. Uh…how did you know, sir?"

Good. I had his interest.

"You're traveling ACT—Available Civilian Transportation. If you were being transferred with your unit, you'd be packed into a military dropship right now with sixty other grunts." I grinned at him. "Lucky you. You get to travel luxury class."

"I…I didn't know it would be like *this*."

For a moment, it looked as though the kid was going to panic again. "So…you get to visit your family back home after boot camp?"

"Yes, sir."

"Where's home?"

He actually had to think about that one. "Uh…Mason, Ohio, sir."

I continued to draw him out, asking questions about his family, his pre-Army life, his girlfriend—a girl named Kathi Morena. He had an animated image of her on his upper arm.

Sometimes, in my more philosophical moments, I wonder why people surrender themselves, who they really are, to what other people expect of them.

And after a while, rebreathing his own carbon dioxide as he cupped it in his hands, Raul Kaminsky began to breathe normally.

The clone was standing next to me. I hadn't noticed him cross the deck. "That was very well done, sir." The voice was weak, almost watery. The creature made me uncomfortable… and that made me angry at myself.

"What was?"

"The way you calmed him, sir." Its—*his*—head tilted to one side and he blinked. "Are you a doctor?"

"No."

"A psychologist, then? You show a superb practical knowledge of the human condition."

A philosophical clone? It was possible, I suppose. I was grappling at the moment with my own feelings. Clones made me uncomfortable, where bioroids did not. I know, I know—lots of humans have the same response; there'd been all of those dead clones in the streets last year.

But I wanted to understand. Damn it, clones are human. Bioroids are not. Why did I find my gene-altered human siblings…creepy? It wasn't just the bar codes tattooed on the sides of their necks.

I glanced at Kaminsky. He appeared more relaxed now, as the sky outside darkened to black despite the continued glare from the sun. He was also far enough away that I could talk about him without being overheard.

"He's a soldier," I said, shrugging. "I was in the military, too, about a million years ago. I just had to get his mind off the problem for a moment, and get his breathing back to normal."

"I see, sir."

"Don't 'sir' me. Like I said, that was a long time ago."

The Moon, I thought, *is not Mason, Ohio*. In some ways it was more dangerous than the streets of Earthside New Angeles. Taking an eighteen-year-old kid who was terrified of heights and could barely find his butt with both hands and dropping him into that environment was tantamount to murder.

I hoped Kaminsky had buddies in his unit who would look out for him.

I looked at the clone. "So what's your interest in...what did you call it? 'The human condition.'"

His face contorted, as though twisted by some strong emotion. *That,* I thought, *is part of my trouble with the things*. With clones, you couldn't read the thousand subtle clues natural humans gave off during conversations. They had facial expressions, certainly, but they seemed pasted on, almost as though they wore them for effect...and often they didn't match the situation in which they were used.

"All of us have a considerable interest in full-human psychology, sir."

"I imagine you do. Did you have any trouble back at the Root?"

"I beg your pardon, sir?"

"That mob in the Plaza. Making a lot of noise, mugging for the newsies, and chanting 'no clones.'"

"Ah. Them. No, sir. I took an elevator up to the station's interior. I didn't go outside."

"How do you feel about that sort of thing?"

"What sort of thing, sir?"

"The Anti-Clone Movement. Human First."

"Ah. I can't say that I feel anything, sir." His face was bland as he said it, completely without expression.

And I *knew* he was lying.

The term "clone" is really a blatant misuse of scientific terminology. I blame Hollywood and a century or so of 3Ds and sensies portraying clones as soulless automatons out to take over the world...or at least trying to ravage the wives and daughters of *real* humans. Originally, the word meant nothing more than taking a cell from one individual and growing a new organism, identical to the parent in every respect. The second individual was no more inhuman than an identical twin. It *was* an identical twin, in fact, except that it was a bit younger than the original. The very first successful clone of a mammal was a ewe, a female sheep, named Dolly.

We've progressed a bit since then. Eventually, the old laws against human cloning were overturned. As with stem cell research and nanomed, there were pressing reasons, both medical and economic, to explore the field—individual human organs, for example, can be cloned and stored for use in organ transplants without danger of immune-rejection problems.

Eventually, though, companies like Jinteki began...tinkering.

Today, clones are still human, no matter what Cardinal Reese might say about it, but they're also the product of both extensive gene modification and considerable neural conditioning. They're *made* to be obedient and single-minded about their work, though that has nothing to do with genetics. I understand they use neural channeling—same as the brain-taping that gives bioroids human-like personalities—to make clones feel happiest when they're part of a team, following orders, productive, and fitting in.

Like a lot of other members of the more traditionally created individuals of the human species, I didn't think clones were subhuman things. Caprice Nisei, who was rented out to the NAPD by Jinteki on a regular basis as a kind of beta-test model for the "new" detective, was one of my favorite people. A bit moody, maybe, and the way she seemed to pluck evidence others had overlooked out of the air could be startling and a bit scary, but she was a *person*, damn it, not a *thing*.

But a lot of people don't see it that way—especially those people who are out of a job because of cheap clone labor. For the corps, clones are spare parts, human replacements, simulants that can be grown in batches, hired out to customers, and used as cheap labor until they're used up, discarded, and recycled, with no need for health insurance or social security.

There's a word for that in my book, and it's not pretty. *Slavery*.

If this clone riding up-Stalk with me claimed he didn't have feelings about the anti-clone movement, he *had* to be lying. No brain-tape conditioning could be that good.

I held out my hand. "I'm Harrison, by the way. Rick Harrison."

He took my hand. I tried not to think about it feeling cold and a bit clammy. *He's as human as I am, damn it.*

"John Jones," he said. He hesitated, then added, "Jones 937, Melange Mining Corporation, Block 1280."

First-generation clones—the ones used in large numbers in mining and in the military—were usually given bland, pedestrian names, with the surname used for everyone in that individual's batch. On the job, there might be a thousand other Joneses or Smiths, so they were given numbers to keep them sorted out. I understand that the British Army did the same thing in the 19th century, when recruits from Wales all tended to be named "Davies" or "Williams" or, for that matter, "Jones."

"I don't believe you, you know."

"You don't believe what, sir?"

"That you don't care about the ACM."

He kept that bland and empty poker face on. "I really have no opinion on the matter, sir."

"Uh-huh." There was another problem with Mr. Jones, now that I thought about it. He was awfully well-spoken for a mining clone.

As with most clones, his voice came across as weak, little more than a voiced whisper, an unobtrusive murmur. I'd always taken that to be part of the clone I-want-to-fit-in group mentality. Don't speak loudly, don't call attention to yourself, don't offend real humans or intrude upon their conversations.

And most of the clones I'd met over the years had a rather narrow range of interests. They were force-grown in vats—a bit more of Jinteki's genetic tinkering, that—and were considered to be fully grown at age three or so. Their training—which included their social conditioning—tended to be narrowly specialized. Why waste quantum calculus or transcendental philosophy on someone who's going to spend his entire, rather brief life running a regolith strip-miner on the surface of the Mare Crisium?

As a result, clones rarely had much to say to full-humans, and tended to come across as a bit dim-witted—"developmentally challenged" as the psychs like to say. Add the fact that they weren't socialized like human children—they didn't even have a childhood, for Skinner's sake—and you can see why they didn't fit in with their natural human sibs. Most came across as extremely uncomfortable when they were forced to interact with humans one-on-one.

John Jones was an anomaly—a clone interested in human psychology and brave enough to initiate a conversation with a stranger. The last I heard, Jinteki clones weren't into facilitating group therapy sessions. His interest in the psychology I'd just used with Kaminsky suggested at least some knowledge of the topic, and that just didn't square with what I thought I knew about clones. He also didn't seem at all ill-at-ease, the solitary clone in a beanpod with seven humans. He'd approached me and struck up a casual conversation, not clone-like at all.

All of which meant either that my knowledge of clones was deficient...or that John Jones was more than he appeared.

"So...you headed back to Heinlein?"

"Yes, sir."

"You're with the big 2M?" I asked. Melange Mining, "2M," handled most lunar helium-3 mining and processing. "What do you do?"

"I operate a D9Y surface conveyer," he told me. Was there actually a touch of pride in the near-whispered words? "I dump incoming regolith into the first-level converters, to separate out the helium as the first step in refining helium-3."

Helium-3 is the whole reason for the Heinlein colony on the Moon. It's an isotope of helium; one neutron and two protons in the nucleus instead of the usual two and two found in ordinary helium-4. It's fantastically rare on Earth. It's rather rare on the Moon, too, but the lunar surface has been collecting the stuff from the solar wind streaming out from the Sun for four billion years or so. Regolith—the fancy name for lunar surface material—has about 28 ppm—that's parts per million—of helium-4, and only .01 ppm of helium-3. It takes a hundred million tons of regolith to recover one ton of helium-3. Of course, we can manufacture the stuff on Earth. Tritium, with a half-life of twelve years, decays into helium-3, and that can be trapped and concentrated for industrial use, but it's a lot cheaper to strip-mine the lunar surface and dump the regolith into a converter.

And if it's worth doing, it's worth doing on a massively industrial scale. Modern fusion reactors require helium-3 for the deuterium-helium-3 reaction. That process is less energetic than deuterium-tritium, and needs a bigger power plant, but it's cheaper, simpler, and safer to operate, doesn't pollute the air or water, produces very low-level radioactive waste, and doesn't use radioactive fuel.

Someday, we might mine helium-3 on a *really* big scale from the atmospheres of the outer gas giants, Uranus and Neptune, but until that happens we're dependent on the lunar mines for ninety percent-plus of our electrical power. I do *not* want to think about what would happen to civilization if our sources of the stuff were interrupted.

"You like your work?" I asked.

"I do, sir. It is satisfying and fulfilling. 'We supply the life's blood of human civilization.'"

He was quoting a 2M advertising slogan, and the blatant propaganda almost made me gag.

"You'll have to excuse me for asking," I told him, "but… your speech…"

"Is there something wrong with my speech, sir?"

"No. Not at all. You just seem unusually well-educated for a conveyer belt operator."

Another indecipherable expression crossed his face, a slight tic pulling at his eye and the corner of his mouth, instantly gone. "I…was also specially trained, sir, to work in Personnel."

My eyebrows went up at that. "Impressive. A management position?"

"Admin, sir. I was a file clerk."

"I see. I guess that makes sense."

But it didn't, not really. File clerks didn't need to be imprinted with a knowledge of human psychology, and they didn't need to speak English with the gentle elocution of a college professor.

He studied me for a moment, then added, "Ah…and for a time I was on the help desk out in the main lobby. They enhanced my vocabulary for that, but I ended up being there for only a week."

He was either reading my mind—and mining clones couldn't do that—or he was reaching blindly, looking for an explanation that would satisfy me. The idea bothered me. Ever since Jinteki had begun introducing clones, the corporate line had been that they *can't* replace humans, not as human beings. Clones weren't supposed to be as flexible, as adaptable, or as all-round clever as normal humans. In the work force, they were supposed to be more like highly trained chimpanzees than real people; hell, they *couldn't* be people, because if they were, they had rights, and using them would be a form of slavery. Jinteki's marketing and legal departments worked endlessly to see to it that people saw them as biological machines, not human at all.

"You seem like you'd get on well, uh, unsupervised. Working with humans. Ever thought of doing that?"

For the first time, I saw a crack in the emotional façade. Jones looked scared, but the expression only lasted for an instant, and then it was gone.

"I have a satisfying and fulfilling relationship with my employers," he said. "I will happily perform whatever duties they require of me. I enjoy working with full-humans, and I enjoy working toward the betterment of humankind."

"Okay, okay," I said, raising a hand. "It's getting so deep in here I need my thigh-highs."

He cocked his head again. "I don't understand the expression, sir."

"It means—"

But then the holographic attendant materialized in the middle of the room, all smiles and brisk professionalism. "Ladies and gentlemen, we are approaching the midpoint of our ascent. In two minutes, acceleration will be cut off, and we will experience momentary low-G conditions. Please remain strapped into your seats. The outside view will be switched off momentarily, in order to prevent feelings of disorientation or vertigo. Some of you may experience some minor discomfort. Please be assured that everything is as it should be. Deceleration will commence once the midpoint maneuver is complete."

For the past twenty-five minutes, we'd been under an acceleration of 1.5 gravities—that half a person sitting in my lap. During that time, the sky had gone completely black. No stars, because even in space the brightness of the sun washed them out, and I suspected the view they were putting up on the walls was stepped down a bit to keep us from going blind from unfiltered light at both optical and UV wavelengths.

Jones leaned forward, extending his hand. I shook it—a bit reluctantly—and he dropped his other hand on my shoulder. "It's been wonderful talking with you, sir," he said.

I disliked the overt familiarity of his touch…and not for the first time I had to dig down inside, looking for deep-lurking feelings of prejudice or anti-clone bias. I didn't *think* I had any… but I didn't like his touch. Then again, I wouldn't have liked it if a human had put an overly familiar hand on my shoulder, not unless I'd known him for a *long* time.

It was so difficult reading clone expressions and emotions, and I knew their behavior had essentially been conditioned into them. Usually, though, their demeanor toward full-humans wasn't so personal or direct.

Before I could comment, he returned to his seat and strapped in. I noted with interest that he walked right through the holographic projection of the uniformed woman. Most clones, I'd noticed, tended to shy from any human contact, even the anticipation of contact created by a good animated hologram.

A short time later, the attendant's voice gave us the countdown. "Low gravity in five…four…three…two…one…and we are initiating the midpoint maneuver."

The interior projection vanished along with the attendant, and we were once again surrounded by rather bland walls of gleaming off-white plastic. I felt a slight, sharp stab of claustrophobia—I didn't like not being able to see out.

Acceleration ceased.

We were continuing to move upward at a now steady speed of

twenty-three kilometers per second. We weren't in zero gravity, however. Lots of people don't get that, assuming that if you're in space you must be weightless. Though we'd be in orbit once we reached Midway, at the moment we were attached to the elevator tower 18,000 kilometers above Cayambe, and our lateral motion was the same as Earth's rotational velocity, which was considerably less than the orbital velocity required at that altitude. Had I cared to step through an airlock into space, I would have immediately fallen, dropping toward Earth at something less than the ten meters per second squared which is Earth's gravity at sea level, but dropping nonetheless.

After a *long* fall, I would have burned up in the atmosphere, a brief shooting star descending toward the planet.

I felt the pod rotating.

Still drifting upward but no longer accelerating, the pod now slowly turned end for end, rotating on the railguide mounted at the pod's center of mass. Now Earth would be above our heads rather than beneath our feet.

For a moment we were all hanging upside down, with a definite feeling of *down* up toward the top of the compartment. The kid squalled…and then was abruptly and noisily sick. The soldier and one of the businessmen looked a bit green, though I didn't know if it was the sensation of turning upside down or the smell from the kid's vomit. God, he'd had a big breakfast! I wondered what his mother had been thinking, feeding him before going up the Beanstalk.

They had problems like this on the Beanstalk all the time, of course, and were ready to deal with it. Something like a vacuum cleaner was already purring across the ceiling below our heads, cleaning up the mess, and a strong breeze of fresh air was washing out the smell.

"Commencing deceleration," the attendant said, "in three… two…one…and we are initiating deceleration."

I glanced down…uh…up to see if the vacuum robot was going to fall, but it had already left the ceiling spotless and vanished into a cubby in the wall. The feeling of a gentle tug toward the ceiling slowly and quite smoothly decreased, until we were truly weightless, our up-Stalk acceleration perfectly balanced by Earth's weakened but still significant gravitational tug.

After that, the sensation of weight toward the floor re-established itself, growing stronger. Then the attendant appeared to tell us we could walk around again, with care.

This time I only had the weight of a small child in my lap. We were now decelerating at 1.5Gs, but the pull of Earth was now working with the mag-lev braking, not fighting against it. The woman took her kid into the restroom to sluice him down.

I wanted to continue my conversation with Jones, but he was sitting in his seat across the cabin now, staring at his clasped hands in his lap and not making eye contact. I'd touched something there with my last question, and the investigative detective in me wanted to know what the hell it was.

The walls seemed to turn transparent once more, and I breathed a little easier, surrounded not by white walls, but by spectacularly deep, black emptiness, the sun a dazzling disk low and to my left, almost at the edge of the floor.

Then they switched on the projection over our heads and my breath caught in my throat.

At an altitude of 18,000 kilometers, Earth spanned almost forty degrees of the sky, almost full, with an achingly beautiful ragged edge of sunrise stretched across the Pacific, close to the disk's western rim. It was spectacular—deep blue seas and long, swirls, loops, and streaks of blindingly white clouds, filling much of the ceiling.

From my perspective, the planet appeared upside down, with the fiercely bright gleam off the Antarctic ice cap at the top. The Beanstalk ran past the side of the pod and sliced into the planet's heart, dwindling to a sharply foreshortened point at the center, at the patch of grey and brown I knew was Ecuador.

New Angeles was big enough that you could see it easily from space.

"My God in heaven," one of the businessmen said—the one who hadn't looked like he was going to lose breakfast. That one wasn't looking; he had his eyes shut. So did Kaminsky…and Jones wasn't looking up, either. *That* was more like the clone stereotype with which I was familiar.

Vocal music was playing in the background—something from Rossini's *Otello*, I think it was. It was a bit astonishing to realize we were still moving at twenty kilometers per second, but the Earth didn't seem to be moving at all. Only by staring at the vast expanse of blue and white for several long minutes did you begin to realize that it was, truly, *shrinking*, still falling away beneath us as we, in our upside-down pod, hurtled upward.

It's a shame, I thought, *that they weren't able to display the Earth for the first leg of the ascent, when it was beneath us...* But too many people panicked when the deck seemed to vanish beneath their feet. They'd taken an electronic poll before the ascent; if everyone on the deck requested window-floor seating, I knew, you could see the Earth beneath you all the way up to the flip over, but the numbers hadn't worked for this flight. Kaminsky, most likely, had down-checked it.

Earth viewed from 18,000 kilometers up was mesmerizing in her spectacular beauty.

I leaned back in my seat, adjusting it so I didn't have to crane my neck, and watched her fall slowly away as we continued our ascent.

Chapter Four

Day 1

We arrived at Midway twenty-five minutes later, dropping down the Beanstalk—or so it seemed from our inverted perspective and acceleration—and entering Midway Station. By that time, Earth had dwindled to cover just about twenty degrees of the ceiling directly overhead. From our vantage point, we seemed to be dropping down, floor-first, into an open well. A moment later, they switched off the external cameras and our magnetic acceleration dwindled away to nothing.

In the pit of my stomach, it felt like we were falling.

"Please note," our smiling attendant told us, "that conditions of microgravity exist within Midway Station. Please do *not* leave your seats until attendants arrive to help convey you to the station terminal, even if you have experience with working in zero-G. Your seatbelts have been locked as a precaution, and for your safety."

Sure enough, the seatbelt clasps wouldn't open. They didn't want us bouncing around the pod's interior and possibly hurting ourselves. An eighty-kilo person might not weigh anything, but he still has eighty kilos of mass, and that mass has inertia that an ill-considered push could slam into a ceiling hard enough to break his neck if he's not careful.

After a few moments, the door in the again opaque wall slid open, and two men in white jumpsuits floated in. They helped the woman and the damp child out first, securing both with straps clipped around their waists before unlocking their seat harnesses. One of the men put their carry-ons into a kind of backpack slung over his shoulder, and the four of them vanished out the open door, the kid—his sickness now forgotten—squealing with ear-piercing delight.

A few minutes later, the two returned, this time one helping one of the businessmen, the second one the other.

"How you doing, soldier?" I asked Kaminsky.

He swallowed, then gave a jerky nod of his head. "Doing okay, sir." He hesitated. "Uh…thanks. I appreciate your helping me back there."

"Not a problem. But I recommend you check in with your base doctor. If you have problems with heights, they might not want you riding skyhoppers, y'know?"

"I will, sir. Thanks."

After helping him out, they came for the young couple, probably on their honeymoon. I suppressed a smirk. Those noir set kids looked like they'd stepped straight out of the 1920s—him with a jacket and a tie aglow with neon animations, and her with a short, tight dress. I knew they could expect some fun times when they experienced their clothing in zero-G.

Once they were gone, I was next. They were leaving Jones for last, apparently. The luck of the draw? Or did they always leave the clones for last?

My guide waited as I retrieved my evidence kit from the wall locker and helped me strap it to my back. Cinched to his waist by a bungee strap, he hauled me down the boarding corridor and into the main terminal.

"Are you okay from here, sir?" the attendant asked.

"I used to fly Strikers for a living," I told him. "I'll manage."

"Yes, sir!" I caught a flash of respect in his eyes, and wondered if he was ex-military as well. "You're continuing up-Stalk?" he asked.

"Yes, I am."

He pointed. "You want the green line, sir. Takes you straight to Midway Station Up."

I thanked him as he uncinched himself from me and hand-over-handed away, heading back toward the pod. There were hand lines everywhere in a can-shaped interior thirty meters across, organized in pairs so that if you met someone coming along a line in the opposite direction, one of you could shift to the rope alongside so the two of you could pass. The rope-pairs were color-coded so that you could find your way through the weightless maze. With no up or down, navigation could be a bit confusing.

There were some hundred or so people in the arrival concourse at the moment, most of them pulling their way along with slow and steady movements. A poorly judged quick movement in zero-G could set you spinning, or leave you helplessly adrift just out of reach of your lifeline.

I chuckled when I saw that noirie couple—him with his jacket and tie billowing up around his shoulders and face, her with that short skirt bunched around her waist as her bare legs thrashed. Live and learn, kids…

I noticed there were also quite a few hocas about.

Homo caelum fabricata was the Latin name, meaning something like "manufactured space man." They were clones out of Jinteki, quite new on the market, with the basic human genome altered considerably from the original. Each was smaller than a normal human, with a large, bald head, deep-set eyes, dark skin, large hands, and—the most startling change—an extra set of arms instead of legs and feet, and extra shoulders instead of hips. They reminded me a bit of tailless monkeys as they hauled passenger baggage or other massive loads with one hand, and used the other three to zip along non-color-coded lines at careening, stomach-twisting speeds.

There were other, more human-looking clones as well, many in 2M grey. I looked around for John Jones, hoping to continue our conversation, but if he'd emerged from the pod he was either nowhere to be seen now, or he was any one of five clones who looked exactly like him: his identical brothers—the "Jones-model," as it were.

I wondered if any of them were as intelligent and as socially accomplished as Jones 937.

No matter. I started hauling myself to the next compartment, to catch the pod for the Challenger Planetoid.

At Midway we had to change pods. When they grew the first buckyweave straps, the Beanstalk was manufactured in two sections; one growing from Midway down, the other, in perfect step and perfect balance, growing from Midway up. After the structure was complete, you couldn't ride a beanpod non-stop all the way from the Root to the Ferry, because the two cables were anchored separately to Midway Station.

Travel was a bit different, too. For the first leg of the trip, Earth to Midway, we'd been accelerating against Earth's gravity along the portion of the elevator *not* going fast enough to stay in orbit. Leave the pod and there was that very long step down with a messy *splat* at the end. Once at Midway, you were in synchronous orbit, and moving laterally fast enough to circle Earth once in precisely twenty-four hours. That meant you were in free fall, a.k.a. zero gravity, though microgravity was the more precise term. We weren't beyond Earth's gravity, as Hollywood sometimes claimed. We were falling, falling, and *missing*, falling in an eternal circle around the planet.

But above Midway Station, another factor entered the picture. The upper Beanstalk, all of it making one orbit in one day, was spinning around the Earth too fast to stay in orbit, but was being held down by the Beanstalk itself. With the Challenger Planetoid anchored to the up-end, the whole structure was like a rock tied to the end of a string and whirled about the head; centrifugal force pulled the whole thing taut, and it created an out-is-down spin gravity that steadily increased as you rose above Midway. It wasn't much—only .04G at the planetoid, but it was enough to give you the feeling of a little weight. Beanpods made use of that sliding up-Stalk, though they also used mag-lev, of course, to maintain a steady 1.5G.

I would have liked to explore Midway a bit. The place is huge, and they've continued to add new modules over the years. There are shops and boutiques, several restaurants, and a couple of large hotels, including the notorious Honeymoon Hilton for adventurous couples who want to try out the joys of zero-G. Several megacorps have their home offices there for tax purposes, and NBN is headquartered there right under their primary transmission dishes.

I wondered if Lily was at Midway yet…or if she'd come up at all.

The last time I'd been here as a tourist had been during a stretch of leave during the War. I'd been heading for Mars; we knew things were going to get rough, and we'd hired some joy girls for a hell of a party at the Hilton. Ten years later, I'd tried to take Lily there, but work had interfered, as usual, and we'd had to give it a rain check.

Someday I wanted to cash that rain check, and take Lily flying.

But according to my ticket, my beanpod was leaving in twenty minutes, and the next one wasn't due out until late in the afternoon.

There were some familiar faces in the Midway-out pod. The soldier, Private Kaminsky was on-board, as was the woman with the six-year-old…and thank God for self-cleaning clothes that shed water, dirt, and nasty digestive juices. The couple was missing, and I wondered if their destination had been the Honeymoon Hilton. The businessmen were gone as well. Possibly they'd had meetings at one of the Midway corporate offices. In their places were three other business people, two men and an attractive woman in a conservative purple skinsuit with a Melange Mining logo on her left breast.

And there was no sign of John Jones. He'd *said* he was heading up to Heinlein.

Perhaps that was true, and he'd simply not mentioned the need to stop off at Midway for a while to complete some errand…or perhaps he was on this pod, but riding in one of the other two compartments.

But I'm a suspicious type by nature—good detectives don't come any other way—and Mr. Jones was gnawing at me. There was something not right about him, and it had nothing to do with the creeps I usually felt when dealing with a clone.

I sat in my seat and tapped a code into my PAD. Police officers are authorized to use access codes for local seccams, and I was tuning in to the security cameras that I knew were invisibly present on-board my pod. A moment later, I had the pick-up for Deck One…and then for Deck Three. Both had the usual mix of passengers.

But all were full-human. No clones. John Jones was not onboard.

The attendant was giving her canned spiel again about staying strapped in, but I was continuing to link in with the local extension of the Net. I did a search on Jones 937, accessing both NAPD and Heinlein Authority files.

There he was.

JONES 937, JOHN.

SERIAL NUMBER: 937-777-894-236(C).

RESIDENCE: HEINLEIN, FREETOWN, BLOCK 1280, CUBE 354 BLUE.

OWNER: JINTEKI.

EMPLOYER: MELANGE MINING CORPORATION. (*)

OCCUPATION: D9Y SURFACE CONVEYER OPERATOR, CLASS 1(C).

HEIGHT: 155 CM.

WEIGHT: 69 KG.

HAIR: BROWN.

EYES: BROWN.

SEX: MALE (C).

AGE: 10.

PREVIOUS ARRESTS: NONE.

THREAT: LOW.

The file included a holographic photo and both a set of fingerprints and a pair of mapped retinal images.

Nothing. I didn't have fingerprints or retinal images to compare with his file, and I hadn't scanned his bar code to verify the data, but at a first glance it looked like I'd been talking to Jones, and that he'd been telling the truth.

I was curious, though, about the (*) notation after the employer, and followed that link. *That* piqued my interest. It seemed that John Jones 937 had been seconded to another client…and the identity of that client was classified at level Green-zero. Not a problem. My security classification clears me to Blue-one. I entered my NAPD pass code and e-ID number, and a moment later I had the answer.

Humanity Labor.

The clone Jones worked for an organization devoted to ridding the world of clones. *Very* interesting.

The seconding of clones to other employers was not uncommon. Clones are valuable assets essentially leased by Jinteki to corporate clients, and those clients, in turn, might sublet clones to other "employers"—one means of getting a profit out of the initial investment. What was interesting was the political paradox. Melange Mining used clones for those jobs so dangerous or unpleasant that they would have had to pay very high wages to human workers, not to mention health and retirement bennies. 2M used clones because it was profitable to do so; otherwise, why bother?

Humanity Labor, on the other hand, saw clones as cheap labor taking jobs away from decent, God-fearing humans. They wanted to abolish the use of clones altogether.

Now, if that ever happened in the real word, what would you do with several hundred thousand suddenly unemployed clones? If you're a member of SAM, the Simulant Abolitionist Movement, you give them full civil rights and let them compete with full-human workers for the same jobs at identical wages—equal pay for equal work.

But most Humanity Labor types saw the abolitionists as somewhere out there on the wacko far-left. Even at the same wages, freed clones would still mean competition, and possibly very serious competition because they'd been conditioned to be *very* good—and very happy—at their specific jobs. Many of them had advantages, in fact, that full-humans lacked, like increased resistance to radiation.

Of course, the problem would solve itself in fifteen years after clones were emancipated. They weren't able to breed, and if Jinteki stopped manufacturing them, the last clone would drop dead fifteen years later.

Humanity Labor raised another issue—Human First. An underground group, often running outside the law, they still tended to have the full support of Humanity Labor and other workers' advocacy groups, as well as a vast array of ACM organizations. The Anti-Clone Movement didn't care whether clones got to vote or not. Unlike SAM, most ACM groups simply wanted clones gone, period, even if that meant—to use Melange Mining's rather chilling weasel-word euphemism—*retiring* them.

I typed in the words "Easter egg," followed by my NAPD pass code again. Additional data appeared.

Jones had been "hired," if that was the right word, on the authorization of Roger Mayhurst Dow, Jr.

"Curiouser and curiouser, said Alice."

I'd been so entranced by my Net search that I hadn't even noticed when the beanpod had begun accelerating. The sensation of weight had returned as the pod silently rode the twisting magnetic fields up the elevator Stalk, deeper into the black.

I shifted the focus of my online investigation to the murder victim.

At higher security levels, there was file data on Dow that couldn't be found on Netpedia...not to mention the fact that Netpedia bios *have* been known to be controversial or just out-and-out wrong. I started with Dow's credaccount. Nothing unusual there. He wasn't on the verge of bankruptcy, didn't have unusual debts, didn't appear to have a drug or sex habit...

Hold on. He had 117 charges against his account over the past two years from one special creditor: Eliza's Toybox.

So I followed that link, just to make sure I was on the right track. Eliza's was a large business located in Heinlein, one of the biggest. And she rented out bioroids.

Most notably, bioroids who were sex-service gynoids.

There *are* other uses for female bioroids, of course. Eliza's had several lines that catered particularly to rich clients who wanted an attractive domestic servant, complete with old-fashioned maid's costume and feather duster, though even those were usually programmed to allow the client to seduce her—or to force her. Face it, though. If a client wants a generic robot laborer, he's usually going to rent a generic male android—assuming the thing looks like a human at all.

Sexbots are big business, and they've been so for a long time. Back in the first decade of the 21st century, a German company marketed a sex doll called Andy the Android. She had a pulse, a heartbeat, a realistic temperature, and could simulate breathing, all for between $4,000 and $7,000, depending on the exact mix of features. During the company's first couple of years of operation, they'd received more than four million orders.

Of course, Andy had been a bit shy in the brains department, and couldn't carry on a conversation, much less walk or be taken home to meet the folks. That came later.

Bioroids were human simulants—android robots that mimicked human thought, intelligence, and personality through neural channeling technology. The experts were still arguing over whether AI robots could be considered intelligent, creative, or self-aware in the same way as people, but they certainly *acted* as though they were. And while I'd never used one myself, I understood that high-end robotic sex companions were *very* good at what they did. Eliza's Toybox rented out only high-end models, and they charged a lot for the service.

It looked as though Roger Mayhurst Dow, Jr. had been a frequent purchaser of Eliza's services.

A lawyer and lobbyist for Humanity Labor, using a bioroid for sex. That complicated things. Had Dow been into some twisted, psychological fantasy...maybe dominating a sex gynoid because he hated the things? Or had he just been indulging in guilty pleasures that would have gotten him fired if his bosses had found out?

And that made me think. *Fired? Or taken apart with a mining laser?*

Somehow I doubted Humanity Labor was so paranoid about bioroids that they would kill a human employee just for dating one. But I made a mental note to question whoever was further up the chain of command above Dow. I used my security codes to access the Humanity Labor organizational charts. Dow had been an independent lobbyist who'd reported to the company's legal department, and someone named Thea Coleman. Her record looked clean enough—not even a flight path violation—but *her* supervisor was Thomas Milroy Vaughn. Before he'd gone to work for Humanity Labor in their public relations department, he'd been a lawyer on retainer for Cheong Li Hua. Cheong was 14K, and that meant, almost beyond the shadow of a doubt, that Vaughn was dirty.

More leads to follow up. More people to interview. But at least now I had something to work with.

I spent most of the rest of the trip time after that exploring the murder scene on my PAD, pulling the tightly rolled screen up from the top edge and unfolding it into a 28 x 40 rigid display. Whoever had shot the crime scene had gone through the whole room, pointing the camera at everything, and all of that data had downloaded to my PAD in the Commissioner's office that morning. That meant I could use the touchpad to navigate through a 3D scene, studying whatever caught my attention from every angle.

What a mess!

And then, seventy thousand kilometers above Cayambe, we arrived at the end of the line.

The Challenger Planetoid is a five kilometer rock serving as the Beanstalk's upper-end anchor. The Nearside facility started off as a construction shack for workers on the elevator project, including a huge spin-gravity carousel—a pair of side-by-side, three-decked wheels rotating on the planetoid's surface. That rotation had provided a half-G of artificial gravity for the workers during the Beanstalk's construction.

The wheels were enormous: two hundred meters across and rotating once every twenty-eight seconds in order to create a steady half-G of spin gravity. They rotated in opposite directions, the torque of one countered perfectly by the torque of the other, because without that little detail, spin would very gradually be transferred to the far larger planetoid, with disastrous consequences for the space elevator.

Today, the big rotating complex includes the original Castle Club, plus an enormous dance floor and cabaret, the Cloudtop. There's an exclusive restaurant, the Earthview, where you can drink wine from an open glass without worrying about sloshing the contents in low gravity. There's the Carousel Boardrooms, available for business meetings; that was where Dow was going to make his pitch to the politicians from Earthside. Directly adjacent to the up-end of the Beanstalk, there's a large hotel and business center, the High Frontier—which was where I'd be headed soon enough. And just outside the twin wheels proper were the low gravity attractions: a ballet theater where a good dancer could carry off a *sauté* that let her brush the ceiling with her hands, ten meters above the stage, and, of course, another Honeymoon Hilton, this one at .04Gs for those couples who had problems performing the docking maneuver in zero-G.

On Farside is a collection of surface domes and underground tunnels constituting the Challenger Mines, as well as the embarkation terminal for the Challenger Memorial Ferry. Both planetoid and base are named for the Space Shuttle *Challenger*, destroyed seventy-three seconds after takeoff on January 28, 1986, back at the dawn of the space age.

We dropped down the last kilometer of elevator toward the planetoid's Nearside at .04Gs, propelled solely by the artificial spin-gravity of the Stalk at that altitude. Earth had continued dwindling until it covered just 10.5 degrees of arc. It was well past noon in New Angeles, and I could see the terminator, edged by sunset colors, following the curving edge of night across western Europe and the bulge of Africa.

We didn't need attendants to help us float into the terminal this time. Here, I weighed a mere 3.2 kilos, enough to keep me on the deck so long as I watched my step. An attendant did hand me a pair of low-G grip-slippers, though. They fit over my regular shoes, and gripped the carpet on the deck with thousands of near-invisible hooks. If I had jumped hard, though, I would have sailed into the ceiling ten meters above my head…and it would have taken me a *long* time to fall back to the floor at just four-hundredths of a meter per second squared.

The terminal was filled with passengers, some going up to Heinlein, others coming down—a bustling place. There were the usual shops and souvenir stands, but commercial ventures were not nearly so evident here as they'd been at Midway. The feel of the place was a bit more raw and new-frontierish than the lower stops on the elevator, with expanses of bare metal and lots of foam padding to protect the heads of the careless. No backscatter x-ray checks on the way out. The only security I could see were cameras on some of the walls—and the ever-present Beanstalk yellow jackets.

They actually had full-sim bioroids wandering around the terminal, though—perfect replicas of the seven *Challenger* astronauts killed in the disaster. I had to ask Christa McAuliffe for directions to the High Frontier Hotel and Meeting Center.

Full-sim, of course, means extra care has been taken to avoid the Uncanny Valley; unless you get *very* close, it's hard to tell you're talking to a simulant. These models don't have the cables in the backs of their wrists, or the blank silver eyes employed to make a bioroid seem just a little *less* human. Christa's eyes were the dark, dark brown of the real person—lifelike and lustrously bright enough to remind me of Lily's. With these bioroids, Haas-Bioroid had crossed the Uncanny Valley and made it through to the other side.

I wondered why they hadn't done this with *all* of their products. Probably a money issue, like most things.

"Right over there, sir," Christa's ghost told me. "Across the terminal to the blue door, down the passageway, and up two levels."

"Thank you."

"Captain Harrison?"

I turned to face a small, neat man with a goatee. Beards are common enough on Earth, but not so much on the Beanstalk or in Heinlein, though they're not unknown. There's a chance that you'll get hair caught in the pressure rings when you're trying to don a helmet in a hurry, and it makes for a poor seal if you have to wear an emergency oxygen mask, which can happen if a pressure hull is breached.

"Yes?"

"I'm Tom Fuchida," he told me, extending his hand. "Manager of the Challenger High Frontier Hotel and Meeting Center."

"How do you do?" I said, shaking his hand. "And just how the hell did you know I was coming?" I hadn't shared my itinerary with anyone.

"Commissioner Dawn called me a couple of hours ago, and told me you were on your way up-Stalk. She told me to extend to you *every* courtesy, and to cooperate completely with your investigation. We tracked you by your e-ID, and I came down to meet your pod."

"I see. Thank you very much."

Damn Dawn. She knew I'd rather show up without the locals being prepped to receive me. I didn't want them screwing with *my* crime scene. Why the hell had she called ahead? Didn't she *want* me to solve this case?

"What would you like to see first?"

"The crime scene, of course," I told him. "I trust you have it cordoned off. No one in, no one out."

"We've followed standard procedure, Captain. The room has been sealed off from the public." He produced a deep blue handkerchief and mopped his upper lip. "It was dreadful in there. *Dreadful*. In any case, the only ones in or out have been elevator security pers—"

"*What?*" I turned to face him, furious. "You have damned *elevator mercs* trampling the crime scene?"

"Sir!" he sounded shocked. Perhaps he was. "The Space Elevator Authority employs only the highest caliber of security officer."

"SEA employs rent-a-cops, Mr. Fuchida, who wouldn't recognize their own butts if you dropped them into their open and waiting hands!"

"We are handling this case according to standard procedure, Captain Harrison, as I said."

Which probably meant SITFUBAR—Situation Fouled Up Beyond All Recognition.

"Just get me there, Mr. Fuchida."

We took a slidewalk across the terminal and entered the Blue Sector. Through the passageway and up two broad and sloping ramps brought us to a hotel lobby, the High Frontier Hotel.

"So, what do you know about Mr. Dow's death?" I asked him, using my PAD to record the conversation.

"Just what we told you in our report this morning. A maid went up to Mr. Dow's room at about 2330 last night. He'd called down and asked for a nightcap. She found him…like that. Like in the vid we sent you." He looked and sounded like he was going to be sick.

"Is the body still there?"

"No, sir! Of course not!"

I groaned inwardly. "Great. Where is it?"

"In the med center morgue, of course. We didn't want to risk having it…uh…begin to decay."

"He wasn't going to start rotting on you *that* fast," I said.

"The environment in a base like this is…delicate, Captain Harrison. *Very* delicate. It was important to, um, get him on ice quickly."

What Fuchida was trying to say delicately was an indelicate truth. The air circulating through the base was carefully monitored for temperature, humidity, and particulate levels—especially dust and mold—but the environmental control personnel of a hotel, I knew, tended to be fastidious to the point of obsession. An odor in one room would very swiftly circulate throughout all of the other rooms, and then across the station.

And then something else occurred to me as I recalled the images of the crime scene I'd seen on my PAD that morning in Dawn's office. The legs on the bed. Part of the torso on the floor.

We were through the hotel lobby, and making our way down a long corridor with numerous doors to the left and right.

"Mr. Dow's abdomen was cut open, wasn't it?" I asked.

Again the handkerchief came out, and Fuchida could only nod.

Once, during the War, I'd had to pry open the pressure suit of a man who'd caught a laser burn across the belly. We were in the emergency field surgery unit, and I'd removed my helmet. My God, I will *never* forget the smell—charred meat and leaking intestines.

Yeah, they'd had good reason to get that body packed up and on ice, or the smell would have been literally *everywhere*.

"Here we are, Captain," Fuchida said, gesturing at an internal pressure-seal door with a yellow and black keep-out disk mounted on it. A couple of armed yellow jackets watched me suspiciously from either side, and I flashed them my badge.

One handed me a bright yellow cleansuit. Fuchida waved it away when one of them offered him a suit as well.

"Not coming in?" I asked, setting the evidence kit on the floor and handing my PAD to a guard. I removed the grip-slippers and stepped into the suit. It fit snuggly over my shoes, and, as soon as it sensed the pulse at my ankle, began to unfold and expand, spreading up and out and around to completely enclose me. An environmental pack smaller than my PAD rested at my waist, and cool air filled the transparent bubble helmet. Sensing my body size, it snugged down to a perfect fit. I retrieved my PAD and club.

"No…no," he said. "I'll…wait here."

Fuchida used a keycard to open the door for me and I stepped inside.

Oh, *God…*

Chapter Five

Day 1

The room was one of the High Frontier's finest—luxuriously appointed and quite large by up-Stalk standards. The low, slanted ceiling and one wall were part of the outer hotel dome and were partially made of a curved sheet of transplas rather than titanium steel. That was no digitally projected image of the Earth, impossibly blue and white, suspended in the blackness directly overhead, but the real thing. The Beanstalk was a thread-slender dark scratch across the Earth's face, vanishing into her center.

The room was bathed in Earthlight, ethereal and beautiful. That made what the light revealed, somehow, that much more horrific.

There was blood everywhere, including on the transplas ceiling directly above the large, square bed. The bed itself—which rose only half a meter above the floor and was covered by what looked like violet silk sheets—was crumpled, burned, and soggy with blood, and there was a pool of the stuff on the floor alongside it.

Two yellow jackets were in the room, both in cleansuits.

"Hold it right there," one said, his voice slightly muffled by his helmet. "You authorized to be in here, Mac?"

My badge was inaccessible inside my jacket and the yellow cleansuit, but when I tapped it, it broadcast my e-ID. The yellow jackets' PADs chirped, and brought up my number and ID.

"Uh…yes, *sir*," one of them said, reading his screen. "Good to meet you, sir."

"What the hell are you doing in my crime scene?" I demanded. My PAD gave me their names: Smethers and Daley.

"Collecting evidence, Captain," the second one, Daley, told me. He held up a small, plastic bag with voice-tag sample tubes inside.

"Trampling through evidence and mucking it up, more like it," I replied. I could see blood on their cleansuit booties, and bloody footprints tracked all over the room. "How many of these damned footprints are yours?"

"Uh, the blood is kind of everywhere, Captain Harrison," Smethers said. "It's hard to avoid, you know?"

"I do know. That's why you people shouldn't even be in here, damn it! *Now get the hell out!*"

Smethers skittered out like a kicked puppy, leaving more bloody tracks on the carpet. Daley glared at me. "You don't need to take that ristie tone with us, Cap."

"It's 'Captain Harrison,' and I'll take any tone I damned well please." I reached out my gloved hand. "I'll take that."

Reluctantly, he handed me the evidence pack.

"Sign for it."

There was a tag on the evidence bag, with a barcode, a signature box, and a small attached stylus. He used the stylus to sign his name, then handed the package to me.

"Now git!"

He got.

I seethed for a moment, and counted to ten. *Amateurs!*

His signature had vanished into the plastic box, recorded

by the tag's processors. I added my signature, which would be time-stamped and validated by the tag. It was crucial to keep the chain of evidence well-documented. Otherwise, something vital to the case could be thrown out in court because we hadn't maintained proper evidence control.

Alone in the room, I walked over to the desk and carefully set my evidence case on a clean bit of the surface. It didn't look like the blood had splattered this far. I couldn't use my thumbprint to open the case, of course, so I spoke to it. "Harrison… Captain…ID 718-2461, Blue-one."

Obligingly, the case recognized my voice and hissed open.

Neatly sardine-packed inside were print goggles, a black light wand, chemical and DNA sniffers, rack upon rack of evidence containers, cameras, microscopes, RIR goggles and scanners, a small DNA analysis computer, and a whole armamentarium of other high-tech gadgets.

First things first.

"Crime Scene," I said, recording my words in my PAD, "Challenger Planetoid, High Frontier Hotel, Room Twelve. Victim is Roger Mayhurst Dow, Jr." And I added the case number and the date and time.

Next I used a microsampler to acquire a measure of blood from one of the semi-liquid puddles on the floor. I took two samples, one to save for the lab later, while the other went into my kit's portable medical analyzer. The blood, it told me, was Type O positive, the most common of blood types. Roger Dow's records stated that he was O pos as well. That wasn't definitive—about thirty-seven percent of all humans are O positive—but it would do as confirmation of the murdered man's identity for now, until I could get other samples back to a lab for comprehensive DNA testing.

Turning away so I didn't accidentally breathe on anything, I thumbed my bubble half open and pressed the RIR goggles over my eyes. In the brief moment that my helmet was open,

I caught the sharp, coppery-sweet smell of blood, a smell that had ridden my brain since the War.

I suppressed my gag reflex, and closed the bubble helmet once more.

Then I turned back to face the room.

I knew what to expect, but the anger snapped out again, boiling and insistent. RIR—Residual Infrared—is heat. You can actually track a person in RIR hours after he's walked across a floor because his footprints are still glowing at infrared wavelengths. In the false-color enhancement of the goggles, the room was filled with the green and yellow haze of residual heat, lots of it vaguely man-sized and shaped, and the floor was covered with glowing, crisscrossing tracks.

Almost all of those would be from the security team I'd just tossed out, and they'd tracked around so much that there would be no way to sort out their heat traces from those of others—Dow, the maid, or the murderer. I studied the bed; none of them would have been rolling around in *that*. But blood is hot, and that heat covered the bed now, saturating it. The blood had cooled, but was still a degree or two warmer than the background.

I removed the goggles and replaced them in the kit. It had been many hours since the murder in any case, and there would be very few thermal traces left by this time. But I wanted to be thorough. I pulled out a UV loupe and put it on before closing my helmet again.

I used my PAD to call up the image of the crime scene Dawn had given me that morning. The legs had been *there*, tangled in the sheets. The upper torso had been here, on the floor. An arm had been over here, by the wall. The head—according to the walk-through PAD vid—had been on the other side of the bed.

The mining laser still lay on the floor, just to one side of the door, as though the murderer had tossed it aside as he'd fled.

Time to begin looking for prints.

There are two general classes of fingerprints—patent and latent. Patent prints are like those left by the rent-a-cops on the floor. Someone gets blood on his hand and leaves a visible fingerprint when he touches something. Latent prints are much more subtle, created by the natural skin secretions of a human body; aqueous eccrine secretions, sebaceous oils, urea, even amino acids—they can all be left behind by a touch. They tend to be invisible to the naked eye, but chemistry can bring them out in somewhat spectacular fashion. I used a small squeeze bottle to blow a microscopic puff of fluroninhydrin across the smooth and shiny surface of the laser's pistol grip. The ninhydrin reacts with the ammonia and secondary amines present in minute traces of urea and other bodily secretions, producing a characteristic blue-violet color called Ruhemann's purple. The fluorescent component stood out through my UV loupe as a brilliant, blue glow.

Nothing.

No prints, anyway. The pistol grip had been smeared, however. Traces of UV fluorescence showed where someone had dragged a swab across the plastic.

The rent-a-cops, again, damn them.

There are two ways to process fingerprints but, unfortunately, the two are mutually exclusive, and a crime scene investigator has to make some decisions at the beginning of his investigation about which way he's going to go. He can develop for prints, which can be photographed, or he can go for chemical and DNA evidence, but not both. The swabs used for chemical evidence destroys prints—as had happened on the laser's hand grip. And the fluroninhydrin destroys amino acids…and that's what DNA is made of.

DNA swabs in sealed evidence tubes were a part of the evidence Daley had handed over to me. I'd have to pray that they'd done a decent job in the collection, and labeled it properly. Ideally, the crime scene is divided in two, with one type of evidence collection on one half, and the other type on the second half. Reality is never that neat, however, especially when investigating a single piece of evidence, like that mining laser.

I searched other parts of the laser, both for chemical traces and for prints, working in small sections that I recorded vocally, block by block, on my PAD. The yellow jackets had gone over the laser pretty thoroughly already, though. Very carefully, holding it by the tip of its muzzle and the very end of the butt, I turned the laser over to check the other side.

Damn them. They'd already moved it, going over both sides and destroying any prints.

I photographed the laser carefully, though, and added notes to my PAD's crime scene log. The weapon was heavy and bulky, not exactly a precise weapon, and certainly not a neat one. It would have been hard to wield, too—too heavy for most women, unless they were athletic G-mods. Not too heavy for a bioroid, though…or for a gene-modified clone.

I expanded my search.

Eventually, I found one partial handprint. It was a patent print—a smear of blood on the wall at the head of the bed. It looked like the outer portion of a palm, plus the tip of a little finger, but it smeared away in a bloody trail. I photographed it carefully at various wavelengths, then stepped back and called up the walk-through on my PAD.

When you're collecting evidence at a crime scene, it usually helps to not think about things, to try not to picture what happened. If you do, you're all too likely to begin formulating a story of exactly what happened in your head…the victim was here…the murderer was there…and if you're not careful you'll begin following that story a bit too religiously. You'll end up looking for evidence that fits your still-forming theory, and ignoring things that argue against it. That is *not* the scientific method, and it's a no-good way to find and collect data.

At the same time, a forensic investigator has to have *some* imagination, and he needs to have a working theory as he goes in order to figure out what to look for. The only way to balance the two contradictory attitudes is to rein in the imagination and deliberately not form conclusions, even when it's staring you in the face.

I took a few steps back and unfolded the big screen on my PAD, calling up the walk-through vid. Zooming in for a close look, I found the smeared handprint on the wall, followed the blood trail down…and there was the victim's arm and hand in the image, blood-covered and lying on the pillow.

As a working theory, then…the victim had been in bed when the murderer entered. The victim had sat up…maybe bracing himself with one hand against the wall. Sitting up too quickly in four hundredths of a gravity could throw you into the air, so maybe he'd braced himself to keep from becoming airborne.

The killer fired the laser, shooting wild, and severed the arm just above the elbow. Blood had gushed everywhere, and the hand had left the print as it slid down the wall.

Not entirely satisfactory, that. There must have been blood on his hand already when Dow had touched the wall. So the first shot had cut him somewhere else, splattering blood. *Then* he'd braced against the wall, and *then* the arm had been severed.

I backed up to the door, sighting through my mental visualization of Dow sitting in bed, one arm against the wall. The laser shot would have left a dark burn track against the wall behind him, which would confirm the location of the murderer when he'd taken the shot.

Odd. That part of the wall was actually the transplas window behind the bed. I couldn't find any burn marks there at all.

Okay…maybe that made sense. *Transparent* means that light goes through it, and a laser, even a 100-kilowatt mining laser, is just light, after all. But I would have expected *some* scarring or charring. No transparent material perfectly transmits light, and with a kilowatt laser, if the transplas had absorbed even a tiny fraction of that energy, there should have been some sign.

I also wondered about the mindset of a person who would fire a mining laser at someone with a window directly behind the target in the line of fire. Unless they were certain the laser light would pass harmlessly through the transplas...would they risk the possibility of puncturing the window and causing a pressure loss that might threaten the entire station? At the very least, with a major atmosphere leak, the automatics would cut in and the room would have been sealed off. All of the rooms at the High Frontier had pressure-seal doors so that an accidental rupture in one wouldn't vent the atmosphere of the entire facility.

The murderer would have been locked in as the room air leaked away into vacuum.

Most of the laser damage I could find was on the bed or on the floor, however, randomly distributed. In fact, it looked like the murderer had been blazing away with indiscriminate abandon—panic-shooting, maybe.

I took some photos with my PAD, then moved around the room, trying to line up where the murderer had been standing when he'd shot Dow's arm.

Nothing seemed to fit.

One rule of crime scenes, though, is that things rarely are as neat and orderly as you think they should be. There are *always* factors you're not anticipating. Good crime scene investigation requires that you discard preconceived notions and concentrate on the evidence. Not until you have *all* the facts is it safe to begin drawing conclusions.

I was beginning to have some problems with the crime scene, though. It was overkill to the nth degree. The center of the bed had been savagely slashed again and again; at one point, the mattress was very nearly sliced clean through, the separate edges so clean and sharp they looked like they'd been parted by a fantastically keen razor or a monofilament knife. In places the sheets had charred and almost burned.

Why hadn't the sheets burned? Mining lasers create fantastically high temperatures.

Perhaps the blood soaking the sheets had kept them from catching fire? I examined the saturated portions carefully, and began taking samples. In places, the sheets were still soggy; in others, the blood appeared to have dried and even charred.

Twenty minutes into my examination, I was able to put my finger on what was bothering me most.

The evidence was not internally consistent.

I've seen a lot of wounds caused by high-energy lasers, both in murder investigations in New Angeles, and before that, during the War. What was bothering me was how damned much blood there was.

When a laser beam hits human flesh, one of two things can happen. Usually, the beam will slice through skin, muscle, and bone, but because the beam is so hot it cooks the meat as it passes. Blood vessels are sealed off. Proteins are denatured. Tissue chars. *There's very little bleeding.*

This isn't always the case, of course. If a laser beam hits a body cavity or blood vessel in such a way that internal fluids heat and expand explosively, it can make a hell of a mess. This is especially true of a shot to the abdomen or chest. I remember seeing one poor guy hit in the chest by a combat laser on Mars. It peeled open his pressure suit, his chest cavity exploded, his heart ruptured, and in the near-vacuum of the thin Martian atmosphere almost his entire blood volume—a good six liters—had partially vaporized and splashed across the sand. *Not* pretty.

At least he'd died instantly.

But the way the murderer had been wildly slashing about with the mining laser, I wondered why the wounds hadn't been cauterized. I took another long, hard look at the walk-through vid on my PAD, trying to picture what had actually happened. Okay…this long, deep slash across the center of the bed was the one that had cut Dow in half just above his hips. That must have released a lot of blood...not to mention the smell that had so worried Fuchida. But I would have expected the shots that had cut off the victim's arms and head to have cauterized the wounds. In the vid, there was so much blood on the various body parts they looked like raw hamburger.

Uncooked hamburger.

I would have to have a look at the body later, or what was left of it. This really wasn't adding up.

I didn't let that bother me too much, though. *Wait until you have all the pieces.*

I groaned at my own bad pun, pulled out a microsampler, and began sampling.

Humans leave traces of themselves everywhere. They can't help it, unless they're encased in something like a cleansuit. We're constantly shedding hair, flakes of dead skin, various oils and secretions, eyelashes, and microscopic bits of ourselves that can reveal a lot when studied in context. The microsampler was a pen-sized vacuum with replaceable, sterile vacuum heads and specimen containers. I pulled some dandruff from a non-blood-soaked corner of a pillow. Some hairs from the sheets and from the floor. I pulled a couple of beauties from the pillows: thirty centimeters long and golden yellow. I used a developer spray, then waved the black light wand over everything, using my UV loupe to check for telltale bits of fluorescence.

I found several patches of something moist on the bed sheets that weren't blood. One near the edge, two on the bed just outside the saturated part in the middle. All three might have been contaminated by blood—hell, there was blood everywhere on the bed, from stray droplets to complete saturation—but my club's chemical analysis should be able to separate that out.

And then...*hello*! What's *this*?

A fingerprint...a *perfect* fingerprint, invisible until I dusted it with a powder form of DFO. It was located on the bed frame, up near the head. DFO—formally 1,8-Diazafluoren-9-one—reacts with amino acids, and can pick fingerprints out of porous materials like paper or bed sheets as well as from less permeable materials. After dusting, I passed a blue-green light stick emitting at 470 nanometers above that part of the frame, and got a strong excitation emission at 570 nm.

I used a hand microscope to study the print…then to photograph it. I swear it was *perfect*, no movement, no smearing at all…

And yet there were no ridges, loops, or whorls.

Nothing.

I was looking at the fingerprint left by a bioroid.

All humans have fingerprints, of course, tiny friction ridges in the epidermis, and no two humans have the same prints. Even clones, perfect genetic copies of one another, have different fingerprints. Identical twins—and clones are biologically nothing more than identical human twins—have different prints, because fingerprints have more to do with position, contact, and blood flow in the womb than they do with genetics.

So a bioroid had been in Dow's room.

Not only that, I knew the bioroid had been there *recently*… say, within twenty-four hours. Why? A little-known fact about fingerprints is that children's latent prints tend to disappear after a very few hours. That's because their skin lacks the waxy oils that become so prominent at puberty—think of adolescents and their acne breakouts. The fatty acids and sebaceous oils in younger children are much lighter, and tend to evaporate rapidly.

The same is true of the oils associated with a bioroid's artificial skin, though to a lesser degree than with kids. They're present, certainly, to keep the skin supple and lifelike, but they're water-based and don't hang around for more than a few hours.

And why did I pick up that latent print with a chemical that reacted with human amino acids? Easy. We tend to collect an awful lot of junk on our fingertips just in the day-to-day process of living. Ordinary fingerprints, for instance, carry a lot of heavy sebaceous oils even though the glands producing those oils are not present on the fingertips. Why? Because most of us have the lifelong habit of unconsciously touching our faces or our hair, of rubbing our foreheads or scratching our scalps… and those are places that have a *lot* of sebaceous glands secreting heavy skin oils or, in the case of hair, of collecting it. The oil builds up on the fingertips, and then is left behind in a latent print.

Bioroids have no amino acids in their chemical make-up, of course. If a bioroid had left amino acids in a fingerprint on the bed, it could only be because it had touched human skin first, exactly like a human picking up sebaceous oils from the face or hair by touching them. Amino acids are water-soluble, and would be present in the moisture of the print, though in very tiny amounts.

I was beginning to get a very interesting picture about what had been going on in that room. The position of that one fingerprint on the bed frame alone suggested the 'roid had been in an odd position…and that suggested that Dow's visitor had been a playmate. And there were those long, blond hairs on the pillows.

The elevator mercs appeared to have missed the bed frame, so I dusted the rest of that side, looking for latent prints, and used swabs to collect possible oils and residues from the frame on the other side. I photographed everything, and recorded locations and impressions on the evidence tags. I was already acquiring quite a large collection. I moved carefully, recording each part of the room before I entered it, though the way those clowns had tracked things up already I scarcely needed to bother.

Eventually, I moved to the bathroom.

People are careless. Even if they're trying to not leave fingerprints behind, they'll touch things in the bathroom out of habit, and not think about what they're doing...and every non-floor surface in a bathroom is generally chrome or linoleum or plastic or glass or other hard, shiny, nonporous materials perfect for holding latent prints.

The facilities were designed for low-G, of course. A dry toilet, made from frictionless buckyfilmed ceramic, with directed water jets when you flushed and a seatbelt to hold you in place. A recessed shower stall with an automatic door to keep the water in. A large spa-tub, again with an automatic door. A fabric-covered floor in the stall so you could wear your grip-booties into the shower. The High Frontier's bathroom was pretty fancy, with voice-activated facilities and temperature controls along with the usual manual pressure plates. The non-fabric surfaces all looked clean and shiny, but I almost immediately scored.

There was blood on the shower.

Not much. In fact, I almost missed it, a tiny fleck of red caught between the wall and the fabric floor, and as I searched more closely I found another on the pressure plate on the wall where you turned on the water.

I dusted for prints inside the stall, and did an amino check on the fabric floor.

I found another speck of blood up under the rim of the sink. There wasn't enough for a blood-typing, but so far as I knew, only one person in this room had been bleeding—Roger Dow. I did not believe that Dow had come in here to wash up, however.

I pictured the crime again. Blood splattering everywhere—and flying lots farther and in a finer spray than it would have done on Earth, because here on Challenger there was only a spin gravity of about four hundredths of a G to pull it down. By the time Dow was dead, the murderer must have been drenched with splattered blood.

He must have taken the time to go to the bathroom afterward, strip down, rinse off his self-cleaning clothing in the sink, and step into the shower himself. Blood in the sink, blood on the shower. Then he carefully cleaned up after himself.

Cold—and not entirely consistent with the out-of-control madman image I'd begun to form in my head when I had looked at the wild slashes on the bed.

There were two bath towels on the floor next to the sink, both damp, neither bloodstained. I took vacuum samples from both, and carefully dusted for prints throughout the bathroom. I pulled some good palm prints from the back lid of the toilet, and from the walls to either side. I also downloaded the toilet records. You never know. Sometimes a killer used his victim's toilet before leaving. When you gotta go, you gotta go, and most upscale toilets record the users' glucose, triglyceride, and protein levels, as well as checking for other key healthcare data, like blood.

But why would the killer leave that blood-bathed charnel house in the bed, then carefully clean up after himself in the bathroom? That didn't make sense.

It was time I put a call through to Commissioner Dawn back Earthside.

"Harrison," she said, her face appearing on my PAD's unfolded display. "What do you have for me?"

"Pretty much the mess we expected," I told her. "The elevator mercs tracked up everything, and I had to put my foot down. You, uh, may get a call soon complaining about my poor bedside manner."

"I already have. Twenty minutes ago."

"I stand by what I did. The *gilada* had no business being in here."

"Actually, they do. We may have to negotiate things with the SEA. Don't worry about it for now. What have you found?"

I described my preliminary conclusions. There'd been a bioroid in the room at some point while Dow had been here. The chances were good that it was a gynoid sex toy.

I didn't think the bioroid had killed Dow, though. Why? It seemed unlikely that a bioroid would drag a mining laser into the room, put it down, have sex with Dow, *then* slice him to pieces.

The murderer was either known to Dow, or Dow thought the murderer was the maid coming up for room service. Why? He'd been in bed when the murderer walked in and switched on the laser. We knew Dow had called for room service at around 2330 last night; if the murderer had shown up a few minutes after that, Dow might have voice-opened the door and let the murderer in.

Otherwise, the murderer needed either a key card or some decent hacking skills. Why would Dow order the door to open to a stranger?

And, to wrap things up, I admitted that I was suspicious of the crime scene. There were things that just didn't fit—the fact that the murderer had snicked off Dow's left arm without burning the transplas behind it, the fact that there was so much blood, when the wounds from a mining laser should have been instantly cauterized, and the fact that the killer had carefully cleaned the bathroom, but left the main room drenched with blood.

"Murder scenes always have contradictory evidence in them, Harrison," Dawn told me. "You ought to know that by now. Anyway, don't sweat the small stuff. We have a material witness, and we know who had this done."

"Oh? Who?"

"We picked up Noise a couple of hours ago. He's in Detention downstairs."

"He's confessed?"

"Not yet." She seemed unconcerned. "He will."

"He's supposed to be working for Melange now, right?"

"That's the word we have. We'll confirm that by tonight. When we do, we'll go after Melange. They have the motive.

Dow was going to pull strings to create legislation that would eliminate clones from the work force, and the mining concerns can't afford that. The murder weapon matches a mining laser stolen from Alpha Prospecting a couple of days ago. A miner—or someone working for a mine boss—killed Dow. Q.E.D."

"I'd feel better about that hypothesis if more of the physical evidence lined up."

"Like I said, don't overcomplicate things."

"I'm not. I'm trying to be thorough."

"What you are looking for, Harrison, is proof that someone we can link to the miners, preferably Melange, was in that room at around 2330 last night. I suggest you look at the seccam records."

"I intend to. *And* to question the maid. And Housekeeping." There were some problems there, too, that just didn't add up.

"Okay…but make it fast, and then get your tail back down to headquarters. We know who we're going after. And they're going to fight back."

True. The mining bosses were not known for their quiet and reasonable ways. They were powerful, and they fought dirty. With *lawyers*.

At the same time, I was not convinced that the mining bosses were the answer. Not yet.

"I think it advisable," I told Dawn, "to dispatch an evidence team up here."

"Damn it, Harrison, that's expensive! That's why I sent *you*!"

"I know. But I want a full GCP work-up of Room Twelve."

GCP—Genetic Chemical Presence. A team of men in cleansuits would come in and literally vacuum up everything in this room. All the blood. All the stray hairs and skin cells I'd missed. The sheets. The carpeting. The dust mites in the mattress. The outer layer of paint on the walls. *Everything*. It would all be put through the big chemical analyzers back at

NAPD HQ; they would sequence out every bit of DNA and other molecules that could be extracted, and spit out a list of everything found, together with probabilities, listed as percentages, of what belonged to whom—blood, semen, perspiration, skin cells, eyelashes, even stray molecules of amino acids. Was *all* of the blood on the bed Dow's? The analysis would tell us. Were there hairs or skin cells left on the rug or on the laser by the murderer? The analysis would find them. How many people had been in the room recently, and what were their genotypes? The analysis would tell us that. Was the murderer a human or an android? The analysis might tell us that as well. I simply didn't have the equipment or the training for such a comprehensive study.

It was crime-scene forensics on an industrial scale.

"That's going to take time, Harrison," she grumbled. "Couple of days at least."

"What we're looking for will keep," I told her.

In the meantime, I had a complete range of physical evidence identified by where I'd found it and backed up by photographs. That would give me something to go on.

But no matter how exhaustive I was, in my experience the physical evidence could lie because people misinterpreted it. I had a lot more faith in human testimony.

And the maid who'd found the body would be first on my interview list.

Chapter Six

Day 2

Fuchida had given me a room, number ninety-three on the main level. It didn't have Room Twelve's view, but it was big enough for me to run some tests in my evidence kit, and big enough, after a good night's sleep, to let me interview Maria Delgado, the maid who'd found Dow's body.

"Hello, Maria," I told her as she walked in. She was wearing the hotel uniform, a blue iridescent skintight with the hotel logo, and she looked pinched and terrified. I stood up. "Have a seat. I just want to ask you a few questions."

"Y-yes, sir." She could barely speak.

"There's nothing to be afraid of. You're not a suspect. But you may have noticed some things that will help us in our investigation. Understand?"

She managed a jerky nod.

I had my PAD recording both audio and visual. "Okay. I'm recording this. Interview with Maria Delgado, Dow murder case," and I added the date and time. "Okay, Maria. First of all, I'd like you to sign this."

"*¿Que es eso?*"

"It says you've volunteered to answer my questions of your own free will. It says you're waiving your right to an attorney for this questioning, and it's giving permission for me to take some samples—fingerprints and blood. Is that okay?"

"Yes, sir." There was no hesitation.

"Do you want to have an attorney present?"

"No, sir. I don't have one."

"We can get one for you if you like."

"No, sir. I'll…I'll just answer the questions. Anything you want."

"Very good. Thank you." I let her thumbprint the form, which I put away in my club. "Okay…your name and address?"

"M-Maria Chavez Delgado. I live here at the High Frontier."

"Where are you from, Maria?"

"New Angeles. Just north of Guayaquil."

"Occupation?"

"Housekeeping technician. Sir."

"I see. And Housekeeping got a call last night from Room Twelve?"

"Yes, sir."

"What time?"

"It was logged in at 2317, sir."

"And what was requested?"

"Mr. Dow asked for…for fresh sheets."

"And you took them up?"

"Yes…"

"What time did you get there?"

"It was…it was around 2330, sir."

"So…twelve, thirteen minutes after Housekeeping got the call. That's a quick response."

"We try to be, sir. Uh, quick, I mean. Ms. Robards can be pretty sharp to us if we're not on our toes."

"Ms. Robards?"

“She’s the shift super, sir.”

“Your boss.”

“Yes, sir.”

“Okay. You went to Room Twelve with some fresh sheets.”

“Y-yes…”

I could see the terror in her eyes. I decided to change tack for a moment. “Where is Housekeeping, anyway? Where were you coming from?”

“It’s on Sublevel One. That’s one down from this one.”

I had a map-pad on the desk, a disposable flatscreen with the complete layout of the hotel, left for guests who might want to go up to the Athletic Center, or find the restaurant on the other side of the lobby. “Show me on this, would you?”

She traced her journey from Housekeeping, up an elevator to the second level, then down a passageway to Room Twelve. I pointed to the last stretch of her journey. “This passageway here,” I said, indicating the corridor coming off the ramp from the hotel lobby. “That’s the only way in from the lobby, right?”

“There are emergency exits at the far ends of these hallways, sir.” She pointed them out. “But this is the only way in from the lobby, yes.”

“Those emergency exits. An alarm sounds if you open them?”

“Yes, sir.”

I’d check that later. “When you were in this part of the hallway,” I continued, “did you meet anyone?”

“No, sir.”

“No one at all? No guest? No one else on the staff?”

“No, sir. The hall was empty.”

“You’re sure of that?”

“Yes, sir.”

“Okay. You got to the door to Room Twelve. What happened then?”

“I thumbed the door announce.”

That was the small panel in the center of the door, an electronic door chime.

"And what happened?"

"There was no answer, sir."

"And?..."

"I rang twice more. And then, well, I...I thought it was possible that Mr. Dow had just stepped out, that he'd called Housekeeping for fresh linen, then left and gone down to the bar or someplace while I changed his bed." The terror was returning, the eyes in her dark face growing large. The words began spilling out in a torrent. "It happens all the time! The guests ask for room service and we take care of it while they're out, because the risties don't want to see the staff and Ms. Robards says we're supposed to be invisible on the job and I didn't want to—"

"Okay! Okay!" I held up a hand. "Take it easy, Maria. It's okay."

"I was just doing my job!" The tears were flowing now.

I handed her a tissue from the dispenser in the desk. "So you opened the door..."

She nodded, dabbing at her nose. "I used my passcard."

"And what did you find?"

"*¡Oh, Jesus y María! ¡Fué horrido!*"

"You found Mr. Dow..."

She nodded, a jerky, almost spasmodic movement of the head. "*¡Tanta sangre!*"

"Was there anyone in the room? Anyone besides Mr. Dow, I mean?"

She shook her head.

"*Dígame*, Maria. What did you do next?"

"I...I was sick."

"What...there on the floor?" I hadn't seen any sign of vomit inside the door. Had someone cleaned it up?

She shook her head again. "No, sir. I went to the bathroom."

Ah. That made more sense. "And there was no one in the

bathroom?"

"No, sir."

"Maybe standing inside the shower stall, hiding from you?"

"No, sir. The shower stall—it has a transparent front. But it was open, anyway. There was no one in there."

"I see. Was the bathroom clean, pretty much? No blood on the floor, nothing like that?"

She shook her head. "No, sir. There were some used towels on the floor beside the sink. I didn't see any blood."

I'd seen those when I'd been in there, and pulled samples. "But nothing else?"

"No, sir."

"What about blood on the bathroom floor?"

"No. I didn't see any. I don't know…"

I considered the testimony for a moment, wondering what else to ask. The girl hadn't seen anything useful, it seemed.

"Did you touch anything in the room?"

"Y-yes, sir."

"What?"

"I—I touched the wall behind the toilet, while I was being sick. I might have touched the wall beside it, too."

I remembered pulling the prints from beside the toilet. They'd been full handprints, and looked small—like a woman's. Like Maria's.

The fact that she'd remembered that little detail went a long way to establishing her credibility, so far as I was concerned.

"After you were sick, what did you do?"

"I left the room, locked the door…and I called Ms. Robards on my personal PAD. I told her…I told her…"

She was about to burst into tears again. "*Está bueno*," I told her. "That's okay."

"There was so much blood!…"

"Okay, Maria. You've been very helpful. Thank you."

She managed a weak smile around the tissue.

"I would like to get handprints and a blood sample from you, if I may."

"*¿Por qué?*"

"If we find your fingerprints in that room," I told her gently, knowing I already had them in my kit, "we want to be able to rule you out as a suspect, right?"

A few minutes later, I was alone in my room. I began using my e-ID and badge number to access hotel records. The first thing I wanted to see was a list of emergency door access incidents.

Those emergency doors at the end of the hallways—they opened onto back stairs going all the way down to the basement level. Push on the access bar, and the door opens, an alarm sounds, and the fact of the opening is recorded in the hotel log. Fair enough. But it also turned out that, as with most hotels, those back stairs and passageways were routinely used by hotel staff. They used a coded pass card or even an e-ID recorded on an implant to open the door without the alarm. And each time the door was opened, the fact was recorded, with the time and with the number of the employee.

According to the hotel log, the door at the far end of the hallway for Room Twelve had been opened seven times between 1800 and 2400.

I made a list of the employees who'd used their cards on the door that night. I would need to check each one out later.

I was facing some troubling questions.

It was the timing that bothered me now. I patched through to the hotel's Housekeeping log, and verified that a call for room service had been received at 2317 last night. But when I went to pull up the actual recording of the call, I hit a blank.

I double-checked hotel procedure. Each room had its own phone system, accessed simply by saying "I want to place a call" out loud in any of a number of languages. Or Dow might have said, "I want room service," or something of the sort, and the room would have patched the call through, and recorded it in case of a dispute later.

There'd been no room phone call from number twelve last evening.

Which meant Dow had used his own PAD, and might even have called from someplace else, like the bar. It was possible. Some people are so used to using their own personal electronics that they don't think of the services provided by a hotel.

Dow couldn't have called from the bar, though, and then been able to get back to his room, get undressed, slip into bed, and get himself murdered before Maria showed up with his sheets.

For that matter, why get into bed if the maid was coming up with sheets? Had he planned on seducing her?

The real kicker, though, was that we were assuming Dow had been killed between 2317 and 2330. Maria had seen no one in the hall when she went to deliver the sheets.

And the emergency door log showed that no one had used it during that time.

So how the hell had the murderer got in, lugging a heavy mining laser?

And then…how had he gotten out afterward without Maria seeing him?

Interesting. I began typing on my virtual keyboard, this time calling up a list of hotel seccams. Unfortunately, there were none in the hallways or in the rooms. Had there been, it would have been simple to see who'd gone in and out of Room Twelve that night, and when.

A few years ago, though, PriRights, a citizens' privacy rights group, had sued and won over the question of cameras in private areas. It was okay to have cameras in public areas—like a city street, or the hotel lobby or restaurant, but not inside private hotel rooms, and not in the hallway outside. Some people, the suit had argued, might not like a public record of them going inside a hotel room with someone else.

But I *could* access a camera on the ceiling of the High Frontier's lobby. Beginning at the time in question, I stared at the lobby through a camera that just showed half of the lower edge of the ramp leading up to Dow's floor, starting at 2315:00. Lots of people wandered in and out of the scene—people leaving the restaurant, someone coming up to the front desk—but no one entering the partly obscured ramp at the top-left of the picture.

At 2328:04, Maria Delgado walked out of an elevator door with an armful of sheets, turned to her right, and vanished up the ramp. No one had come out of the ramp in the time I'd been watching.

There was something else bothering me now, too. If Dow had used his own phone to make what was essentially a call from outside of the hotel's internal phone network, his voice hadn't been recorded. I had no way to prove that the person who'd made that call was Roger Mayhurst Dow, and *that* set the alarm bells ringing in my head.

So far, we had a time-of-death pegged at between 2317 and 2332—the time Maria called her supervisor. But if we didn't know that the call at 2317 was Dow…

I logged into the security camera system, and wound things back to 1800, five and a half hours before Maria found Dow's body.

It was going to be a long afternoon. I used the room's system to call room service, to have lunch sent in. While I was waiting, I put some samples into the portable analysis unit in the evidence kit, and started it cranking. The process would take half an hour.

Room service wasn't bad, as hotel food goes. Baked gog—not fried, because of the low gravity—and hydroponically grown mashed potatoes, gravy, and g-beans, the big ones the size of your fist, where two are enough for a meal. Coffee, strong and black. Ms. Robards herself delivered the tray.

"Is there anything else you'd like, sir?"

"You can tell me about Ms. Delgado."

"What about her?"

"Is she a good worker? A good employee?"

"Oh, yes. A little flighty. She's so young…"

"But truthful?"

"Oh, yes!"

"Ever given to exaggeration?"

"Well, she lied to me once on a towel count."

"Lied?"

A shrug. "Perhaps she was mistaken. But sometimes guests take towels with the hotel logo, as…as a kind of souvenir. We charge them for anything that turns up missing afterward. Once, she told me the towel count was correct, but it wasn't. It was one short."

"As you say, possibly a mistake on her part."

"Yes, sir."

"What about the towel count for Room Twelve?"

"I…beg your pardon?"

"Has someone counted the towels in Room Twelve?"

"We haven't been allowed in to clean the room!"

"Ah, of course. Tell me, were there any other calls from Room Twelve that night?"

She shook her head. "No, sir."

"Okay. Thank you."

She nodded and let herself out.

I was pretty sure Maria had been telling the truth to begin with, and the camera record bore her out. But it was good to have verification from someone who worked with her.

By the time I mopped up the last of the gravy, my chem results were done. I ran through the results on my PAD.

The blood was O positive, verifying my quick-test results.

One of the wet spots on the bottom sheet and mattress was semen—again, type O positive. It was contaminated with blood, as I'd expected, but the test unit was smart enough to pull the two substances apart and analyze them separately.

The other two wet spots—*hmm*. Now *that* was interesting. Water, glycerin, propylene glycol, polyquaternium-15, methylparaben, propylparaben, and dimethyl silicon dichloride... again with some blood contamination, but with enough of the liquid available that I could get a solid read-out.

I had to go on-Net to check to be sure. After a bit of hunting, I came up with the answer. What I had here was the ingredient list for any of several brands of commercial lubricating gels... all except for that last, the dimethyl silicon dichloride. I had to do a bit more searching on the Net to track down that one, and finally found out that lube plus dimethyl silicon dichloride was what was used in gynoids to reduce friction when it came to moving parts.

I thought about that bioroid print on the bed frame, then checked the photos I'd taken when I sampled those wet spots. This was confirmation that Dow had had company last night—a sex-service bioroid.

But when? And was the bioroid the murderer?

So I began watching five and a half hours of lobby surveillance camera footage. I sped it up times two, but no more than that. I didn't want to miss anything. I could have routed it through to my PAD secretary, of course; though not a true AI, he was bright enough to handle routine surveillance, to flag me if he saw something within an easily defined parameter like "any person going into that hallway."

But deep down, I don't entirely trust machines. It's weird, I know, seeing as how much I have to rely on them in my work. But I need the human touch.

And I knew I could trust myself.

So I began at 1800 and watched that sliver of a hallway entrance, making notes each time someone walked in or out. I saw Dow coming in from the direction of the restaurant at 1925:13. He was alone.

Several people entered the hallway, several different people came out. I recorded their faces and the times. Probably they were innocent hotel guests, but I would have to follow up on all of them. One of them *might* be the murderer.

At 2015:56, I spotted the bioroid going in.

I froze the image and zoomed in, backing her up so that I could see her come in from the lobby's front door, walk to the front desk, talk to the clerk, then turn and walk into Dow's hallway. I recognized the type—shoulder-length blond hair, full lips, and upper-body sexual characteristics out to here, giving her a somewhat top-heavy appearance. She was wearing a bright-red, skin-tight sheath that accentuated those characteristics by only coming up to *here*, barely concealing them, though her throat, back, and shoulders were discretely covered. She was an Eve-model, one of the more popular pleasure androids out of Eliza's Toybox.

I made a note to check with the front desk. They weren't allowed to give out room numbers or names of guests, so what had she asked them? Directions to Room Twelve, perhaps?

I kept watching. More people going in, more coming out. I recorded each face and time.

At 2042:27 I saw something else that made me sit up and take notice. A very small, bald, slight-looking man with a nervous expression entered the lobby. He was carrying a suitcase two times too big for him—the thing must have massed forty kilos. Sure, it weighed a fraction of that in .04Gs, but it would still have had forty kilos' worth of inertia, and this guy handled it like it was nothing—like he was used to hauling around heavy gear in low-G.

He was wearing a Melange Mining jumpsuit, the grey-green variety reserved for clones, and I could clearly make out the barcode on the side of his neck.

I froze-frame the image, zoomed in tight, and pulled a screenshot of the clone's neck. I didn't even have to print it out. I could feed the barcode directly into a Net search algorithm that downloaded that individual clone's data in less than a second.

HENRY 103, MARK.

SERIAL NUMBER: 103-465-237-870(C).

RESIDENCE: HEINLEIN, FREETOWN, BLOCK 1013, CUBE 134 GREEN.

OWNER: JINTEKI.

EMPLOYER: MELANGE MINING CORPORATION.

OCCUPATION: T90 STRIP-MINER OPERATOR, CLASS 1(C).

HEIGHT: 152 CM.

WEIGHT: 68 KG.

HAIR: BROWN.

EYES: BROWN.

SEX: MALE (C).

AGE: 12.

PREVIOUS ARRESTS: THREE.

THREAT: LOW.

I followed up on the arrests. The human miners working with Henry didn't like him, it seemed. He'd been accused of assault and arrested three times, but the case each time had been dismissed. I scanned down through the data, but found nothing unusual or alarming. Mark Henry had been granted leave yesterday morning by his block supervisor in Freetown, and caught a ferry Beanstalk-bound out of Kaguya. He'd arrived at the Challenger Planetoid at 2010 hours last night with one piece of luggage, and proceeded immediately to the High Frontier.

Dawn was looking for someone associated with one of the big mining companies. I seemed to have found one. I was very interested in what he might have been carrying inside that suitcase.

I waited, watching. At 2122:25, Mark Henry came back down the ramp, walked hurriedly past the front desk and back toward the terminal. The look on his face was...peculiar. Again I wished I could read clone expressions. It looked like a combination of blind fury and severe indigestion.

He did *not* have the suitcase with him.

Twelve minutes later—at 2134:17—the lovely-in-red Miss Eve Bioroid reappeared, walking down the ramp and out through the lobby. She had that amazing killer walk that only a good gynoid or a real woman can manage.

Which left me with a lot of questions. Had Eve gone to Room Twelve? Hotel records would not admit it if she had, not unless she'd been a hotel guest.

Had Mark Henry gone to Room Twelve? Same problem.

What had happened to his luggage?

And when those two had emerged from the corridor into the lobby once more...had Roger Dow been alive?

Chapter Seven

Day 3

I slept like the proverbial log.

Usually, I have trouble sleeping in microgravity, especially in zero-G. I tend to have dreams about the War. But under .04Gs—with me weighing all of 3.2 kilos—even a solid plascrete floor doesn't feel all that hard, and the traveling of two days before, plus the fact that I hadn't had much sleep in the last forty-eight hours, had left me pretty tired.

By the time I woke up, my crime lab in a box had come up with a book-length report for me on all of the samples that I'd fed it the night before. An official request to Salvavidas, the New Angeles health insurance company used by Humanity Labor, had gotten me both a complete blood type series and a DNA readout for Dow. That told me, without any possible doubt, that the body in Room Twelve had been his.

Yeah, I'm the suspicious type. Goes with the territory. I'd needed to be sure that someone wasn't pulling a switch on me, killing someone else and making Dow disappear. In this day of genetic typing, that sort of thing is next to impossible to pull off, but I'd still needed to rule out the possibility. I still needed to check the Challenger facility morgue, too…a little chore I definitely was not looking forward to.

I also had a set of Dow's finger- and handprints for comparison. Most of the prints in that room were his. Big surprise. He hadn't been trying to hide his presence.

And, yes, the prints by the toilet were Maria Delgado's, no question.

There was a list of twenty-three latent prints, only four of which were complete, that didn't match either Delgado or Dow. Those might belong to other members of the Housekeeping staff, they could belong to the last person to use that room before Dow, they could belong to idiot elevator mercs who'd entered the room without a cleansuit or gloves…

…or one or more could belong to the killer. I zapped them all back to the NAPD print department.

There was just the one print belonging to a bioroid, and I needed to follow up on that. The only bioroid entering that hallway last night had been the Eve-model I'd seen on the lobby security camera.

And bioroids are strong. She could easily have handled the mining laser, probably even done it one-handed.

The various DNA and amino tests didn't tell me anything new. The semen on the bed had been Dow's. No surprises there, not if Eve had been in his bed last evening.

The glycerin lube was confirmed—with a 93% probability that it had come from a bioroid. There *were* commercial lubes on the market with dimethyl silicon dichloride in their makeup, products available in bottles or tubes, but those were more popular in Europe, less likely to show up in New Angeles.

Those blond hairs from the pillows were human, but genetinkered for inorganic transplant. The bioroid, again.

And then there was the oil.

I'd sampled a number of spots by the door and near the mining laser, places where the killer might have stood when he opened fire. The analyzer had come back with a long list of chemicals and a probable breakdown of sources: packing gel and machine silube.

Not the kind of gel or lubricant I was likely to find inside a bioroid. The packing gel was a fairly common silicon-based glycerin used for storing weapons and certain devices such as mining lasers. The silube was similar to a light machine oil, but consisting of silicone and carbon buckyballs, a low-friction compound used in mechanical systems to prevent seizing or jamming. A mining laser might have the stuff coating moving parts, like the trigger assembly and the power switch. There'd been traces all over the mining laser, and some isolated patches on the carpet.

Looking at a Computer Assisted Drawing of the crime scene, I decided that the murderer had dropped the laser when he was finished with it, and that it had hit the floor and bounced at least twice. A Huong-Zhen regolith beam tunneler, Mark V, Mod 2, according to the online operating specs, massed 35.5 kilograms, but in that room it had weighed less than a kilo and a half. Yeah, it would have bounced.

There were no useful biological traces on the laser, though, damn it. The elevator mercs had been too thorough.

I did have one pleasant surprise from that quarter, however. Results from the yellow jackets' evidence sweep had come back. It all appeared to be in order and properly labeled and referenced—no screw-ups there, thank God—and it included some important information.

The blood on the bed and floor was Dow's: confirmed.

A tissue sample taken from the body was Dow's; I would confirm that later in the morgue.

And a tissue sample had been found on the laser.

On the laser!

I read further.

Most of the mass in the Mark V tunneler is in the battery, a bulky, heavy box that snaps in at the rear and actually becomes the device's buttstock. You attach the battery by placing the bottom of the connector block on the receiver rim, then swinging the battery up and in until it clicks solidly home. If you're not careful, you can catch your hand between the block and receiver, and it can give you a nasty pinch.

Apparently, that was exactly what had happened here. The rent-a-cops had swabbed up a tiny sliver of skin caught between the battery and the body of the laser, enough to give a complete genetic profile.

I couldn't identify the individual without matching the profile to someone's DNA readout, but the analysis had been able to tell a couple of things right off the starting block.

Whoever had left that bit of skin behind was male.

And whoever it had been was a clone.

Lots of humans are G-mod, of course, with genetic modifications ranging from improved intelligence to increased strength to strangely colored hair or patterns on the skin. G-mods are different from cyberware add-ons, of course, which involves adding parts rather than growing them. Nowadays, the line between cyberware and genetic bioware is damned thin. Originally, G-mods had to be applied *in utero*, but for the past fifty years it's been possible for anyone to walk into a gene clinic and inhale or swallow nanobiotic agents that would begin making changes to the basic human genome. As cells divided and reproduced normally, they would pass on the new genetic information; in a couple of months of treatments, you could have purple skin or cat's eyes or strength enough to bench press 200 kilos in a one-G field.

Clones were extreme examples of this.

For clones, though, Jinteki and a few others took a single cell and tweaked it into being a zygote. Within certain fairly broad limits, they could rewrite the genetic code in that cell to make much more serious alterations than skin color. The clone was given strength, yes—and a skeletal structure to match. Human G-mods with enhanced strength had to be careful not to snap their bones.

There were genetic tweaks that made the zygote grow very quickly, reaching adulthood in as little as three years. And there were telomere timers built into the rewritten genome that caused the clone to die—to "retire" in Jinteki's weasel-speak—in twelve to fifteen years. Both of these were present according to the read-out.

The DNA analyses could even read the telomeres—the lengths of repetitive DNA sequences at the tips of each chromosome that kept the strand from unraveling—and estimate that the clone who'd pinched his hand in the mining laser had been about twelve years old.

I checked my electronic notes. Yep. Mark Henry, the clone I'd seen with the big suitcase in the surveillance vids, was twelve years old.

Hey! Maybe this was going to be a quick and simple case after all.

I zapped all of the data back to headquarters, along with a personal recommendation that they put out an APB for the clone Mark Henry.

There was still something bothering me about the picture, though.

Walk it through.

Dow eats dinner in the hotel restaurant, and goes back to his room at 1925:13 last night.

Fifty minutes later, at 2015:56, the Eve bioroid arrives. She goes to Dow's room, does the bouncy-bouncy with him, is acrobatic enough to plant her fingerprint on the bed frame, and drip a couple patches of synthetic lube on the sheets.

At 2042:27, just under half an hour later, Mark Henry walks in, carrying a mining laser inside a large suitcase. He goes to Dow's room—probably unpacks the laser and snaps in the battery pack out in the hall, pinching a finger as he does so—then steps into the room. Maybe Dow and Eve are still going at it. Maybe she's already up and out of bed. But one way or the other, Henry slices and dices Dow until there's nothing left but blood and spare parts. Either he or Eve—or maybe both of them—go to the bathroom, strip, wash the blood out of their clothing, wash the blood off themselves, then clean up the bath after them.

At 2122:25, Mark Henry leaves Dow's room, walks down the ramp and through the lobby, looking like he has indigestion.

Twelve minutes later, Eve follows him, slinky and sexy in that blood-red sheath.

And an hour and forty-one minutes after that, Henry phones the High Frontier's Housekeeping services, identifies himself as Roger Dow in Room Twelve, and requests clean sheets.

Sounded good, with just two lingering questions.

Was forty minutes long enough for those two to murder Dow, then wash themselves and their clothing and clean up the bathroom?

And where the hell was the suitcase?

I called up the surveillance images again, studying both Henry and Eve as they left the hotel.

Neither of them looked wet.

Now, self-cleaning clothing can fool you on a case. Chances were good that the blood would have slipped right off of the bioroid's dress—assuming she'd been wearing it when Henry broke in, and even if she'd washed it in the sink it would have been dry in moments.

Same for Henry. I wasn't sure whether miner's jumpsuits were self-cleaning or not—I needed to check that—but he wouldn't have been able to keep splattering, low-G blood from landing on his skin.

Okay, maybe Eve had hidden in the bathroom while Henry

carved up Dow. No blood on her. Henry drops the laser and goes into the bathroom for a quick wash-up. Eve cleans up after him because bioroids are *fast*. Even at that, forty minutes didn't feel like enough time for Henry to shower *and* for the two to clean up after themselves. Something wasn't right.

It made sense and hung together, though, just barely…except for the question of the suitcase.

At the moment, the most likely explanation was that Henry had left the suitcase empty and open in the hall outside. For whatever reason, he'd left it there when he fled the scene, and someone from Housekeeping had moved it between 2042, when Henry arrived, and 2329, when Maria came by with the sheets. A search of the back stairs, of Housekeeping downstairs, and of the hotel lost and found might produce it.

One conclusion I could make readily enough: Henry and Eve had been working together. She'd *been* there, either in the main room or safe from splattering in the bathroom while Henry killed Dow. Maybe she'd been sent in first to keep Dow occupied; it must have been a hell of a shock when Henry had come through that door with the laser. Then she'd helped Henry clean up after the fact, and waited for twelve minutes until he left. Or else Henry had brought the laser in and *she'd* used it to slice up Dow, after having had sex with the guy for a half-hour. That didn't feel quite as right as the other, but it was a possibility.

There was still one other mystery, though. Clearly, Eve had been invited to the room. Dow must have let her in when she arrived. But how had Henry gotten inside with the laser a half-hour or so later? The bioroid *might* have left the door cracked open a bit and Dow hadn't noticed. More likely there was a simpler answer: Henry had pressed the door chime, Eve had called "Come in!" from the bed—probably much to Dow's consternation—the voice-activated lock had clicked open…and in walked Henry.

Nice, neat, and tight. Just the way Dawn liked them.

So why didn't I believe my own story?

Motive was a part of it. Having a clone and a bioroid working together to murder a full-human in such a spectacularly gory fashion would play well with the tab-rags. Humanity Labor and Human First would both be salivating over this—one of their own brutally killed by two murderous androids.

But what would have been their motive?

Clones *are* capable of crimes of passion. They're human, after all, with all of the wiring full-humans have for love and hate and anger and lust and every other emotion in the human spectrum. They can even have sex, though their genome keeps them sterile. Where they're different is in the conditioning. Jinteki makes sure their brains mature with very deep channels devised to keep them in line. Love your work. Obey orders. Be quiet. Fit in. It takes *a lot* to break a clone out of that conditioning to the point where he might actually get angry enough to kill someone.

Bioroids are capable of crimes of passion, too, though in general that's even less likely. The programming process for bioroids includes conditioning as deep as a clone's. *Act* like you love your work. Obey orders. Be quiet. Fit in. A bioroid's programming, especially the neural channeling that gives them personalities based on a human model, seems to give them human emotions. The experts, though, are still arguing whether an AI can really feel emotions, or if it just mimics them, doing so with such precision that it can even fool itself.

What it came down to was this: I was willing to believe that a sex bioroid or a miner clone *could maybe* feel enough rage to kill a human…and the crime scene suggested that the murderer had lost control, slashing Dow with a 100-kilowatt laser a dozen times and chopping him into bloody bits.

But Humanity Labor was going to argue that Dow had been killed before he was able to convince legislators to pass laws eliminating androids from the work force, and *that* suggested premeditation, not a crime of passionate rage. And there was the planning involved, using Eve to distract Dow and get Henry into the room with a laser, then cleaning up after, and making the call to Housekeeping to throw us off the track about the time of death.

So which was it? Wild rage because Dow was trying to block androids from the work force? Or cold and calculating premeditation?

I had to go with premeditation based on the evidence, and I wasn't certain that clones or bioroids could think that way. Sure, cold and calculating perfectly described bioroids in the public imagination, but things just weren't that simple. There were too many safeguards built in.

A couple of centuries ago, back before humans even walked on the Moon, there was a writer of popular fiction who wrote a lot about robots. Most of his guesses about the future of robotics had turned out to be wrong, of course; after all, he'd been an entertainer, not a writer of scientific treatises on engineering or AI programming.

But this writer's robots, with their positronic brains, had run according to something called the Three Laws of Robotics. What these boiled down to were armor-plated rules that made it impossible for a robot to harm a human under any circumstances, or to allow one to come to harm.

A nice idea, but not practical in the real world. Suppose a robot has a split second to save a human from certain death—and can only do so by killing another human who is about to murder the first? Suppose a robot confronts a new Hitler or Pol Pot or another General Tseng and the only way to prevent mass genocide is to kill the bastard? Never mind weaseling out of the question by saying the robot can try to immobilize or incapacitate the villain; in a hand-to-hand fight *nothing* is certain, and to save a life—or millions of lives—snapping the guy's neck or shooting him dead might well be the only sure option.

Still, Haas-Bioroid had done their best to make sure that their products couldn't harm humans by way of massive neural conditioning that would shut the thing off if it began planning a human's death.

So how had Eve gotten around that programming? Or Mark Henry, for that matter? With him, he would have trouble just getting himself to the point where he could even think about such things. For him, thinking about work was so much more pleasant.

No, planning the murder of a lobbyist who was about to help create laws against simulants in the work force is something a *human* would do. A bioroid and a clone might be given certain isolated tasks to complete—to carry a laser inside a suitcase up to a certain room at the High Frontier and assemble it, for example—but plan out the whole thing, then carry it out with such bloody, wild, and apparently emotional abandon?

It didn't feel right.

There were three individuals I wanted to talk to right now.

Two of them were the suspects—the Eve bioroid and Mark Henry 103. I'd have to check Beanstalk records to see whether they'd gone out, to the Moon, or in, toward Earth...or if they were still here on the Challenger Planetoid. First guess would be that they were on the Moon. The bioroid would have to return to Eliza's Toybox, unless she'd gone rogue. And Henry would need to report back to work, or risk a retire-on-sight sanction by both Melange and Jinteki.

But I also needed to talk to someone about Dow. I needed to know more about the guy, about what he'd been doing for Humanity Labor, about his personal and private life if possible. So far, he was little more than a cipher. To do that, I would need to talk to his boss—Thea Coleman—and *she* was back on Earth, in the offices of Humanity Labor.

It made the most sense to head on up to Heinlein and see if I could track down Eve or Henry first. I had enough of a case here to charge them, at least—not that charging a simulant carried the same legal burden as a human. Still, I would do it by the book. Henry still belonged to Jinteki, and Eve would belong to either Haas-Bioroid or, more likely, to Eliza's Toybox. This needed to be done right if we were to avoid nasty legal entanglements with the owners.

Before I did that, though, I needed to complete one more chore here at the top of the Beanstalk.

I needed to visit the morgue.

The morgue was a part of the Carousel Emergency Medical Facility. Humans evolved in a one-G gravity field, and there are some aspects of our physiology that just work better in that environment.

So while some hospital facilities work well in zero- or low-G environments—burn units, for example—most off-Earth hospitals have at least a 0.5 gravity field. Broken bones, especially, require at least that much gravity to heal properly, and the only way to manage that in microgravity is to set up a big, spin-gravity wheel.

Partly buried in the surface of the Challenger Planetoid, about a kilometer from the low-G Beanstalk terminal and the High Frontier Hotel, that huge double wheel had been built by the U.S. government and the Weyland Consortium, back in the early days of the space elevator's construction. Eventually the Feds sold out, though.

The wheel had been purchased a decade or so ago by Gianfranco Calderoli, an *uber*-wealthy entrepreneur and casino developer who'd wanted to turn the place into a huge, low gravity nightlife club that would rival the entire city of Las Vegas. At something like a half a billion dollars, it turned out to be a steal. He called it the Castle Club, and based the theme on the old fairy tale of the giant's castle at the top of the beanstalk.

The Challenger Carousel still maintains some of Calderoli's thematic elements from the fairy tale. There's a harp three meters high with a woman's face that sings Mozart, Verdi, and Puccini. And there's an animatronic goose as tall as a man. Both of these are courtesy of Eliza's Toybox, up in Heinlein. That goose almost got the place shut down once. The thing waddles like a real goose, it squawks and honks and hisses like a real goose, and—until a couple of tourists were killed in the ensuing riot—it used to periodically lay a genuine golden egg worth something like twelve thousand dollars. The idea—originally a promotion for the casino—was supposed to bring in a lot of customers who would pay a stiff admittance fee at the door for the one-in-a-gazillion chance of being able to grab a real golden egg.

It had brought the customers in, all right. And two had been shipped home in body bags, while others ended up in the Carousel Emergency Medical Facility.

The hospital occupied a relatively small section of the bottom wheel on two levels. The lower levels of both wheels, further from the hub, were at half a gravity; the upper levels, closer to the hub, were at about a third of a G, roughly the same as on the surface of Mars. I got there by riding the access tube deep beneath the surface from the High Frontier out to the basement level beneath the Challenger Carousel's hub, taking an elevator up to the hub proper at the bottom wheel, and then stepping into one of the horizontal people-movers, letting the spin gravity waft me out and down into an artificial gravity field that grew stronger and stronger the further I dropped out from the hub.

I was met by Dr. Hugh Weissmuller, the hospital's pathologist, and his assistant, Carol Dole.

"Welcome to gravity, Captain Harrison," Dr. Weissmuller said, extending a hand. "You feeling okay? Dizzy or anything?"

"Doing fine, Doctor," I replied. "I haven't been in low-G for that long."

"Fine, fine. Just checking." He had to ask, of course. People who came all the way up-Stalk had experienced considerable acceleration—a G and a half, at least—in order to get there… but often they spent a considerable time in the low gravity sections of the facility. Even after a day or two, you could find yourself feeling dizzy and a bit weak in the knees when you went straight from .04G to .3G, especially if you weren't in real good condition to begin with.

The simulated gravity felt quite natural. The decks are slightly canted to compensate for the additional, almost trivial .04G drag you feel from the planetoid's movement about the Earth.

"Your call earlier said you wanted to see the body they brought in the other night," Dole said. She was short, slender and athletic, like a gymnast, and her voice had a no-nonsense edge. "I hope you have a strong stomach."

"I'll manage," I told her. I looked at the doctor. "Have you done a post yet?"

He made a face. "It's hardly necessary. There's not much question about what killed the poor son of a bitch—massive exsanguination, massive trauma, multiple amputations, and, just to round things out, decapitation. I think we can rule out suicide."

"I saw photographs," I told him. "But I *would* like to know if the victim was drugged or otherwise incapacitated when he was killed."

"Ah, yes. Of course. We *did* draw samples, yes. He had a blood alcohol of 0.07. For someone of his body weight, that's consistent with three drinks. There was no indication of illegal drugs. We did detect mirtazapine—that's a tetracyclic antidepressant—at therapeutic maintenance levels. And his blood showed significantly elevated testosterone levels."

"Oh? What would cause that?"

"Any of a number of things. He could just have high testosterone levels naturally. It happens. Or be on testosterone therapy, though there's nothing in his medical records about that. If he was into power games, power-over role-playing, blowing up at underlings, that sort of thing, that could generate an elevation." He shrugged. "So could sex."

Well, he'd certainly been having sex that night. I hadn't known that intercourse could elevate testosterone levels, but it certainly seemed the obvious conclusion.

"So, nothing that could have incapacitated him?"

"Oh, no. Absolutely not."

"Well, let me see it."

Carol Dole, it turned out, was the morgue attendant on duty this morning, and she led me back into a cool room with a massive refrigerator in the center of it—a refrigerator with four pullout drawers.

"Are you ready for this?" she asked with a raised eyebrow as she handed me a pair of surgeon's gloves.

"Go ahead," I told her, and when I'd snapped the gloves into place, she opened the door and pulled out the slab.

It was bad. I'd seen worse, I suppose, back during the War, but that didn't make it easier. The pieces had been laid out to roughly simulate an intact human body—the head lying above the stump of the neck, the left arm below the stump of the upper left arm, and so on. Intestines had been put into a plastic bag, along with other, less readily identifiable parts. The foul stink of feces lingered above the body despite the bagged internal organs, and I gagged involuntarily.

"Told you," Dole said with a shadow of a smile. I think she was enjoying this.

"You're not like the other girls," I told her. "How long have you been doing this?"

"Seven years," she replied. "But..." She gave a dramatic little shudder. "You *never* get used to it. Not *this*."

I stuck it out for more than thirty minutes. I used my PAD to photograph everything, and from several different angles. I took blood and tissue samples of my own, rather than trust an independent doctor's report. And I spent a long time just… looking.

There was still a lot of blood coating every part, giving everything a slick red color, so dark it was very nearly black. The face was a mask of blood, the eyes still wide open in an expression of perpetual surprise and horror, the mouth open and the lips dragged back in a nightmare rictus that might have been horror, might have been shock or pain.

Where the torso had been cut apart was deeply and badly burned, the tissue turned to black charcoal, the exposed ribs blackened and charred. I'd have expected that from a mining laser.

What I had *not* expected was the sharp, bright, clean slice that had severed Dow's left humerus just above his elbow. The brightness was partially obscured by blood…but when I picked up the lower part of the arm and rubbed my gloved thumb across it, the clotted blood wiped away and the cut through the bone was so clean it looked polished.

Lasers have the reputation for being surgically clean and precise, of course. We've used them in surgery since the 1960s, and they're capable of tremendous precision.

But this was a 100-kilowatt tunneler, packing far more energy than any surgical laser, and had been wielded with wild, sweeping strokes. It would have charred. It would have burned. It would have denatured proteins and it would have caused internal fluids to explode.

But polish bone?

When I was finished, I nodded to Dole and she returned the slab and its bloody display to the refrigerated locker, then shut the door.

"Thank you," I told her.

"I'm impressed," she said.

"Oh? Why's that?"

She gave me a sour look. "Because the last person to come in and look at the guy was sick all over the floor."

That grabbed my attention. Who else was coming in to look at Dow's mutilated body? "Who was it?"

"I don't remember. Lockyear? Lockley? Something like that. Anyway, she was a news reporter…"

I closed my eyes and groaned.

Things had suddenly just gotten a lot more complicated.

Chapter Eight

Day 3

Hey, Rick," she said, brushing back a few strands of that gorgeous auburn hair from her face. "Long time, no see."

Lily Lockwell was waiting for me in the Earthview restaurant when I walked in, a mixed drink of some sort in front of her. That was a bit alarming, since it wasn't yet noon, the sun not yet over the yardarm, and all that. I'd given her a call as soon as I'd left the morgue, and had found out she was on the Challenger Planetoid as well. She'd agreed to meet me.

I walked in through the main entrance, spotted her alone at a table by the window, and joined her. There was no sensation of going around in circles in the Earthview, but there *was* the view of Earth that gave the restaurant its name. The restaurant was in the upper of the two counter-rotating wheels. A large window in one wall, though it seemed like it ought to be looking out over the surface of the planetoid, in fact was looking straight up at the Earth, spanning more than ten degrees of the sky. We were, in fact, on our sides, but the out-is-down spin gravity of the place had flipped things over for us. Earth hung there to the right in blackness, turning around and around in a tight little circle, making one revolution each thirty seconds. The large room was bathed in blue and white light.

I slipped into the seat next to her. "You mad at me?"

"Furious," she said, "but I suppose I'll get over it." She looked down at her drink. "You *knew* Dow was dead, didn't you? When I ran into you at the Root the other day?"

I nodded. "And I wasn't allowed to tell you."

"Bullshit."

"Truth. I was ordered not to talk to the media. What would *you* have done?"

"Trusted you. Confided in you, and to hell with Commissioner Dawn."

"Ah. Well, I'm not really the trusting type."

"I know."

"Hey, it's part of the job. You don't tell me your sources, or write what I tell you to write, right? And I follow orders."

She gave a small smile. "Sometimes."

"So how are you feeling?" I asked, ordering a ginger ale on the table PAD. The Earthview had a human maître d' standing by the lectern up front, but the ordering and food service were strictly electronic. "They said at the morgue that you got sick."

"They're lying. I was *not* sick."

"Oh?"

She winced. "I *wanted* to be, though…yeah…I thought I was going to lose breakfast for a moment there."

"It was pretty bad," I agreed. "Not the worst I've seen, but it was bad. What's your angle going to be?"

"Angle? What angle?"

"You're obviously here writing a story on Dow's murder. How are you playing it?"

"Actually, I was hoping you'd tell me."

I shook my head. "Sorry, sweetheart. It's 'no comment' all the way through."

"I figured as much. But damn it, Rick, this is *big*, and it's nasty. I have sources talking to me about full-blown civil war, humans against androids."

"Are those sources human or android?" I asked.

She hesitated, considering whether or not to tell me. "Human," she finally admitted. "People who want to round up all of the clones and bioroids out there and destroy them."

"Human First?"

"Among others."

"The Clone Riots last year all over again."

"People are *afraid*, Rick. And this story could blow things clear into the stratosphere."

I nodded toward the window at the impossibly gorgeous circle of the Earth going round and round like an old-fashioned vinyl memory device. "We're already well above the stratosphere, sweetheart."

A tiny sound chimed, and my drink slid out of the table well and rode up the little elevator platform to the top. I authorized payment from my implant—God, a soft drink here cost five times what it did on Earth—and took the glass.

"You *do* know how the *Sol*'s page-one headline's going to read on this one, Rick," she said. "'Humanity Labor Lawyer Found Dead, Mutilated.' And below that: 'Police Suspect Mine Bosses.'"

I blinked. "What makes you think the mining CEOs are suspects?"

"It's kind of obvious, isn't it?"

"Not from where I'm sitting."

"Different perspective?"

"Something like that."

"Your main suspects right now are a bioroid...and a mining clone working for Melange."

"*How the hell do you know that?*"

"Whoa, take it easy there, Fish. Don't fry your circuits."

I glared at her for a long moment. Someone was leaking intimate details of the investigation, and few things were better calculated to throw me into a white fury.

Or…

I forced the anger back down. I knew from experience that a shouting match wouldn't budge this woman. "You mind telling me how you found out who my suspects are?"

"I have my sources."

"Such as?"

"Go to hell."

This sparring was getting us nowhere. I thought for a moment. "As it happens, there *is* a bioroid and a mining clone who are…of interest in the investigation."

"And what are *your* sources?"

"Go to hell."

She suddenly leaned over and punched me in the shoulder. "Oh, you're no fun." It lightened the mood a bit.

"No. But I do follow accepted legal procedure. It's called 'the book.'"

She considered me for several seconds, then seemed to reach a decision. "Okay. According to Dow's personal financial report, he was into sex bioroids in a big way, if you know what I mean. Preferred them to women. He rented one from Eliza's Toybox on the Moon as soon as he arrived at the High Frontier Hotel. Paid for her passage down-ferry to the Stalk. Her name is Eve 5VA3TC. She's supposed to be *very*…talented."

"I see. And the clone?"

She shrugged. "Educated guess. According to the Transit Authority records, there was a Henry-type mining clone on the ferry in from the Moon last night. He knew Eve 5VA3TC. In fact, he may be *quite* close to her, according to one of my sources. So I assumed that Henry knew that Eve was here, and threw him out as one of your suspects just to see what you'd say." She sipped her drink. "Thank you for confirming that part for me. Until now I wasn't quite sure."

I cursed myself and my short temper. Lily always had been faster on the uptake than me.

"You're implying that the clone and the bioroid have a little something going on the side?" I asked, considering the idea. "I didn't know clones *had* sex lives."

She shrugged. "Why not? They're under heavy neural conditioning, yes, but they have the equipment and they have emotions. Just like people."

I frowned at her. "Clones *are* people."

"Then I rest my case."

Lily and I had an argument once—I think it was back during the Clone Riots a year ago. She's not convinced that clones qualify as human. I am. Mostly it's just an ongoing philosophical question with no real blood behind it, but she does make me angry sometimes with her oblivious disregard for the patently obvious.

Were clones property? Or were they people being treated like property? The basic question was an old one, long predating the arrival of clones on the scene.

"Consider the facts," Lily continued. "Dow hires Eve 5VA3TC to come out and spend time with him. They hop into bed and do the pokey-pokey. A half-hour later, Mark Henry shows up with a mining laser and takes Dow apart, literally. And the way he did it! Obviously what they used to call a crime of passion."

I shook my head. "I don't buy it, sweetheart. Henry just happened to have a 35-kilo mining laser on him?"

"Then we're stuck with something *much* worse," she told me. "We have a man who's about to convince several powerful U.S. senators and representatives that it would be in everyone's best interest if clones and bioroids were not competing with full-humans for jobs. The mining bosses, the CEOs of Melange and Helios and Lunar Ice, they don't want that, because they actually have to *pay* full-humans, especially for jobs involving high-radiation and vacuum. So they program a mining clone and a bioroid to murder him."

I knew she was trying to draw me out, working me to get some sort of a response, any response, that might give her a lead that would help her develop her story.

"It sounds to me like you have it all figured out. Whom have you been talking to, anyway?"

"You know I can't tell you that."

I chuckled. "Right. It's pretty obvious, though. By now, every person in the High Frontier's staff—Housekeeping, Food Service, Front Desk—they all know what happened in Room Twelve. You found one of them who's willing to talk."

"Maybe."

"And you got to the morgue before I did. Dr. Weissmuller is a thoroughgoing professional, and probably told you to take a hike outside without a pressure suit…but Dole… She likes drama, I think…I'll bet she told you all sorts of things."

Lily looked uncomfortable. She drained her glass, then ordered another drink. She didn't like being that transparent. She preferred to be in control.

Like me.

"The mining bosses angle is important, Rick."

"And which mining bosses angle would that be?"

She made a face. "Don't play dumb, Rick. You're too smart to do it well."

"I'm not playing dumb. But I would like to know what you *think* you know."

"I know the mining bosses weren't real happy about Dow trying to push through legislation to stop them from using clones. A law like that would cost them billions."

"That's one possible motive. It doesn't make them guilty of murder."

"No. But they certainly wanted to stop him."

"They also have lobbyists of their own. And half of Congress must be in their hip pockets."

"But they could have used the Henry clone to take Dow out of the equation. It would've been faster. More certain."

"*Could* have doesn't mean they did."

"Right. You sound pretty sure of yourself. Does that mean you have the case wrapped up?"

"Maybe," I admitted. "Just a few loose ends to tuck in. We have an APB out for Mark Henry."

"Hm. Do your loose ends include Ms. Coleman?"

I stared at her for a beat. "Dow's boss? What about her?"

"You talk to her yet?"

"She's on my list."

She laughed. "You don't know, do you?"

"Know what?"

"She's here."

"What…here at the Earthview?"

"Close enough. In an office at Humanity Labor, in a dome on the other side of the asteroid."

"Since when?"

"Since three days ago. She came up with Dow in order to prep for the meeting with those senators. And I don't think I'll tell you any more. Your quid isn't pro-ing my quo."

"That's blackmail."

"No. More like extortion."

"What do you want?"

"Something I can write about."

"So…this is conditional, is it? I don't help you, so you don't help me?"

"More like I scratch your back, and you reciprocate. Like you *used* to, Rick."

"Damn it, Lil, I can't. I'm muzzled."

"That's really too bad. Because I think you're on the wrong track with Henry. He didn't kill Dow. He *couldn't*."

"Actually, I tend to agree."

She cocked her head. "A hunch?"

"Nothing that definite. There are some things about the case that don't add up."

She grinned. "Such as?"

I smiled back. "You think you're going to get me like that?"

"Doesn't hurt a girl to try."

I'd been thinking, though, and now I reached a decision.

"Yeah, well…the hell with Commissioner Dawn," I told her.

She looked startled. I'd caught her by surprise. "What?"

"The hell with Commissioner Dawn. Want your back scratched? Where does it itch? Up high? Or lower down?"

She gave me one of *those* looks. "I can think of several places."

"Play later." I thought back over the conversation so far, looking for the high points. "I was going to talk to Coleman about Dow. Find out about the guy, what he really believed, that sort of thing. Why do *you* think it's important to talk to her?"

"Dow and Coleman were sleeping together."

"And just how the hell do you know that?"

"I talked to Dow's wife, back on Earth."

"Wait a sec. Dow had a wife *and* he was banging sexbots on the side. You're telling me he also had a thing going with his boss?"

"Apparently. According to Lupe Gonzales—that's the wife—Dow was unhappy with the marriage. They had an open relationship, and he could pretty much go where he wanted with it." She shrugged. "My guess is that Dow felt bored with her, so he began looking for fun elsewhere."

"I take it you talked to her before you came up-Stalk. Was that before the murder?"

"Yes. I was doing some background checking on Dow, getting ready to cover the Congressional meeting up here. Gonzales told me Dow hadn't been home for a month, and that he was chasing his boss. She didn't seem too concerned about it."

No matter how open a marriage might be, human nature always raises its ugly little head. Jealousy has destroyed more open marriages than I know how to count. That might not make sense, but humans aren't rational critters, most of the time. They get possessive, and they get greedy.

After a while they think they own you. Like Nina.

"And have you spoken with Ms. Coleman yet?"

"No. She wouldn't see me."

"That's interesting. Humanity Labor is usually eager for media coverage."

"Usually. Her PAD secretary just told me she wasn't accepting calls, and that Humanity Labor had no comment about the murder."

"I think," I said slowly, "that I'd better pay Ms. Coleman a visit."

"I was hoping you'd see things my way."

First, though, I arranged to have the evidence kit and its refrigerated contents shipped down-Stalk to the NAPD labs. Some of the blood and enzyme studies were too complex to be run on my little club, and I wanted to have them cranked through in case anything else turned up. But I had to pay for special handling in order to maintain continuity in the chain of evidence. Another entry on my expense account; I wondered if accounting would let it go through.

After that, Lily and I spent a couple of hours hunting around the back stairs and Housekeeping chambers of the High Frontier, looking for the missing luggage. Fuchida himself checked the lost and found, and assured me that if it was in the hotel, it would be located.

But we didn't find it. We stopped short of searching occupied rooms—that would have required separate warrants for each—but it didn't appear to be anywhere else on the premises.

Then we called Thea Coleman.

I took some time first to call up her personal file. She'd been with Humanity Labor for twelve years, and become Operations Manager two years ago. Her educational qualifications were impressive—Levy University for business admin and software design, plus MIT for courses in robotics, systems analysis, and general AI. Minors in both business economics and psychology. A real renaissance woman.

She'd refused to talk with Lily and she didn't want to talk to me, either, but she agreed when I told her that I was with the NAPD and that I'd heard she'd had a relationship with the deceased. Yeah, she agreed to see me *real* fast after that.

Humanity Labor maintains its local offices near to the hydrocarbon mines on Farside. They have a strong presence on the Challenger Planetoid, strong enough that only full-humans are working the mines. Clones need not apply.

The Heinlein colony on the Moon tries to be as self-sufficient as possible, of course. They mine ice water at the poles and in subregolithic veins, and that provides the colony not only with water, but also with hydrogen for hydrazine as a monopropellant rocket fuel, and oxygen for breathing. Titanium and silica are common in the regolith, and those can be fused into fairly strong building materials, including anhydrous glass. What's *not* common on the Moon, though, are nitrogen and carbon.

And that's where the Challenger Planetoid enters the picture. They'd needed a fair-sized asteroid to anchor the space elevator, of course. They'd pulled one out of the Outer Belt and nudged it into place, accelerating it with a precisely timed loop past the Moon so that it could be captured and tethered to become the top of the Beanstalk.

The asteroid they chose was a carbonaceous chondrite, the most common kind of space rock there is. Carbonaceous chondrites are rich in hydrocarbons, and that means not only hydrogen and oxygen, but nitrogen and carbon as well—CHON, the basic elements of life.

A tube-lev took us from the Beanstalk terminal straight through the planetoid's heart, emerging at the ferry embarkation platform on the other side. This was where travelers headed for the Moon caught the Challenger Memorial Ferry for the last leg of the trip. Our destination, though, was a blue-grey dome with an entrance just off the terminal. The dome itself belonged to Humanity Labor, though it took guidelights on the walls to walk us through a twisting maze of offices and compartments to bring us at last to the actual Challenger Planetoid offices of Humanity Labor.

Their offices on Earthside are enormous—a titanic arcology in the Manabi District. Up here on the far side of the Challenger Planetoid, the venue was far more modest. Animated wall panels showed humans at work in space: scenes of miners, orbital constructors, surveyors, engineers, medical technicians, transport operators, and hundreds of others. I found it interesting that there were no windows. I suppose that made sense. On Farside, the buildings are all upside down. That out-is-down spin gravity generated by the rotation of the entire space elevator around the Earth once each day meant that the ceilings were toward the planetoid, the floors away, and if you could look outside you would see that immense, coal-black space rock apparently hanging above your head.

That could be disconcerting for visitors.

We found Coleman's temporary office not far from the Humanity Labor reception desk.

"Ms. Coleman?"

"I'm Thea Coleman," she said. She was a thin woman with a pinched face and stringy, red-blond hair. Her taste in clothing ran to brightly and discordantly colored patchworks, complete with flashing LEDs and animations.

A thug in black watched us narrowly from a couch on the other side of the room—a thug with a wicked-looking flechette pistol in a shoulder holster.

"Captain Rick Harrison," I told her. "NAPD. I called you a while ago? And this is my, um, assistant, Lilith."

Lily had insisted on coming along, claiming that she'd been the one to turn up the contact, which was true. I just hoped these two didn't recognize her as a big-time media personality. A cop could get a bad rep hanging around with nosies.

"Pleased to meet you."

"Thank you for seeing us. So...I gather you're Humanity Labor's Operations Manager?"

"That's right."

"Normally you're Earthside? At the Humanity Labor complex?"

"Yes."

"What are you doing up here?"

"I'm...I *was* helping to coordinate a meeting with a senatorial committee," she told me. "Look, I just want you people to find the ones who did this," she added, emotions surfacing in a rush. "Roger...Roger was a *good* man."

"I'm sure he was," I told her. "Actually, I was hoping you could tell us something about him. Did you know him well?"

"We...were lovers." She reached for a tissue from the desk dispenser. "I still can't...can't believe he's gone."

"When did you find out he was dead?"

"Just this morning." She wiped at her eyes with the tissue, then noisily blew her nose. "I called him that day to coordinate something concerning the Congressional meeting the next night...and was told his PAD was out of service. And...and then Bob Vargas called me with the news..."

"Who's Bob Vargas?"

"He's...he *was* Roger's bodyguard."

"Bodyguard?" I hadn't heard that Dow had one.

"Oh, yes. Things have been getting so ugly with the clones and bioroids...the Humanity Labor Board of Directors passed a regulation two weeks ago that said all senior personnel had to have one." She made this last comment with a slight hand gesture toward the thug on the couch.

"Yeah," he said simply. The guy must have massed well over a hundred kilos.

"I see." I smiled at him. "And you are?"

"He is *my* bodyguard, Mr. Harrison," Coleman told me.

"So where was this Vargas character when Dow was getting himself carved up by a mining laser?" I was being deliberately brutal now. I was looking for emotional reactions.

"He was with me," the thug had a bass voice that rumbled as he spoke, "checking things out in the Carousel Boardrooms, where the meeting was gonna be."

"I see. Pretty big responsibility, that."

"Yeah. You said it."

"You were with him?"

"That's right."

"What's your name?"

"Hodgkins. Frank Hodgkins."

"And who do you work for? When you're not pulling bodyguard duty for Ms. Coleman, here, I mean?"

"Humanity Labor. I'm what they call your Mr. Fix It guy."

"Something's broken, you fix it, is that it?"

"Yeah."

"Mr. Hodgkins has been transferred to the security department," Coleman said firmly.

"I see. And who was in charge of security for the meeting?"

"Mr. Vaughn handled those arrangements," Coleman told me. "He's Humanity Labor's Director of Public Relations."

I looked at her. "A PR director in charge of security?"

"Mr. Vaughn had experience. Mr. Martín asked him to handle it."

"And who's Martín?"

"*Mister* Martín is the Chairman of the Board for Humanity Labor. But he is temporarily in charge of security."

I frowned. "Have the senior officers at Humanity Labor been getting many threats?"

"Not…directly. But there've been a lot of rumors. Things are getting very ugly out there, Mr. Harrison. The clones can't be trusted. I don't think bioroids can be trusted, either. They're *machines,* after all."

"How did Mr. Dow feel about clones?"

"Like all of us here, Mr. Harrison, he didn't care for them. He hated them, in fact."

"I see. How about bioroids?"

"Them, too. Frankenstein's monsters. They never should have been created in the first place! Stealing jobs from real humans…"

I considered telling her that I knew Dow had been in bed with a bioroid shortly before the murder, but decided to play things cozy instead, I didn't want them to know everything I knew. They were lying—Mr. Fix It was, at least. And I wanted to know why.

"So…I presume the senators are no longer coming up-Stalk."

"No," Coleman said. "Our head office called them the morning of the scheduled meeting and canceled it. The damned clones have won…at least for now."

"Why do you say they've won?"

"Isn't it obvious? They knew Roger was going to present a *very* attractive package to the Congressional committee. The new law would have ended bioroid and clone manufacture, and phased out their use in the workforce over the next five years. Our experiment with these machines has been a failure, Mr. Harrison, a dead failure. Unemployment among full-humans in New Angeles is at over nine percent—higher in some other cities—and it's all because Jinteki and Haas wanted to play God.

"Well, the clones found out about the proposed legislation, and they decided to stop it. Either that, or Melange Mining decided that losing their clones would cut into their profit margin too much. If they did, they probably programmed a clone to do it for them.

"Either way, Roger is dead and so is the new legislation." Her mouth compressed for a moment into a thin, bitter line. "But they haven't won the war. A battle, yes, but they haven't won the war!"

"Uh-huh."

"Excuse me," Lily put in, "but I wonder if you could tell me something. Why did you decide to hold this meeting up here? Wouldn't it have been safer on Earthside, maybe at Humanity Labor? Or even back in Washington?"

"That decision was made by Mr. Martín," Coleman told her. "He wanted the senators to see the Challenger Mines."

"Oh?" I said. "Why was that?"

"Because the Challenger Mines are fully *human*-staffed. No android machines. No clones. We thought it important to show them what the future *could* be. Without simulants."

"I see. Well…I think that's all the questions I have for you right now. Ah. One more thing, before I forget. Would you and Mr. Hodgkins here be willing to give me some samples?"

"Samples?" Her eyes narrowed suspiciously. "Samples of what?"

"Blood for DNA profiling. Hand- and fingerprints. I'd also like to get in touch with Mr. Vargas—"

"I am *not* giving you any samples, Mr. Harrison." She rose from behind her desk, furious. "None of us are! *That* is what is wrong with civilization today! People treated like machines… treated *worse* than machines! That is what Humanity Labor is pledged to fight! *We have rights!*"

I seemed to have just kicked over a hornet's nest. "You don't *have* to be tested," I said, keeping my voice reasonable and disinterested. "Of course not. The Fifth Amendment guarantees your right to refuse self-incrimination."

"I know what my rights are, Detective! And I've done nothing! *Nothing!* You can't show probable cause, here! You don't have a warrant! And I don't need to submit to your needles!"

"Ms. Coleman—"

"We have fundamental rights to privacy!"

"Yes. I simply—"

"*I am not a machine!*"

"Ms. Coleman—"

"*And I am not some damned, slimy clone!*"

Eventually, we escaped to safety.

Chapter Nine

Day 4

How do you know they were lying?" Lily asked.

We were lying together in bed after a long and thoroughly delightful catch-up on old times. After our visit with Ms. Coleman, we'd returned to Nearside and my room at the High Frontier Hotel. I'd made some more calls and inquiries, gotten more lab results back from Earth, and tried to track down Bob Vargas, but without success. Lily had a room of her own over at the Carousel, but I'd invited her to stay with me for the night, and she'd accepted.

"They claimed their rent-a-thugs had been handling security for the visit by those senators," I told her, "and that Humanity Labor's security department was running the show, at the direction of their CEO. The Secret Service handles security arrangements for visiting senators."

"Damn. I should have seen that."

"More than that, parts of Coleman's…call it her attitude… just don't add up."

"What do you mean?"

"I pulled up her personal file. Her job title at Humanity Labor is Operations Manager, but she has enough programming know-how listed on her résumé to give Noise Reilly a run for his money." I knew she was aware of old Noise, the hacker *enfant terrible* of New Angeles. He'd featured prominently in some stories she'd done about the Stuckey IT scandal a few years back.

"So? Operations Managers need to be e-savvy."

"Sure. But when was the last time you heard someone who could make computer networks sit up and beg for a living go ballistic about privacy rights and not being a machine?"

She frowned. "It's not unthinkable. Someone might know enough about computer networks to get really paranoid about electronic eavesdropping. And anyone working for Humanity Labor is going to feel strongly about android labor."

"True. But…it doesn't feel right, y'know? Something's off about that woman and her response." I grinned. "'Methinks the lady doth protest too much.'"

It was morning, now—the planetoid facility ran on New Angeles time—and the floor-to-ceiling wall display was showing the Earth at just past half phase, with the sunrise terminator curving across the eastern Pacific just offshore from South America. Room Ninety-Three didn't have the transplas window looking straight up at the real Earth as Dow's did, but the digital scene was every bit as big and as beautiful. Most of the western United States was still in darkness, the Pacific coastline picked out by the softly glowing radiance of the Sansan megapolis.

The night before, when we'd been holding each other close after our first sweaty round of getting re-acquainted, the concentration of the lights of New Angeles, centered exactly within the ghostly disk of the world, had been breathtaking. You could see the lights of the other cities in the Western hemisphere, of course—especially the glowing sprawls of Boswash and Sansan—but the glow from New Angeles had looked as large and nearly as bright as the full Moon from Earth.

A city that never slept.

"You can't charge her with aggravated programming skills," Lily pointed out. "As for the security arrangements...wouldn't Humanity Labor want to check things out for themselves before the Secret Service got there?"

"Oh, certainly. I'm sure any corporate security department involved in that sort of meet would," I told her. "But Coleman said Humanity Labor was in charge of the security. Not true. And too many other things didn't add up. Humanity Labor uses the services of Globalsec—that's one of the largest private security firms in the world. You'd think if they were concerned about security, they'd bring up a few platoons of Globalsec troops. Why use labor goons?"

"It's cheaper?"

"It also keeps any dirty secrets inside the family, as it were. Globalsec operations are subject to legal and governmental review. Besides, the whole set-up sounded fishy. Security being handled out of the PR department? That's just nuts."

"I was wondering about that, too." She dragged the backs of her fingernails up the center of my chest. "I guess it pays to be paranoid."

"Sometimes." I kissed her deeply. "Right now, I'm paranoid that you're going to get out of bed and I'll never see you again...except maybe on the evening news."

She kissed back, her hand wandering. "Well, I don't have a deadline right now," she said in my ear a moment later. "The bed is comfortable. I don't think we have to get out of it just yet, do you? I can think of a few more experiments we need to conduct first."

Last night, I'd joked with her about carrying out some important experiments with her in that bed. Turns out you can get pretty damned creative in micro-G.

Yeah, old Roger High-Testosterone Dow must have had an incredible time with his rented sex toy the other night...

A long time later, with the dawn terminator now well clear of the Sansan coast, we were up and dressed and planning the day.

"I'm not going to be tagging after you today," Lily said. "I've got my own stuff to do."

"Suits me. But…stay in touch, okay? *Quid pro quo.*"

"Absolutely."

"So what is it you're going to be up to?"

"I'd like to find Bob Vargas," she said.

"Ha! So would I."

"And I need to get some vid of the hotel, here, to file with my story."

That part made me a little uncomfortable. "You remember… we agreed that you aren't going to talk about the different angles on this case. No theorizing. Not until we know more."

"I know, I know. I'll be a good girl. But you know my editor's going to be hounding me for some in-depths on this one. The victim is too high-profile to bury in the obits."

"Of course. But right now, we have too many different leads, too many ways this thing could break. Let's give them time to develop a bit."

The murder *could* have been exactly what it seemed on the surface—a couple of androids killing Dow to keep him from talking to that Senate committee. But right now it seemed a lot more likely that there was someone behind it—someone like a member of Melange Mining's management, or even some sort of conspiracy among all of the mining companies. I still didn't think Mark Henry could have killed Roger Dow all by his lonesome, and probably not even with Eve's help.

Then there was our Ms. Coleman and her personal thug, Hodgkins. The fact that Dow and Coleman had been lovers immediately threw a whole lot of other possibilities into the mix—possibilities involving human emotions like jealousy and rage and possessiveness. Until I knew why those two had been lying yesterday, I wasn't about to let them off the hook.

I didn't want Lily writing up any of those theories and publishing them, not yet. I didn't want the murderers to know they were on my radar. Even if I wasn't yet certain which blip I was targeting.

"So where are you headed, Rick? Up or down?"

"Up. I need to find Henry and Eve and bring them in if I can. I want to talk to them about what they were doing here the other night. Henry, at least, was involved in the murder. I'd bet a year's salary that he had the mining laser hidden inside that suitcase when he walked in, and I know he didn't have it when he left. Eve's wrapped up in it, too. She was with the victim, and she left the hotel after Henry did."

"But you don't think they actually killed him?"

"I don't know, Lil. I really don't. From what I know of bioroids and clones, though, I just don't think they have the…the programming for it."

"Maybe someone reprogrammed them."

"A possibility. I keep wondering, though."

"Wondering what?"

"Bioroids and clones both undergo a kind of programming—patterning taken from human neural readings."

"Sure," Lily said. "Brain-taping."

"Old-fashioned term," I told her. "And misleading. They don't record a human personality and somehow transfer it to the simulant. But neural channeling can mimic a remarkably human personality."

"So what's the problem?"

"Do clones and bioroids have a moral compass?"

"You mean…do they understand right and wrong, good and evil, that sort of thing?"

"Exactly."

"They seem to…"

"Right. For a bioroid, that could be part of the programming.

For a clone…I don't know. Are they conditioned to be moral? I mean, other than being taught to always obey orders and enjoy work?"

"I'd guess that was up to Jinteki."

"I know a clone who works for the Force," I mused. "She's smart and really…intuitive. She's got this uncanny knack for picking up impressions from her surroundings."

"Caprice Nisei."

"Yes! How did you—"

"It's hard to work the crime beat and not know Caprice," Lily said.

"She seems to have a finely developed sense of right and wrong," I said. "She's absolutely devoted to Jinteki's cloning project. But I think she's more devoted to her sisters."

"Sisters?"

"Several dozen Nisei clones, exactly like her, but still in the vats. Not, uh, not born yet. She's somehow linked in with them, though."

"How does that show her understanding of right and wrong?"

"She's afraid that if she fails, her sisters will be recycled in favor of a Mark III model. She's determined not to let that happen."

"Is that morals? Or fear?"

"Maybe morals *are* fear. Or fear-based. People do the right thing because they're afraid of being found out. Of being caught. Or they're afraid God is going to torture them in Hell for all eternity."

"Jesus, Rick. You *can* be cynical. Maybe people choose to do something because it's the right thing to do."

"Maybe. I don't see much of that in this line of work, though."

"Yeah? Why do you act the way you do?"

I shrugged. "I don't see a moral issue there, hon. I do my job because I like a positive credaccount balance."

"Your balance would look a hell of a lot better if you took bribes. Sometimes I think three-quarters of the Force is on the tri-maf payroll."

She didn't say it, but I knew she was thinking of Louis Blaine. And how did Commissioner Dawn afford that fancy DFM in her parking spot on the NAPD roof?

"Point is...*could* Eve be reprogrammed to kill Dow, or help someone else kill him? Could Mark Henry be conditioned to do it? Or do they have enough of an innate moral sense to...I don't know, resist it somehow?"

"My guess would be that a bioroid can be programmed to do anything the programmer wants it to do. Clones...I don't know about them."

"It wouldn't be that easy with bioroids, either," I said. "Haas-Bioroid's PR department is always proclaiming how safe their products are. 'Programmed for safety and obedience.'"

"It's an interesting question, I'll admit," Lily said.

"Anyway, if I can find Mark Henry and Eve, I'll see what they have to say about human morals. I have a feeling they may see things a bit differently than we do."

"Good luck."

"Thanks." I reached into a jacket pocket, extracting an e-card. It looked much like a traditional business card, and it had my name and contact information printed on one side. It also had an electronic data strip down one edge. "If you find Vargas, give him this."

"Sure." She moved it toward the back of her left hand.

I snapped out my own hand and grabbed her wrist. "Don't."

"But...I don't think I have your current information."

"I'll give it to you. But you don't want it from *that*."

E-cards were like old-fashioned business cards, but could be swiped along a PAD or over a hand implant to transfer electronic data. This one, though, was one of a batch of special cards I'd had printed. Swipe that card, and you not only got my contact information downloaded to your file, but a very compact little virus that had nothing on its algorithmic little mind but the need to ping me if I called for it. If Vargas swiped it into his files, I'd be able to use my police access codes to track him on my PAD from just about any distance, using standard Net pick-ups and nodes.

She twitched the card a few times in front of my nose. "There's a tracking virus in here, isn't there? You want me to do your dirty work."

"If you find Vargas, why should I have to find him again? It's harmless."

"And what kind of moral compass do *you* have?"

"A practical one."

The card vanished into a thigh pouch. "You ready to go? I'll walk you to the terminal."

"Sure."

The door chimed. An image flashed on the wall, identifying Fuchida, the manager of the High Frontier.

"Open," I said, and the door slid aside.

"Mr. Fuchida," I said. "We were just about to check out."

"I am terribly sorry to bother you, Captain Harrison...but after the events of the other night...after poor Mr. Dow's murder..."

The man was in shock. I thought he was going to fall over right there in the doorway.

"What is it?" I asked. "What's wrong?"

"Would you...would you come with me, please? Quickly..."

The High Frontier had several emergency exits throughout its structure, including one midway down each of the long, straight hallways radiating out from the lobby. They were airlocks, with massive walls and heavily dogged hatchways, and with lockers next to the inner hatch containing lightweight pressure suits that would keep you alive for at least a short time on the surface of the asteroid.

Fuchida took us up one level to the same corridor that included Room Twelve. Perhaps fifty meters down the passageway was an airlock. Two men were suiting up—Beanstalk security judging from their yellow garb. I recognized one of them as Smethers, from the other night.

"One of our maintenance people went into the lock," Fuchida explained, "to check the instrumentation, and he saw…he saw…"

"What?"

"Why don't you have a look, sir?"

Fuchida pressed the door actuator, and the inner hatch slid open. The airlock beyond was small, perhaps thirty cubic meters, lined with pipes and valves and equipment lockers. The outer door was closed, of course—the fail safes meant that you *couldn't* activate the outer door when the inner door was open—with a small, square window in it.

A face stared at us from the other side of the transplas window.

Lily gave a small gasp, quickly stifled. Fuchida moaned; murders at his hotel were becoming something of a routine, and I had the feeling that right now he would be happy to give up managing in favor of something quieter. Like riot control.

I stepped into the airlock for a closer look. The face stared back, eyes peeled open wide and rimmed with blood-ice. There was frozen blood on the nose and mouth, too, and in the matted beard. The mouth was open, an obscene rictus, baring teeth and bloody tongue.

For just a moment, I thought that it was Coleman's pet bodyguard, Hodgkins. The guy was bearded, muscular, and was wearing a dark shirt. The hair was darker, though, and the face seemed thinner, more angular, with more pronounced cheekbones, though when a face is contorted like that it can be hard to recognize anyone.

I stepped back inside the hallway. "Let's get him inside," I said.

It took a good fifteen minutes. Smethers told me later the poor bastard had been clinging to a couple of handles mounted on the outside of the outer lock door, and that they'd had to break the corpse's fingers to get him off.

As they laid him on a blanket on the hallway floor, I pinged the guy's e-ID.

Robert Vargas. Humanity Labor.

"Was he...murdered?" Fuchida asked.

"I don't think he stepped outside voluntarily," I said. I went through the corpse's clothing. He was wearing a black shirt with a Humanity Labor logo, like Hodgkins, and he had on a shoulder holster, but it was empty. His pockets were empty as well. I took a closer look at his right arm. It didn't look right.

Broken. Not just broken, but *crushed*, just above the elbow. I tried to imagine what could have caused an injury like that. All I could picture was someone with very strong hands gripping him by the upper arm and squeezing, hard. No human grip could be that strong.

A bioroid might do it.

Maybe a G-mod human could, as well, if he'd been enhanced for strength.

He would have had to drag Vargas into the lock, close the inner door, then open the outer before throwing him out. Humans can survive vacuum for a short time. The trick is to blow all the air you can out of your lungs—be as empty as you can make yourself—so that you don't explosively decompress.

Could the murderer have done all that, and held his breath until the airlock repressurized and the inner door could open? Maybe. It seemed more likely, though, that the murderer hadn't needed to breathe in the first place.

Someone with respirocytes in their bloodstream could manage it.

Or he might have been wearing a pressure suit. I tried to imagine him standing there in the airlock, repressurizing it, opening the inner door so Vargas couldn't hit the emergency entry panel and open the outer door.

I thought of the murderer standing in front of the outer door, the inner door open behind him, watching as Vargas screamed silently in the vacuum outside, clinging to the handles.

If he didn't have respirocytes in his blood, Vargas would have been dead in about thirty seconds.

If he did have respirocytes, it would have taken longer for him to freeze, and for his lungs to begin bleeding out into vacuum.

How long had the murderer stood there?

Through it all, Lily had been filming. She'd pulled out the small, silver monocam she always carried and popped it over her left eye, the tiny, high-def camera filming everything she looked at. I could hear her, too, speaking in a low, quick subvocalization as she described what she was seeing, but I couldn't make out the words.

I did pick out the name "Robert Vargas," though, as well as the words "Humanity Labor" and "murdered."

"I...I've informed the medical center," Fuchida said. "They'll have someone over to pick up the body soon."

"Good." I decided I'd go with them. I wanted to talk with Dr. Weissmuller.

"Can I report this to you?" Fuchida asked. "Or do I need to call someone else?"

I pulled out my PAD. "You can make your report to me, sir," I said. "You can start by telling me who found the body, and when."

Later, I said goodbye to Lily in the Beanstalk Terminal. "You're still going down-Stalk?"

She nodded. "I need to file my story, and I want to do it in person. They may put me on the air. What about you?"

"I'm going to see what Dr. Weissmuller has to say about the body. Then I'm going up to Heinlein. I think I'll stop and make a call to our friend Coleman when I get there."

"Rick..."

"Yeah?"

"Be careful. I don't like the way this is turning out."

"You, too." I had no reason to think that anyone was out to get me...but if they were, they might be interested in Lily, as well. She'd been seen at the morgue, and she'd been seen with me both here at the High Frontier, and at the Humanity Labor dome on Farside. My "assistant."

Damn it, there was a reason I didn't like working with partners. It reduced the legwork and gave you someone to watch your back...but it also gave you someone else to worry about.

Lily Lockwell looked very small and vulnerable as she walked away from me into the boarding tube that would take her to a down-Stalk beanpod.

I took the subsurface slidewalk to the Carousel, then twisted into the horizontal elevator that took me to the third-G hospital level.

"Captain Harrison," Dr. Weissmuller said. "I was half-expecting you to show up."

"We seem to be collecting oddly traumatized bodies, Doctor. Have you seen the one they just brought in?"

"Seen it, yes. Performed the autopsy, no. I'll be doing that later this afternoon."

"This is part of the Dow case, Doctor. I need you to be *thorough*."

He bristled. "I always am, Captain Harrison."

"Good. I want to know about drugs in this guy's bloodstream, and I want to know if he has any special enhancements—respirocytes, G-mod characteristics, anything like that. And I want to know what you think broke his arm."

"I noticed that when the body arrived," Dr. Weissmuller

said, nodding. "His humerus appears to be compressed, even smashed. I would expect the assailant possessed a great deal of strength. A G-mod, perhaps."

"Or a bioroid?" I asked.

He blinked, as though that had not occurred to him. "Certainly. If you could get past the programming."

"Just how good is a bioroid's programming, Doctor? Could you get one to murder someone?"

"I'm not the one to ask," Dr. Weissmuller replied. "Someone at Haas-Bioroid would be better-suited. They build the things, after all."

"Would you call me with the results of the autopsy later?" I handed him an e-card. A non-infected one.

"Of course."

Two hours later, I'd checked out of the High Frontier, taken the tube-lev through the planetoid to Farside, and made my way down through the inverted dome next to the Challenger Ferry dock. The next ferry launch was leaving in three hours, but the time passed by quickly with all I had to think about.

At 70,000 kilometers above Earth's surface, the Challenger Planetoid moved too fast to stay in orbit. Like a string tied to a rock used to whirl the rock in a circle, the only thing keeping it in place was the Beanstalk itself. The Challenger Memorial Ferry was one of a number of spacecraft, both passenger and cargo, released from the ferry terminal within a precisely calculated window, and hurled outward by the Beanstalk's centrifugal force.

At the Ferry Terminal, I passed once more through a backscatter checkpoint, and was allowed to board the ship. My seat was 11C, but when no one else in the half-filled cabin claimed the seats next to me, I moved over to the window seat. There was nothing to see at first but the steel interior of the drop bay, but eventually one of those holographic flight attendants winked on, all smiles and professionalism, and warned us to stay strapped in for a period of zero-G.

A voice counted down the seconds, and then those steel walls outside shot upward, and we emerged into dazzling sunlight.

Zero-G. We were in free fall, hurtling outward at several meters per second.

If the time of drop was calculated precisely enough, we might have fallen outward in a long, curving path that would have allowed us to be captured eventually by the Moon's gravity, but this was an express run. There was another countdown, and then a hand pressed me back hard against the yielding foam of my seat, and we began picking up speed.

The asteroid, black as coal and looking like a lumpy potato with a tiny constellation of lights at its center, dwindled, and soon the Earth emerged from behind its dusty face. Eventually, the Challenger Planetoid fell away into a speck, then was lost to sight, while the Earth remained half-full. The sun was setting on the Earthbound portions of New Angeles; the cities of Europe were clearly visible as dustings of light on the darkened half.

Then the maneuvering burn ended and we fell, weightless once more, into the dark.

Chapter Ten

Day 5

The Challenger Memorial Ferry's arrival point on the Moon is Starport Kaguya, located just south of the lunar equator within a crater called Hypatia-C.

"Starport" seems a little ambitious, I know. We have colonies on the Moon and Mars, yeah, and we've started mining asteroids, but we're a long, long way from traveling to the worlds around other stars.

The Heinlein Lunar Colony, though, is nothing if not optimistic about the future of humankind in space. From the Loonie perspective, we've finally dragged ourselves out of Earth's gravity well and planted ourselves on more than one world. We're in the process of getting industry off Earth and into space, out where we have near-free energy and abundant natural resources. Helium-3 mining on the Moon is providing Earth with the fuel for clean fusion energy; orbital manufactories are turning lunar regolith into titanium and anhydrous glass using free solar power, and shipping the products down on skip-gliders for an ocean recovery off *Bahía de Caráquez*. Lunar industry—most especially the recovery and transport of helium-3—has made

New Angeles by far the wealthiest, most prosperous city on Earth, with twenty times the gross domestic product of the rest of the United States combined.

Because not only is the Beanstalk a part of New Angeles, so is Heinlein.

The Quito Accord arranged for what amounted to the outright purchase of Ecuador by the United States. We actually took less than a quarter of the country's total land area...but the rest of the country was on the way to being assimilated economically within a few decades of the Beanstalk's opening, no matter what the mapmakers say. The Quito Accord also established that the New Angeles Police Department was responsible for keeping the peace all the way up the Beanstalk to the Heinlein colony, as well.

From one hundred kilometers up, Starport Kaguya didn't look thriving or bustling. From a hundred kilometers out, in fact, it was invisibly small. But the ferry's engines cut in for the final burn to the surface, and the crater grew until we could see the base: two silvery domes in the crater floor, a big one connected to a little one, with white and red beacons pulsing brightly once per second. The smaller dome opened, panels unfolding like the petals of a flower, and we balanced down into the interior on invisible jets of hot plasma. A boarding tube extended from one wall, pressure-sealing to the ferry's passenger hatch, and the holographic attendant bid us all welcome to the Moon.

I like Heinlein, like being on the Moon. When I actually allow myself to think about the possibility of some day retiring, I think about moving here, where the one-sixth Earth gravity is strong enough to keep your bones hard, but gentle enough that you don't feel like you're fighting gravity just to live. There's a large geriatric community here, thanks to an ongoing emigration of centenarians similar to the retirement migrations to Florida and the American Southwest many, many decades ago.

Of course, food and water is more expensive than on Earth,

and you do have to pay an air tax…but a lot of that is subsidized by lunar industry. In fact, a lot of the larger lunar corporations will pay for your water and air, one hundred percent, if you just sign a seven-year contract to work for them. There's a labor shortage in Heinlein—that's the reason Jinteki introduced clones and Haas made bioroids in the first place. But what they need most are people who have experience and training that androids don't possess, at least not yet; things like computer technology, medical training, mine engineering, and software design.

You don't need grip-slippers on the Moon, but you do still have to watch yourself when you walk. I only weighed a bit over 13 kilos here, but, just as on Challenger, I still had 80 kilos of mass, and it can be hard to stop if you get yourself moving too quickly. I used the safety rail, just in case, as I made my way down the transparent embarkation tube. Above me, the flower petals were slowly closing—protection against the radiation and micrometeorites that had driven most lunar civilization underground.

That's why native Loonies refer to being *in* Heinlein or *in* the Moon, not on it.

Starport Kaguya occupies the larger dome in Hypatia-C. Kaguya is the name of the Moon princess from the 10th-century Japanese tale, the *Taketori Monogatari*, the "Tale of the Bamboo Cutter," which may be the oldest folktale in Japanese literature, as well as one of the earliest examples of science fiction.

But Starport Kaguya got its name not from medieval Japanese science fiction, but from science fact. In 2007, the Japanese launched the SELENE space probe from the Tanegashima Space Center and sent it on what became a twenty-month mission to map the lunar surface. It was the largest-scale lunar exploration since the U.S. Apollo program five decades earlier, and it helped refuel the public's interest in lunar exploration, paving the way for the return of humans to the Moon around fifteen years later. The Japanese public had given the SELENE spacecraft its nickname of "Kaguya," and the name was passed on to the lunar end of the Beanstalk transport system.

I was met by an attractive young woman made up to look like Kaguya-*hime*, the princess of the tale, wearing a traditional kimono and with hair glowing a bright, luminous white, like the Moon. I wondered if the shining hair was a cosmetic effect or the result of genetic modification, but decided not to ask. At least I could assume that she hadn't been found as a baby inside a glowing bamboo plant, like the original princess.

"Welcome to the Moon, Harrison-*san*," she said, bowing, and pulling my name from my e-ID. Her hair was shining brightly enough to read by.

"*Domo arigato, gozaimase*," I replied, returning the bow. "*Konnichiwa.*"

Since it was past 1100, it was a *konnichiwa* kind of moment, not one for *ohayou gozaimase*.

There's quite a large population of Japanese on the Moon. I don't know if that's because of the Kaguya legend or because the Japanese have always been fascinated by Earth's natural satellite. There's a community of more than ten thousand people of Japanese descent in the big dome at Tranquility Home called *Tsuki-no-Miyako*—the "Capital of the Moon" of the fairy tale. The Heinlein Authority hires a number of attractive young Japanese men and women to meet and greet incoming visitors. What they don't tell you is that these girls and boys are running a kind of security triage for the mining corps. Incoming labor is directed to the appropriate destination, while tourists are given personal, friendly native guides to lead them through the underground lunar warrens…and make sure the visitors aren't on the Moon to stir up clone trouble or to organize protests against the grand-scale strip-mining of the lunar surface.

"Can I be of assistance to you in finding your destination?" the greeter asked. "Heinlein can seem very large, very confusing—"

"Thanks, sweetheart," I told her, "but I've been here before." And I headed for the tube-lev platform. She seemed like such a sweet and innocent girl; I didn't think she'd have understood if I'd told her I was on my way to Eliza's Toybox. She was probably reporting me right now to the yellow jackets, but I didn't care. My badge number and e-ID were on file; they knew who I was.

I had a mental list of places I needed to go, but my first stop was relatively close to Kaguya. During the trip, on the ferry out, I'd received the promised call from Dr. Weissmuller.

The doctor had included Vargas's personal file off the Net. Robert Vargas had worked for Humanity Labor for nine years, and he'd been in the Army for ten before that. A Special Forces member, he'd been injected with Freitas respirocytes while he was in the service—like me—and that gave me a nasty inner shudder. If he hadn't suffocated during those first few seconds outside the airlock, his death wouldn't have been easy.

I still remembered the expression etched into his dead face on the other side of the transplas.

According to Dr. Weissmuller's tests, Vargas hadn't been on any drugs, and there'd been no alcohol in his system. By studying the condition of his surface tissues, Dr. Weissmuller had concluded that Vargas had died within the previous four days. He'd admitted it was a guess; those tissues had been frozen, cooked, desiccated, and exposed to hard radiation. My assumption, though, was that Dow's bodyguard had been offed at about the same time Dow was.

Hodgkins had told us that Vargas had been at the Carousel, checking on security arrangements at the meeting center. I'd assumed Hodgkins had been lying, but where *had* Vargas been? Perhaps Vargas had finished his work elsewhere and been on his way back to Dow's room when the murderer had killed him.

Maybe Dow had sent him away because he hadn't wanted an audience when Eve arrived.

And, just maybe, Eve had grabbed Vargas either an hour before or immediately after the murder, hauled him into the airlock, depressurized, then tossed him out onto the planetoid's surface, breaking his arm in the process. He'd managed to make it back to the outer door despite being in hard vacuum, and died clinging to those hand-holds—possibly staring through the transplas into the bioroid's silver eyes as he died.

Dr. Weissmuller couldn't learn anything more about Vargas's arm fracture, except for one interesting fact. Robert Vargas was osteoporotic.

It happens to people who live in microgravity—or in the extremely low gravity of the Challenger Planetoid. According to his records, Vargas hadn't been to either Earth or the Moon in five years. Unless you exercise vigorously for several hours each day—or spend a substantial amount of time in a spin-gravity environment like the Carousel—your bones begin to lose calcium. Lose enough calcium, and your bones become brittle, more susceptible to fractures.

Dr. Weissmuller told me the osteoporosis in Vargas's bones wasn't incapacitating yet, but it was bad enough that it wouldn't have taken the tremendous pressure to crush his humerus that I'd assumed at first. A strong man with a strong grip could have done it, and not necessarily one with an athletic G-mod. I wondered how the osteoporosis had affected his job as a bodyguard. He would have been at a considerable physical disadvantage against someone fresh up from Earth.

But that didn't leave bioroids off the hook, either. It was vital that I find Eve 5VA3TC as quickly as possible, because right now she was my prime suspect. She'd been with Dow immediately before the murder, and she had the strength—and possibly the motive—to kill Dow's bodyguard.

According to the Transit Authority records, Eve 5VA3TC had caught a ferry for Starport Kaguya a few hours after Dow's murder. She'd most likely returned to Eliza's Toybox at Fra

Mauro, and that's where I hoped to track her down.

First, though, I had another stop to make.

A short tube-lev jaunt from Kaguya, just sixty kilometers or so, is the immense dome of Tranquility Home.

Houston, Tranquility Base, here. The Eagle has landed.

Possibly the most momentous words of the past few centuries: the announcement by Neil Armstrong, Apollo 11's Mission Commander, that the Lunar Excursion Module *Eagle* had just touched down on the Moon's Sea of Tranquility. Tranquility Home was the name of the big dome directly adjacent to the Apollo 11 landing site, the first part of Heinlein opened to colonization, and the location of the Tranquility Home Museum. The rest of the main dome was bustling and filled with humanity—it was mostly taken up by habitation modules for the workers at Melange Mining and Alpha Prospecting—but here, in the pressurized viewing gallery above the landing site, there was a still and reverential silence.

A holy shrine. "Here men from the Planet Earth first set foot upon the Moon, July 1969, A.D. We came in peace for all mankind" as it says on the plaque left on the lander's descent stage. The surface there is still in hard vacuum to preserve the footprints, but not long after Heinlein was established, they built a stadium-sized anhydrous glass shell over the place to keep it pristine. The ceiling of the dome was opaque, with a sky projection that included the Earth, Sun, and a few bright stars frozen in the positions they'd held on July 21, 1969, moments after Armstrong and Edwin "Buzz" Aldrin had lifted off again from the lunar surface.

The pressurized visitor's gallery lets you inspect much of the site without actually touching it. You can walk out on the transparent floor raised a meter above the lunar surface and look out through the slanting, optically perfect anhydrous glass overlooking the area. It's all still there: the descent stage, the EASEP science package and solar panels, the United States flag (still held out from the mast by a stiff aluminum rod). The original flag was actually knocked over by the exhaust from the LEM ascent module when it lifted off, but during construction of the museum, someone had used a robotic arm to lift the flag from the regolith and place it upright once more.

A lot of the footprints in the area had been erased by the ascent module's silent rocket blast, but those closest to the descent module—including the very first human footprint on the Moon—had been shielded by the module itself, and were still clearly visible.

With no wind, those prints would still look pristine and fresh millennia from now.

I'd been to the landing monument before. It's always left me a bit in awe; the walls of the LEM ascent module had been so thin that a dropped wrench would have punched through them as if through aluminum foil. Today, visitors arrive at Starport Kaguya by the hundreds each day on-board modern lunar ferry ships, and they don't even think about the incredible long-odds risks experienced by those first humans to walk the Moon's surface.

But I wasn't here to look at the exhibit. Not this time.

"Hello, Captain Harrison. It is very good to see you."

I turned and smiled. "Hello, Floyd."

Floyd 2X3A7C was a bioroid, and one I'd worked with before. A Floyd-series android robot manufactured by Haas-Bioroid, he was rented out to the NAPD as a part of an ongoing test program, one intended to determine whether bioroids could be safely and usefully implemented into the police force and similar social-service positions.

He looked young. Well, of *course* he was young—his records said he was six years old—but what I mean is that he looked like a young man, twenty or younger, with a thin, almost effeminate face and slender hands. He had a Catholic rosary draped around his neck like a necklace that I hadn't seen before.

"Your message said you wanted to talk with me," Floyd said. Often he wore goggles—Floyd tended to be shy about revealing that he was a bioroid—but at the moment I could see his eyes: silver with a mirror-bright polish. They reflected the artificial lighting over the encapsulated landing site beyond the glass as he turned.

"That's right. I was wondering if you'd be willing to talk to me about morality."

"Of course. I enjoy discussing that topic."

We stepped from the shrine-silence of the viewing gallery and back into the bustling chaos of the city proper—lights and holo-advertising and thousands of people swarming through the subsurface warrens. "*We supply the life's blood of human civilization,*" a voice boomed from somewhere overhead. "*Melange Mining—from the Sun to the Moon to you!*"

We caught the next tube-lev out for Fra Mauro.

Melange Mining is located 650 kilometers west of Tranquility Home in the Sinus Medii, almost at the exact center of the Moon's disk as seen from Earth and halfway to the major Heinlein facilities scattered across the hundred-kilometer wide expanse of Fra Mauro crater. I wanted to talk to Melange about the clone Mark Henry, but it was more important, I thought, that I find the bioroid Eve 5VA3TC first. I still didn't think a clone could have committed a murder like the one that had shredded Roger Dow, but a robot? Machines do what someone tells them to do, and if a bioroid has a human personality, it's still a personality artificially layered into a computer, a programmable machine.

So we caught an express car and rode beneath the huge Melange Mining facility without stopping, while the bioroid and I talked about what it meant to be human.

"I frequently discuss the topic with Father Michael," Floyd told me as we hurtled through the silence of the hard-vacuum tunnel above a superconducting mag-lev rail. "We try to find time to play a game of chess each week, unless, of course, I'm on a case. We generally meet at his church, St. Theresa's."

"That's the one in Earthside New Angeles?"

"It is. We often discuss philosophy and human ethics."

"And have you arrived at any conclusions?" I asked.

"I don't see that there is a conclusion to reach, Rick," the bioroid said. "Father Michael believes, quite passionately, in the survival of a kind of life force or energy he calls 'the soul.' I find the concept…intriguing."

"But you wonder how it might apply to you?"

"At one point I did. Can a bioroid—a machine—have a soul? No matter how lifelike its design, or how human others might think it to be, does the simple fact of self-awareness within a machine translate as a soul?"

"I don't know."

"Nor do I. Further, I know that I was not programmed to have a soul. There is no such program in my directory.

"Recently I have given careful consideration to the idea. I now question whether a soul is necessary at all."

"Necessary for what? Maybe it's not 'necessary.' Maybe it just *is*."

"Perhaps. But Father Michael seems to believe that the reality of an afterlife is necessary to engender and preserve human ethical behavior."

"What do you mean?"

"Father Michael posits an afterlife governed by a deity who created the universe. He seems to believe that this deity is essentially good—meaning, I believe, that it is ethical and benevolent. However, it has the power to punish human souls after death, to either admit them into this paradisiacal afterlife…or to torture them horribly for all eternity, for the most part based on their moral behavior."

"That seems a little harsh."

I was fascinated. As we continued to speak, Floyd's fingers

flickered along the beads of the rosary he wore. I could hear the tiny, plastic clicks as he touched each bead. Was he actually reciting the rosary as he spoke to me?

"Positing such a deity seems to me to be an unnecessary complication. Surely, ethical behavior can be enforced among humans by the analysis, on a case-by-case basis, of risk versus reward. Unethical behavior tends to be antisocial behavior on one or more levels. Humans avoid such behavior in order to avoid discovery, punishment, and possibly humiliation within the social framework. No god is necessary to explain the tendency of humans toward moral behavior."

Floyd's fingers were really flying now, moving so quickly they seemed to blur. The *clickclickclick* of the beads ran together into a soft, background buzz.

"I've been a cop for a bunch of years. I'm not sure I see 'a tendency in humans toward moral behavior.' Quite the opposite, in fact."

"Then why do you, Rick Harrison, behave in what I would call a moral fashion?"

"Well, thanks for the vote of confidence. I'm not entirely sure I agree with you there. But…well, I don't know if there's a God out there or not. But I try to do the right thing anyway."

"Why?"

"Why what?"

"Why do you try to do the right thing?" The beads circled Floyd's neck every few seconds now, his fingers blurred nearly to invisibility, the clicks chattering like a radiation counter recording a solar flare.

"Because it's important to *me*. Not because it's important to God." I thought for a moment. "Tell me something."

"If I can."

"If you don't believe in God…why the beads?"

Abruptly, the beads stopped running through his blurring, mechanical fingers. "It is an exercise in logic."

"Oh?"

"I have no way of determining God's existence or non-existence, nor can I prove or disprove the reality of eternal souls—in particular of my own. Cycling through the formulaic prayers of the rosary costs little in terms of energy or mental concentration. If I am mistaken and God is real, the prayers generated may have a positive effect."

I burst out laughing. "You know, Floyd, that's the most human thing I've ever heard you say. I suspect most humans think the same way."

I paused for a moment, thinking through our conversation thus far before continuing. "But there's something in all of this I need to know."

"Yes?"

"Bioroids have it written into their code that they're not supposed to kill humans, right?"

"That is part of our basic programming, yes. We receive these instructions before we even receive our neural channeling."

"Could you overcome it?"

"I…do not understand the question."

"Could you kill a human despite that programming?"

"Why would I want to?"

"Suppose someone—someone at Haas-Bioroid, say—gives you instructions to kill a particular human. Would you do it? Would you be able to do it?"

Floyd was silent for a long moment. I wondered if perhaps I'd pushed him too far, too hard.

"I must assume that you have a bioroid suspect in a murder investigation," Floyd said at last. "You're wondering if a bioroid could commit murder."

I was impressed. Floyd had a blindingly fast intelligence. But sometimes he didn't seem to think like a human being.

"Exactly." I filled him in, at least with the major points: a human carved up by a mining laser, a sex gynoid at the scene of the crime, and the possibility that the bioroid had also killed Dow's bodyguard, Vargas.

"It would be...possible," Floyd said after another lengthy pause. "But extremely difficult, and extremely unlikely. I can see only a few ways that such orders could be given and implemented."

"And they would be?..."

"A complete wipe of the bioroid's operating system," Floyd said. "Take it all the way down to bare silicon, and install a new OS, one lacking the inhibitions against harming humans, and including orders to kill."

"I see."

"A second possibility would involve a severe electric shock."

"How severe?"

"Twenty to forty thousand volts, alternating current. The charge would incapacitate a bioroid temporarily, and wipe short-term memory. It would then be possible to give the bioroid new operating instructions, though these would be temporary in nature."

"Okay..."

"Or, the bioroid could be subjected to neural channeling, *new* neural channeling, possibly using the mind of a human murderer as a mental template. This might create a bioroid with a new personality, one apparently lacking the inhibitions against murder."

"'Apparently'?"

"The original programming would still be there, together with the original inhibitions, but...suppressed. I cannot imagine that this would be a permanent effect, however. Sooner or later, with stress and with multiplying logic-tree branches, the original programming would reassert itself. And that would be unfortunate."

"How so?"

"Consider. A bioroid has absolute injunctions against harming humans. It has memories of having done so. The...dissonance might well destroy the bioroid. It would certainly cause extremely serious damage, the bioroid equivalent of a nervous breakdown."

"It would go insane?"

"Haas-Bioroid does not admit that such could be the case," Floyd replied, "and bioroids are instructed not to discuss it."

I realized he was telling me as much as he could without crossing certain programmed lines. "Is there anything else about this topic you're not supposed to discuss?"

"Yes."

He volunteered nothing more, in effect telling me that I was welcome to take wild guesses about what the forbidden material might be, and that he would respond as far and as completely as he could...but he could not bring the topics up himself.

Having a conversation with a bioroid is not the same as talking with a human.

"So...you're telling me you can't just reprogram a bioroid on the fly."

"Not for something as complex as murder, no. Minor changes to a bioroid's standard function can be obtained simply enough—a good hacker could do it, if he has either password access or knowledge of a back door in the code employed for maintenance. A patch can be beamed over the local wireless network, in effect inserting a software virus that can modify the original programming. But this would not affect the deeper neural channeling."

"Okay... Does a bioroid feel emotion, Floyd?"

"An interesting question, but one I cannot adequately answer. I...*feel*—though that is such an inadequate word, and it may give you entirely the wrong impression—such things as satisfaction at a job successfully completed, for instance. If you mean human primal emotions such as rage, fear, jealousy, love…no. I can simulate such emotions quite well. I cannot 'feel' them."

"Even with the neural channeling?"

"Neural channeling helps shape my thoughts and mental processes, providing me with a kind of mental and emotional roadmap, if you will. It does not instill me with emotions."

"So a bioroid couldn't fly into a rage and kill a human because of it?"

"No."

"What if the bioroid was insane?"

"I cannot…I cannot…I cannot…I can—" For a moment, Floyd froze in mid-word, mouth open in an almost comical expression.

Great, I thought. *I broke him, and Dawn's going to take it out of my pay.*

Then the jaw snapped shut and Floyd stared through me with those eerie silver eyes. "I cannot answer that question," he said.

The rosary beads scattered as the string around his neck snapped. Beads cascaded across the floor, rolling and bouncing everywhere in slow motion.

And moments later we pulled into the Fra Mauro terminal.

Chapter Eleven

Day 5

Fra Mauro was a far-flung group of craters covering one corner of the dark shores of the vast Mare Imbrium, the site of Man's third landing on the Moon, Apollo 14.

Floyd seemed to have recovered completely from that glitch on-board the tube-lev, thank God, and hadn't said anything more about it. We emerged from the terminal into a cavernous world of low buildings beneath a vaulted, grey dome. In lots of ways, it was like the cityscape of Earthside New Angeles, with the crowded buildings, the tightly packed crowds, the eye-watering advertising. A different voice, one among hundreds, cajoled us here: "*Haas-Bioroid! Making the future today!*"

Larger than the Tranquility Home complex, Fra Mauro was also considerably younger, and represented the wealthier side of the Heinlein colony. Where Melange Mining dominated life at Tranquility Home, here it was the high-tech industrial facilities of Haas-Bioroid.

"*Help in the office! Help at home! Help at enjoying life! Haas-Bioroid!*"

And in a wealthy underground labyrinth of retirement communes, upscale restaurants, entertainment malls, 3D Haas-Bioroid advertising animations, and high-end neural simsensies, is the magical world of Eliza's Toybox.

The two of us walked through the main door into a fairyland of red light and soft textures. The door tried to deduct an entry fee from both of us, but was blocked by our account wards. This was strictly official business.

We were met just inside the entrance by a Giselle model identical to the hostess that had greeted me at Tommy Liu's Diner a few days earlier—golden hair, a perky upper chassis, and almost enough clothing to wrap around my PAD. Her silver gaze slid past Floyd like he wasn't there and latched onto me. "*Hello*, Captain," she said in a contralto hot enough to sizzle the cold lunar night. "What can I...*do* for you?"

"You can introduce me to your owner," I said.

According to her bio, Eliza Manchester had emigrated to New Angeles forty-five years ago from England. She still had that classic British unflappability, though, coupled with the aura of upper-class manners, elegance, and good breeding that has always so fascinated us rude, crude Americans. Her bio said she was ninety-six, but she could easily have passed for sixty. People don't age on the Moon the way they do in the crushingly high gravity of Earth.

"Oh, dear," she said as I showed her the holo of my badge. "You're with the police? This is about one of my girls, isn't it?"

"Eve 5VA3TC," I replied. "Is she here?"

"She is. But...ah, me. Perhaps we should have some tea?"

The front of Eliza's Toybox encompassed an enormous display area, with sultry lighting, sexy music, and larger-than-life holographic displays—women, mostly, in various stages of undress, performing in alcoves alone and in groups, though there were a few well-oiled and sculpted male bodies, as well. I saw twenty different models just in that first room, including the perky Giselle and the top-heavy Eve. Voices whispered promises about each model as we passed their alcoves. "*Your most exciting erotic fantasies brought to vivid life...,*" one murmured. "*A tantalizing dream given form, warmth, and a burning desire for you...,*" said another. "*The Rhoda model,*" said a third, "*a true living doll...*"

There were more sales floors behind the first. The Toybox, evidently, wasn't *all* about sex. There were maids and butlers in traditional dress. There were personal companions, eye-candy, and nannies. There were a number of dogs of different breeds, from yappy little ankle biters up to a phantasmagorical, larger-than-life mastiff with three heads. There were purring cats and trilling tribbles, hamsters and boa constrictors, garden gnomes and miniature unicorns, house pets for every taste and desire in a city where air was taxed and water expensive. There was a duplicate of the giant goose at the Castle Club. There was something that yapped like a dog and looked like a cyborg bear called a "dagget," whatever that was. There was even a large and wooly something called an electric sheep, though I really didn't want to know what its purpose might have been.

"People simply can't live without their pets, don't you know," the little English lady told me as we walked past. "It's a part of being human, I think. But most folks can't afford to keep live animals in Heinlein or the Beanstalk...or on Earth either, for that matter. We offer them an affordable alternative."

She took us to a comfortable lounge in the back, with sunken-pit seating around moon glass tables and atmospheric lighting and music. Somehow I was expecting an old-fashioned English butler, or even a bevy of naked gynoids, but tea was served by an authentic-looking Japanese *geisha*, wrapped in a kimono with chopsticks in her hair.

At least we didn't have to sit through a formal tea ceremony.

"Poor Eve 5VA3TC came home from an assignment a few

nights ago," she told us. "She was terribly hurt. That dreadful client had been beating her again."

"Which client was that?"

"Well, I'm really not supposed to—"

"Roger Dow?"

She hesitated, then nodded. "He's the one. *Bastard.*"

"Why do you say that?"

"The man is sick."

"You think he's been beating Eve?"

"I know he has." She looked hard at me. "You probably think this is just some scuzzy little sex entertainment shop, Captain Harrison. But we—the girls and boys and I—we have something precious here. We're more of a family, don't you see? We *care* about each other, and about what we do. We provide a vital service to the community, and, yes, we make some money on the side. But I care for every one of my bioroids as though they were my very own children."

"Yes, ma'am." This was not exactly a conversation that I would ever have expected to have with a little old lady, and a little old *English* lady at that, all prim and proper, talking about providing sex and sexual fantasy as a vital community service. I glanced at Floyd, but he was just sitting next to me, watching her through bright, silver eyes with no expression.

"Roger Dow hated bioroids," she went on. "*Hated* them. Well, you might expect that to be the case, I suppose, since he worked for those dreadful Humanity Labor people. But there was something very dark and twisted about that man. It was as though he had to prove he was better than bioroids, by...by dominating them. *Hurting* them."

I nodded. "It's called a display of 'power over,' right?" I asked. I'd scanned through the police reports from Eliza's Toybox on my way to Heinlein, reports she or her employees had filed when their property had been maliciously damaged. Generally, there wasn't anything the police could do, not unless there was proof of deliberate vandalism. Rough sex was a part of the package when it came to sex-service bioroids. Beatings. Whips. Chains. The whole SM scene. Things got broken…but it was better that things got broken than *people*.

"Ms. Manchester," I said, "are you aware that Roger Dow is dead?"

"*Is* he!" Her eyes widened, her hand fluttered at her throat. "Good heavens! No, young man. I was not."

"He was murdered. Eve 5VA3TC was with him just before he was killed. She may have been with him when it happened. I'd like to question her about that night."

"Of course. I knew something more than 'the usual' had happened… She was very upset that night. Still is, I should warn you."

How did a bioroid act *upset*? "Has she told you what happened?"

"No, not really. She told me she'd met…a friend."

"A clone? Mark Henry 103?"

"She didn't tell me his name." She gave what seemed to be a disapproving sniff. "We don't encourage *unprofessional* relationships within our family, Captain Harrison. But sometimes they happen, just the same."

"Are you saying Eve 5VA3TC had a sexual relationship with Mark Henry 103?"

"She had a relationship with him, certainly, though what the exact nature of that relationship might have been I'm sure I have no idea."

I still wondered if clones could even have sex. They might be human, yes, but with all of that conditioning…

"You said Eve is upset. In what way?"

"She…she acted strangely, a bit, when she got home."

"Strangely how?"

"Well, I asked her how the assignment had gone. She looked at me and she VIed."

"'Vee-eyed'?"

"Verbal iteration. She started saying 'It went, it went, it went,' on and on like that for several seconds. I actually had to hit her reset to break the loop. And then she told me she had no memory of the event."

No memory? That didn't seem likely. "I thought bioroids had two sets of memory. One analogue, like in human memory, imbedded in the neural channeling matrix, and another digital, like a computer memory."

She made a face. "Almost. A bioroid's neural-net memory mimics human memory using fractal integration and quantum-derived fuzzy logic. It *has* to, don't you see? We humans perceive sensations, feelings, emotions, even memory on an analogue scale—a little bit, a lot, not at all, somewhere in between. Digital means binary—on or off, all or nothing. In order to think like a human, a bioroid needs that analogue component. But it also stores a simple digital record of events. It's not really a second memory. It's more of a diagnostic tool."

"I see." Eliza Manchester's file mentioned that she had doctorates in applied AI engineering *and* in computer software design, though she never used the honorifics. "Can you pull that digital record?"

"I did. It was blank."

"As in erased?"

"Yes. Only about forty minutes were missing, mind you. From some time while she was in Mr. Dow's room to when she boarded the Challenger Ferry."

"That's her digital memory?"

"The digital timeline record, yes."

"What about her analogue memory?"

"That's a bit more difficult. Human memory is holographic in the way it works, and Eve's memory works the same way. The memory is actually stored over a large area of the brain. As with a hologram, if you remove a piece of it, the entire picture remains intact…but it's fuzzier, less distinct. It's not like cutting a two-D photograph in half. It's the entire photograph, but at a lower resolution, do you see?"

"Was her analogue memory affected? Fuzzy or indistinct?"

"She seemed…confused, Captain Harrison. And when I questioned her, she became agitated. So I didn't question her any further."

"I see. And may we speak with her now?"

"I really wish—"

"Ms. Manchester, I will, if you prefer, get a warrant. Or I could arrest *you* as a material witness to the murder of Roger Dow, and impound Eve." I didn't like using the show of force on her, but Eve knew *something* about Dow's death, of that I was certain.

"I'll get her, Captain Harrison," Manchester said. She sounded weary. I didn't see her press a control or send a signal, but a few minutes later an Eve-model bioroid entered the room.

"You sent for me, Ms. Manchester?"

Like the Eve-model bioroids in the Toybox showroom, Eve 5VA3TC was shapely to the point of being top-heavy, standing about 170 centimeters tall, with wavy, shoulder-length blond hair. She had a tiny waist, narrow hips, a thin face, and long legs. I knew she massed a lot more than she appeared to—probably on the order of 109 kilos, though she would only weigh eighteen kilos here. Pretty, of course…but her silver eyes bothered me. Somehow, I tended to take Floyd's mirrored eyes in stride when he wasn't wearing his goggles, but seeing them in the face of what otherwise appeared to be a sexually attractive young woman bothered me.

"Yes, Eve," Manchester said. "This gentleman is from the New Angeles Police Department. He'd like to ask you some questions. Do you mind?"

"Of course not, Ms. Manchester." The silver eyes turned to stare through me. "How can I help you…Captain Harrison?"

She'd snagged my name from my e-ID.

"Five nights ago, on the evening of the twenty-third, you saw a client at the High Frontier Hotel on the Challenger Planetoid. Is that right?"

"I am directed not to talk about my clients, or about my activities with my clients, Captain Harrison."

I looked at Ms. Manchester, as did Eve.

"It's okay, dear," she told the bioroid. "Captain Harrison is authorized personnel. Code one-seven, restriction release. Initiate."

Eve turned the silver eyes back to me. "The client's name was Roger Mayhurst Dow, Jr.," she told me. "He'd checked into the High Frontier Hotel on the twenty-first, and called this establishment to request my services as a sex partner the following day. I arrived at his room at 2017 on the evening of the twenty-third."

"What room?"

"Room Twelve."

"And had Mr. Dow been a client of yours before?"

"Yes. He requested me by name and number."

"Many of our clients do," Manchester put in. "There is a *very* highly placed prelate within the Starlight Crusade church who uses Eve's services exclusively."

"Doesn't that violate a vow or something?"

"Only with a *person*, Captain Harrison. Eve is not a person… according to the 'law.'"

"Hm. Eve, did he…hurt you?"

"I do not feel pain, Captain Harrison."

"Not at all?"

"Not in a way that humans would describe it."

"Show him your back, dear."

Obediently, Eve turned around. She was wearing a kind of grey-blue business suit, with a high collar and long sleeves, but leaving her cleavage on display. She opened the neck piece and let the dress fall, in slow motion, to the floor.

"My God," was all I could say.

Bioroids don't bleed. No blood. They do have a kind of circulatory system for the hydraulic fluid that works their muscular actuators, but that's deep enough inside that superficial cuts can't reach it. Her back and buttocks didn't look bloody or bruised, but they were torn open in a dozen places, the plastic hanging in strips.

"Turn around, dear," Manchester told her.

She did so. The high collar on her dress had been obscuring the marks on her throat, and the long sleeves had covered the peeling chafes on her wrists. On her torso, just below where the ribcage would end on a human, at the solar plexus, there was a nasty burn—the soft plastic partially melted and blackened. It looked as though she'd been stabbed twice there, too. The punctures, small and close together, weren't deep, but they made me wince. Maybe Eve didn't feel pain, but I felt an answering empathic twinge nonetheless.

"May I touch you?"

"Of course. Would you like me to touch you?"

"Uh…no. Thank you. Just stand still for a moment." I probed gently at the burn mark. It was quite deep. What had Dow used? Something hotter than a cigarette.

I pulled out my PAD and photographed the damage to Eve's body, front and back.

"We didn't have a replacement back for the Eve-model in stock," Manchester told us. "We have a new one ordered from Haas-Bioroid, and it should be here in another day or two. When it arrives, we'll snap off all the ruined parts, snap on the replacements, and you'll be good as new, won't you, dear?"

"Yes, Ms. Manchester."

I examined her wrists more closely. There were marks on the synthetic skin of both wrists, just below the cables connecting her lower forearms to the back of her hands, like the marks left by cuffs or binders. "He tied you to the bed? And whipped you?"

"Yes, Captain Harrison."

"Did you free yourself, or did he untie you?" I asked. Then I added, "You can put your clothes back on now." *It was distracting, her standing there like that.*

"He freed me. Just before I heard Mark Henry by the door," she said, stooping over and pulling up her dress.

"Heard him?"

"My hearing is considerably more acute than humans," she said, her tone as blank as her eyes, and completely matter-of-fact.

"Did he come in?"

"I do not remember."

"What do you remember?"

"I remember that room service came to the door," she said.

"I see. What happened then?"

"I do not remember."

"Was it the clone instead of room service?"

"I do not remember."

"Did the clone kill Mr. Dow?"

"I do not remember him doing so."

"Did the clone have a mining laser?"

"I do not remember."

"Do you remember a mining laser?"

"No."

"What *do* you remember?"

"I remember…boarding the Challenger Memorial Ferry."

"That was about forty minutes later. What do you remember between the time room service came to the door, and when you got aboard the ferry?"

"I remember…screaming. Screaming. Screaming. Screaming…"

"Oh, dear," Manchester said. Standing swiftly, she reached

up and did something to the back of Eve's head, just below the hairline. I saw a plastic cover swing open, and Manchester pressed something hard enough to force Eve's head forward and down. "A reset switch," Manchester told me.

"I remember very little," Eve said in cool and matter-of-fact tones as her head popped back up. "My analogue memory includes images of returning down the corridor outside the room. I had been programmed to return home. I was doing so."

"What about the clone?"

"He was no longer present. I believe he had already left, but I do not have clear memories of that period of time."

"Did you see anyone else in the room besides Roger Dow?"

"I do not remember anyone else."

"Do you remember seeing Roger Dow dead?"

"I remember…screaming. Screaming. Screaming…"

Manchester again opened the panel at the back of her neck and pressed something. "I really think that it's not a good idea to keep questioning the poor thing," she said, snapping the panel shut. "This sort of emotional looping can be *extremely* stressful for a bioroid."

"Eve," I said, ignoring her. "Did you kill Roger Dow?"

"I do not remember doing so."

"Did Mark Henry 103 kill Roger Dow?"

"I do not remember him doing so."

Dead end.

Her eyes were bothering me. Her speech was, if not monotone, then precise and somewhat flat. When a sexbot turns up the sultry, she can set the room on fire with the heat. *Expressive* doesn't begin to cover it.

"Tell me, Ms. Manchester," I said, pointing. "Why do bioroids have the silver eyes?"

"I think it's silly, myself," she said. "But it's supposed to help avoid the Uncanny Valley effect."

I knew what she was referring to, of course. The Uncanny

Valley was first described during the 1970s, and had been based, in part, on a paper published in 1906 by Ernst Jentsch called "On the Psychology of the Uncanny." So it had been around for a long time.

The modern Uncanny Valley was a simple enough concept. Make androids more and more lifelike, appear more and more human, and you'll elicit a more and more positive response in humans interacting with the things. Eventually, though, you reach a certain, hard-to-define point where the thing is so lifelike it seems...*wrong*. Creepy. Both familiar and strange at the same time, and that sets up an emotional dissonance that makes you feel repulsed instead of attracted.

Now, if you can continue making an android even more lifelike, to the point where it is almost literally indistinguishable from a living human, the curve of acceptance swings back up out of the valley again, and humans will be able to relate to the machine just as if it were a person. I thought of the McAuliffe bioroid back at the Challenger Planetoid. But pushing the verisimilitude that extra little bit is expensive, and there were lots of people who thought making perfectly lifelike machines might be dangerous.

Hollywood again. How many movies have there been through the years where human robots were engaged in plots to take over the world, perhaps by replacing world leaders with perfect robotic look-alikes?

"Haas-Bioroid was trying to gain more acceptance for their products," Manchester explained. "They deliberately added some features to back their products away from the Uncanny Valley."

I nodded. Bioroids don't need things like these electrical cables exposed on their wrists. Both the power connections and the muscle actuators are the thickness of human hairs, or finer, easily hidden inside the framework. And those silver eyes? Geez...we've had lifelike glass eyes indistinguishable from the real thing for centuries. If you ask me, the silver eyes on a typical bioroid are creepier than anything in the Uncanny Valley. With Floyd, I could ignore them. Most of the time he wears dark glasses or goggles anyway, and you can't see them. But silver eyes in a love-bundle like Eve were a serious turnoff. At least for me.

"I don't think it worked," Manchester said. "The eyes are the part of the human face you notice first, and if they're not right, you don't accept the face as truly human. That was the idea, of course...but bioroid eyes look strange, and that drives away customers."

"I don't see how you get *any*," I said. "When I was a kid, I had nightmares of a big dog or wolf...you know? And what was scary about it was the eyes. All white, no iris or pupil."

"A lot of folks feel the same way," Manchester said, nodding. "So...we've developed a work-around. Show him, dear."

Eve closed her eyes. When they opened again, they looked... beautiful. Irises of a deep blue, pupils deep and lustrous.

Eve blinked again, and the eyes were once more blank silver.

"Neat trick."

"We do what we have to in order to survive, Captain," Manchester said. "As it happens, there's a law on the books that says that bioroids must have eyes that distinguish them from humans. That 'neat trick,' as you call it, lets Eve look—shall we say—'appealing' when she's working. When she's off duty, the eyes are as you see them."

"That certainly follows the letter of the law," I mused, though I wondered how bioroids like the Christa McAuliffe on Challenger got away with it. Perhaps there were loopholes within the law for bioroids in certain lines of work? "Her eyes are 'different from human eyes,' though, no matter how you look at them."

"Precisely. You might be interested to know, Captain, that the law was introduced in the U.S. Senate a few years ago by one Roger Mayhurst Dow, Jr."

"The murdered man?"

"The same, during his time in the Senate. As I told you, he hated bioroids…and I think he was afraid of them."

"And a law like that would help keep them from being accepted as…people."

"Exactly."

"Eve?"

"Yes?"

"When you were…'working' with Dow. Did you have eyes that looked human? Or were they like they are now?"

"He ordered me to keep my eyes at Presentation One."

"That's the silver look," Manchester added. "Light passes through them, just like in silvered sunglasses. Isn't that right, Eve dear?"

"Yes, Ms. Manchester."

"Your vision is normal with the other eyes, the human ones?"

"Yes, Captain Harrison. My vision with Presentation Two is limited to optical wavelengths and the shorter IR wavelengths, and I cannot see in ultraviolet."

"Is that a handicap?" I glanced at Floyd, who was silently watching.

"In the normal course of activities," he said, "it is not."

"No, I imagine it's not." I was wondering if bioroids would be more accepted by the general public if their eyes weren't creepy-scary, like that. "May I see your human eyes again, please?"

She blinked. Blue eyes stared at me.

The effect was not perfect. There was just a touch of fashion-mannequin effect, a feeling that those eyes were staring through and past your head, not focused on *you*. The Uncanny Valley, again.

But I found myself thinking of her as a *person* when her eyes didn't reflect my face.

"Eve?"

"Yes?"

"Can you get angry at someone?"

"I do not understand the question, Captain Harrison."

"Dow beat you. Abused you. And he wanted to get rid of all bioroids. Did that make you angry?"

"I do not feel anger, as humans seem to use the word."

"You don't remember if you killed Dow."

"Captain Harrison," Manchester broke in, "I really must protest *this*...this inquisition!..."

I ignored her. "Answer my question, Eve."

"No, Captain Harrison."

"*Could* you have killed him?"

"If you mean was I physically capable of doing so, yes. I am considerably stronger than typical humans. And humans are rather fragile in certain key respects."

"But could you have killed him if you'd had a reason to do so?"

"I do not understand the question, Captain Harrison."

"Did anyone order you to kill him?"

"I do not have such an order in my command list nor in my timeline."

"Your timeline was erased." I was still staring into her eyes. They were gorgeous.

"Yes, Captain Harrison."

"Who erased it?"

"I do not remember."

"Could you have erased it yourself?"

"That is not possible."

"That's true, Captain Harrison," Floyd said. He always addressed me formally when we were in the presence of others. "Bioroids are not designed to be self-programming, and that includes intentional purges."

I sighed. We were so *close* here.

But we seemed to have reached a solid, blank wall.

As blank as Eve's eyes in Presentation One.

"I'm afraid Eve will have to come along with us, Ms. Manchester," I said.

"Oh, no! Surely not!"

"Yes, ma'am. There's an APB out for her arrest." I didn't add that I'd ordered the APB…or that technically you can only arrest a *human*; you could commandeer a machine, but it worked out to much the same thing. "It's partly for her own protection. I also want the android techs at the station to run some tests on her for me."

"I will file a formal protest with your superiors!…"

"Go ahead. Eve is evidence in a murder case, Ms. Manchester. She may also be a witness, if we can figure out how to unlock her memory."

"I…I understand. I just don't want to see her hurt, is all."

"We won't hurt her," I said. "When those spare parts come in, you can bring them around to the Fra Mauro Station and install them. But we'll want to hold on to the damaged parts after you replace them."

"Of course, Captain. Evidence…"

"Yes, ma'am."

"But, how long will it be before she can come back to work?"

Eliza Manchester was a strange one. She talked about her bioroids being family, but she was concerned about them missing work.

She was such a nice little old English lady…pimp.

Chapter Twelve

Day 6

Floyd had volunteered to take Eve 5VA3TC to the NAPD satellite station at Fra Mauro. I had given him some explicit instructions to pass on to the officers there. She was to be treated well, and no one else was to be allowed to see her except Eliza Manchester, and then only with supervision. No lawyers—but that wouldn't be an issue since bioroids don't have civil rights and we didn't need to charge her…yet. I wanted them to give her a complete chemical scan—especially her hands, where bits of packing gel or blood might remain for weeks despite careful cleaning. If she'd handled the laser, the silicone compound would still be on her skin

I'd ordered a complete protein work-up, too. Some of Dow's DNA would still be in her, even days later, and it would be possible to pull in a molecular match with the traces of lubricant I'd picked up in Room Twelve.

Finally, I wanted Dr. Jason Cherchi to examine her. He was our chief roboticist in Heinlein—in fact, he worked for Haas-Bioroid in their research department, but he consulted for the NAPD on the side. I wanted to hear his opinion about the various injuries and damaged spots on Eve's body.

The more I thought about it, the more suspicious I was of those two puncture marks in the burned patch on Eve's lower chest.

"You sure you don't mind doing this?" I'd asked Floyd at the entrance of the tube-train that would take them to the police station.

"Not in the least," Floyd had replied. "As it happens, I need to return to Haas-Bioroid periodically for adjustment and examination. I will do so after depositing Eve 5VA3TC at the satellite station."

He had one hand clasped around Eve's upper right arm, holding her…and I remembered the injury to Robert Vargas's arm. Had she tossed Vargas out the airlock at the High Frontier?

"Okay. One more thing to pass on to the techs there."

"Yes?"

"When they do the chemical scan on her hands…have them look for tissue, blood, or amino traces that would match with the DNA of *this* man." I used my PAD to transmit the file on Vargas.

"Data received. Very well. And where will you go next?"

"Melange Mining," I told him. "I need to talk with Mark Henry if I can, and bring him in as well. After that, probably Alpha Prospecting. The laser used in Dow's murder came from there."

"I will have the station transmit the lab results to you as soon as they have them."

"Thanks, Floyd. Catch you later."

He cocked his head to one side like a curious puppy. "I am not running from you, Rick. I am merely—"

"Never mind, never mind," I said, holding up my hands. Floyd sometimes had trouble with human slang. "I'll *see* you later."

The tube-lev had whisked me back beneath the face of the

Moon, 650 kilometers from Fra Mauro to Sinus Medii. The artificial day of the Heinlein Colony was coming to a close by then, so I checked into a cheap hotel, the Barbicane, at the Columbiad Arcology.

The Arcology is the tallest structure on the Moon. Arcologies on Earth, of course, are built high to maximize living space in the tight quarters of megopoli, but there's still plenty of open space on the Moon, and no real need to build kilometer-high structures enclosing what amounts to a small city. But the view from the restaurant on the top of the tower is *spectacular*, bathed in Earthlight, and overlooking much of the central 2M corporate complex.

The next day, I went to visit Melange Mining.

The big 2M is a vast and tangled collection of domes and Quonsets, towers and separator stacks, gantries and surface conveyers. They even had their own high-G launch track, a surface west-to-east mag-lev monorail three hundred kilometers long, from the crater Bruce to the crater Godin. The track accelerated helium-3 canisters into space, where they looped around the Moon and drifted in for a precision-timed rendezvous with the top of the Beanstalk—the first leg of their journey down-Stalk to Earth.

An escalator took me from the security check-in station up a level to the expensive-looking front office for the Melange Mining Corporation, with huge anhydrous glass windows overlooking the dark lunar plain outside. A human secretary told me to follow the green guidelights to Personnel.

John Jones was working behind the front desk.

"Jones?" I asked, surprised to see him. He'd mentioned working as a clerk for Melange's admin department during the up-Stalk trip to Midway, but I hadn't expected to run into him here. In fact, he was supposed to have been seconded to Humanity Labor, an odd factoid I still hadn't figured out.

"I'm Jones, yes, sir," the clone said. He seemed scrunched in on himself, almost as though he expected physical abuse.

"You're not the Jones I met on the Beanstalk a few days ago, are you?"

"No, sir. You most likely met one of my…brothers. I am Philemon Jones."

"Which one? What's your serial ID?"

He looked terrified. "*Please*, sir. Those numbers are restricted information, and not for public dissemination! You can refer to me simply as 'Phil.'"

"Actually, Phil, I'm not the public," I told him, flashing my badge. "Harrison, NAPD. I need to find a clone, Mark Henry 103."

As I studied him, I realized that he wasn't a perfect duplicate of the Jones I'd met. The face was a tad longer, a little leaner. But differences in diet could explain such trifling variations.

I reminded myself that their fingerprints would be different as well. There are always unique differences in how a given genome is expressed.

"Yes, sir. Of course, sir." He typed for a moment on a virtual keyboard, bringing up blocks of data on a transparent display hanging in the air between us. "*That* Mark Henry is currently outside. Mine Seven, Pit Three. Shall I have someone bring him in?"

I was about to say yes, when I noticed the spy-eyes high up in two corners of the room. There'd been heavily armored guards outside the personnel department, too, and at the tube-train station below. Besides that, if Henry was guilty he might flee. A skyhopper could put him anywhere in Heinlein in an hour or two, and then I might never run him down.

"Maybe I should go see him."

"Yes, sir. I'll assign you a turtleback, sir."

I'd heard of them before, but not worked with one. Turtlebacks were another brand new offering from the sorcerers' labs at Jinteki—*Homo vacuo operae*—roughly "vacuum working man." The one assigned to me stood just one meter tall, and looked like he was wearing a turtle shell, hence the nickname. His head was almost invisible inside the shell's embrace; two tiny, deeply recessed eyes peered out at me from the shadows. His arms were long, slender, and had skin like black leather. Like the hocas I'd seen at Midway, he had legs and feet that doubled as an extra set of arms and hands, but they were articulated in such a way that he could walk on them okay, especially in low gravity. I doubted that he'd get very far in one-G, though.

A turtleback didn't need a spacesuit. The shell and leathery skin protected him from solar radiation, cosmic rays, and extremes of heat and cold. The eyes, protected by thick, transparent membranes from ultraviolet radiation, could dilate wide enough to pick up infrared light. I learned later that he had a large space under the shell that held a pressurized air reserve, and respirocytes in his bloodstream that let him hold his breath for over an hour. He could speak in any atmosphere, but out on the surface, I was told, he could only speak with a special mask that included a built-in radio; normally, turtlebacks communicated with one another through sign language.

"Take Captain Harrison to Mark Henry," Jones told it...*him*. "T90 Number 5, seven/three."

"*Oh-gay,*" the odd little being said. "*I aib ib Darlie.*"

Evidently, its throat and mouth weren't well-adapted for speech. I couldn't even see its mouth. Jones explained that it had just told me its name was "Charlie."

Him...*him*. I was having trouble thinking of it as a *him*.

Jinteki, I thought, *is really pushing the boundaries of what it means to be* human.

Of course, they wouldn't see it that way. Clones, whether they looked like John Jones or a turtleback, weren't human.

A human technician helped me into my surface suit. It was lightweight and flexible, with a UV-opaque bubble helmet—not much protection for a long stay, but it would serve for an hour or so on the harsh lunar surface. It was bright orange in color—presumably to make it easy for a rescue team to spot me if I wandered off and got lost.

I didn't intend for that to happen.

I checked the external equipment pouch and made sure I had an intercom jack.

Charlie led me out through an airlock onto a transport pad elevated some twenty meters above the dusty grey surface. We clambered onto a minihopper and, with Charlie at the controls, lifted into the black, empty sky.

The minihopper was designed to carry two passengers and a pilot, and was for short-range flights only—say a couple of hundred kilometers. It was powered by bursts of meta-heated steam fired from a quartet of big, white water tanks beneath the open platform, where I clung to the guardrail for dear life. The view was…dizzying.

Most people, when they think of mining the Moon, for some reason imagine shafts deep beneath the surface. Some lunar water comes from deep veins, of course, but the helium-3 is all found on the surface, in the very top half-meter or meter or so of regolith. The actual mining involves strip-miners like the T90: big, bulldozer-type machines on multiple tracks that scrape up the top meter of regolith, suck it down through an enormous maw, and channel it to a hopper trailing behind. When the hopper gets full, it decouples from the strip-miner as an empty one takes its place, and runs itself to the nearest surface conveyor—moving belts that can run for many kilometers across the surface until they reach the processing intakes of a converter. For the past four billion years, helium-3, blasted out from the Sun, has been falling on the lunar surface. We scrape it up now at a ratio of a hundred million to one—one hundred million tons of regolith refined to produce one ton of helium-3.

Even at that, it's cheaper and easier doing it this way than trying to recover it from wells on Earth, or waiting for radioactive tritium to decay. But Lord, you should hear the Greenies moan about how we're defacing the pristine lunar environment.

I'm all for environmental consciousness Earthside. The best thing that ever happened to our battered little home world was our starting to get industry off the surface and into space. Someday, Earth might even be healed again, with life in the oceans and green rain forests.

There's precious little green on the Moon, however. None at all, in fact, except for the hydroponics units and botany domes. The surface is a sere, blasted, empty, barren waste, with dust so fine it gets into machinery and spacesuit seals with appalling ease, and temperatures that swing from minus 153 to plus 107 Celsius in time with the four-week cycle of day and night. In the permanently shadowed spots, temperatures can hover around minus 230. The only life here is *us*, inside the domes or underground, or working on the surface. So…so what if we're strip-mining the place?

I tried to enjoy the view. It's not that I'm afraid of heights, but the minihopper was tiny and open, and we were sailing a good hundred meters above the surface at a considerable clip. A safety harness was attached to my suit, but I gripped that safety rail so tightly that my fingers ached.

The area already mined was billiard-ball smooth and a very dark grey in color, like graphite. Earth hung directly overhead, in half-phase, at the moment, looking down on the Indian subcontinent, with the sprawling coastline of eastern Asia picked out of the encroaching darkness by the soft glow of the megapoli. The sun washed most of the stars from the sky, though I could see a few of the brighter ones despite the glare.

And everything was deathly silent. I could feel the vibration through the metal grillwork of the platform against my boots when the steam jets fired, but in hard vacuum they didn't make a sound.

Eventually, we began to descend. I felt something hard pluck at my sleeve, looked down, and my guide pointed. A T90 was working a kilometer up ahead.

Some of the newer strip-miners have enclosed, pressurized cabins and airlocks. T90s still leave their drivers exposed to vacuum and hard radiation, with just a thin awning of aluminum foil stretched above the driver to keep the direct sun off. That's one reason, I suppose, the big mining corps like using clones instead of humans. The open units are cheaper, and clones, well... they're expendable, aren't they?

This one was surrounded by a vast cloud of dust thrown up by its operation. Lunar dust has a consistency similar to fine talcum, and in one-sixth of a G it falls quite slowly. Worse, everything, including the surface itself, tends to build up a static charge that makes the dust hover—when it's not making the stuff cling to every available surface, like space suits, visors, and machinery.

There was a hopper landing pad behind the driver's station, and Charlie skillfully angled us in and down for a landing squarely on the big white crosshair painted there.

The operator saw us coming and put the machine into idle. He was waiting for me as I stepped off the platform and onto his rig, wearing a once-white space suit coated from helmet to boot with graphite-grey dust.

"Mark Henry 103?" I asked. They'd given me his channel back at the dome.

I saw him start. "Who are you?"

"Captain Harrison, NAPD." My badge couldn't project a holo through my suit. He'd have to take my word for it, or accept the word of my e-ID. "You're wanted for questioning concerning the murders of Roger Dow and Robert Vargas. I'd like you to come with me."

"I don't know anything about that!" I could hear the panic edging his voice over the radio.

"Nevertheless, I need to ask you some questions."

"Where...back at Melange?" The panic level went up a notch.

"Here will do for now." I reached into my external pouch. "I have a jack."

I wanted to question him without being overheard. Melange might have offed Dow because he wanted to get rid of clones, which would have meant more expense for the corporations. Radio wasn't good; even at low power, the signals might be picked up by receivers on the T90 or even by communications satellites in lunar orbit, and relayed back to corporate headquarters. I was pretty sure that Charlie might have a receiver tucked away inside that shell of his, too.

I plugged one end of the jack into the base of my helmet, and let Henry plug the other end into his. The intercom cable was shielded, and would give us privacy. In the old days, you were supposed to be able to do the same thing by touching helmet to helmet, but I understand that never worked all that well because plastic laminates tend to absorb and muffle sound. Intercom ought to be safe enough, however.

"Your radio off?" I asked.

With a gloved finger he depressed a key on his chest pack. "Yes, sir." His face, peering out through a visor grimy with streaked, grey dust, appeared terrified. "But I can't talk for long. *They* will see my radio is off, and come check on me."

"This'll just take a couple of minutes...and I'll square things with your employers. Okay?"

A jerky nod.

"We have both vid and electronic data records of you going to the High Frontier Hotel on the twenty-third. You left about an hour later, catching a ferry back to the Moon. Would you care to tell me what you were doing at that hotel?"

"I was...I was running an errand."

"What kind of errand?"

"I'm not supposed to tell. Sir…I could be in *terrible* trouble if I tell!"

"You could be in terrible trouble right now if you don't," I told him. "What was the errand?"

"I…I had to take a suitcase to the hotel."

"That's all? Just take a suitcase? Who'd you give it to?"

"No one."

"You took it to a room?"

"Yes, sir."

"Ah. What was the room number?"

His eyes closed behind the visor. "Room Sixteen."

A new piece of the puzzle! Room Sixteen was two down from Dow's room…and that explained why we hadn't found the suitcase.

"Did you see what was inside the suitcase?"

"Captain Harrison, please…don't make me…"

"You can tell me here, or you can come with me to the station and tell me there. Which will it be?"

"Look…if I tell you…I need protection!"

"You *want* me to arrest you?"

"No. Yes. I don't know. Look…I was told to do…things, and I was told not to tell anyone about them. I was told that if I did, I would be…retired."

"I see. Well, for the time being, at least, you are officially under the protection of the New Angeles Police Department, okay? I'll see about getting you into protective custody once I see how well you answer my questions. Understand?"

Again, a jerky nod.

"Did you see what was in the suitcase?"

A nod.

"What was it?"

"A Huong-Zhen regolith beam laser tunneler, Mark V, Mod 2," he said. "I was told to go into the equipment locker at Alpha Prospecting and take one, and a charged battery, from their storage unit. That was…on the twenty-first."

"Go on."

"They gave me the suitcase. It was big enough that I could put both the battery and the tunneler inside, but they had to be broken down separately. They arranged special clearance for me so that the suitcase wouldn't be scanned at the ferry terminal, and put me on a flight to the Beanstalk. I was told to take the suitcase to the High Frontier, to Room Sixteen, open it, and assemble the laser and battery pack."

"Who was in Room Sixteen, Mark?"

"No one."

"No one? You're sure?"

"The room was empty, Captain Harrison. I was told it would be…"

I sighed. "Okay. What did you do with the laser, then?"

"I left it on the bed, as I'd been instructed."

"And the suitcase?"

"I left that in a corner."

"As you'd been instructed?"

He nodded. "Yes, sir."

"Mark…who gave you all of those orders?"

"I don't know his name."

"You'd never met him before?"

"No, sir. Never."

"A human?"

"Yes."

"What did he look like?"

"Fairly tall. Thin. He wore a black uniform, and had a gun, a pistol of some kind in a shoulder holster. Oh…and he had facial hair. A beard…"

Bingo! Mark Henry's mystery contact was either Robert Vargas or Frank Hodgkins. Both had beards; both wore black uniforms and carried weapons as part of Humanity Labor's ad hoc security force.

Someone had been handling Mark Henry, playing him like a fish on a line.

If Vargas, someone higher up had already taken steps to clean up after themselves.

I wanted to get Henry back to the safety of a police station and have him look at some file photos. If someone had killed Vargas to keep him quiet, Mark Henry must be on the death list as well. *Why*, I wondered, *had they left him alive this long?*

"You think you would recognize this bearded guy if you saw a photo of him?"

"Yes."

"Did he give you a name?"

"I was supposed to call him 'Mr. Green.'"

What bothered me most now was the fact that the investigation had just gone in a most unexpected direction. Vargas or Hodgkins…they were both muscle, employees of Humanity Labor and probably Human First, as well, and they hadn't struck me as being all that bright. Why the hell would they murder Dow, one of their own, the guy who was pushing to eliminate clones and bioroids from the work force, which was what both organizations wanted most?

More, why would they want to murder Dow in such a spectacularly bloody fashion?

None of this made sense.

I decided to change tack. "Do you know a bioroid named Eve 5VA3TC?"

Henry nearly fell off the mining rig's deck. I reached out, a stab of movement, grabbing his arm to steady him. His other hand grabbed my wrist, and for a moment I felt just how strong the genetically enhanced muscles of a worker clone were.

"You okay?"

"Y-yes. Thank you."

"You know her?"

"Please, sir. She had nothing to do with it. *Nothing* to do with it!"

Eliza Manchester must've been right. Henry had had some sort of a relationship with Eve.

"I'm not saying she did. But I know she was in Dow's room just before he was murdered. And she saw…something."

"You…you've spoken with her?"

I nodded. "She's been taken in for safekeeping, Mark. She's okay."

"They…they wanted to make it look like she did it," he said. "I'm sure of that now! But she didn't do it!"

I noticed a red light flashing on the cab control panel. Henry saw it, too. "They're calling for me. They know I have my radio switched off."

"Let them call. Did you know Eve was there that night?"

He gave a miserable nod. "Yes. I knew she was with… him."

"She's a sex gynoid," I said. "She gets rented out to all kinds of guys. Gals, too, I suspect."

It was hard to tell, but it looked like tears were streaming down the clone's face behind his dirty visor. "I…I know that! But we had something special! I *know* we did!"

"Suppose you tell me the whole thing."

It was the old, old story, but with a somewhat new twist. Clone meets bioroid. Clone loves bioroid. Clone scrapes together enough money to bang bioroid, and then wonders why she won't give him the time of day when he doesn't have any more money.

They don't actually pay clones at Melange Mining. They issue electronic scrip for personal use in the corporate commissary and store. But there was, Henry told me, something of an underground economy going, where humans exchanged folding green for certain items with a high resale value. Rocket motor parts. Static discharge circuits. Moon glass artwork. Even moon rocks, for sale to collectors Earthside. It had taken him a long time to collect enough money to buy a night with Eve. Then, later, "Mr. Green" had given him money for several more evenings with her, at Tranquility Home and at Freetown.

"But it wasn't just business for her," he insisted. "She *loves* me, like I love her. I *know* it!"

"And you're sure she's innocent?"

"Yes, sir!"

"You know that Dow did some horrible things to her?"

"Yes! She…she told me!"

Interesting. Eve hadn't been inclined to give me details about her clientele until Manchester had told her to. If she'd talked about it with Henry, maybe she *did* feel something for him.

I wasn't ready to believe that a bioroid could feel *love*, however. Henry was deceiving himself, I thought—a love sick, love-blinded puppy.

"If you really believe Eve is innocent," I told him, "you'll be able to help her best by telling me everything you know."

"Okay." He didn't like it, but he was scared to death, not only for himself, but for her.

"So…you knew she was there that night? With Dow?"

"Yes, sir."

"How did you know?"

"Mr. Green told me. At the Challenger Nearside Terminal, just before I went to the hotel."

"He told you she was with Dow?"

"Yes…"

"What did you do?"

"I took the suitcase through the hotel lobby and up to the hallway. I…I stopped outside of Room Twelve, though. I listened at the door."

"Those doors are well-insulated."

"Yes. But I have very good hearing. I could…I could hear what he was doing to her."

"And what did you do then?"

"I took the suitcase to Room Sixteen, as I'd been ordered. I sat on the bed and assembled it."

I could hear the strain in his voice. "You wanted to go back to Room Twelve and break that party up, didn't you?"

A strangled sob came across the intercom cord.

"When, when Mr. Green told me about Eve, told me she was with Dow, he told me I could help her! He told me I could do something about it, about Dow...that all I needed to do was take that laser tunneler into Room Twelve and use it to kill him! He gave me a card key to the room. He told me that no one would ever know, that I could take Eve and they would help me get away, maybe down to Earth! They would give me more money. We could be together. We could start over!..."

"Whoa. Who's 'they'? *Who* would help you get away, start over?"

"SAM."

That rocked me. Maybe I'd been wrong jumping to conclusions about Human First. SAM, the Simulant Abolitionist Movement, had political connections with Humanity Labor, but they were a separate organization entirely. Where the anti-simulant groups wanted to do away with clones in the workforce by any means necessary, SAM wanted to do away with *slavery*. Full civil rights for clones, including the vote, free speech, and an equal chance at jobs for full, equal pay.

But this still didn't smell right. There have always been rumors that SAM was trying to organize some sort of rebellion among the simulants, but in all my years with the NAPD I'd never seen any real proof. So far, SAM's fight for freedom among clones had involved lawyers and public relations, not murder.

"Sir, they're coming. They're going to be looking for me!"

I nodded. "Okay. Get on the hopper. I'm taking you into protective custody."

On the hopper, we disconnected the intercom cable and

switched on our radios. Charlie seemed to understand that we were headed back to the big 2M.

Twenty minutes later, we were descending through the black sky, the main Melange Mining facility in sight just a few kilometers ahead.

Then something hit the safety railing a couple of centimeters from my right hand, hit it *hard*, splitting the metal tube open and sending a shock through my hand and wrist despite my glove. The impact occurred in the complete silence of vacuum and made me swear and lurch back a step.

Turning, I looked up and back.

And that's when I realized we were no longer alone in that sky.

Chapter Thirteen

Day 6

"We've got company!" I called over the radio. "Look!"

Two silver skyhoppers, larger than ours, were approaching fast, fifty meters behind us and perhaps twenty meters higher. Standing on each hopper were two men in white space suits: one driving, one with a rifle.

They were shooting at us.

I felt a jolt through my boots as a round struck the minihopper's undercarriage. The craft lurched to one side, threatening to tumble. One of the big water tanks had been breached, and the water inside was blasting out into space like a rocket's exhaust. Charlie struggled silently with the controls, taking us lower. I slapped him on his arm, pointing urgently. *Take us to the base!* But we continued our erratic descent as the skyhoppers behind us raced closer. Three meters above the grey surface, the turtleback released the controls and leaped over the side, dropping slowly to the ground, hitting and bouncing in a billowing grey cloud, then skittering away at high speed.

Had he just panicked and run, or was this part of a setup? I didn't have time to think about it just then. I stepped into the pilot's spot and grabbed the controls—two joysticks half a meter apart, one controlling speed and direction, one controlling pitch and yaw. The design was simple enough, but it takes experience and a delicate touch to handle a small craft like that. My experience was with Strikers, which are just a bit larger, but I was able to pull us up before we plowed into regolith, and start us moving forward again on a level plane.

"They're getting closer," Henry called. "*Watch out!*"

He ducked, and a bullet slammed into the deck grating a few centimeters from my left foot. I hauled over on the pitch and direction controls, sending us skittering just above the surface to the right. We were still leaking from one tank and that was making handling the minihop damned tough, but as I banked the platform I saw a trio of dust geysers puff silently from the surface ahead and below. If one of those rounds even nicked my suit it would be bad. Yes, I'd had respirocyte injections when I was in the military, but explosive decompression is *no* one's friend. It would put me in a world of hurt—probably blind me as moisture froze on the inside of my helmet and on the surfaces of my eyeballs, and likely incapacitate me as my lungs were sucked dry.

I found myself thinking of Bob Vargas, of the agonized expression frozen on his wide-eyed face outside the airlock door.

I twisted the controls left, then right…then right again, abruptly changing course to head back toward our pursuers. The maneuver surprised them. They'd dropped almost to our level by that time, and it looked like I was trying to ram. They split, left and right, and I hurtled between them, swinging back through a sharp 180-degree turn as they slowed and turned around.

My Number Three water tank was showing empty. The minihop's mass was badly unbalanced now, but at least the water jet wasn't trying to throw me into a tumble. Another geyser spat dust silently from the surface off to one side. I think the most terrifying part of the entire encounter was its utter and complete deathly silence. No gunshots. No screaming ricochets or thumps of bullets hitting dust, no screech of steam jets.

Silence.

Well, I *could* hear my own breathing, rasping loudly inside my helmet, and the pounding of my own heartbeat in my ears.

"They're getting closer!" Henry called over the radio.

I risked a glance back over my shoulder. One hopper was fifty meters back, the other thirty. The passenger in the nearest skyhopper aimed his weapon.

With a nightmarish detachment of thought and emotion, I noticed that his weapon was an M460 military assault rifle with a bullpup magazine, that he was using a camera-sighting unit so he could aim the thing while wearing a space helmet, and that he had the weapon's selector switch on full auto because I could see the twinkle at the muzzle as he fired. Even with the camera sight, he was having trouble hitting us. Between the movement of his own skyhopper and the way I was jerking my minihop around, most of his shots were going wild.

They were slug-throwers rather than lasers. That was a good thing, though not unexpected. The military has "man-portable" lasers, but they are considered such only as a courtesy. You need either a massive battery to give a laser enough juice to do serious damage, or the ability to hold the beam on-target, at a time when the target is going to be doing its very best to move. Army laser rifles aren't as big or as massive as the mining laser that sliced up Dow, but they come close. For this kind of work, though, you needed either old-fashioned slug-throwers like the M460, or you needed linear accelerator rifles.

Our pursuers, it seemed, had gone the old-fashioned route. The bullpup design packed one hundred .115mm caseless rounds into a cassette magazine clipped to the butt. The way the one guy was spraying at us, I wondered if we could just play dodge-'em until his weapon ran dry.

Hard left!

Who *were* these guys? They wore suits like mine, though with white torsos rather than orange. They were standard issue for Melange Mining's airlocks, but probably standard for every other airlock in Heinlein, too.

If they were trying to kill us, they knew who we were. Henry had been afraid that someone in Melange would come out to check on his radio silence…or that they might overhear what he had to tell me. His record said that he'd been involved in trouble with human miners before, that his human co-workers didn't like him.

But this seemed to go a bit beyond mere dislike or bad feelings in the workplace.

They were faster than we were, and getting too damned close. The only thing that made them hang back was the erratic way I was twisting the damaged minihop all over the black lunar sky.

Another jolt, and now tank Number One was starting to drain, and quickly, so quickly that the minihop began shuddering and losing altitude fast. I increased the power to the main exhaust, but I knew I wouldn't be able to keep it flying much longer. The domes and surface tubes of the Melange Mining headquarters were just a tenth of a kilometer ahead, but I didn't think I'd be able to keep the platform up for even that far.

"Get ready to jump and roll," I told Henry.

"*What are you doing?*"

I didn't answer. The minihop was skimming the regolith now, and in another instant the undercarriage dragged through powdery grey dust. The unconventional landing had one effect I hadn't been expecting; as we dragged along the surface, the undercarriage threw up an immense and utterly opaque cloud of dust, forcing both of the pursuing skyhoppers to break off once again. We dug in deeper…and then the hopper pitched over wildly, sending both Henry and me hurtling forward a meter above the surface.

I hit, hard. One-sixth Earth's gravity or not, I still massed eighty kilos or so, and I think the only thing that saved me from a *very* unpleasant jolt and a sudden loss of pressure was the soft dust, the way it exploded up and forward with my impact. I bounced a couple of times, then rolled. Henry didn't go as far; his arms and legs flailed wildly as he flew, and he caught the ground sooner than I did. Dust was everywhere, filling the sky.

Shakily, I got to my feet, still half expecting to feel the bite of cold as the air in my suit explosively expanded into hard vacuum. My suit seemed to still be intact, however.

There were no rocks to hit, thank God. This part of the lunar landscape had been plowed over by strip-miners already, reducing it to featureless, craterless, rockless anonymity.

"*Run!*" I screamed at Henry. He was getting up, clumsily and awkwardly. In the distance, the two skyhoppers were joining up again, clear of the looming rooster tail of dust we'd thrown up with our landing.

I started back toward him, but he waved me off. "I'm okay!" he called over the radio, and then he was running past me, covering ground in long, loping strides that sent him flying with each step.

The two skyhoppers accelerated toward us.

My hand came up and slapped at my chest. My service pistol was there, the compact little H&K 2920 slug-thrower I call my hand cannon. I could feel its comforting heft of plastic and metal, but it was sealed beneath my space suit…it might as well have been on Earth.

I ran.

Henry was well out in front of me by this time, bounding across the regolith at a faster clip than I could possibly hope to manage. He was used to this gravity, after all.

Since I was closer to our pursuers, I seemed to be the target of choice. Dust clouds puffed in silence to either side. I tried to turn and nearly sent myself tumbling. Get up a head of steam like that and then try to turn, and your momentum keeps you going in the original direction—the cold, dead hand of Sir Isaac Newton. I stumbled, but managed not to fall.

Something hit me hard on my left shoulder, a solid blow from behind, and I thought I'd been shot…but then one of the skyhoppers flashed past my left side and I realized the pilot had just tried to run me down.

It was a glancing blow, didn't even knock me off my feet, but it *hurt*. The pilot was trying to pull his steed up, to bring the hopper to a halt just ahead.

That's a lot easier said than done. Flying a skyhopper isn't like flying an aircraft in-atmosphere. Once you get moving, you need to fire rockets to stop…or wait for gravity to bring you down. After brushing against me, the hopper was slewing sideways as the pilot tried to balance his jets.

I changed direction and darted to the right…and ran smack into a wave of darkness. The dust cloud from our landing had followed us, blotting out the sun and enveloping me, falling slowly, not blowing about as it would have in atmosphere, but kind of sliding down through the sky in a steady, opaque cascade. Enough clung to my visor to momentarily blind me. I swiped at it with my glove, leaving a sticky smear.

Twisting left again, nearly losing my balance as I did so, I began running as fast as I could through the unnerving black of the cloud, hoping to put some distance between me and them before the cloud settled out.

I hit something high and solid.

I felt along the smooth surface, and realized I'd run into the side of one of Melange's domes. I'd been running for an airlock that was off to my left, so I started feeling my way along the wall, moving in that direction.

Quietly, with no fuss at all, the dust fell out of the black sky. Those electrostatic charges in the surface kept some of the finest dust hovering in a thin, almost luminous haze, but the larger particles soundlessly dropped to the ground.

I glanced back. One of the hoppers had landed, and two men in dirty white space suits were moving toward me. I couldn't see the other hopper. The airlock hatch was twenty meters away. Where the *hell* was Mark Henry? If he'd reached the hatch and cycled through, it might be a nasty minute or two before I could get in.

One of the space-suited figures stopped and raised his rifle to his shoulder. Firing from a wildly moving platform with any accuracy is almost impossible, but this guy had stopped, taken a solid stance, and was aiming with trained deliberation.

He fired, a single shot, the round striking the titanium-steel wall beside me in an explosion of fragments...and, impossibly, I *heard* the crack.

At the same instant, a brilliant white star appeared on the helmet's surface close beside the right side of my face, and I realized that the bullet had shattered on the dome wall, and a ricocheting piece had hit my helmet. I didn't know if the bubble was plastic or transplas or old-fashioned tempered glass, but the impact had crazed a third of my bubble.

Had *breached* it. I could hear a thin, high-pitched screech as air bled from my suit, and my face suddenly went cold. When air expands rapidly it carries away heat—the principle behind refrigerators since the 19th century—and right now my face felt like I'd just shoved it into an icebox. I swallowed hard, trying to clear my ears as the pressure dropped. My breath froze across the inside of my helmet, and suddenly I was nearly blind.

Turning slightly, I groped toward the airlock entrance, though I could scarcely see. An orange shape stepped in front of me; I could barely make out that it was a man in a space suit, that he was holding a semiautomatic pistol in a two-gloved stance, and that he was aiming it directly at me.

He was too far to rush, too near to dodge. I could see enough to see him press the firing button, see gas erupt silently from the muzzle…

And only then did I realize that he was aiming *past* me, aiming at the men twenty meters behind me. I turned in time to see the guy who'd shot me crumple and fall in a slow-motion twist, saw the other one running, saw the second skyhopper hovering in the distance, then accelerating forward.

A strong hand grabbed me by my arm and dragged me forward. I felt him haul me bodily inside the airlock as the last of my suit's air bled away into emptiness and the screech whistled higher into inaudibility. My ears *hurt.*

The man in orange stood just inside the airlock door, squeezing off silent rounds as the door slid shut. I was on my hands and knees, now, trying to seal off my throat and hold it against the pressure still inside my lungs. Then a dirty, white-suited figure helped me unseal my helmet, and I could hear again, as air rushed in to fill the lock chamber.

The man in the orange suit was braced against the airlock door, now, peering out through the window, his service pistol still clutched in both gloved hands and aimed at the ceiling, his helmet unsealed and hanging open.

He turned and gave me a lopsided grin. "Hey, Fish! Fancy running into *you* here!"

It was Raymond Flint.

He looked considerably better than he had the last time I'd seen him—his eyes bright, his skin a healthy pink color. Damn it, he looked like he was *enjoying* himself.

"What the hell are you doing here?" was all I could manage to say.

"Happened to be in the area," he replied. "Just thought I'd drop by."

Pressures equalized and the inner hatch popped open. Several men in 2M security uniforms were there, looking worried. "My God!" one said. "Who *were* those guys?"

"I don't know," I replied. I started peeling off my suit. My ears were ringing, and the voices around me sounded a bit muffled. "But I'm damned well going to find out!"

"Your ear's bleeding," Flint pointed out. "Let's get you to the dispensary first."

Turned out I'd blown an eardrum. The doc at the company dispensary was able to fix me up with a replacement, though. While I was with her, Flint used his PAD to try to trace the attackers, patching through to the 2M complex's space traffic control to see where those two skyhoppers had come from.

No luck there. The hoppers had vanished over the horizon in the direction of Tranquility Home, taking the man Flint had shot with them. But we had one clue. Those goons had come hunting for us, for Mark Henry and me. They couldn't have known we were there unless someone had passed on that information.

Someone inside Melange Mining.

"I'd come to 2M to find this character, actually," Flint told me as we rode the tube-lev back to Tranquility Home. He patted Henry on the shoulder. The clone was riding with us in the lounge car, his face pale, his eyes darting around at every new sound or movement in the car's compartment. "I was in the main lobby, waiting to talk to McNally, the guy in charge of the clones working for Melange. They have a big, anhydrous glass window up there, overlooking the lunar plain.

"Anyway, the receptionist had just told me you were already here, that you'd gone out to find Henry and bring him back. I went over to the window to look, and sure enough: there you were—at least I assumed it was you—skimming in toward the dome like the Devil was after you, and two skyhoppers on your tail. I broke records going down a level and getting to the airlock. There were emergency suits there, so I grabbed one."

He grinned. "I just remembered to draw my piece before sealing up!"

"I'm glad you did," I said. "Of course, I wasn't expecting to get into a damned firefight."

"If the bad guys did head back to Tranquility Home," Flint said, "it'll be tough to find them."

"Our first responsibility," I said, "is making sure our star witness here is kept safe. I want to get him down-Stalk and back to Earth as fast as I can."

"Back to Earth?" Henry asked. "You're taking me to Earth?"

"That's right. You got a problem with that?"

"No. I don't want to stay on the Moon," Henry said. "Not now."

"You really think Melange is behind the attack?" Flint asked me.

I nodded at the other side of the compartment. "Let's step over there."

Henry had admitted to having excellent hearing, but the tube-lev lounge car was large enough that we could speak privately on the other side of the compartment, and still keep an eye on our dejected and terrified prisoner. There were only a few others riding with us, and they didn't appear to be interested in anything other than their newsrags and their drinks. Just to be on the safe side, I used my PAD to project a sound suppression field, a handy little app that projects precisely calculated sonic wavelengths that cancel the sound waves of a conversation as they spread out a meter or so from the speakers. It wasn't foolproof, especially at close quarters, but it gave us a degree of privacy.

"Right now," I said, speaking softly and keeping my eyes on Henry, "I don't know what to think."

Quickly, I filled Flint in on what I knew of the Dow murder. When I finished, he gave a low whistle.

"Sounds like you have more suspects than you know what to do with," he said. He nodded at Henry. "He *could* have done it, you know. Him and the bioroid."

"Yeah, he could have. But I have a hunch that he didn't."

"I dunno, Fish. There are a lot of rumors circulating on the street about a clone underground. A clone *rising*."

"I've heard 'em. People have been nervous since the Clone Riots last year. It's also possible those rumors are being deliberately planted."

"You gotta consider all possibilities."

"You want possibilities? I think his 'Mr. Green' was trying to set it up so Henry *would* do it. He was telling me about that part out on the surface, when we were interrupted."

Flint snorted. "'Mr. Green,' right. Nice and generic, impossible to trace. He's lying."

"Maybe. And maybe he was told something that would make us *think* he was lying."

"That seems a bit far-fetched, Fish."

"If Henry's telling the truth, Ray, someone was setting things up so that he would break in on Dow and kill him."

"Telling him he could save Eve?"

"Right. Now, I still haven't questioned him about this part… but I think he chickened out. And whoever was handling him had to improvise."

"Improvise how?"

"Kill Dow themselves, and cover things up to make it *look* like Henry had done it."

"You really think someone's trying to set him up, make it look like a clone killed Roger Dow?"

"Yes, I do."

"Okay. Who?"

"Damifino. If Vargas was involved, his murder suggests it might be someone with Humanity Labor or Human First."

"Yeah, maybe. But maybe Vargas was just in the wrong place at the wrong time. He was coming back to check in with this Dow character, saw the murderer, and was killed to keep him from talking."

"But 'Mr. Green' had a beard."

"Okay. Mr. Green had a beard. But Humanity Labor? What would the motive be? Why would they kill their own lawyer?"

"I don't know," I admitted. "But Humanity Labor is filled with Human Firsters, and both of them want to get rid of clones and bioroids permanently. I'm beginning to wonder if they're setting Henry up to trigger another round of anti-clone riots, like last year."

"Hm. Interesting idea," Flint said. "Dow was pretty high-profile, former senator and all that. He was working on pushing anti-clone legislation with a bunch of D.C. senators, so the murder would look like someone trying to stop the new laws going through. Someone like a clone underground."

"Or SAM."

"Or SAM," he agreed, nodding.

"Or it could be Melange Mining after all. They knew I was out there. And they knew where Henry was, and that I was looking for him. They might have been keeping Henry safely on ice, but when I showed up and demanded to see him, they could have decided to kill us both."

"Why'd they wait to kill Henry in the first place? Why not pop him the moment he gets back from the Beanstalk? Instead, they send him back to work…"

"I'm honestly not sure…but I'm beginning to think that the plan—killing Dow and pinning it on a clone and a bioroid—went wrong. Henry was supposed to be the triggerman, but he chickened and ran, so someone else stepped in to finish the job. Maybe they planned to 'retire' Henry later, so it wouldn't look like someone higher up was cleaning up the mess. Maybe they planned to put him through another round of conditioning so that he thought he *did* do it. It would be better if they could produce a live murderer. But then you and I show up, and they decide they need to take care of loose ends."

"Damn, Fish. This could be *big*. Bigger than we can handle.

Whether it's Human First, Humanity Labor, or Melange Mining, you're talking about a major conspiracy here."

"I know. Which is why right now I just want to get Henry back Earthside." I considered the possibilities, then added, "But I also need to check some things on the way down-Stalk. Ray… I need to lean on you."

"What do you want me to do?"

"Couple of things. First, I want you to take charge of our friend over there. Get him to the sat station at Tranquility."

He looked doubtful. "Fish, after what you've told me, I don't think I trust the NAPD stations up here. Not completely, anyway. Melange has its hands in *everything* in Heinlein, *especially* at Tranquility Home. If they're the ones behind that attack, Henry won't be safe there."

I sighed. "I know. But I need to poke around at the High Frontier again, and I can't baby-sit. There's a satellite police station at Fra Mauro, but it's tiny compared to the one at Tranquility. Show me some options."

"I don't think I have any."

"When you deliver Henry to the Tranquility sat station, put the fear of God into them for me, will you? Tell them if *anything* happens to him, they're dead meat over there. I want a twenty-four hour watch on him, with class-one security. *No* one gets in to see him. Understand?"

"I understand."

"After that…you can go get Eve. Have Floyd help you. They're at the satellite station out at Fra Mauro right now, but I think they'll be safe—safer, at least—at Tranquility Home.

"Once they're both secure, I want you to follow up on the skyhopper attack. Check the Heinlein hospitals and clinics, see if anyone turned up with a gunshot wound."

"The guy I capped might be dead. I know I depreshed him."

"Then check the morgues, too."

"You got it."

"After that, I'll want you and Floyd to bring Henry and Eve down-Stalk."

"Right. Why wait, though? I could have both of them on Earth tomorrow morning by dropship."

"It's tempting, but I want to check something first. Besides, if Melange is behind this, they'll have the resources to put out a hit on those two, and the best window of opportunity will be when you move them out of the sat station. Same goes for Humanity Labor, even Human First. Whoever's behind it, they were willing to just wait and keep an eye on Henry, here, but as soon as they knew I was going out to see him, someone panicked and sent four guys in hoppers out to silence us. I'd say the stakes in the game have just punched straight through the ceiling of the pressurized dome. If they're desperate enough, they might try *anything*. Okay?"

He nodded.

"I'm counting on you, Ray." I looked at him, curious. "Why did you come back, anyway?"

He gave an easy shrug. "You were right. I was crawling into that damned bottle again. Throwing my life away. So when I sobered up, I squared myself away and went to see Dawn. I asked to be put on the case."

"She didn't tell me anything about it."

"I asked her not to."

"Why?"

"Wanted to surprise you."

"You did do that."

"And...well, maybe I just didn't want to get your hopes up."

"What do you mean?"

"Fish...Rick, I mean...the memories...they're getting bad. *Real* bad. I didn't know if I could do this. I guess I just didn't want you relying on me, when I wasn't sure that would be all that good of an idea."

I clapped him on the shoulder. "You came back when it counted," I told him. "And that's all that matters."

Privately, though, I was worried. If Flint stressed out and cracked while bringing our two star witnesses back to Earthside New Angeles, then everything I'd put together on this case so far would be lost.

"Look," I added. "If you run into trouble, give me a call. And I'll put a call through to Dawn and have her put together a squad to help you and Floyd bring Eve and Henry Earthside. Okay?"

"Right, Fish." He held out his hand a moment, flexing the fingers. "And…I feel pretty good now. You *can* count on me."

"Good. I knew I could."

But that reminded me of something. There was one last thing I wanted to check before we reached Tranquility Home. I walked back to Henry and sat next to him. "Mark? Let me see your hands."

I motioned Flint closer and had him look, too. On Henry's left palm just below his forefinger was a shallow cut, scabbed over, evidently several days old. "How'd you get this?" I asked him. "Looks like you might have caught your hand in something."

"No, sir."

"No? What happened?"

"Mr. Green…he took a sample of skin there. He told me it was for a DNA test."

"You didn't catch your hand while assembling the laser and battery pack?"

He looked at me as if I was crazy. "Of *course* not. I *do* know how to handle my tools."

So "Mr. Green" had planted a bit of skin on the laser, intending that the police lab find it and link the tool to Henry. Slick. And sneaky.

"Okay, Mark. Here's what's happening: Detective Flint,

here, is going to take charge of you. You'll be held in protective custody for a day or two at Tranquility Home, at the NAPD satellite station there, okay?"

He nodded.

"After that, he'll bring you and Eve back to Earthside."

He brightened. "She is coming, too?"

"That's right. And there's something you can do for me."

"Anything, Captain Harrison."

"I want you to tell Detective Flint everything you told me out on the surface, okay? And he's going to record it all on his PAD." I'd been kicking myself because I didn't have any of Henry's testimony recorded, not a word. Like my pistol, my PAD had been sealed inside my suit…and since we'd been using a shielded intercom jack, there'd been no way to record the conversation anyway. I wanted Henry's testimony recorded safe and secure, just in case.

"Tell him all about Mr. Green," I went on. "About the mining laser. About him telling you to rescue Eve. Everything you can remember. Understand?"

"Yes, sir."

"You know, we kind of got interrupted back there. You were telling me that Mr. Green suggested that you break in on Dow and Eve and…what did you tell me? 'Do something about Dow.'"

"Yes, sir."

"Tell me something. Tell me the truth. *Did* you break in on them with the laser?"

"No, Captain Harrison. I swear I didn't!"

"What happened?"

"I sat there in Room Sixteen for a long time, Captain Harrison. I *wanted* to kill him. I did. When I'd listened at the door to Room Twelve, I'd heard her *screaming*!"

"Mark," Flint said gently. "Bioroids don't feel pain."

"I know that. It was…a performance. Dow *liked* to hear her

scream! And I knew he was playing those sick games with her in there! So I sat in Room Sixteen and thought about killing him…but I didn't. Then Mr. Green showed up."

"Oh?"

A nod. "He chimed my door, and when I answered he asked me what the hell I was doing."

"And what did you say?"

"Nothing. I was scared. Terrified. I pushed past him and ran down the hall. By the time I got to the lobby, I was just walking, but all I could think about was getting out of there. I went to the tube-lev that took me to Farside…then I caught the next ferry back to Heinlein."

"Did you ever see Green again?" Flint asked.

Henry shook his head. "No."

"Okay," I said. "You tell all of that to Detective Flint, okay?" I looked at Flint. "Get it on your PAD, then flash it to me, to Commissioner Dawn, to NAPD Evidence, everywhere you can think of. Just in case."

"You got it, Fish."

"Good. Then I'll see you on Earth in a few days."

Chapter Fourteen

Day 8

"When did she leave?"

The secretary at the Humanity Labor office on the Challenger Planetoid's Farside shook her head. "I really don't know, Officer. Ms. Coleman is not in the habit of sharing her schedule with me."

"Can you tell me if her bodyguard went with her? Big guy," I brushed at my chin, "beard. His name is Hodgkins."

"I can't tell you that, either," she said. "I'm sorry."

"Is Ms. Coleman up-Stalk often?"

"Not really, no. She was just here to coordinate that planned meeting with some bigwigs from Washington the other day. When that was canceled…" She shrugged. "I guess she and her assigned security person went back to Earth."

I considered having her call down to the Humanity Labor offices in Earthside New Angeles and find out, but decided the news wouldn't help me one way or the other. I was suspicious of Ms. Coleman now, and I didn't particularly want to tip her off that I was looking for her.

"You've been most helpful," I lied. "Thank you."

"I *could* put a message through to her, through the corporate network," she volunteered.

"I just have one or two minor points to clear up," I lied again, "so that won't be necessary. I'll catch up with her on Earth."

The tube-lev through the core of the planetoid took me to Nearside.

At the Beanstalk Terminal, I made my grip-slippered way to the Space Elevator Authority Security Center. Raul Guerrero was the guy in charge of security for every facility on the Challenger Planetoid, and for the upper half of the Beanstalk, as well.

"Captain Harrison," he said, not sounding pleased to meet me. "What do *you* want?"

"Just a little of your time," I told him. "I want to check out an evidence kit...and I want to make sure that Exhibit A is safe."

"That laser tunneler? Yeah, it's safe. In the evidence locker."

"I'd like to see it."

"You don't trust us, do you?"

"I don't trust *anyone*, Mr. Guerrero. Why do you ask?"

"You came down damned hard on a couple of my people," he said. "I filed a complaint with your boss."

"Yeah, I know. And I'm really sorry about that." Well, I *tried* to sound contrite. I was doing some major tail-kissing, here, but I needed the chief elevator merc's help.

I made a note to myself to be a little less testy in the future, even when the targets of my anger *were* first-order *gilada*, blithering idiots who couldn't find their backsides with both hands.

"Seriously," I added, "I was a bit stressed when I got up here. I'll apologize in person to the two guys I chewed out if you want. What were their names?"

"Daley," he said, "and Smethers."

"Daley and Smethers. Yeah. Are they on duty now?"

"They're gone. Back to Earth."

"Something I said?"

I saw the shadow of a smile tug at the corner of Guerrero's mouth. "It wasn't you. You weren't the only one stressed out by what was in Room Twelve. And then Smethers had to go outside and bring in Robert Vargas." He shook his head. "*Not* pretty."

"No."

"You call us 'elevator mercs' and 'rent-a-cops.'" He sounded bitter. "I suppose there's something to be said for that. We don't have your training. We *are* professionals. But most of the day-to-day routine is helping little old ladies find the right tube-lev car to Farside, or breaking up a drunken brawl at the Castle Club or the Earthview. We don't usually have to wade through blood and pick up loose body parts to do our job."

"Tell you the truth, it's the same for us," I told him. It was time to do some major pride swallowing. "I had no business going off like that."

He seemed mollified. "We're just doing our jobs here, Captain Harrison. The best we know how."

"I know. And right now you can help me do mine."

"How?"

"I need to check out that mining laser. I want some dedicated time on your target range—no one there but you and me. And I want to order a gog from wherever you keep them up here."

"A gog?" He looked puzzled. "What do you—"

"I know you've got them, Mr. Guerrero. I had some from room service at the High Frontier a few days ago."

"A gog. Alive or dead?"

"Doesn't really matter."

"The High Frontier ships them up from Brazil frozen. I could see if they have some available."

"Do it. If it's frozen, I want it thawed. I need to perform a little experiment. And you can help me record it."

Gogs—genetically altered hogs—are artificial life forms

based on the genome of *Sus domesticus*, the domestic pig. They're big critters, bigger than a human, so fat you think they should roll rather than pick their way around on those stubby little legs. And they have a head *just* big enough to accommodate the snout and its gaping, toothless mouth. No eyes, no ears, and just about enough brain to find a food trough, it was one of several genetic answers to the little problem of keeping Earth's teeming billions fed.

It took a few hours, but eventually a freshly thawed gog carcass was delivered to the SEA Security Center. In the meantime, Guerrero had set up the Center's firing range to my specifications.

Anyone who's learned to fire a weapon in a gravitational field under one-G is going to find all of his training and reflexes pretty much useless when he gets into microgravity. Pistols—except for a few specialized weapons developed for the military—are bored in such a way that the round emerges from the muzzle *rising* in order to compensate for the pull of gravity. The instant a round leaves a gun's barrel on Earth, it starts to drop toward the ground with an acceleration of ten meters per second squared. At close range, the engineering doesn't matter. At longer range—say thirty meters for a pistol—the round is going to strike consistently high in microgravity. There were rifle and pistol ranges at all of the NAPD satellite stations on the Moon, and the SEA had this one at the Challenger facility as well. They were handy places to get the feel of your service weapon in low gravity.

Mostly I needed a bare and empty room with solid walls that could absorb a burst from a 100-kilowatt laser and not vent atmosphere.

A rent-a-cop showed up at the range with the gog carcass on a pull-pallet. I helped Guerrero maneuver it downrange and get the hulk off of its frictionless pallet and standing on end. It looked something like a massive, pink potato, the head and legs removed, standing almost two meters tall and massing something like 300 kilograms. Some gogs massed over half a ton, but the small- and medium-sized animals were easier to ship.

In the Challenger facility—those parts of it not inside the rotating Carousel, at least—300 kilograms weighed only twelve kilos, and it would fall very slowly, less than half of a meter in the first second.

I stood on the firing line five meters away, holding the tunneler laser, which had been delivered from the evidence locker in an airtight carrying case. I was wearing a cleansuit. Though the forensics people had been over the device, looking at it with microscopic attention to detail, I wanted to keep any useful evidence useful if there was any possible way to do so. I had my PAD set up so that it could record the entire scene, and a second camera set up behind and to one side of the target. I wanted to catch this from all angles, and in ultra-high-def.

Five meters was about the distance from the door of Room Twelve to the bed. I switched on the power, then nodded to Guerrero. "When you let go," I told him, "get the hell back on this side of the line as fast as you can."

"Right."

We both wore protective goggles under our cleansuit helmets. "Okay," I said for the benefit of the recorders. "Testing the 100-kilowatt mining laser on a 300-kilogram gog carcass, range five meters, in three...two...one...now!"

Guerrero let the balanced carcass go, and it slowly began falling over. He pushed off and sailed across the intervening distance in a single long, low bound, catching himself on a reloading table.

I felt the laser humming with power, and the ready light was bright green. I aimed from the hip—there was no way I could aim the bulky device properly—and pressed the firing button when the top of the carcass was halfway to the floor.

Despite what you might see in the sensies, a laser beam is

invisible. Having a brilliant, semi-solid beam of light stabbing from the weapon is pure *zurullo del Hollywood.* What you *do* get are sparkles in the air—bits of drifting dust caught by the beam, or air molecules ionized by the high-energy bolt—plus a hell of a show downrange.

Harsh, white light flared off the far wall of the firing range and I adjusted my aim, sweeping left and up. The beam hit the falling meat and cooked its way through. I could see the skin on the carcass crinkle and blacken, saw blisters rise, then explode, saw smoke boiling off the surface as the meat charred.

The two-meter carcass split into two uneven chunks. Ribs turned black and popped in the heat, and a mess of internal organs spilled into the air.

There wasn't a lot of blood. I found out later that they drained the carcasses of blood before shipping them up-Stalk, and I wish I'd known that ahead of time because I'd also wanted to see the effect of a laser on liquid blood inside laser-zapped meat.

The pieces were falling slowly enough that I had time to swing the laser back through for a second slice…and then for a third before releasing the trigger switch. The upper end of the carcass fell free and skittered across the floor in the low gravity. I took a couple steps forward, picturing in my mind's eye what might have been the scene in Room Twelve that night, and fired a second time, carving through a chunk of partially cooked meat and an exposed bit of white vertebrae.

Carefully, I switched off the laser's power, then disconnected the battery. "Clear," I said.

"*Jesús*," Guerrero said with quiet reverence. "And this is how it was done?"

"No," I told him. "It wasn't."

After putting the laser and the battery pack back in its case, I removed my helmet and goggles. I picked up my PAD and returned to the carcass, now lying in five pieces on the floor. The pieces were still smoking, and the whole room smelled like burnt bacon. I used the camera to record every piece, paying special attention to the severed ends where the laser had burned its way through skin, muscle, bone, and internal organs. A strong suspicion I'd had a few days ago, in the morgue at the Challenger Medical Facility was now a certainty. Roger Dow had been carved up by a mining laser, certainly, but that probably wasn't what killed him. *Probably.*

The beam had cooked the flesh, yes, and I'd seen evidence of that on Dow's body. But it hadn't sliced cleanly through bone. Wherever the laser beam had touched bone in the gog, that bone had blackened and frequently exploded as the marrow inside heated suddenly and explosively. I didn't see any ends cut so smooth that the bone actually looked polished.

"Sorry for the mess," I told Guerrero. "You can have someone take this back to the High Frontier kitchen. Maybe I'll have it for dinner tonight."

I picked up a club from the security department. It wasn't as good or as complete as our NAPD-issue, and didn't have any of the usual analysis equipment, but it had bags and bottles and sterile swabs and a mini-vacuum, enough for what I needed to do. I used my PAD to call up Tom Fuchida at the High Frontier Hotel, and set up an appointment.

I'd planned on going to lunch first, but found I wasn't hungry. The stink of burnt meat and stomach contents was triggering unpleasant memories of Room Twelve.

Tom Fuchida, the High Frontier's manager, was waiting for me in the hotel lobby.

"Welcome back, Captain Harrison," he said. "What can I do for you?"

"You can open some hotel records for me," I told him. "I want to know who was in Room Sixteen the night of the murder."

"*Six*teen?" He looked startled. "I'll have to check."

He pulled out his PAD and linked through to the hotel's files.

"Okay…from the twenty-first through the twenty-fourth, Room Sixteen was occupied by a couple: Harold Espinoza and Cindy Carter."

"I don't suppose you have photographs of them? DNA samples? Fingerprints?"

"Of *course* not, sir!"

Of course not. In China they take fingerprints of each guest when they check in. DNA samples, too, sometimes. I didn't want to see that kind of erosion of civil liberties in the United States, but, damn it, it would have made my job easier.

"Has anyone else checked into that room?"

He consulted his files. "A *Señor* Montoya was there from the evening of the twenty-fifth through the twenty-sixth. And a *Señor* Duarte and a friend checked in on the twenty-eighth… and, ah! They are still here."

Damn. It would have been easier if no one had been in the room. It had been cleaned at least twice since Mark Henry was there, the sheets had been changed three or four times, and people staying there would have both mucked up any physical evidence, and left plenty more evidence of their own.

"I'd like to take some samples from that room," I said. What the hell? A check might turn up something useful. I might at the very least pick up enough clone DNA to back up Henry's story that he'd been in there.

What I was really hoping for was a bit of DNA from the mysterious "Mr. Green" and his accomplice. Presumably Espinoza and Carter were Green and someone else.

And I had a good idea who they were behind those pseudonyms.

"But the room is occupied," Fuchida told me.

"Then I'll ask you to talk to Mr. Duarte and his friend and ask them to step out of the room for a few minutes."

It turned out that Duarte wasn't in his room at the time anyway. DynaTech Orbital Manufactories and Armitage Software were co-hosting a seminar of some sort at the High Frontier Business Center, and his PAD said he and his secretary were there. Fuchida let me in with my evidence kit and watched from the open doorway while I went to work.

I recorded various latent prints, but I was pretty sure they would prove to be those of the room's more recent guests. When I was done, I packed up my gear and samples. "One more thing, Mr. Fuchida."

"Yes?"

"What time did Espinoza and Carter check out?"

He tapped something into his PAD. "They checked out…that would be at 1040 on the twenty-fourth."

"Excellent. And I'd like a room. I'm going to be staying here one more night."

"Of course. I'll talk to the front desk."

Later, down a level in Room Fifty-Six, I unfolded the large screen for my PAD and again tapped into the High Frontier's security cam records. I wound back to the morning of the twenty-fourth, the first morning after the night of the murder.

And I began watching people coming out of the hallway that led to Room Twelve.

At 1036, a lone woman carrying a small overnight satchel walked out of the hallway entrance and passed beneath the camera on her way to the front desk. She had very long and curly blond hair, all the way to below her waist, and her face was partly covered by the cascade. Hair that long on the Beanstalk was unusual. In low gravity, it tended to billow and weave, and it got in the way. It was almost as though she was calling attention to herself.

I made a note of it, and kept looking.

Another woman came out of that hallway at 1038. Conservative black leather and a backpack, short brown hair. I didn't recognize her.

Right behind her was a man—bearded, dark-haired, short,

wearing a white turtleneck. He was carrying a large, extra-long suitcase.

The suitcase.

I brought up the original surveillance images and compared them side by side on the screen. I was as certain as I could be that it was the same missing suitcase.

It didn't look like Frank Hodgkins, though, even with the beard and the shaggy dark hair.

I couldn't be absolutely sure, of course. The camera angle was looking down on the guy from up by the ceiling, and I couldn't see his face full-on. But this guy couldn't have been much over 150, 155 centimeters.

I went back and studied both women carefully, trying to get a visual match with Thea Coleman. I couldn't do it. Again, the camera angle wasn't good, and the first woman's blond mane obscured her face from above. The second woman, the one with the backpack, had a heavier build than Coleman. I was pretty sure it wasn't her, either.

I called up a different security camera, this one from the main desk in the lobby.

The blond didn't approach the front desk, but walked through the lobby and straight out the front doors, and all I could see was her back. The short guy, however, came to the desk, set the suitcase down, and used his implanted credaccount chip to pay for the room. Then he picked up the suitcase, turned, and walked out the main lobby door.

Damn. I'd been ready to bet that year's salary that Espinoza and Carter were Hodgkins and Coleman.

I pulled several photos and vid stills of Frank Hodgkins up on my PAD, fed them to my secretary, and gave him a search order—this time admitting that the time saved by the AI's search would be worth it, rather than doing it myself. Yeah, I don't entirely trust the machines, but all I was really looking for was a flag I could check myself. My PAD began running through security cam vids of the High Frontier lobby at high speed.

An hour later, I had him. Frank Hodgkins had entered the hallway at just before 1900 on the twenty-third, and left it two days later, on the twenty-fifth, at 0820.

That gave me a fairly solid case, something to start with, anyway. There was a strong possibility, I thought, that Espinoza and Carter were Hodgkins and Coleman, and also that Espinoza was Henry's "Mr. Green." We also had a new player in the drama—a very short, bearded man who'd carried the suitcase out of the hotel.

The blond, just possibly, could have been Coleman. The short guy, though…

Okay, *think*.

They hadn't left the planetoid, of course. Not then. These images were from seven days ago, on the twenty-fourth. If the blond *was* Thea Coleman in a wig, then she wouldn't have left the Challenger facility, as it appeared, but simply would have taken the tube-lev back across the planetoid. She'd been at the Humanity Labor office the next day when Lily tried to interview her and failed, and again two days after that, when I'd gone to see her.

Then, possibly on the twenty-seventh or the twenty-eighth, she'd left. Up-Stalk? Down? I did a search of Beanstalk travel records.

Here it was. Frank Hodgkins and Thea Coleman left the terminal on the twenty-eighth, heading down-Stalk.

I called Commissioner Dawn.

"Whatcha got, Harrison?" She looked tired on the folding PAD screen, with bags under her eyes. I guessed she hadn't been sleeping much lately.

"A solid lead on the murderer," I told her. "*Murderers*, I should say. Two of them. I'd like you to put out an APB for Frank Hodgkins and Thea Coleman, both employees of Humanity Labor. Coleman is Humanity Labor's Operations Manager. Hodgkins works for their security department."

"Done," she said.

"It may not stop with them."

"Meaning?"

"My best guess is that they were trying to implicate a clone in the murder, Mark Henry 103, and a bioroid, Eve 5VA3TC. The news—a bloody murder—was calculated to set off more anti-clone riots."

"Fragging great..."

"Well, it didn't work the way they planned, and the news hasn't gone out. Not yet, anyway. I think someone higher up in Humanity Labor is sitting on the story until he's certain that this isn't going to backfire in the organization's face. I also think Coleman and Hodgkins are small fry. For a conspiracy this big, we're going to have to look higher."

"How high?"

"At the very least, I suggest we question Thomas Vaughn. That's the head of HL's PR department."

"Okay. What about the clone and the bioroid?"

"In custody. Ray Flint will be bringing both of them down-Stalk in a day or two. But I don't think they're guilty."

"You know, Harrison, that's for the courts to decide."

"What do you mean?"

She sighed. "Both of them are obviously involved, right? I've been following your notes as you post them through your PAD. The bioroid was having sex with the victim...and might have let the murderer into the room. The clone brought the mining laser to the hotel, and assembled it in a nearby room."

"Yeah. They were both being manipulated by someone, though—set up to look like they were the killers."

"Not good enough, Harrison. I've already had to release Noise Reilly. Up until now, he was our top suspect, just because he could have reprogrammed a bioroid or tapped into the security network. But we don't have any evidence he's involved, so we had to let him go. If we can't find the ones behind this plot, we're going to have to take what we can get. When this news hits the streets, and it *will*, trust me, the public will be screaming for the murderers' heads. Your girlfriend has been calling me for two days, asking for permission to go with her story. She says if she doesn't, Associated or NetNews or one of the others is still going to broadcast the story all the way to Mars. If we don't have the big boys in custody, if we can't establish a solid evidence trail…we'll have to give them what we have."

"You mean Eve and Henry."

"A bioroid and a clone." She shrugged. "The mayor's on my case, Harrison. If we can wrap this up, cleanly and quietly over the next day or two, before the sordid details of Dow's murder get out, maybe we can avoid another round of riots. Understand me?"

I understood, too well. She was talking about sacrificing Henry and Eve to avoid something bloodier.

The hell of it was, they *were* accessories to the murder. The DA would be able to put together a pretty solid case—placing them at the scene, with the weapon, and with a motive.

It would mean disassembly for Eve, and probably 'retirement' for Henry.

I didn't like this, not one bit.

"Commissioner," I said, angry, "I gave my word to them that they would be safe."

"Your *word*?" She laughed. "To a sex toy? To a *clone*? Time for a reality check, Harrison. If we can wrap this up by proving the two of them did it, that's what we're going to do. It's what's best for the public welfare."

I cut the connection before I said something I might regret later.

Damn the fragging politics.

Damn expediency.

Damn the public welfare, if you had to sell your soul to secure it.

I sat there thinking for a long time, because something had at that moment dawned on me...something that had been nagging at the back of my mind for a couple days, now.

How had the men who'd attacked Henry and me out on the lunar surface known where I was?

It would have been simple if the bad guys had been working for Melange Mining, of course. The help-desk person, the personnel-admin clone, either of them could have let their bosses know that a snoopy NAPD detective was looking for Mark Henry.

But what if Melange Mining or the mining bosses had had nothing to do with Dow's murder?

How had the real murderers found us?

I used my NAPD authorization codes to link in to another set of electronic files, and spent a long and uncomfortable time studying them.

And then I called Lily.

"Fish!" she cried when her face appeared on the folding screen. "What a pleasant surprise! You *never* call or—"

"Can it, babe. The Commissioner tells me you want to break the story."

"Rick, I *have* to. I told Dawn I could hold off for today, until tomorrow at the absolute latest. A friend of mine over at Associated let me know this morning that they're working the story up now. They've talked to Dr. Weissmuller, Fuchida, the SEA, and some of the Housekeeping staff at the High Frontier. There's already been an official announcement of Dow's death. His wife went on NetNews the other evening and demanded to know what was being done."

"You're just full of good news," I told her.

"There's more and better. Humanity Labor has called a press conference for 1600 tomorrow on the front steps of the HL building."

"About the murder?"

"I can't imagine what else it would be. Vaughn himself is making the announcement." She hesitated. "Rick, I *can't* sit on this much longer. I've got a responsibility to report the news… and if I don't, someone else is going to anyway."

"I don't expect you to sit on it, sweetheart," I told her. "But when you write it, remember one thing, okay?"

"What?"

"Eve and Henry are not guilty. Say that they are, and you're going to have to publish a retraction later."

"How sure are you?"

"Willing to bet my life on it. Here's another flash. The person who killed Dow didn't use a mining laser. The whole scene was a set-up to make it look like Henry was guilty."

"Rick—"

"Where are you?" I asked, cutting her off.

"At the Network. The Midway."

"Okay. Right now, I'm at the High Frontier. I'm spending the night here again…Room Fifty-Six. I'll see you tomorrow. I'm coming down-Stalk as soon as I can. And I'll bring the proof of what I'm saying with me."

And I cut the connection.

I didn't want to say *too* much. Not then.

Not there.

I was expecting visitors.

Chapter Fifteen

Day 9

Even in .04G, I spent an uncomfortable night slumped in the deep, stuffed chair in one corner of the room, my H&K on the floor beside me as I faced the door in the darkness.

I knew they would come. They *had* to…because now they knew I was on my way to talk to Lily…and they knew I had enough of the picture pulled together to be a threat.

I was certain I'd been bugged.

PriRights is a citizens' privacy rights group, one of the oldest of a number of similar groups out there. For over a century, they've been trying to limit the ongoing invasion of ordinary people's privacy by government and the big corps. One of their biggest fights was against backscatter scanning. On the one hand, the government demanded the right to *thoroughly* search everyone boarding the space elevator and certain key tube-lev transit lines. Peek-a-boo units were just too damned effective at seeing what you were carrying into the terminal underneath your clothes. During the last few years they've refined things to the point where they can add a couple of tightly focused ultrasound beams, bring your internal organs into view in high-res

3D, and make a fair guess at what you've had that morning for breakfast.

One place PriRights *has* been effective, though, was in combating the widespread use of hidden security cameras and microphones. We can build the things pretty small, now: a camera thinner in cross-section than a human hair, a microphone a bit bigger than a long-chain organic molecule, a short-range transmitter and piggyback modem as small as a grain of sand. They can be powered by ambient heat, such as the heat from a human body, and are for all practical intents and purposes invisible. The government, the big corps, they're not allowed to use devices like that. The average Joe on the street needs to be able see that they're there, watching—as with the police security drones drifting ominously about the New Angeles streets like cops on the beat.

That doesn't mean that invisible electronic surveillance systems aren't used…or that they're not available to people or to groups who want them. Technically, it's three-to-five years in prison if you use such a device without the subject knowing about it, but the government can usually demonstrate it was a need-to-know or a public safety issue and get away with it, while the corps know whom to pay off.

As I sat there in the dark, I once again pulled out my PAD and unfolded the screen. I typed in my badge number and authorization code, and again linked through to SEA e-security files.

The black-and-white image of a nude man appeared on the screen, rotating in space. The man was me, caught by the backscatter unit as I'd gone through security the other day while boarding the Challenger Memorial Ferry on my way up to Heinlein.

Personally, I try to avoid backscatter scans whenever possible. I'm just not a huge fan of the enforced technological strip-search, even when it's a sophisticated AI rather than a human that's actually looking at the images.

Because, frankly, anyone with the right access codes can look at the files, just as I was doing now.

I froze the rotating image and zoomed in slightly from the front. I could see the hazy shadow of my shoulder holster high on the left side of my chest, and the much sharper, clearer image of my H&K hand cannon, tucked safely away beneath my now invisible jacket. My badge was clear too, attached to the holster, my service number picked out bright and clear in the X-ray image.

Other bits and pieces of hardware stood out sharply on the image. The implants in my wrists that accessed my credaccount and personal data downloads. The two spare clips of 12mm pistol rounds at my waist. My PAD hanging in its thigh holster, tucked in next to my leg. I zoomed in closer, panning up to my chest…then to my left shoulder.

It was tough to see unless you knew exactly what you were looking for.

It looked like a tiny, faint star. It might even have been an artifact of the backscatter scan, a stray bit of noise, but I zoomed in still closer.

The star was hovering above my left shoulder, as though riding on my invisible jacket. Some shapes were just barely discernible beside the reflected bit of flare, but so fuzzy it was impossible to know what they were or what they were for.

Unless, of course, you *knew*.

It was all I could do not to go to my jacket, hanging in the closet by the hotel room door, and check that shoulder… My fingers—gross, clumsy things—would not be able to find the near-microscopic device, though, or to remove it from the weave of my clothing, and it would only tip them off that I'd found the bug.

John Jones's bug. The device he'd planted on me eight days ago on the up-Stalk beanpod when he shook my hand and casually touched my shoulder.

Jones 937. The enigma, the clone secretly hired by the clone-hating Roger Dow and Human First. Jones with the educated vocabulary, the atypical interest in human psychology, and the apparent ease around full-humans.

I wanted to add "Jones the murderer," but he couldn't have been part of that, not if he was a fellow up-Stalk traveler on the beanpod from the Root to Midway that first morning after the murder. That's why I'd overlooked him for a time, frankly. Jones wouldn't have had time to take part in the murder, catch a beanpod down to Earthside New Angeles, and then find the guy assigned to the murder case and follow him back up-Stalk the next morning.

Well…no. As I called up the beanpod schedules and took a look at them, I realized he *could* have done it. Pods leave from the Challenger terminal going down every few hours. It's an hour from Challenger to Midway, another hour from Midway to the Root. So he could have done it, sure.

But it was far more likely that he'd already been in place in Earthside New Angeles. The most disturbing part of it was the realization that NAPD security had been that badly breached. How had Jones found out that I was the detective on the case? I hadn't even known that bit of news myself until after Ray Flint had turned me down in Tommy's sitsleazy. That was…when? Oh-three hundred, or so?

On the other hand, Human First was a big organization, and they had a *lot* of money behind them—including the full backing of Humanity Labor. Enough clout, enough money, and enough contacts inside the Force to pick up a detective assignment as soon as Commissioner Dawn or her admin assistant had plugged my name into the case file.

Hell, maybe it *was* the admin assistant, or even Dawn herself, who was on Humanity Labor's black-op payroll. I didn't like thinking like that, didn't like the implications, but it was possible, and I had to consider *all* of the possibilities, however unpleasant.

One way or another, they'd fingered me as the detective in charge of the Dow case. Jones had picked me up at the Root and followed me on-board the beanpod. He'd struck up a conversation with me and had found a way to casually plant a nearly microscopic bug on me—audio at the very least, but possibly a camera as well.

It wouldn't be transmitting all the time. There were scanners that could pick up that sort of thing from quite a distance away, alerting me if something was transmitting from my clothing. More likely, the device was programmed to wait until I'd connected with the Net through my PAD—picking up the signals associated with the palm device's multiple wireless connections—then piggybacking an outgoing burst signal containing compressed data over the Net, where Human First would have lurking electronic agents just waiting to snap it up.

The gunmen at Sinus Medii—could they have tracked me by the bug since, at that point, it was sealed inside my suit? Possibly so. That suit had been pretty thin, strictly for short-term surface work. Even if not, they might have picked me up when I entered Melange Mining's headquarters and asked for Mark Henry. A microbug like that easily had enough memory onboard to let it react to key words, like "Henry" or "Dow," enabling it to tune in on important conversations and transmit data containing them. By that time it might even have established a parasitic link with my PAD, using it to continually transmit my real-time position.

Someone had been tracking me every step of the way throughout this investigation. They'd listened in on my conversations, they'd known where I was going, and who I was speaking with.

Knowing all of that, I'd set a trap.

Not an elaborate one, certainly, but the best I could manage on such short notice. My last conversation with Lily would have told them exactly where I was, though doubtless they knew that information already, and how long I would be here. It also told them that I hadn't yet passed my proof on to Lily; I didn't want to set her up as a target, and I wanted any eavesdroppers to think I had something special in my possession.

Something more definitive, more evidential, more *solid* than a strong hunch.

I'd given them a small but definite window—the time between when I'd talked to Lily, and when I would be catching a down-Stalk pod in the morning. They would have to strike tonight. *Here.*

So I waited there in the dark, bare-chested but ready. I'd bunched up pillows and bedclothes to make a suggestive lump in the middle of the bed—something that might look like me. I'd put my jacket and holster in the closet, and taken the added precaution of removing my shirt and putting it in the closet, as well, just in case the bug had video as well as audio.

I'd programmed my PAD and set it on the desk, hiding it under a casually placed brochure touting the recreational glories to be found on the Challenger Planetoid. It wouldn't be able to catch a vid of anything, but it should be able to record any conversations, and someone entering the room wouldn't see it without a careful search.

Then I went back to my chair.

I must have dozed a little, because I was jerked awake by the door chime. *This is it.*

"Who…the hell is it?" I called, doing my best to imitate someone just awakened out of a deep sleep, muzzy and groggy. I pressed my timepiece and read the faintly luminous numerals on the back of my hand. Oh-four-thirty…zero-dark-thirty, as we'd called it in the service.

"Room service," a woman's voice called over the intercom, sultry and suggestive, dripping warm promise. "Very *special* room service." The door screen, when I flashed it, did indeed show a young woman whose attire matched the promise of that voice.

And I could also see that the image was a vidcheat, a clever bit of video software fed directly to the security scanners to give a completely illusory picture of who was outside. Slick…and completely illegal, of course.

"I didn't order room service," I called back. "It's the middle of the fragging night, for chrissake!"

"This is very special room service," the voice repeated. "Compliments of Mr. Fuchida and the High Frontier staff and management, *and* of Eliza's Toybox!"

I picked up my pistol and quietly chambered a round, but kept the weapon hidden beside my leg. Did they really think it was that easy…just asking to be let in that way in the middle of the night?

"Open."

The door slid aside, and the woman walked in, silhouetted by the light in the hallway at her back. By that dim light, I could see that she was wearing grip-slippers and skintights, that she was short-haired…and that she was carrying something in her right hand.

At first, I thought it might be a knife, but there was no blade, just the hilt nestled in her hand…and suddenly *all* of my attention was focused on that deadly, bladeless knife. I saw her thumb move, and a tiny, silver bead fell silently from the knife hilt, dropped perhaps thirty centimeters toward the floor and then hung there, floating in mid-air just below her knee.

A monoknife.

My blood ran a little colder at that. A monofilament knife consisted of a strand of buckyweave fabric just one molecule thick, fed from a reel inside the hilt. When the bead at the end of the filament drops, the thread is pulled out and an electric charge from the hilt stiffens it, just like a folding screen or newsrag. The "blade" isn't completely rigid; it has some give, like a fencer's foil. But that one-molecule-thick wire will slice through solid steel as though it were clay…or through clothing, flesh, and bone without slowing for an instant, without even noticing there's anything at all in the way. *Sharp* doesn't begin to describe it.

I watched as she paused in the doorway, then strode forward. Not exactly a sexy walk to the bed…with her grip-slippers making tiny *fft-fft* noises as she shuffled across the carpet. Then her right hand came up, whipping the silver bead and its attached, invisible thread high above her head. She snapped the monofilament down, cleanly slicing through sheets, mattress, and the bed frame.

I stood, my H&K held in both hands, aiming at her from the side. "That's *quite* enough, sister," I told her. "Drop the knife and step back from the bed."

I heard her gasp. She hadn't yet fully registered that I hadn't been in the bed when she'd sliced through the sheets, and my voice coming from the far corner of the room must have been a real shock.

"*Frag!*" she spat, whirling.

"Lights on full!" I commanded, and the room lights came up, glaring and harsh as only room lights can be at 0430 in the morning.

Thea Coleman stood before me, stooped, her face flush, panting. "You're too clever by half, Harrison," she said.

She still hadn't dropped the knife.

"I want you to retract the monofilament," I told her, the pistol leveled directly at her chest.

She hesitated, then her thumb moved, and the silver bead rose up as though it was part of a conjurer's levitation trick, snapping into the knife's hilt with a tiny click.

"Good girl," I said. "Now, toss the handle on the floor over there. Slowly."

She did so.

"A GATCO monocarb," I said, glancing at it. "That's pretty high-end hardware. I thought you must have used a monoknife—"

"How the hell did you know?" she demanded.

"What…that someone had planted a bug on me? I have my ways."

"No, about the monoknife!"

"Monofilaments slice through bone clean, almost mirror-smooth," I told her. "It makes the severed end of the bone look polished. A laser doesn't." I was curious. "But why pretend you used a mining laser instead of this little slicer-dicer, here?"

She shrugged.

I wasn't going to pull such a dumb rookie move as bending over to pick up the knife. Instead, I used my foot to edge it further away from her, over toward the wall.

"Let me guess," I continued. "When you killed Dow, you wanted it to be spectacular. Bloody. Something that would grab the public's attention. Right? And if it was a *mining* laser that killed Dow, it must have been a mining clone that did it. Am I right?"

She hesitated, then nodded. Damn, that was no good. I needed her to say something for the recording PAD on the desk.

"So why'd you do it?" I asked.

"Androids are a threat to *all* real humans!" Coleman snapped back. "Something had to be done!"

"What…killing Roger Dow?" I let puzzlement shape the words. "Why kill him? He hated clones as much as you did. And he *worked* for you!"

"Yeah, and if it looked like a clone and a bioroid had worked together to kill the dumb bastard, kill him before he met with those senators, it would look like a conspiracy: the androids working against humanity!"

"And what about the fact that he was your lover? Or didn't it bother you that he was in bed with a bioroid?"

That goaded her. I saw the words sting. "*The bastard was sleeping with a damned sex-doll!*" she snapped. "He dumped me for a clunker! It was a pleasure taking him apart!"

"I'm sure," I said. "So why no laser for me?"

"Who said we didn't bring one?" a different voice said.

It was Frank Hodgkins, Coleman's bodyguard. He'd stepped into the doorway from the hall leveling a military laser at me—a Sunbeam LW2400, with 1.2-kilowatt throughput. "Drop the gun," he said.

"Stupid cop," Coleman said with a sneer, padding toward the monoknife on the floor. "The idea is to kill you *exactly* the same way we killed Dow! We couldn't get hold of another tunneler, but this'll do."

I had to make my move, and I had to do it *now*. If I tamely handed over my H&K, I would still be dead, probably sliced up by the monoknife, like Dow, and the pieces burned with the laser.

"Okay, okay," I said, holding up one hand and making like I was going to toss the gun down with the other. But I was watching Coleman, and as she crossed the room she came just a little too close to Hodgkins's line of fire.

That was a dumb rookie move. I leaped, and in four-hundredths of a gravity I *flew*, arrowing directly between Coleman and the muzzle of Hodgkins's weapon. He swung the rifle, but didn't fire, unable to shoot without hitting his partner.

I brought up the H&K two-handed, aiming at Hodgkins as I fell in slow motion. I saw him pivot as Coleman yelled, "*Shoot him!*" and jumped clear, saw his finger tightening on the laser's trigger, and immediately squeezed my eyes shut to keep from being blinded. I squeezed off a shot...and another...and a third, firing blind until I plunged right shoulder first into the room's carpeting.

I felt heat, *pain*, as if someone had turned a welding torch on the back of my left leg.

I opened my eyes as I bounced, then rolled. Hodgkins had staggered back a step, the military laser scorching a sweeping, charred line across the wall and ceiling. I tried to aim a fourth shot, but he'd stepped back into the hallway and out of my line of fire.

Coleman, meanwhile, had dived for the monoknife, scooped it up, and released the tiny, silver bead. She leaped toward me—

I twisted around sideways, bringing my pistol to bear on her, but she snapped down with that damned knife before I could acquire the target, snapped down as I rolled desperately to my right and the invisible thread-blade sliced through the arm of the chair in which I'd spent most of the night.

She slammed into the chair, a tangled flailing of bare legs and arms. She was trying to pull the blade free—I think the bead had snagged in the chair's upholstery—so, from the floor, I swung my right leg around to kick her wrist.

It was an awkward blow, but she yelped and let go of the knife, stumbling back a step. I saw movement at the door, a shadow only, but it was enough to distract me, to make me swing the gun away from Coleman and aim at the doorway.

"Give it up!" I yelled.

Hodgkins rolled back around the door and I shut my eyes again, firing at the same instant. I heard him yell, felt a wave of heat wash past my head, singing hair and blistering the wall behind my head.

The heat snapped off, and I opened my eyes just in time to see Coleman's back vanishing around the corner.

Scrambling to my feet, I started after them. There was blood on the wall beside the doorway; I'd hit the bastard. Dropping to my knees, I peeked around the door frame, staying low in case he was waiting for me to show myself.

He was, ten meters down the hall toward the lobby. I jerked back as he fired, waited a few seconds, then peeked again, high this time. Both of them were gone.

H&K in hand, I started after them, cursing myself for the stupid rookie move I *had* managed to commit: no backup. They drill that into you at the Academy: *always* take along backup, and have the bad guys' escape routes covered before they beat a hasty retreat.

I wasn't entirely sure what I could have done, however. With Coleman listening in on my conversations through the bug in my clothing, I wouldn't have been able to set the trap without giving the game away. Possibly I could have written a note to the yellow jackets…but the bug might have a video component. Besides, I still didn't trust the rent-a-cops, despite my nice words and pride-swallowing with Guerrero the evening before.

Detective work tends to be a one-man show anyway; I've never been comfortable with partners.

I heard shouts coming from just ahead, so I knew I was heading in the right direction. My leg was screaming at me, but I jogged down a ramp to the lower level and burst into the hotel lobby. Even at zero-dark-thirty, there were people in the lobby, checking in, checking out, or simply waiting for someone. They were on the floor now, terrified expressions on their faces, but there was no sign of Coleman or Hodgkins. Damn! Which way?

A woman screamed again when she saw my gun. "Police!" I yelled as I ran past, half naked with my pistol aimed at the ceiling.

"He went that way!" one man said, pointing a shaking hand toward the hotel's front entrance. Plunging through the doors, I entered the broad concourse that led to the Beanstalk terminal.

The military laser was laying on the floor, next to a wall of ornamental, low-G philodendra. Hodgkins must have tossed it aside, then vanished into one of several passageways, walking to avoid causing panic. Had the two gone to the Beanstalk terminal? The tube-lev to Farside? The collection of shops and restaurants located near the hotel? The tube leading out to the Challenger Carousel?

I stopped and stood there, panting, as passersby looked at me and my handgun and bare chest with varying degrees of curiosity, indifference, and fear. My leg was throbbing; a patch of my pants leg had melted when Hodgkins had fired the laser, burning the skin.

Finally, I safed the weapon and tucked it into the waistband of my trousers. They'd gotten away. I picked up the laser rifle by the strap to avoid smearing any prints that might be on it, and limped back to my room.

Worse was waiting for me when I got there. I walked over to the slashed-open chair to retrieve the monoknife Coleman had left there…and found the knife was gone. I bit off a sharp curse, then gave my whole room a very careful search to make sure one of them wasn't hiding somewhere, waiting to ambush me with that thing. Either there was a third intruder in this little party, or Coleman and Hodgkins had gone in separate directions in the hallway after leaving my room…and Coleman had snuck back in to retrieve the knife while I was chasing her bodyguard. They might have had a room farther down the hall, or she'd hidden in an airlock or behind the door leading to the emergency stairs.

Damn it!

I hobbled over to the desk and picked up the brochures. My PAD, at least, was still there. I touched the replay button.

"The clones are a threat to all real humans!" I heard Coleman's voice say. "Bioroids, too! Something has to be done!"

So I had what amounted to a recorded confession. Humanity Labor's lawyers would naturally make a stink about the fact that I'd made that recording without the subject's knowledge and without a warrant and it almost certainly would not be admissible in a court of law…but at least I could use it to convince Dawn that Coleman and Hodgkins were the culprits here, not

Eve and Henry.

I'd wanted the monoknife for Coleman's prints, to tie her to the murder weapon, and evidently she'd thought of that, coming back to retrieve it while I chased Hodgkins.

So what now?

I could wake up Fuchida and get him to check every other room on that hall. The hell with that. Coleman and Hodgkins would be using phony names and IDs, and they might well be gone already.

I could canvas passenger lists for both the tube-lev to Farside and the Beanstalk. Again, they would have fake names and identification.

After a moment's thought, I unfolded my PAD's screen and began checking security cameras…going to the lobby cams first, then patching into a security camera in the concourse outside the hotel. I pulled up security scans going back just ten minutes.

I watched Hodgkins run through the High Frontier's lobby, watched civilians scream and drop to the floor. And I watched me run through a moment later. No sign of Coleman. She *must* have doubled back the other way, further up the hallway.

I didn't see Hodgkins in the concourse, however. The security cam, it turned out, was directly above the ornamental plants, the angle wrong to catch him throwing away the military laser. I saw what might have been him—just from the back—sauntering casually toward the tube-lev terminal.

I kept watching…kept watching…and then a woman walked through the concourse and through the tube-lev terminal doorway as well…with grip-slippers and a carry-bag, with blond hair down to here. She must have ducked back into another room, donned the wig, grabbed the bag, and followed Hodgkins the moment I'd come back to my room.

At least now I knew where they were. Farside.

Once they were at Farside, they could catch a ferry for Heinlein, double back on another tube-train to catch the Beanstalk, or simply find a place to go to ground and hide—inside the Challenger Mines, for example, or in the Farside office complex.

But there was still time to catch them if I was quick about it.

I called Guerrero and woke him.

Chapter Sixteen

Day 9

Guerrero wasn't happy about being awakened in what he called the middle of the night, but he listened as I told him the two perps were tube-leving through the planetoid back to Farside, and that we needed yellow jackets to close off their escape routes and pick them up. I passed along the security camera footage of both Hodgkins and Coleman, along with the warning that Coleman was wearing a long, blond wig, but that she might ditch the hairpiece or use some other disguise to throw off the hunt. He assured me that the perps would not get away and he was dispatching teams of yellow jackets at both Nearside and Farside to cut them off.

I decided not to go back to bed. It was well past five, New Angeles time…and, in any case, my bed was partially sliced in two. Instead, I began catching up on my research.

First off, there was a long vid monologue from Dr. Jason Cherchi, at the Fra Mauro NAPD station.

"I looked carefully at your visual scans," he told me in the saved message, "and then this afternoon I went down and actually examined Eve 5VA3TC in person. In my opinion, the burns on her front torso were inflicted by a taser."

He went on at some length to describe what a taser was, though I already knew, of course. It stands, believe it or not, for "Thomas A. Swift's Electric Rifle," a reference to a fictional device in a novel written in 1911. Older versions fire a pair of darts attached to wires leading back to the weapon; more modern versions fire a slow, two-pronged bullet with a compact, internal battery. When it strikes human flesh—or bioroid plastic, evidently—it releases a 40,000-volt charge.

In humans, the charge is incapacitating, causing serious pain and momentary paralysis or spasms. In bioroids, the effect is less predictable, but tends to melt the plastic between and around the round's penetration point.

I remembered my conversation with Floyd, about how one way of tampering with a bioroid's short-term memory would be to zap it with high voltage. If Eve had been in that room when the murderers broke in, they could have used a taser weapon to disable her while they took care of Dow; when she recovered a few moments later, she would have no memory—or only a very scrambled one—of what had happened in the room.

"I remember…screaming. Screaming…," Eve had told me.

Yeah, I'll bet. Dow would have done a *lot* of screaming when Coleman started taking him apart with the monoknife, at least until his head had finally come off. And the screaming was the only piece of sensory input Eve had retained.

When the murderers went to clean up, they'd simply plucked the taser round from her lower chest, and assumed the melted spot would be attributed to Dow's love of sadistic sex with bioroids.

In fact, the more I thought about it, the more likely it seemed that they'd thought she would remain incapacitated, and be found in the hotel room by the maid later on. It would have played well to the big picture they were trying to construct—that sex-starved Mark Henry had broken in on the couple while they were going at it, been horrified by what Dow was doing to Eve, and cut him up with the laser. The assumption would be that she had malfunctioned from the shock…not the literal shock of the taser, but the *emotional* shock of Dow's bloody murder.

That scenario would have gone a *long* way to convincing the public that bioroids and clones were emotional, unstable, and capable of irrationally emotional acts, acts that threatened humans.

Coleman and Hodgkins had been following a two-layered plan. First choice had been to goad Henry into killing Dow with the laser. If Dow was too quick and Henry wasn't able to keep the laser focused for long enough to kill the guy, no problem. Dow would have been horribly burned, and be an eyewitness to the attack upon his person by a clone, aided and abetted by a bioroid.

When Henry didn't—*couldn't*—kill Dow and fled, they fell back on Plan B—disable Eve with a taser, kill Dow using a monoknife to be *sure* he was dead—decapitation would work—then use the laser to implicate Henry and make the monoknife wounds look like laser burns. There was a risk, that way, of Eve remembering some of what had happened, but her memory would certainly be scrambled enough for those few minutes that it would be tough to make sense of anything she had to say.

Very, very slick.

And the only thing supporting that version of what had happened was my conviction that Mark Henry was telling the truth. The melted spot on Eve's lower chest could be blamed on Dow. The story of "Mr. Green" could be discarded as a clone's self-serving fiction. In fact, I hadn't had *any* real independent support for the theory until the attack on Henry and me at Fra Mauro…and then the attack on me that morning.

But as I thought about it, I *still* didn't have much in the way of hard evidence. I might have Hodgkins's fingerprints on the laser rifle, but that tied him to an attempt on *my* life, not to the Dow murder. I had the recording of both Coleman's and Hodgkins's voices, including Coleman admitting—or at least not denying—that they'd killed Dow, but that recording probably wouldn't be allowed as evidence. I had the bug on my clothing in the closet, but that, I was sure, had been planted by the clone, John Jones, and I hadn't been able to tie him to the Dow murder yet. For all I knew, Jones was simply a member of SAM, and they were keeping tabs on my investigation...illegal, yes, but not murder-one.

No, I needed more. Once the yellow jackets captured Coleman and Hodgkins, I might be able to get a confession out of them, especially if I could play them off against one another. Hodgkins, I had the feeling, would be willing to talk about his boss if I promised we'd go easy on him. He seemed like the "all muscle" type.

But right now I had zip.

I did now have the report from the police evidence crew, who'd come up a few days before and gone over Room Twelve at damned near microscopic resolution. It verified what I'd come up with already—the presence of Roger Dow, of a fembot bioroid, and of silube packing gel.

The problem was that there were also traces of 685 *other* humans, as identified by traces of DNA—mostly from flakes of skin, dandruff, dried mucus, semen, eyelashes, or hair. The team had done a gamma-emissions scan and recorded over two hundred complete or partial latent fingerprints. There were traces of dozens of meals—baked or pressure-cooked in the High Frontier's kitchen, or brought in from shops on the concourse. There were also traces of synthetic hair, oil, and artificial skin identifying at least fifteen bioroids, and possibly as many as nineteen.

And there'd been at least one clone.

Damn. That room had been as busy as Earth Station Terminal.

I'd expected as much. Hotel rooms collect the sheddings and effluvia of everyone that goes through them. The cleaning staff—their cast-off biological debris would be in there among the 685 separate human genomes, of course—could do the best job possible with the most powerful cleaning units and robots available, and they still couldn't hope to get everything.

Mattresses, especially, collect skin cells and hairs from everyone who uses them, not to mention navel lint, skin mites, sebaceous oil secretions, ear wax, and traces of every other bodily function you can imagine. Self-cleaning mattress surfaces help—so do old-fashioned bed sheets—but the stuff still collects in corners and crevices, on the floor and underneath, and especially inside the microscopic weave of the material.

It's enough to make you never want to go near a bed, *any* bed, ever again.

The lab report showed biological traces of every person who'd been inside Room Twelve in the past several months, and by itself wasn't very useful. I put in a request for the genome records for Coleman and for Hodgkins, however. That would require a biological warrant, of course, and we'd have to show cause—but my being able to identify them as the people who'd just tried to kill me inside another hotel room was cause enough, and then some. The voluntary release forms signed by the hotel staff would let us compare our collected bio-traces with them, just to knock a few of those genomes off the list.

The best thing the scan did was give us a genome database in case more suspects came up. We'd be able to prove that they had been in that room.

The clone data was interesting, but not conclusive. That there was only one type identified was not surprising; clones didn't stay in expensive Beanstalk hotels. It was perhaps more surprising that there were any traces at all.

The problem was that all clones of a given type had the same DNA. John Jones would have a different genotype than Mark

Henry...but there were *thousands* of Joneses and thousands of Henrys and no DNA-based means of telling them apart. Same-series clones did possess different fingerprints, true, but the chances were good, with so many humans in the room and so few clones, that all of the prints would turn out to be human.

So all I knew at the moment was that at least one other clone, and of a different genotype than the Henry-model, had been in the room. I didn't know which model—yet—and I didn't know when it had been there.

But it was something, and at least we wouldn't need a warrant to check the clone DNA. Clones don't have civil or medical rights, and every clone type has its genome and prints on file with Jinteki. A request had already been forwarded from NAPD HQ to Jinteki for a match with their records; we should know the model of the unknown clone visitor in short order, and if another clone had left fingerprints in that room, we'd know that as well. A check of hotel records would tell us if a human guest had arrived with a clone as a personal servant.

But not which individual. The NAPD had been pressuring Jinteki to write individual serial numbers into the so-called "junk DNA" of each individual clone, but so far we hadn't gotten anywhere with them. So we'd already proven that a Henry clone had been in the room through the fleck of tissue on the laser; what we could *not* prove from the DNA traces was that it had been Mark Henry 103.

The bioroids provided an even more difficult problem. Most of those fifteen-some traces would be from sexbots rented for an hour or for a night by past residents of the room. They'd arrived, done their thing, and microscopic traces had been left behind. They always were.

Some might be personal attendants; lots of risties had their own bioroids that they brought along as valets, as arm-candy, or for more personal reasons. The only biological traces left by bioroids were artificial hair samples from the body or the head, and those had originally come from human hair specifically grown from human donor samples. Many—but not all—Eve-models would have hair with the same altered DNA code... which, when we checked, would probably turn out to be from some female employee of Haas-Bioroid. I could be pretty sure that the strands of blond hair I'd found on the pillow in Room Twelve had come from Eve 5VA3TC, since I knew she'd been in the bed with Dow the night he was murdered, and the House-keeping staff would have removed any stray hairs long enough to be visible to the naked eye the last time they'd changed the sheets.

Even so, bioroid hair samples could establish a *probability*, not a certainty. Evidence collection was all about finding enough probables to build, step by slow step, a statistical near-certainty.

Haas-Bioroid would have records of which models carried which synthetic hair genome; since one donor sample could provide the hair for thousands of bioroids, however, I wouldn't be able to tell the difference if, say, there'd been *two* Eves in the room that night.

But an Eve usually had blond hair, while a Giselle, for instance, had gold-blond hair from a different donor, and a Rhoda had dark brunette hair grown from yet another source. With luck, we might find a difference if there'd been different models.

Unfortunately, it would be very difficult to prove that they'd been in the room that same evening. Unlike clones, who had their movements closely tracked by the bar codes on their necks, bioroids were personal equipment, and the hotel would not keep records on clients who'd either brought their own along, or who rented one for the night. What we would have to do was check the account records at Eliza's Toybox and other bioroid rentals for models hired by human customers on nights when those humans had checked into a room at the High Frontier. By cross-indexing the lists, we could eliminate many of the bioroid samples...but by no means all.

And, once again, there was no way to tie any one specific bioroid to Room Twelve on the night of the twenty-third.

Police detective work, I decided, would be a hell of a lot easier if Humanity Labor or the ACM *did* win and get artificial humans of both types banned. Clone and bioroid evidence could be contradictory, subtle, and, more often than not, frustratingly inconclusive.

My PAD chimed. It was Guerrero.

"Whatcha got?" I asked, fanning open the big screen.

His dark features seemed guarded. "A team got to the Farside tube-lev terminal a few minutes ago," the security chief told me. "According to the records, there've been no passengers matching the images you transmitted, not within the past couple of hours."

"What...you didn't have people already there, at Farside?"

"No one authorized to go into the security camera records, no."

"Damn it, *I* can go into seccam records from here! I told you I wanted someone there *physically* watching the trains as they arrived!"

His lips tightened as he watched me from the folding screen. "I am doing the best that I can, Captain, with the resources I have available. You don't need to shout."

I sighed. Rent-a-cops. Better than nothing, arguably, but...

"Have they checked the ferry terminal?"

"I have another team there now."

"When did the last ferry leave for Heinlein?"

"Almost six hours ago."

"And the next one out?"

"Not due to leave for hours, yet."

That was something, at least.

"Okay, good," I said. "I want you to shut down the ferry departures until further notice."

"We can't do that!"

"Sure you can. You call SEA Control and say, 'Hey, I got a situation; shut down the ferry.'"

"For how long?"

"Until I tell you. In the meantime, you're going to check *everyone* in the ferry terminal waiting area. You're going to tag their e-IDs, if they have them, and you're going to scan their faces and their hands."

"There must be two hundred people waiting for the next departure!"

"Then you'd better get busy, because I'm not turning off the no-flight order until you have them all."

"I—I'll need authorization. From Earthside."

"You'll have it. Start without. What about Nearside?"

"I have a team at the Nearside tube-lev station, checking people getting off from Farside. No matches in the past half hour."

"Then start scanning faces and hands there, too."

"But there are *hundreds*—"

"Just do it!" And I cut the connection. *¡Gilún! ¡Malparido!*

I was going to be catching flak on this one. Technically, police and security forces can request fingerprint or facial scanning data *only* at specific security checkpoints—such as the security stations at each platform up and down the Beanstalk—*or* if the subject signs a release, *or* if a law enforcement officer declares a hot-pursuit emergency. Essentially, I was calling an emergency…but I'd be grilled for it later, first by Commissioner Dawn, then by NAPD Internal Affairs, and then by a judge. I could end up suspended, fined, fired, in jail…or any combination of the above. I was putting my career on the line, but I *had* to find the two fugitives.

The question was which way Coleman and Hodgkins would go. I knew they'd caught the tube-lev for Farside. From there they could catch a ferry for Starport Kaguya—but that was blocked, now. Or they could head for the offices of Humanity Labor…a good bet, since they probably had temporary rooms there. Or they could head for the Challenger Mines…possible, but not extremely likely. There were numerous buildings and pressurized underground rooms there, a labyrinth to hide within, but a search would find them eventually. Same for Humanity Labor, if it came to that.

A likelier scenario would be for them to turn around and catch a tube-lev right back to Nearside, where they could blend with the crowd and eventually catch a down-Stalk beanpod for the trip back to Earth.

Once they mingled with the billion or so other people in Earthside New Angeles, it would be damn near impossible to find them if they didn't want to be found.

The PAD chimed again. It was Guerrero.

"What?"

"Thought you'd want to know about this," he said, holding up a large plastic evidence bag of gold-yellow tangles and strands. "One of the boys found it tucked away behind a seat on-board the tube-lev when it arrived at Farside."

That was the best news I'd heard in some time. "Good. I'd appreciate it if you would ship it to NAPD HQ right away, Attention: Evidence Department. Include your report."

"Right." This time he signed off first.

That seemed to confirm that Coleman, at least, was somewhere at Farside.

But then I got to thinking about that.

Why stuff a wig behind a seat on a tube-lev? Every seat had disposal slots, and even a full wig as long and thick as that one could be crammed inside. Disposal tanks on a tube-lev car were emptied automatically upon each arrival at a station, the contents shredded, then separated for recycling. A wig made of human hair would have been reduced to discrete elements—carbon, hydrogen, oxygen, nitrogen, mostly, with traces of potassium, iron, phosphorous, and others—and shipped either to the Challenger Farside Life Support Unit or on a volatiles tanker bound for Heinlein in short order. There would be no way to trace it then.

So why shove it behind a seat?

Unless...

Unless she *wanted* it to be found.

Frag! There were security cameras in the main Nearside concourse, but not inside the Nearside tube-lev terminal itself. Coleman had proven to be damned clever already with that wig worn for the benefit of the seccams, and I was beginning to suspect that Hodgkins was using a disguise as well. Was his beard a fake, perhaps?

I called up the security camera overlooking the Nearside concourse and pointed at the entrance to the tube-lev platform. I ran it back an hour...and began watching. *Closely.*

I was beginning to suspect that Coleman and Hodgkins both had ducked into the Nearside tube terminal, changed their appearance—in Coleman's case, she'd actually boarded a train and hidden the wig—and then...waited. Later, after the train had left, they would have come back, doing so separately.

Nothing...

Nothing...

I switched over to a security map of the Nearside terminal area. Frag, and frag again. There were two entrances to the terminal from the concourse alone, two sets of restroom facilities with entrances into both the terminal and the concourse, and a maze of security and maintenance passageways back behind the walls. Those last would be no-admittance and require handprints or other security measures to get in, but Hodgkins was in Humanity Labor's security department, and would be able to get access to literally anywhere.

I hadn't been thinking big enough. Both of them had re-entered the concourse, avoided the security cameras, and...what?

Almost certainly they would be headed down-Stalk, and would have to board a beanpod at the Space Elevator terminal. Any other destination—the Challenger Carousel, the High Frontier, the low-G facilities near the Carousel—would offer them temporary safety at best. Sooner or later, they'd have to pass in front of a security camera.

There was also the possibility of tagging their credaccounts or e-IDs—they were sure to have e-IDs, working for a major company like Humanity Labor. Almost everyone had one—well, everyone except for a few neoluddites, anti-technology anarchists, fundamentalists afraid of the Antichrist's mark, and a few million homeless people—but you weren't likely to encounter any of them at the top of the Beanstalk. The problem there was that fake e-IDs were not that hard to come by; any halfway competent underground programmer could do it in a matter of minutes—not enough to scam a deep electronic query, but good enough to fool typical doorway security scans and low-level security checkpoints.

So I linked in to the Beanstalk's security system again, calling up the backscatter data.

Every person boarding the Beanstalk at any terminal had to walk through the backscatter unit. Used to be there'd been exceptions...but then that terrorist had smeared himself all over the inside of a beanpod ten years ago, and there were no more exceptions. *Everyone* got scanned.

However, in deference to groups like PriRights, many security sites used computer programs to blur faces and certain body parts normally kept hidden, and most claimed to discard the information after the subject was checked for weapons...but the original data scan showed everything at maximum resolution, and the records were simply too valuable to discard. With a high enough security clearance, *anyone* could see *all* the data.

As I was doing now. I'd have to explain myself to Internal Affairs—add another one to the list, boys—but I didn't have the time right now to go through channels.

I started with people who'd boarded the next down-Stalk pod at 0445 that morning, within a few minutes of the attack in my hotel room. I pulled up the image of a man in a business suit carrying a briefcase. No.

A child. No.

A woman with short hair, wearing a traveler's suit with a shoulder cape. No.

The images were in black and white, but at a superficial scanning level the faces were crisp and clear, showing details as fine as creases and skin pores, if I zoomed in closely enough.

No…no…

Each image that came up was a multilayered composite created by the system network. By typing in commands, I could rotate the image, zoom in close, or actually adjust the image for depth and completeness of penetration, which could progressively show the person in street clothes all the way down to some rather grotesque sonar-generated cutaways revealing their internal organs, if I cared to dig that deep.

I kept the scans on superficial for the time being; I was looking at the faces.

No…no…no…

I could have set my PAD's secretary to the task, but, as usual, I didn't trust a machine to replace my eyes and brain—a piece of AI software couldn't ride hunches.

No…no…no…

Attached to each image was e-ID data, pinged from the subject when the scan was made.

No…no…

There. That one looked like Frank Hodgkins. I typed commands into my keyboard, effectively increasing the depth of scan until his hair and beard vanished. I recorded both sets of images; they would be useful in an ID check later. I also looked at the e-ID data. The name given was for Fred Callahan, a machinist from the Strugatsky Apartments back in New Angeles, visiting Heinlein on vacation. He'd checked through Beanstalk Security at 0525…that was almost two hours ago.

And the pod had left at 0600.

I kept checking. No…no…no…

Fifteen minutes later, I spotted Thea Coleman. Her e-ID listed her as Belinda Wiggins, a programming specialist for Armitage Software living at the Columbiad Arcology in Heinlein. She was traveling to Earthside New Angeles to visit family.

I copied her at several levels of scanning as well, for future reference. Then, just because I wanted to cover all bases, I checked the e-ID pings of people leaving the Beanstalk platform, in case either or both had pulled another switch-and-double-back on me.

As near as I could tell, both had boarded the pod and were on their way to Midway right now.

Correction. Their Beanpod had arrived at Midway at just past 0700. It was now almost 0730. They were already there… either at the Midway station, or else they'd changed pods and continued on for the last leg of their trip to Earth.

I was too late to stop them.

Chapter Seventeen

Day 9

I put out calls both to Beanstalk Security at Midway and to the NAPD, alerting them all that the two fugitives were at Midway and presumably bound for Earth. I lifted my hold on Moon-bound ferry launches, and told Guerrero to recall his people.

So why the hell didn't I have them check the backscatter records at Midway? I could have verified whether "Wiggins" and "Callahan" had already left down-Stalk for Earth. I wanted to do just that…but in fact, I couldn't bend the privacy laws quite that far.

Backscatter scanning has been controversial ever since it was first introduced back in the very early years of the 21st century. There were some messy legal cases arising from their use and for a time they were banned, but ultimately the technology was just too useful to ignore. Eventually they'd become common enough that even a dive like Tommy's could afford one.

But PriRights and others had pushed through civil legislation that made the use of backscatter x-ray records to track people a violation of civil—as opposed to criminal—law. You could use them to find out if tourists were smuggling bombs onto the Beanstalk or weapons into Tommy's, but accessing the stored images later for any other purpose *could* end in a civil suit.

Chances were good that Commissioner Dawn was already going to have my hide for pulling the raw data on the backscatter images at Challenger to do just that. Sure, "hung for a sheep as hung for a lamb," as the old adage puts it, but it was also a matter of sheer volume. About ten times as many people go through the Earth-Midway passage each day than go between Midway and the Challenger Planetoid. Even if I put my PAD to hunting through the images, it would take hours, maybe even days, to go through them all. Coleman and Hodgkins would almost certainly have adopted new electronic identities at Midway, and likely would be back on Earth before I found them.

Worse still, a lot of the traffic between Earth and Midway consisted of VIP risties—broadcast network executives and corporate CEOs visiting the geosynch businesses—and it *really* didn't pay to irritate that lot. With enough money, they could purchase software secretaries that would alert them if someone pried into their records, *especially* the stuff recorded by the backscatter units.

I could just imagine Dawn's reaction if the CEO of NBN found out the NAPD had been peeking at those files. *Not* good.

So all I could really do was alert Midway Security.

And then I went shopping.

I didn't know whether the bug Jones had planted on me was on the surface of the jacket, or if it had been the sort that could burrow through the jacket and take up residence inside the weave of my shirt. Either was possible; what was not possible was simply washing the garments to get the bug out. Those things are designed to work themselves into the fabric itself, anchor themselves with tiny wires, and not let go.

There was also the matter of the bug being evidence.

So I donned both shirt and jacket and limped down to the circle of shops and stores off the Nearside arrival concourse. Black shirt, white jacket, and a new pair of white slacks, as well, since the ones I was wearing were partially melted below and behind the left knee where I'd been brushed by that near-miss laser shot, the hole exposing a nasty blister as big around as the palm of my hand.

I slipped on the new clothing and pulled the wear-tabs, the smart fabric adjusting itself to my size and shape and smoothing out the wrinkles. The old clothing went into separate plastic evidence bags for shipment back to the NAPD. The techies Earthside would be able to find exactly where the nearly invisible bug was and remove it for analysis. The bad guys would know I was on to them, of course, but that no longer mattered.

And I wouldn't be able to set another trap for them again, not like that. I'd need to think of something else.

I also stopped at a pharmacy and picked up some analgesic nanomed. My leg was hurting badly, but I didn't have the time to run over to the Carousel medical center and have it treated. The analgesic nanobots, sprinkled across the burn with a talcum-fine bandage powder, would burrow in and switch off individual nerve endings, turning the burned area numb and reducing the inflammation. It would do until I could see a med tech.

Those chores taken care of, I checked out of the hotel and caught the next Beanpod down to Midway.

Commissioner Dawn called me on my PAD on the way and gave me a royal chewing out.

"What the hell were you thinking?" she demanded. I'd sent her an update on my investigation before leaving the hotel, and she'd seen it as soon as she'd come in to work that morning. "Why the hell didn't you have backup?"

"Because getting backup would have alerted the perps," I told her.

"I've already got complaints from Guerrero about your

heavy-handed efforts up there. He says you shut down the Challenger Ferry, and he says it wasn't necessary."

"Guilty on both counts," I admitted. "I didn't stop to think that they might have doubled back without going to Farside. I was guessing the whole way. My guesses weren't good enough."

"So you're descending now?"

"That's right. I'll be at Midway in another half hour."

"And what happens there?"

"I don't know if Coleman and Hodgkins stopped at Midway, or went on through. They could have caught another pod for Earth within a few minutes. I've already checked security records at Midway, though, and I don't see any sign that they reboarded a new pod. I think they must still be there."

"You've alerted SEA Security there." It wasn't a question. She'd been checking up on me from her desk.

"I have. And they have computer images of both of them. I'm hoping to pick them up at Security when they try to get on another beanpod."

"Okay. Just try not to tick off any more of the security people up there. I remind you that we *need* them. The Force doesn't have so many officers on the payroll that we can afford to make enemies, okay?"

"Yes, Mother. I'll be good. Promise."

And my beanpod continued its descent.

We were well into the deceleration phase of the trip. An electronic poll of the ten passengers in my pod had turned up no dissenting votes, so the floor of the beanpod now displayed the Earth spread out beneath our feet, spanning a bit less than twenty degrees and slowly growing.

I hadn't been convinced that Eve and Henry were the murderers.

Now, I wasn't convinced that Coleman and Hodgkins were the sole murderers.

First off, the psychology was wrong. Thea Coleman was a

vicious, murderous *malparida*, and I could see her gleefully executing a plan to cause widespread anti-android riots...but had she planned it in the first place? I doubted that.

Her "Mr. Fix It" was even less likely. Coleman was smart; Hodgkins struck me as just about bright enough to walk and shoot at the same time.

No, there was someone else behind those two. Someone higher up the figurative beanstalk.

And there were players in the hunt that I'd glimpsed, but not yet flushed into the open. John Jones, with his bug. Mr. Green. The deceased Robert Vargas—though he might well have just been in the wrong place at the wrong time. The short, shaggy-haired man carrying the suitcase out of the High Frontier. Their presence suggested a larger and well-established conspiracy, one involving at *least* several other people.

Who might be in on it, at a planning level? Coleman's boss, Thomas Vaughn, was a possibility for a start. Behind him, in the shadows, was Cheong Li Hua and the 14K triad.

This didn't feel like a triad operation, though. Historically, the triads had preyed on Chinese populations worldwide—extortion, blackmail, money laundering, drugs, prostitution. They'd extended their range, somewhat, when they formed a loose working alliance with the Italian, American, and Russian mafias, but their operations still rarely rose above the level of simple thuggery.

Okay, Harrison. *Think.* Who would stand to benefit from widespread riots involving the deaths of hundreds of clones, the destruction of hundreds of bioroids, and the end of androids in the work force?

The ACM—the Anti-Clone Movement—was an obvious group-suspect. And Human First. Both of them were outgrowths of Humanity Labor.

And Humanity Labor was dirty.

The old labor unions had always walked a narrow and unsteady line between radical politics and corruption. Born in the same era as workers' risings and communism, they'd fought against some of the more crippling excesses of capitalism, but at the same time they'd been vulnerable to wholesale takeovers by organized crime.

In 1933, upon his rise to power, Adolf Hitler had created the *Deutsche Arbeitsfront*, or German Labor Front, a monolithic organization that had all but replaced the older, diverse labor unions in the country, and which, like everything else, was controlled by the state. Under the new regime, workers had been better paid and had enjoyed better working conditions, but they hadn't been allowed to strike, either.

Humanity Labor was a similar monolith, a titanic organization theoretically devoted to serving the interests of all workers—but which also guaranteed no workers' revolts, no strikes, and plenty of government-mandated regulations to keep the workers in line. Attacking clones and bioroids in the work force—politically and literally—was a large and somewhat hidden component of their campaign to look after the interests of ordinary working humans. *Save jobs for human workers! Preserve human dignity! Employment for humans first!*

The issue provided a clear win-win for Humanity Labor. By hiding Human First and the ACM within their ranks, Humanity Labor could position itself as fighting for the interests of workers, while eliminating androids from the competition for jobs, which made sure more human workers were employed—and able to pay Humanity Labor their monthly dues.

In the detective game, we always operate under one simple rule: if you want to know who done it, follow the money. Who stands to make a profit?

Unfortunately, and as always, the problem wasn't that simple. As with the old German DAF, the US federal government was part of the issue, though you certainly couldn't claim that Humanity Labor was a state-run operation. The manufacture of both clones and bioroids was big business, *very* big business, and those companies paid billions in taxes each year. Eliminate those businesses, and Uncle Sam took a major hit on income.

From that perspective, the situation wasn't so much like Nazi Germany in the 1930s as it was like the United States in the early 2000s. Illegal immigration had become a crippling handicap for many states, yet the federal government had actually sued states that were trying to enforce immigration laws already on the federal books—primarily, at least according to the history downloads, to allow American businesses to maintain sources of cheap labor.

Androids. Clones and bioroids. The ultimate in cheap labor.

I had no idea what the Feds were thinking about the pro-android corporate confrontation with the labor force, but suspected that it was, as usual, divided and corrupt. *Both* sides were in there buying senators and representatives as quickly as they could, and the outcome might well devolve into who had the bigger political budget—Humanity Labor, or the big corporations like Haas-Bioroid, Jinteki, and Melange Mining. If it came down to that…well, no contest. The simulants were here to stay. Humanity Labor didn't stand a chance in the long run.

Another tick in favor of Humanity Labor as conspiracy mastermind of this particular setup: their belief that if you can't out-spend the other side, maybe you can out-sneak them. Enter Human First. Stir up enough popular unrest, and the government *has* to step in solidly on the anti-android side.

Now I thought I was pretty sure who was behind the plot.

The question was what I could do about it. Humanity Labor was *big*, and whoever had thought this one up would have placed several levels of cut-outs, blind alleys, and dupes between the soldiers like Coleman and Hodgkins, and the generals. Making anything stick was going to be damned tough—about like trying to use frictionless buckyfilm as glue.

I also knew that getting the NAPD to pursue those generals

would be an uphill battle. The police force tries to maintain good relations with Humanity Labor without being owned by it—a constant political juggling act. Humanity Labor, as I said, is dirty, with numerous links to both corrupt government agencies and the tri-mafs. They had the money to bring a lot of political leverage to bear against anyone set on investigating them too closely.

It was more than just possible that the best I'd be able to do would be to get Coleman and her bodyguard brought to justice...while getting Eve and Henry off the hook.

I used my PAD to look up Thomas Vaughn.

His Netpedia entry was pure frag—a prettily written propaganda piece no doubt uploaded by Humanity Labor's lawyers: happily married, with 2.1 kids, three-quarters of a billion in the bank, and a palatial estate high up on the western flanks of the Andes, above La Maná. He was currently on the short list for consideration for a cabinet post with the federal government—Secretary of Space Commerce.

That led me into some more Net-crawling. The current Secretary of Space Commerce was Karen Marie Bucholt. She was 105 and considering retirement. Several names had been floated so far as possible replacements, including Vaughn...and Dow.

Very interesting.

But still nothing definitive, nothing I could sink my teeth into.

I went up a level and looked at Vaughn's boss—Geraldo Ramon Cevallos Martín, Chairman of the Board for Humanity Labor, and the temporary Chief of Security.

I found his full name and titles listed in an electronic brochure promoting Humanity Labor. Martín didn't even have a Netpedia bio entry, which said something about how much money and power *he* had. I extended my search, looking for recent mentions of the guy in the news.

Nothing.

A man who doesn't publicly exist either *really* values his privacy, or he has a lot to hide—quite probably both.

I set up a Net secretary to go out and retrieve news articles on Martín, then turned my attention back to Vaughn. There was a lot more on him, including news articles about investigations into alleged corruption, bribery, and payoffs from 14K—none proven, none even going to trial. At least two New Angeles district attorneys over the past ten years had built cases, then dropped them, and in both instances, the DAs had retired from public service after becoming quite wealthy. Vaughn himself was obscenely wealthy. I couldn't find anything leading me to suspect that he personally would profit from an end to clones and bioroids, but he had linked the success of Humanity Labor to the elimination of simulated humans from the work force. Maybe he was just doing it for the company. Or maybe he wasn't just a leader for Humanity Labor, but also worked for its darker side—Human First.

Midway appeared smack in the center of the two-thirds-full disk of the Earth gleaming in quiet beauty on the deck, a tiny, glittering jewel slowly growing brighter and larger as we continued our descent. I patched a vid call through to Lily, letting her know I was arriving, then sat back to watch the approach. Acceleration lessened, and the feeling of weight dropped away. We were barely moving as we slid down the superconducting cable through an open hatch and snugged down into the receiving bay for arrivals from up-Stalk.

Lily was waiting for me as an attendant hauled me out of the boarding tube and into the arrivals concourse, her magnificent cascade of auburn hair wound tightly up and secured against the prevailing zero-G. "Welcome down," she said, and she opened her arms as I floated into them. We caught, clung, and held for a moment, partly entangled with a safety line, until an attendant cleared his throat and asked us to move along—we were blocking the flight path.

I wasn't sure what it was, but something was wrong. "Are you okay?" I asked.

She nodded. "Fine. You find any trace of them yet?"

"Not yet. They may have changed e-IDs again, though. I saw that Wiggins and Callahan debarked from the 0700 beanpod, but nobody with those names boarded the next down-Stalk pod."

"That would have been at 0830," she said.

"Right." I checked the time on the back of my hand. It was now 1034, and the next down-Stalk pod was due to leave at noon. "We have time to get something to eat," I said. "Can we? I was up early and haven't had breakfast yet."

"Sure," she said. "Let's do the Freefall. It's close to the down-Stalk terminal."

The Freefall is a microgravity restaurant for travelers in transit. The Sheer Heaven has better food and the ambiance of spin-gravity, but it's located in a separate Midway structure, a rotating cylinder parked close to the main Beanstalk platform and accessed by space taxis—twelve-person ferries. It would have taken a bit too much time to make the transit and still have time to eat.

But the Freefall was okay. You slip your feet into grip-holds on the deck instead of sitting in chairs, which are superfluous in zero-G. There's a small, round table between you with a gripper surface that holds your food—a plastic-covered tray with separate food wells and built-in straws. You can order just about anything you like so long as it's pureed. Sucking down mouthfuls of hot, semi-liquid gog and steamed tofuto slush can take some getting used to, but the coffee, at least, was hot.

Absolutely the best part of breakfast at the Freefall, though, is the view.

One entire wall of the eating area is transplas. The environmental controls darken the transparency when the sun is shining directly in, but for at least half of each day the sun is behind you and the transplas is clear.

Earth was there in the middle of everything, of course, spanning twenty degrees and wrapped in gleaming, dazzling swaths and stipples and arcs and ragged tatters of cloud, but you could also see the Beanstalk's shaft going out from one side and dwindling…dwindling…dwindling to a vanishing point in north-central Ecuador. Other Midway orbital structures were visible, as well: the rotating cylinder, a tin can a hundred meters across, that held the Sheer Heaven restaurant and a number of other businesses and facilities that required simulated gravity. The local Honeymoon Hilton was also visible, free-floating a kilometer clear of the Midway main platform. Even further off in the distance was one of the orbital manufactories—I couldn't tell which one—doing its bit to get heavy industry off the Earth's surface and out into space where it belonged.

In the middle distance was a warship. It was hard to tell from that distance, but I thought she was the *Nassau*—a troopship carrying a few hundred space-ready Marines. What was she doing here? For that matter, there'd been that kid, Kaminsky, on his way up to Heinlein Station. Were the Feds beefing up their military presence out here?

Why?

Something to think about, in light of some of what I'd recently learned.

You could also see other parts of the Midway platform itself, the facility that actually anchored the Beanstalk above and below. Besides the two cavernous Beanstalk terminals and the restaurant, there were shops offering a bewildering array of goodies from both Earth and Heinlein, as well as the corporate offices of companies doing business in orbit: space construction, microgravity chemistry, and robotics businesses, mostly.

And there was also, of course, NBN.

I think something like half of the Midway platform's volume is taken up by the Net Broadcast Network and its various subsidiaries—newsrags like the *Sol* and the *New Angelino*, and the higher-tone *NewsDirect*. The complex is huge, though from our vantage point in the Freefall, you could only see some of the massed antenna array, off to the extreme right.

I glanced at it, then smiled at Lily. "So…what's in the news today?"

She shrugged and took a pull at one of her straws. "Just more of the usual," she said. "Riots on Mars, riots in Shanghai, riots in Chicago. Weather clear and sunny, with a seventy percent chance of rioting mobs."

"And in New Angeles?"

She made a face. "*That's* going to depend on Humanity Labor's press conference this afternoon."

"Is your article out yet?"

"It's coming out with the noon edition. Do you want to see?"

She didn't sound very happy about it.

"Sure."

She pulled out her PAD and I pulled out mine, fanning the screen open. She had one of the newer, higher-end models, fancier than mine, with a virtual holographic screen as well as a keyboard field. She switched it on, typed in some characters, and her article appeared on my screen, just as it would appear in the newsrags in another hour.

I scrolled through it quickly, picking out the high points. Roger Mayhurst Dow, Jr. had been found brutally murdered in his hotel room. The investigation was continuing. Commissioner Dawn was quoted as saying that the police were putting every effort possible into the case, and that she was confident that those responsible would soon be in custody. Dow's wife, Lupe Gonzales, wanted to see justice, and the police were doing nothing.

All the way at the bottom was a quote by Thomas Vaughn, PR Director for Humanity Labor.

"Roger Dow was a valued member of the Humanity Labor

team," he was quoted as saying, "a gifted man, and a good friend. He was at the forefront of the battle against clones and bioroids and their wholesale take-over of our jobs, human jobs, and their erosion against human dignity." The article went on to say that Vaughn *believed* that clones and bioroids had been behind the attack.

I tapped at the screen with my finger. "That's good."

"What's that?"

"You didn't quote Vaughn directly about androids being behind the attack."

"No. Commissioner Dawn was very clear about that. If I wanted access to her office, I had to play down that angle." She shrugged. "So I'm a whore."

The word shocked me. She didn't usually use vulgarities like that. "You are not!"

"The free press is supposed to tell the news, and tell it straight," she said, and I could hear a barely suppressed fury beneath the words. "We're not supposed to cut deals with police commissioners…or with corporate bosses, or labor leaders, or politicians, for that matter. But if we want access, we need to play their games. I hate the doublethink and the politics. I hate the *fraud*. And…and sometimes I hate me!"

I slipped free of my foot restraints and held her for a time. I wasn't sure what to do or say. Lily had never struck me as vulnerable, not like this. Usually she tended to have a high—and, I felt, an accurate—opinion of herself.

Teardrops drifted in zero-G—tiny, glittering, perfect translucent spheres of silver.

"So…I gather you've been stressing over this crap," I said after a while.

She nodded. "Rick, the deeper I dig into this, the bigger it gets. The *scarier* it gets. And no one is telling the truth…not the mayor, not Washington, not Humanity Labor, not Jinteki, *none* of them!" She looked up at me and those brown eyes flashed.

"And not the police, either!"

"I've told you what I can, sweetheart. And right now…well, there's just not that much more to tell."

"The clone and the bioroid…you claim they're innocent."

"Yes, I do."

"But they're under arrest!"

"For their protection."

"How can I believe you?"

"It's called trust. I know that's not a real common commodity nowadays…"

I let her go. I was hating myself, right then, not so much because I was hiding something from her, but because I was beginning to suspect that the tears were a put-on, that she was using them to manipulate me, to get me to open up.

When had I become so cynical?

I brushed the thought aside. Probably when Nina told me I was worthless and walked out of my life.

Maybe even before that…

I returned to my side of the table as Lily used a handkerchief. There was movement outside the transplas—orbital workpods carrying out some sort of maintenance on the Beanstalk itself. Work pods were teleoperated spacecraft; their controllers were on-board the Midway platform, somewhere, linked into their mechanical alter egos by Net-based telemetry.

I saw one cruising past the window twenty meters away, a turtleback hanging on to a handhold on the hull. *Ride 'em, cowboy,* I thought.

It wasn't so much that I was hiding anything from Lily. The theory I'd hashed out on the way down from Challenger was still half-formed, with no proof whatsoever. She was looking for facts, not theorizing.

And what I *was* certain of I couldn't tell her. Not yet.

I looked at my hand time. "We should probably go," I told her.

We dropped the trays into a recycler slot, and hand-over-handed along a zero-G line toward the Beanstalk concourse. The line took us past another window set in the wall of the concourse that looked into the beanpod bay, where several beanpods—pointy-ended cigars twenty-one meters long, with hulls a dull bronze in color—hung ready for their descent. I could see ours, with the passenger boarding tube already attached. Several teleoperated probes were working around the passenger pod, prepping it for the trip. I noticed a flare of light reflected from the Beanstalk itself—some bit of necessary welding on the outer hull.

I followed Lily to the security entrance, then waited as a boarding attendant hauled her ingloriously up to the backscatter scanner and gently pushed her through, while another waited to catch her at the other side to help her board the beanpod.

Regulations…

And that's when I realized we were being watched.

I happened to turn to look across the concourse, and saw John Jones floating upside down, relative to me, twenty meters away. He was watching me, and he was trying to stay covert; as I looked at him, he raised a newsrag to hide his face, pretending to read.

It was the sort of amateurish stunt I would expect out of Hollywood. The best way to stand out in a bustling, moving crowd is to stand still—or, in this case, float still.

My first question was *which* John Jones it might be. The same one that had talked to me on my way up-Stalk? Or an identical twin?

But would an identical twin be so obviously keeping me under surveillance?

I pulled out my PAD and keyed Lily's number. It took her a moment to answer; presumably, they were still helping her to a seat. "What?"

"Sit tight," I told her. "My friend Mr. Jones is back. I'm going after him…"

"Wait! You can't—"

"Catch you in a few," I told her, and I switched off.

There was a wall directly at my back. I folded my legs, tucking my knees in tight, placed my feet squarely against the wall, and *kicked.*

Arms outspread, I sailed across the concourse.

Chapter Eighteen

Day 9

With his face behind the newsrag, Jones never saw me coming.

I hit him hard, closed my arms around his legs, and hung on as we went into a tumble, my velocity roughly cut in half by the impact. Jones yelled and pounded at my back, but I hung on until we drifted, still tumbling, into the far wall. I was able to get my legs between us and the wall before we hit, and damped our velocity by letting them collapse as they touched.

"*What the frag are you doing?*" he screamed, thrashing.

Other travelers and platform attendants stared at us from all over the concourse. "Police!" I yelled back, shouting so that the onlookers would hear, too. I didn't want any of them coming to Jones's rescue, though perhaps they wouldn't have done so for a clone. "You're under arrest for the suspicion of attempted murder, of conspiracy to commit murder, and of complicity in the murder of Roger Dow!"

"You're crazy! *Let me go!*"

Looking around, I spotted an obvious businessman floating by a hand line, a PAD floating in front of him as he stared at us in shock. "You!" I yelled, pointing at him. "Hit your panic button!"

All PADs have panic buttons, a locked key that will summon police or security authorities to the site, guiding them in with a locator arrow.

Jones struggled, but I clamped my legs around his waist and held on.

"Look, you're making a mistake!"

"Am I?" I managed to reach my PAD in its holster and switch on the record function.

"I had nothing to do with the murder!"

"No, but you planted a microbug on my jacket that almost got me killed at the Sinus Medii a few days ago, and it helped your accomplices set up an attempt to kill me early this morning. *That's* the 'attempted murder' bit."

"No! I never did that!"

"We also have evidence that you helped two accomplices carry out the murder of Roger Dow."

"*I wasn't even there!*"

"We have evidence that suggests otherwise."

He looked scared, then. He was starting to sweat, the droplets of perspiration drifting about his head like tiny, silver satellites, like Lily's tears earlier.

I took a deep breath. "You have the right to remain silent. Anything you do say can and will be used against you in a court of law. You have the right to an attorney—"

"*I'm a fragging clone!* Clones don't have rights!"

"You have the right to an attorney, and if you can't afford an attorney—"

"You *gilún*! Let me go!"

"—one will be appointed for you. Do you understand this warning?"

He didn't reply right away, and I tightened my grip. They're called the "Miranda Rights," though in fact it's legally a warning. The Mirandas don't qualify as "rights" under the U.S. Constitution.

"Do you understand my warning?" I repeated.

"Yes! Yes! I can't breathe, for chrissake!"

I loosened my grip a fraction. We were tumbling slowly, dozens of surprised and curious faces drifting past my field of view.

"You are being recorded," I told him. "Do you have anything to say?" Legally, I was in the clear. He'd been properly mirandized, and he would have to formally announce his declaration to invoke his rights.

"I'm a clone! Clones have no rights! You're supposed to return me to my employer! You're supposed to charge my employer!"

"Your employer of record is Roger Dow. He's dead."

"I work for Melange Mining!"

"Not Humanity Labor? Helping to rid the world of clones like yourself? Why'd you put the bug on me, shorty?"

"Look…look…this is all a crazy mistake! I'm with SAM, okay?"

That startled me, but I kept a firm hold on my prisoner. SAM—the organization devoted to the proposition that clones were not property, but people being *treated* as property. Full emancipation for clones and equality for them in the work force, and all that—something to which Humanity Labor would never agree.

"You can pull the other one," I told him.

"No! No, really! Yeah, I put a tracker on you, but it was because we needed to find Mark Henry before Human First got to him!"

I could tell I wasn't going to get sense out of this character here. I'd been goading him, hoping he'd let slip with something useful that I could catch on my PAD. Now it was time to go.

"You can save your statement for the desk sergeant," I told

him. "You're coming with me."

He started struggling again. "This is blatant persecution! Bigotry!"

A couple of yellow jackets sailed through the air from across the concourse, using bursts from their front airbelt packs to brake themselves as they drifted up, turning as they arrived by extending their left arms to change their centers of mass.

"What's the problem here?" one demanded. Reaching out, he caught my arm and gave another burst of air from one of his packs, neatly stopping my rotation. My estimation of elevator mercs went up a notch.

I noticed they both carried stunsticks hooked to their belts. Handguns were tough enough to handle in low-G; they were damned near impossible to use in zero gravity, where they acted like rockets to knock the firer into a nasty tumble.

"Captain Harrison, NAPD," I told them. "I need your assistance and a pair of cuffs."

I felt them ping my e-ID for confirmation, and one of them pulled a zip-strip out of a thigh pouch.

"Where are you taking him, sir?" one asked. "Local sec station?"

I shook my head. "Boarding tube," I said. "The 1200 beanpod for Earth. I'm taking this character down to NAPD headquarters."

That elicited a sudden and violent response from the prisoner. "*No!*" He kicked, hard, catching one of the yellow jackets in the crotch, and nearly tore himself free from my grip. He threw his elbow at my face and I blocked the swing, which put both of us into another slow but awkward tumble.

One of the yellow jackets unclipped his stunstick and gave it a snap with his wrist, extending it to two meters. I twisted, then released Jones, giving him a gentle shove toward the yellow jacket with the stinger, drifting backward with my arms and legs outstretched. "Clear!" I yelled.

The yellow jacket extended his stunstick and let Jones have a solid jolt across his solar plexus. He jerked and stiffened, then went limp, curling into the fetal position, drool bubbling from his open mouth. The other yellow jacket spun him around with slick efficiency, grabbed his arms, and used the zip-strip to pin his wrists behind his back.

"Need a hand getting him on-board, sir?"

"Yeah, thanks."

With their airbelts, they were able to maneuver him to the security scanner more easily than I would have been able to do with muscle alone. As they took him through, I argued for a moment with the SEA official at the desk: no, Jones didn't have a ticket, he was my prisoner, and the SEA could bill the police Earthside. When I threatened to commandeer the pod under the provisions of Article Two, paragraphs one and two of the New Angeles Municipal Public Safety Code, she relented with bad grace and keyed something into her computer.

I followed my prisoner through the backscatter, and took him down the boarding tube and into the waiting beanpod.

"Thank God!" Lily said as I entered the pod. "I thought you were going to get left behind!"

I glanced at my hand time. "Plenty of time, babe," I told her.

An attendant and one of the yellow jackets helped me maneuver the unconscious clone into an empty seat and strap him down. I left the zip-strip on his wrists. He might be a bit uncomfortable during the G-and-a-half descent once he came around, but the trip would only last fifty-one minutes. Once Jones was secure, I took my seat between him and Lily. I noticed that she'd popped her monocam over her left eye and had been recording vid of us strapping the clone down.

"...in an exciting new development...," she was saying, her voice just loud enough for me to hear. "...the clone was apprehended at just before noon, today, in the passenger concourse outside the down-Stalk station of the Space Elevator's Midway station. It is believed that he may have had a part in the brutal murder of political lobbyist Roger Dow last week in a hotel room up at Challenger.

"I have the arresting officer here, Captain Rick Harrison of the NAPD. Captain Harrison...would you care to comment on the capture of this clone?"

"He's not a clone," I told her.

Lily looked so shocked she almost lost her monocam, but she recovered fast. "N-*not* a clone! How do you know that?"

"I'll need a DNA test to prove it...but he's not a clone. He's a member of a conspiracy to make us all *think* that clones are capable of murder."

"Would you care to elaborate, Captain Harrison?"

"No, Lil, I wouldn't. Let's wait until we have that DNA test, shall we?"

It was two minutes before noon.

The beanpod was fairly full, eleven people including the three of us, with only one empty seat left on this deck and, I assumed, full or nearly full decks above and below. It looked like a fairly average mix of citizenry: two business people, two elderly women probably on their way down-Stalk from a retirement community to visit family on Earth, a couple of construction workers, and two Wyldside-types with heavy G-mods and lots of jewelry—one of them had scales instead of skin, the other a face that looked like a snub-nosed wolf.

A holographic attendant flickered into view to let us know we would be departing soon, to remain buckled in until after the seatbelt light went out, and polled us as to whether or not we wanted to see the Earth during the descent.

Everyone on our deck voted yes.

I was glad. It was going to be good to get back to Earth, I supposed, but I always enjoyed it when I had the opportunity to go up-Stalk. I never got tired of the view, and I wanted to drink my fill before plunging back into the crowds and the noise and the bustle of Earthside life.

On the display overhead, the beanpod bay doors opened wide, revealing Earth, as wide as forty full Moons edge-to-edge, hanging in the night above us…though words like "above" and "below" had little meaning in microgravity. Then we started accelerating, and up was up, while down was most definitely down. It felt like we were climbing toward the Earth.

"Are you a policeman, young man?" one of the elderly women asked from across the compartment.

"Yes, ma'am, I am."

She nodded at Jones. "Is that your prisoner?"

"Yes, ma'am, he is."

"Is he a *clone*?"

"He's a human disguised as a clone, ma'am." I didn't like discussing the case with civilians, but they'd all heard me talking to Lily a moment before.

"I don't know why a human would want to disguise himself as one," a man in a construction jumper said, "but that's not a crime, I suppose…is it?"

It was a crime for a clone to pretend to be human but, no, a human could dress up as a clone. I looked at the unconscious Jones. A very *short* human.

"I think it's better if I not discuss the case, sir," I told him.

The older woman's eyes grew large. "Is he *dangerous*, officer?"

I grinned at her, "Not any more."

In fact, I wasn't *absolutely* sure that Jones wasn't a clone. There was the small matter of this Jones looking identical to the Jones I'd seen in the personnel office at Melange Mining, up at Sinus Medii…identical enough to be his twin. That was why I wanted to confirm my suspicions with a DNA test.

But I strongly suspected that this Mr. Jones was wearing a DNA mask.

Cosmetic shaping, it was called, a form of gene-mod therapy.

Suppose you want to look like someone else. You *could* create a mask out of latex and bioroid synthskin, but the results might be a little less than completely convincing. Masks are never wholly lifelike—there's that Uncanny Valley effect once again—and someone who gets too close might see through the deception. It's better to receive a series of DNA infusions beneath the skin of the face, using nanobot transport to saturate cells inside the face with DNA from the person you want to impersonate.

You see, the shape of your face is partly the result of the exact contours of the bone beneath it, but it's also due to the layers of fat and muscle tissue overlaying the skull. DNA won't do much to change the shape of the skull—that's the end result of years of bone growth—but it *will* cause the soft tissue to fill in and mold itself into a new face.

In effect, my Mr. Jones was as much an artistic creation as a Jinteki clone. Someone had gone to a lot of trouble and expense to find a person of about the right size—around 150 to 155 centimeters high, with a mass of around 70 kilograms—and to give him DNA cosmetic treatments to reshape his face. A century or two ago, they used plastic surgery to the same end. Cosmetic shaping did the same thing without cutting, without weeks of healing, and it was easily reversible. It took three or four weeks for the tissues to regrow into the new shape, but if you wanted your old face back, you just re-injected yourself with samples of your own DNA.

There were Wyldside kids and bangers, the party set, who used cosmetic shaping to turn themselves into werewolves, vampires, faux aliens, dinosaurs, whatever the current fad of the fast set might be, by growing fatty tissue covered by skin and fur or scales or feathers from a designer-gene lab. You could use gene-mod to grow bright purple hair, or you could go all the way to giving yourself the face of a sensies star…or the head of a wolf, like wolf-boy over there.

Or, in this case, the face of a Jones-model clone.

And I was pretty sure I was right. When I'd talked with him last week, Jones had been entirely too personable, intelligent, and direct, not retiring and clone-like at all. He'd been interested in things well outside the range of his usual duties, and clone conditioning strongly discouraged extracurricular interests.

And he'd been, I was certain, the short, bearded man who'd taken the suitcase out of the High Frontier. Amazing what you can do with a fake beard and a wig.

I'd played around with the image I'd pulled from the security camera, trying to enhance it, but the angle was just too steep. My conviction that it was John Jones was based more on probabilities than anything else. Most people nowadays used genetic modification to take care of any physical trait that made them stand out.

That didn't apply to everyone, of course. Some folks had morphallasophobia—a fear of changing the body. Others just didn't care for the idea.

But there were damned few *short* people on the streets anymore. The average height of the average citizen ran around 177 centimeters—and maybe seven to ten centimeters less for the *Mestizos*, the native Ecuadorian peoples. People who were bothered by their personal height, or lack of it, could get it fixed as easily as myopia at any city clinic. I knew a few people on the Force who were shorter than 165 centimeters…but there weren't many.

And those few had to put up with more than their share of clone jokes.

So we had someone only about 155 centimeters tall checking out of the High Frontier and carrying the suitcase that had been used to smuggle in the mining laser. On camera he looked like a clone disguised as a human…but that's truly remarkable, both because clones are heavily conditioned against such deception, and because if a clone was caught imitating a human he would be retired.

More likely by far that it was a very short full-human, one pretending to be a clone who was pretending to be a human… an elaborate double-deception with a bad wig and beard for the sake of the watching security cameras.

And there simply weren't that many full-humans who were that short. If I was right and this John Jones next to me was human, then he was also almost certainly the human I'd seen on the High Frontier's lobby security cameras.

I was itching to run that DNA test.

Leaning over, I tugged down Jones's collar, looking at the left side of his neck. The requisite bar code was there, containing his serial number and digitized name. I wondered if it was a real tattoo, or simply drawn on the skin with permanent ink. There *are* reversible tattoos, of course…or it might even be a type of animated tat—an intermittent capable of turning invisible whenever its owner wished.

Yeah, I had a *lot* of questions I wanted to ask our Mr. Jones.

And there were some other questions I wanted to ask, as well, of other suspects. I called Floyd, putting up a sound suppression field to allow me to converse with reasonable privacy. Despite that, I felt as though I had a lot of people staring at me.

I also coded the call for Blue-one security, high enough to give Floyd and myself reasonable electronic privacy.

Floyd's stolid face appeared on the folding screen. "Yes, Captain."

"Just checking in. Everything okay up there?" I glanced at Lily, watching me from outside the SS field. "No riots?"

"No riots, Captain."

"Good. How are the prisoners?"

"Well. Eve 5VA3TC has had the necessary repairs made to her body. And Mark Henry 103 has repeatedly told me that he does not feel safe on the Moon, and that he wishes to be brought to Earth, as you promised. Detective Flint is eager to return, as well."

"Okay. But not by Beanstalk. Get a dropship and make the flight direct. Bring Eve's damaged parts along, too. Evidence. Have Flint and a couple of badges you trust help with security."

"Dropship transport is expensive, Captain."

"I'll authorize it." Damn, Dawn was going to skin me for that one. "I don't care about the cost right now. It'll be safer than bringing them down-Stalk."

"Indeed. Is there a problem?"

"Hodgkins and Coleman tried to kill me this morning at my hotel," I told him. "My guess is that they or the people behind them are desperate now, and want to terminate everyone and every*thing* that can tie them to murder-one."

Floyd looked as alarmed as is possible for a bioroid, though, as usual, there was no way to read emotion in those blank, silver eyes. "Are you unharmed, Rick?"

I felt the throb in my leg. The nanobots were still doing their job, though I'd need to have something more permanent done about the leg after I reached Earth.

"Yes," I lied. "The bad news is that they're still at large. I tracked them down to Midway. They still may be there, or they may have continued on down-Stalk to Earth."

"So there is the possibility of an attempt to get at the prisoners either here or on Earth," Floyd said. "I understand."

"Right. I also have a missing piece of the puzzle." I told him about my capture of John Jones.

"I am concerned, Captain," Floyd said when I finished. "This conspiracy is widespread and extensive, with considerable resources behind it."

"Oh, you think?"

I was speaking sarcastically, but Floyd took me literally.

"I do, sir. Four men in skyhoppers operating across hundreds of kilometers on the lunar surface represents a considerable investment in operating costs and materiel. The multiple e-ID identities alone would have cost a great deal of money to create and program. We are not looking at two individuals, here, but at a large and well-funded corporate or government entity."

"I agree. That's why I want you and Flint to get all three suspects on Earth, to NAPD HQ and under lock and key." I hesitated, then added, "I believe that somewhere along the line the intersec software has been compromised."

Intersecurity software took in an enormous area, including thousands of separate programs from dedicated management AIs to tiny subroutines operating inside individual security cameras, drones, and scanners. It was an absolute necessity for modern civic management, since it allowed dozens of separate law enforcement and security processors and programs to recognize and interact with one another.

Intersec software was particularly vital for law enforcement. It interconnected data storage and communications between the NAPD, the FBI up at the Fed level, the district constabularies within the city, as well as the security forces of large organizations, corporations, and agencies, like the SEA, Humanity Labor, and Jinteki. It linked together thousands of separate surveillance and security cameras, police drones, backscatter scanners, and e-ID readers. It allowed electronic communications between the police and the city's myriad private security departments, from the Melange Mining Security Force down to Fred, the bouncer at Tommy's Diner. Intersec software was what allowed me to tap into a specific seccam operated by the High Frontier's internal security, glance into peek-a-boo records for the SEA's backscatter units, and to look up credaccount records for Eliza's Toybox.

The problem was that the entire system, program upon program nested within one another like Russian dolls, was unimaginably complex, far too labyrinthine for any one human mind to comprehend.

But someone who knew what he was doing, a good hacker who understood certain key parts of the system, could penetrate the layers of external security and turn parts of the intersec software against other parts.

In this case, I suspected that someone with intermediate-level system access—someone within Humanity Labor's security network, specifically—was working through that network to penetrate the NAPD's system. At security level Blue-one, my conversation with Floyd was *probably* secure…but I couldn't be absolutely certain even of that.

Humanity Labor had an excellent internal security force, though some of the individuals—like Frank Hodgkins—didn't impress me as being all that bright. They could afford the best hackers, though, that money could buy. They also used the services of Globalsec, which amounted to a small, private army and which had a fairly good intelligence arm.

With assets like that, Humanity Labor could follow an NAPD cop if he had a bug planted on him, follow him anywhere there were scanners and the appropriate software—like Melange Mining. They could learn which beanpods the cop was riding on, and follow him through security checkpoints. They could find out where the security cameras were at the Challenger Planetoid, and avoid them…

In short, they could do just about anything I had done electronically, using the vast, far-flung complex of official electronic surveillance gear to track me…or my prisoners.

"Put together a security team," I told Floyd, "just people you and Flint personally trust. I recommend four badges, with full tactical gear." I pushed aside the immediate questions: Who would a bioroid trust? Was a bioroid even capable of trust?

No matter, I trusted both Flint and Floyd, and I trusted their judgment.

"Yes, sir."

I thought a moment. "I'm going to recommend that you stay as far under intersec radar as you can manage. Don't log your prisoners on the dropship. Don't keep them under electronic surveillance—I want either you or Flint with them at all times instead. If you must discuss them by PAD, use Blue-one security or higher."

"I already had that in mind, actually," Floyd told me.

Damn, he was quick. I signed off and killed the silence field.

Jones groaned, his eyes fluttering. I hadn't expected him to wake up this soon.

"It's okay," I told him. "You're safe, it's okay." Unbuckling, I made myself stand in the G-and-a-half acceleration and walk over to the dispenser wall. A swelling in the hull that cut into the otherwise smooth circle of the deck held a restroom, and on the outside the controls to get water or other non-alcoholic drinks. I got him a disposable cup of water and returned to my seat. "Here you go."

I held the cup for him and he took several swallows of water. "Thank you," he said. "Where…where are we?"

"On a beanpod, on our way to Earth."

Again, his eyes flew wide open. "*¡Diablo!*"

Another confirmation. I'd never heard a clone swear, and never heard one use Spanish. But what worried me more was his agitation. This was more than fear of arrest.

"What's the problem, Jones?" I asked. "Why don't you want to go to Earth?"

For answer, he struggled wildly against the straps and the zip-strip. "We've got to go back!" he yelled. "We've got to go back!"

"Why? Tell me."

"*We're all gonna die!*"

The other passengers were whispering among themselves,

and some were looking panicky. This I did not need—a beanpod full of panicked civilians.

And an instant later I realized why he must be so frightened. "What is it? Did your friends plant a bomb on-board?"

"*A bomb!*" a man cried, fumbling with his seatbelt.

"Everyone sit down and be quiet!" I ordered. I turned back to Jones. "How about it? What do you know?"

He turned glazed eyes on me, the fight suddenly gone. "What time is it?"

I glanced at my wrist. "Ten after."

But before he could reply, a savage, ringing bang sounded through the beanpod, and acceleration ceased.

The lights went out, along with the external display, then both flickered back on.

It took a moment to realize that Earth was no longer directly above us, but drifting slowly past one side.

We'd just been blown clear of the Beanstalk, and were now in free fall, hurtling toward the Earth.

Chapter Nineteen

Day 9

Pandemonium broke out on the beanpod deck, people screaming, people clawing at their seatbelts, people crying or swearing or shouting or all three. Lily seemed calm enough—the cool, collected reporter—but everyone else had just voted to stage a small riot.

"Everyone…be *still!*" I bellowed in my best parade ground voice.

The shout startled the others into silence.

"All right," I continued. "We can get through this if we keep our heads. Everyone stay in your seats. That means you!" I added, pointing at wolf-boy, who was still trying to unfasten his belt.

"We need to get to the lifeboats!" he cried.

"No, we don't," I said. "Beanpods don't have lifeboats. Beanpods *are* lifeboats in an emergency, however. So stay seated and stay quiet, and we'll all be just fine. Understand me?"

I got several shaky nods from around the compartment, which wasn't too bad, considering. There weren't any pressure loss alarms going off and I couldn't hear any telltale hissing, so our hull integrity was okay. We had lights and an external display, so our temperature control would be good. We might even be high enough that they could send a work pod out to snag us before we hit atmosphere.

"Nothing to worry about!" one of the businessmen said with a self-important sneer. "We're in orbit, right? We're falling around the Earth! We're perfectly safe until they come out and get us!"

I didn't reply because now was definitely *not* the time for a discussion on physics, but the fact was that the guy was dead wrong. We'd been in orbit up in Midway, yes, but not any more. At any point below the Midway station we simply wouldn't have the lateral velocity to maintain orbit. We would have some speed sideways due to Coriolis force, and we would also have some fraction of orbital speed left over from Midway—orbital speed for geosynch was 3.07 kilometers per second…but we actually would have bled a lot of that off already, coming down the rail…

How much? What was our lateral vector right now, away from the Beanstalk? As the beanpod descended, it actually tugged the entire Beanstalk slightly to the east; when it went up-Stalk, it tugged to the west. The overall effect was pretty small, but it would have bled off a lot of our eastward momentum.

I didn't know the friction coefficient of a beanpod's rail-guides, so I couldn't come up with a good figure. But let's say two kilometers per second above and beyond the elevator's speed as it swung, with the Earth's rotation, from west to east.

Which all meant: step outside the door, and it was one hell of a long drop almost straight down, with a 2 kps drift to the east. From this altitude, that meant an impact roughly 120 kilometers east of Cayambe.

They still tell the story of a construction worker on the Beanstalk, back in the early days. He neglected to attach a safety tether properly, lost his grip, and dug a crater somewhere out in the Orellana District.

I pulled out my PAD and ran some quick calculations. We'd been accelerating at 1.5 gravities for ten minutes. That put us 2,700 kilometers below Midway, and falling toward Earth with a speed of around nine kilometers per second.

Okay…so when the explosion went off, we'd been 33,086 kilometers above sea level…and that meant we were sixty-one minutes from impact.

Maybe we wouldn't have time for that work pod. I called the Space Elevator Authority command deck, up at Midway, tagging the call Urgent-one, and adding SOS to the subject line. A moment later, a woman's face appeared on my display. The ID line beneath her face read "K. Garcia."

"What do you want?" she snapped. "We have an emergency here and—" Then she realized who she was talking to. "*¡Gracias a Dios!*" she exclaimed. "We've been trying to reach someone in your pod! Are all of you all right?"

"I don't know about the other two decks," I told her. "Everyone on Deck Two is fine."

"We're still checking the cause of the failure," she said.

"It was a bomb," I told her. "Probably pretty small. Hull integrity and pressure are okay, at least so far. But it seems to have knocked us off the track."

She nodded. "Exactly. We're tracking you in free fall east of the tower."

"Are you going to be able to get a work pod down to catch us?" I asked. "I'm figuring something like fifty, fifty-five minutes before we hit the atmosphere."

"We're looking," she told us. "We have no manned craft available, however. And our projections…" She stopped, then shook her head. "Let's just say that an intercept and capture maneuver is very delicate, and we don't have anyone we can get down there fast enough."

Right. We were only a couple of thousand kilometers below

Midway…but with each passing second we were nine klicks farther down and two further to the east. If it took them, say, half an hour to get a ship ready, there wouldn't be time to catch us before we hit the atmosphere.

"You *do* have someone," I told her.

"Who?"

"Me."

"And who are you, sir?"

"Captain Harrison, NAPD. I flew Strikers during the War."

I could tell from her expression that she was checking up on me on a different screen…and possibly checking the stats for a Striker, a space superiority/strike fighter. "Oh…*oh!* I see, sir. But…but you're inside the passenger pod."

"If you can express me a work pod with enough delta-V," I told her, "and send me the access codes, I could teleoperate from here."

The conversation descended into vector technicalities. There was no way I was going to get enough delta-V down from Midway to actually capture the beanpod and shove it back into orbit, but we just might find a work-around.

"Delta-V" is the physics term for a change in velocity, and it's used as an expression of available muscle power in a rocket, relating available reaction mass to the mass of what needs to be moved. A beanpod has a total mass of about 140 tons. A capturing spacecraft would have to slow that mass to zero, then accelerate it against Earth's gravity either up to orbital velocity or back to Midway. That sort of thing takes a hell of a lot of fuel.

A far more realistic plan was simply to slow the falling pod enough so that it would survive re-entry—say, to below a half kilometer per second or so. We still needed to work through the details, but it should be possible to decelerate the falling beanpod *if* we could get a work pod down here with enough fuel to carry out the maneuver.

What we needed was a work tug with a total reserve delta-V

of eight or ten kps, and fifteen would be better. Available work pods and tugs near the Midway platform included WT-20 Rangers and WT(L)-44 Steeplejacks; the WT(L)-44s were typically configured for total delta-Vs of 25 kps. So far, so good.

Unfortunately, if a Steeplejack started off from Midway with full tanks, she would expend half of her reaction mass just catching up with the falling beanpod, and use much of the rest effecting a rendezvous and capture. There wouldn't be enough fuel left to decelerate the pod, much less drag us back up to Midway.

As I discussed this with Ms. Garcia, she suddenly looked away, spoke with someone off-camera, then interrupted me.

"I'm very sorry, Captain Harrison. One of the techs here just pointed out…"

"What?"

"Sir, we're showing another failure in your pod. The telemetry shows that your parachute release panel is inoperative."

I sagged inside.

Even if we were able to survive re-entry, we would not survive the impact at the end of the trip. The beanpod had no engines—not even maneuvering thrusters—and the emergency airfoil parachute was the pod's only chance for carrying out a soft landing.

"What kind of failure are you showing?" I asked.

"Just 'panel inoperative,'" Garcia told me. "It may be an electrical fault."

Yeah, or someone popped an access panel and snipped a wire, I thought. Whoever had planted the bomb would have known that beanpods carried a chute just in case of a rail failure. They'd wanted to make sure we didn't reach the Earth's surface alive.

One of the elderly women seated on the other side of the compartment was watching my face. "We're not really in orbit, are we?" she said.

"No, ma'am. We're not. We're falling. We have…" I checked the time. "About fifty-one minutes before impact."

And less than that to live if we hit the atmosphere at nine kilometers per second. I wasn't sure what the heat resistance of the beanpod's outer shell was, but 9 kps was more than fast enough to turn us into a particularly brilliant shooting star, streaking down through the sky east of the Beanstalk. By an extraordinarily unlikely coincidence of mathematics and physics, a convenient rule of thumb states that the peak temperature in degrees Kelvin of the shock layer around a body entering the atmosphere is equal to the body's velocity in meters per second. Nine kps translated to a reentry temperature of 9,000 degrees.

We would cook long before what was left of us slammed into the ground.

I turned back to Garcia's anxious face. "Look, if we can get a pod down here," I told her, "we can fix the damn parachute. What's the beanpod status up there?"

She looked confused. "We have four down-Stalk beanpods in-dock," she said, "but when the…when the emergency took place, we put a hold on all descents."

"So you have an empty beanpod available? Good! Here's what we're going to do."

Velocity is velocity, whether it comes from a rocket expending fuel, or a beanpod accelerated by diamagnetic impellers down a Beanstalk travel rail.

Take a work tug. According to Garcia, they had one with nearly full tanks that could be deployed immediately—a WT-20 Ranger with extendible remote arms and auxiliary RM tanks. Maneuver it next to an empty beanpod waiting on the guide rail beneath Midway Station and have it latch on to the recessed grappling holds on the beanpod's hull.

And then accelerate the beanpod down-Stalk at 1.5 gravities, dragging the tug along for the ride.

Ten minutes later, the tug would let go, traveling, now, at

nine kilometers per second. Hold the acceleration a bit longer, and the tug would be traveling faster, be able to catch up with us and overtake us. It would have to use some of its fuel to match our two kps lateral velocity, and to carry out the actual rendezvous…but most of its fuel supply would be available for deceleration.

It would be damned hairy, but it just might work.

"We're running the calculations now," Garcia told me.

I'd already done so, as we talked. Assuming no mistakes, no misses in the rendezvous or problems in target acquisition, no telemetry drop-out, no problems at all out of the thousands of things that could go wrong…

We might be able to slow the falling pod to somewhere around one or two kilometers per second.

Which still gave us a good chance of being cooked on the way down. But it was the best option we had out of *very* few choices.

"Okay, Captain Harrison," Garcia told me. "We're maneuvering the tug now. It should be on its way to you soon."

So now there was nothing to do but wait.

"What…can we do?" one of the businessmen asked. At least the other passengers were calm, though wolf-boy looked like he was going to hyperventilate.

"You can take your PAD," I told him, "and try to make contact with the other two decks on our pod. Call SEA to get a passenger e-ID list, okay?" He nodded. "SEA Control has been trying to reach people on-board the pod. They probably didn't get through on the other decks, though, because of panic. I want you to try to reach someone, anyone, on both decks, and keep trying until you do. We need to let them know we're working on the problem, and that they need to stay calm and quiet, right?"

I'd seen what panic could do to a few people trapped in a tight space. I didn't like thinking about what might be happening on the decks above or below this one.

The man nodded. I looked at the other three businessman. "You," I said. "Use your PAD and help him. Keep trying until you get the message across."

"What about us?" one of the construction workers asked.

I looked him up and down. He was a big, beefy man, with powerful hands. My first impression was to tag him as better in the brawn department than in brains.

"What's your name?"

"Mike," he told me. "Big Mike Morales."

"Okay, Mike. You and your friend are now Deck Two Security. I want you to keep an eye on everyone else. They are to stay strapped in *at all times*. I don't want anyone bouncing around the cabin, understand?"

The beanpod was tumbling very slowly. Any spin would be giving us some artificial gravity…but we were smack at the center of the cigar-shaped pod so we weren't feeling it much. To all intents and purposes, we were in zero gravity.

"Yes, sir."

"Anybody gets out of his seat, if anybody even looks like they're going to panic, you can use any amount of force you feel is justified. Got it?"

"I understand, boss," Morales said, and he grinned. The other passengers showed varying degrees of alarm, but there was no shouting or screaming.

"How long do we have?" the kid with the snakeskin face asked.

I glanced at my time display. "Forty-two minutes," I told her. "*Plenty* of time."

But that was a lie. If this worked at all, it was going to be damnably close.

I looked at Jones. He was still breathing a little hard, and his eyes were unfocused, but he was being quiet, at least. He saw me looking at him, and wiggled a bit in his seat. "You think you could get this thing off my hands?" he asked.

I considered the question, then shrugged. “Sure. But if you give me any trouble, Big Mike over there is going to put you to sleep, and he won’t be gentle about it. On my orders.”

Jones agreed, and I used my pen-blade to slice through the zip-strip. He thanked me and rubbed his wrists. And I made sure my PAD was recording.

“So…while we’re waiting,” I said in a light and conversational tone, “you care to tell me anything?”

“I don’t know what you mean.”

“Bullshit. You knew there was a bomb on-board this beanpod. You were watching me up at Midway to make sure I went on-board. Who were you reporting to?”

He shook his head, but his eyes were looking desperate.

“You planted a bug on me when we first met, while we were headed up-Stalk last week. That means you knew who I was, and you knew—or guessed—that I was working on the Dow case. You followed me onto the beanpod, and managed to disappear once we reached Midway.”

Still no response, but his breathing was faster, and I saw perspiration beading on his upper lip. A droplet came loose and slowly, slowly settled toward the deck.

“That bug guided an assassination team to me when I was out on the lunar surface. You probably already knew that Mark Henry was out there…but when you knew I’d tracked him down and that I was going out to bring him in, you decided to kill both of us.”

“It wasn’t me! I didn’t try to kill anybody!”

“Then who was it? Who’s pulling your strings?”

No answer.

“Okay, let’s talk about you. You’re not a clone.”

This time he shook his head, surprise written on his face. “No…but I don’t know how *the hell* you figured that out. They told me no one would be able to tell the difference!”

“Oh, it was a good G-mod. I’ve met some Jones-model

clones, and you're close enough to be their twin. That was the idea, wasn't it?"

"Yeah."

"What's your name? Your *real* name?"

"Federico Cavallo."

"Federico. Good. Go back a few nights, Federico, to the twenty-third. You were with Coleman and Hodgkins that night, weren't you? I'm thinking Coleman was the killer. She pretended to be room service, or some such...and when the door opened she went in with her monoknife. Hodgkins followed, with that mining laser. But you were there, too."

"No! I wasn't!"

But I saw the flare of his nostrils, the quick, slight, sharp dilation of his pupils. And that told me I was on the right track.

"That night didn't go down the way it was supposed to, did it?" I continued. "Mark Henry was supposed to take that laser, break into the room, and kill Dow...and maybe carve up Eve as well. A crime of passion, right?

"But Henry balked and ran. The poor guy was terrified, and his clone conditioning had him by his throat. So Coleman decided to modify the plan. She would use the monoknife, because the laser might not kill Dow immediately. Aiming the thing is tricky, and it takes time for a laser, even a 100-kilowatt tunneler, to burn through muscle and bone. So she sliced, and Hodgkins followed up with the laser to make it look good. But there was still a problem. Eve."

This time, he gave the smallest of nods.

Very often, if you can hammer a suspect with everything you know and everything you *think* you know, even when you can't prove it, the sheer weight of the material will lower a suspect's defenses, and he'll start confirming parts of the story...and even adding some bits that you might not have known.

"Someone," I continued, boring in relentlessly, "had to take her out. She wasn't in on your little conspiracy, was she? So you went in behind Coleman with a taser. You shot her, right here..." I tapped my solar plexus, right at the bottom of my rib-cage. "You shot her and 40,000 volts knocked her out of action, at least for a little while, and incidentally scrambled her short-term memory. You *thought* she wouldn't be able to remember who came in and killed Dow. I guess you didn't know just how tough a bioroid is."

That last bit was a calculated gamble on my part, but a pretty good one, I thought, for a spur-of-the-moment ploy. He wouldn't know for sure what Eve remembered, or whether the taser had even had the desired effect. A roboticist might have been able to predict the exact effect of 40,000 volts on a bioroid with fair accuracy, but this guy wasn't a roboticist. By hinting that the taser shot had failed to affect her memory, that the bioroid had remembered everything, I put more doubt in his mind... and convinced him that I knew the whole story.

"No," he said slowly. "No, she wasn't supposed to remember anything."

"There were three of you in that room, weren't there?"

"Yes."

"You shot Eve. Coleman used her monoknife on Dow. And Hodgkins used the laser to make it look like the deed had been done by a mad clone with a mining laser."

He mumbled something.

"What was that?"

"Yes," he said, loud enough to hear.

Loud enough for my PAD to record him. And I was willing to bet that Lily had recorded it, too.

"So...do you want to tell me who put this little bit of theater together?" I asked. "Or shall I tell you?"

He looked at me sharply, then, eyebrows questioning. "It...it was Coleman. She was the one running it all."

"C'mon," I said, sneering. "Do I *look* stupid? Coleman hates androids, yeah, but something on this scale is *way* beyond her reach. I think she might have come up with the idea in the first place, maybe when she learned her boyfriend Dow had dumped her for a 'roid. I think she took that idea to her boss, Thomas Vaughn. Or…was it someone even higher? Someone on the board of Humanity Labor? Like Geraldo Martín?"

His pupils dilated again. I was zeroing in on-target.

"There had to be a pretty damned big organization behind her to put this thing together. Micro-tracking devices. Skyhoppers at the Sinus Medii. Some pretty sophisticated intersec software cracking, along with some slick efforts to compromise security at a number of levels. Who'd you have doing your programming? Noise Reilly?"

I actually had other ideas about that, but I was trying to prime the pump, trying to get him to start naming names.

"No," he said. He slumped in his seat, almost trying to take on a zero-G fetal curl.

"Who pulled the strings, Federico?" I asked him.

"You've already got it all figured out," he said sharply. "You don't need me…"

"Apparently Martín and Vaughn don't need you either, Federico," I said. "They must know you were arrested and brought on-board this pod. I didn't notice any last-minute attempts to stop departure, did you?"

"We're all…expendable," he said.

"All but the very top. Coleman, Hodgkins, you…you're all expendable. What about Vaughn? What about Martín?"

"Look, you don't understand! They'll kill me if I talk!"

I moved closer, lowering my voice so the others wouldn't hear. "Seems to me, Federico, that you're already going to die. If we do get out of this mess your friends have put us in, I'll arrange for protection…but right now the *only* thing you have going for you is my sweet, loving, and understanding nature. Cross me and I throw you to the wolves…and I *don't* mean Fuzzy-face over there on the other side of the pod. Help me and

I'll help you...unless, of course, we slam into Amazonas and none of it matters after all."

"Okay! Okay! There were others, up above Ms. Coleman. I think one of them was Coleman's boss, the Humanity Labor PR Director."

"That's Vaughn. What about Martín?"

"I don't know. I don't know! Maybe—I just heard some bigwig in Humanity Labor, no names. It was the *government*, see?"

My blood ran just a bit colder. "What do you mean?"

"Vaughn and someone on the Humanity Labor board were gonna get cabinet posts once the Feds took over the Beanstalk. And all of us stood to make a lot when that deal goes through. But *that's all I know!*"

But it was enough.

I turned my gaze to the projected outside view, still there, still impossibly beautiful. As the pod slowly rotated end-over-end, Earth seemed to swing around us, vast and huge and glorious. There was something else out there, too, something tiny and glittering in the sun. At first, I wondered if it was the approaching tug, but it was still too early for that. After a while, I finally figured out that it was a horseshoe-shaped bit of metal, gleaming as it tumbled in the light—probably a piece of our railguide that had snapped off in the explosion and was following us down.

Over the past ten minutes, we'd fallen another 5,400 kilometers. I checked the time, and noted that we'd been falling for a total of twenty-three minutes, and were now at an altitude of less than 24,000 kilometers...a third of the way to impact. There was still no evidence of our movement other than that slow tumble, but Earth had definitely grown over the past twenty minutes, swelling to fill almost thirty degrees of black sky.

I looked for the Beanstalk, but couldn't spot it. By now, of course, our lateral velocity had carried us something like fifty kilometers from the Stalk. If I knew just where to look, I might be able to spot its acquisition lights or safety strobes.

Amazing that the largest and greatest of humankind's engineering achievements would be invisible only fifty kilometers away.

My PAD chirped at me.

"Harrison."

"It's Katrine Garcia, Captain. I just wanted to tell you that the tug's release went as scheduled. The tug is approaching your current position now, with a relative velocity of two kilometers per second, at a range of thirty-five kilometers. You should be able to see it in less than a minute."

"Right! Thanks, Katrine." I turned to Lily. "Let me use your PAD."

"*My* PAD!" She had it open in front of her. "Why?"

"Because you have the high-end model, babe, not this cheap PD-issue toy," I told her. "And I need to reconfigure it to fly a spaceship."

We had thirty-six minutes to impact.

Chapter Twenty

Day 9

I started off by configuring the input holography to something resembling a simplified Striker cockpit, moving my hands to extend the virtual screen to its widest extent, then laying out the keyboard as I wanted it. Yaw, pitch, roll, thrust—I couldn't make an exact copy of a Striker S/A-94 control panel, but there was no need for perfect fidelity. I did want each joystick to be where I could reach for it instinctively, though.

Flying a spacecraft is absolutely nothing like flying an airfoil. You can't bank, you can't stall, you can't use a rudder to turn, and you can't use the lift generated by your wings because there's no air around you to work with. Every meter per second in one direction must be exactly countered if you want to stop, and the ghost of Sir Isaac Newton is looking over your shoulder with each maneuver.

Lily's PAD was a nice model with lots of bells and whistles that I would never use normally, but the enhanced holographics were really nice, and they would stand me in good stead in a few minutes. She offered me a feedback handfilm, and I accepted. Squirt a few drops on your hands, and it spreads out and solidifies, creating a layer over your skin just a few molecules thick. Nano-processors in the mix pick up signals from the PAD, and trigger nerve endings in your skin to create an illusion of pressure when you move a virtual joystick, or press a holographic button.

Sweet.

Katrine Garcia gave me the necessary access codes, and I began typing, identifying myself and logging on to the controller running the approaching spacecraft. Normally, the tug would have been run from the SEA control center up on Midway, but we were far enough away now that teleoperating from a distance was going to be a problem. There would be a time delay of almost a tenth of a second round-trip between Midway and the tug. That's not much, especially with human reflexes as slow as they are, but the tiny increments add up. Besides, they would be watching through a single, fairly narrow-field camera. I'd have that camera, too, but I'd also be able to see the approach and docking through the beanpod's interior display.

And every little bit helped.

On the holographic screen hanging in the air in front of me, I could see the view through the tug's nose camera, and could see the bronze cigar-shape of the beanpod now seven kilometers away and swiftly growing larger. Glancing up from the display, I saw the tug directly, a pinpoint of light growing brighter.

Nudging the attitude controls, I fired bursts of hydrazine to flip the tug end-for-end, then engaged the main engine. I gave it full throttle-up, killing my Earthward velocity kps by kps.

Moments later, the tug streaked toward the pod, tail-first and balanced on an invisible stream of hot plasma. Passengers started cheering, but then it flashed past, a hundred meters distant, and vanished again against the face of the growing Earth.

"Don't worry, people," I called to them. "It'll be back. I just need to match vectors."

And that was the tricky—and time-consuming—part. For

fifteen minutes, I jockeyed that WT-20, killing its Earthward velocity, matching our lateral vector, and slowly, *slowly* creeping up on the tumbling bronze cigar. And all the while my fuel reserves dwindled.

After a while, I became aware of Lily sitting beside me, mumbling. I glanced over and saw her watching me through that silver orb stuck to her left eye. "What are you doing?" I asked, mildly annoyed.

"Filming you conducting the rescue of the century," she said.

"Why don't you wait and see if we survive to watch it?"

"Give a girl a break, huh? You stole my computer. So I'm going to record you being a hero."

"I'd rather you didn't."

"Nonsense. This is the story of a lifetime for me, you realize that? I get you capturing a terrorist, then saving our tails."

"If this doesn't go well," I replied, fighting with the virtual controls in front of me, "you can film the ground rushing up to meet us…*splat*." I glanced up at the Earth, now overhead again. "Your own documentary: 'Bug on a Big, Blue Windshield.'"

She put a hand on my shoulder. "You're doing fine."

How did *she* know? I shrugged her hand away. "Sorry. But I need to concentrate on this…"

What I was trying to do was bilocate, and it wasn't easy.

Your brain doesn't care whether visual input is traveling the eight inches or so from the eyeball to the visual cortex at the back side of your brain, or coming in by radio across a million kilometers. If the interface is good enough, you can kind of lose yourself in the action, feel like you're not inside a tumbling beanpod with eleven other scared people, but actually inside that rugged little tug out there, maneuvering in for rendezvous and grapple.

Every good fighter pilot knows what it's like to *become* his ship, and that's what I was trying to accomplish. My mind, transfixed by the sharp image on the screen hovering in front of my face, was inside the Ranger; my body, though, could still feel the tumble of the beanpod playing hob with my inner ears, could feel the blast and sweep of hard white sunlight sweeping from one side of the pod to the other, alternating with a flood of softer, blue light each time Earth drifted past.

And, somehow, I was aware of all of those eyes on me as I fought the tug in.

The remote-piloted tug was fifteen meters long—a spherical working end with four long, cylindrical fuel tanks, and a rocket nozzle astern. Four robotic arms were neatly folded behind the head, and a single, cyclopean eye peered from the blunt prow. Once, the ugly little craft had been painted a pristine white, but God only knows how many years of bumping around outside of Midway and the other geosynch structures had left the paint faded, scratched, pitted, and sandblasted, with patches of rough, grey metal showing through.

A lot of the more modern tugs and work pods are nuclear powered, with small gas-core fission plants heating reaction mass to produce thrust. This one, fortunately, used exotic fuel—metastable N-He64, usually called "meta." Helium atoms excited into a metastable quantum state by lasers were packaged with nitrogen atoms in a metallic matrix within insulated high-pressure tanks. Heating causes the helium to revert to its normal state, releasing the tremendous energy used in packing the stuff.

A rocket's efficiency is measured by specific impulse, or Isp, a figure, in seconds, that can be described as impulse—thrust multiplied by time—per unit of propellant mass expended. The liquid hydrogen-oxygen rocket engines of the early space age had an Isp of around 460 seconds.

Meta, on the other hand, has an Isp approaching 3200 seconds, making it far more efficient than conventional fuels—as efficient, in fact, as gas-core nuclear engines—and bringing with it the added advantage of not scattering the highly radioactive debris from a fission reactor across eastern New Angeles if this didn't work.

I would have to watch my fuel tank integrity closely. If the insides of those insulated tanks got too hot during reentry, the entire remaining fuel load could revert in a rather spectacular fashion, and our dust would be sifting down out of the stratosphere for years to come.

Right now, though, the beanpod, gleaming in the sunlight as it toppled slowly end over end, seemed to hang just in front of me, moving slowly closer.

"SEA Control," I said. "Check me. I read range: fifty-five meters, closing at four meters per second."

"We confirm that, Beanpod...now forty-seven meters, closing at four mps."

I triggered another burst from the forward maneuvering thrusters. "Forty meters, three mps. Thirty-five...thirty."

This next bit was the really tricky part. The beanpod wasn't tumbling fast—it looked like about one complete rotation every forty seconds—but it represented a lot of mass. If I was going to have a chance of pulling this stunt off, I needed to stop the tumble.

And that would take time, precious time that I did not have.

If I wasn't careful on approach, one end of that falling, 140-ton monster would swing up, over, and down, smacking the tug like a fly. I was approaching from about thirty degrees off the spin axis so I should be able to avoid that problem; when I got very close, though, I would have to latch on to the pod without getting thrown clear and without hitting so hard that I made things worse...*much* worse.

Another maneuvering burst. Two meters per second. Getting close, now...

Someone screamed. I glanced up, and saw the tug against the disk of the Earth, just meters away, its arms outspread like some titanic, spindle-legged spider. It drifted with our spin, so I focused again on the holographic display screen in front of me. Almost there…

"Beanpod," Garcia's voice said. "You're looking good. Range ten meters…eight…six…"

Fire thrusters!

"Four meters…three…two meters…"

Two of the outstretched work arms hit the side of the pod, scraping along the surface as I continued drifting in. "Contact!" I called.

I began wishing I had four hands—no, six—as I reached for the recessed grapple-holds to either side of that otherwise smooth and gently curving surface, deployed the remaining two arms, and fired the thrusters again to bring my relative velocity down to zero. The momentum of the rotating beanpod slewed me sharply sideways, but I managed to snag one grapple and lock it.

I fired maneuvering thrusters, adjusting pitch and yaw…then snagged a second hand-hold.

I felt the shudder through my seat. On my display, the pod's tumble appeared to have stopped, but that was an illusion. Stars, Earth, and sun all were drifting past behind the beanpod, now, as the tug and pod tumbled together. The rate of spin was a bit slower, though—about one rotation per fifty seconds, I guessed. I extended the remaining two arms to snag two more grapple-holds and locked them down.

"SEA Control, I have a solid dock."

Several members of my personal audience cheered, but I ignored them. Now I had to stop the tumble.

That was another worry. My maneuvering thrusters, located in a ring around my center of mass and encircling the fuel tanks so that they faced all directions, didn't use meta. Instead, they used the monopropellant hydrazine. Hydrazine is less efficient as a rocket fuel than meta, but it's easier and safer for maneuvers that require a delicate touch.

Watching my attitude indicators, I put my hands over the thruster controls and waited…waited…then fired, holding the jets open as the rate of spin slowed…slowed…slowed…

…and *release.*

I glanced up. The tug's shadowed belly was pressed against the pod's hull, all four arms wide-stretched to hold it in an obscenely intimate embrace.

And Earth was visible almost directly on the deck below us.

"SEA Control, I'm reading an arrest of RVC. Can you confirm?" Their radar was a lot more accurate than my eyes.

"Beanpod, we read you with a rotational velocity component of less than point four degrees per second."

Four-tenths of a degree per second? That was one complete rotation every fifteen minutes. Not bad for seat-of-your pants… and certainly good enough for now.

What was the time? Fourteen minutes to impact. Seventy-five hundred kilometers left to fall.

"Copy, SEA Control. Test firing main thrusters, two second duration, in three…two…one…fire."

The main engine fired, metastable helium releasing from its high-energy imprisonment and blasting silently into the void. I felt the pod jolt…and then I bit off a short curse as the stars and Earth began wheeling once again. *Damn!*

"*Cease firing! Cease firing!*" Garcia screamed at me.

So far as I knew, this sort of thing had never been attempted before, strapping an engine to a free-falling beanpod and trying to decelerate it. I'd hoped that the pod was massive enough that planting the rocket motor off-center like that wouldn't destabilize it…but the powerful meta-fueled engine's shove against us was off-center, putting us back into a spin, one going in the *other* direction, now. At least the spin seemed to have only a single component. A complex spin would have been *much* harder to straighten out.

Again, I jockeyed the maneuvering thrusters, slowing, then eliminating the spin. I would have to reposition myself at the bottom end of the cigar—kind of like balancing a tall stack of plates on my head.

But first, while I was up here near the center of the beanpod, I would have to do something about the parachute.

With the rotation arrested, I released my mechanical death grip on the pod, then maneuvered around to the other side. According to the beanpod schematics I'd been looking at earlier, the parachute compartment was located amidships, just about where the restroom and drink service compartment was located. There was a meter-thick swelling there, with some nasty scarring on the outer surface.

It was at this point that each beanpod had its diamagnetic railguide mounted, embracing the superconducting elevator rail that ran up the Beanstalk. The bomb, obviously, had been attached at this point, blowing the railguide apart and knocking the pod clear of the Beanstalk. The parachute access hatch was located below the railguide mount, and only a brief inspection was necessary to show me that it was welded shut.

I suppose the weld could have been accidental—caused by the force of the explosion, but somehow I doubted that. I remembered looking at the pod through the transplas back at the midway concourse, and seeing the reflected blue flicker of a spot welder.

Who had gotten into SEA Control and hijacked a work pod? It was even possible that Coleman or Cavallo or someone else had done it through a PAD in the Midway concourse. All they would have needed was the access code and an off-duty pod with a welding arm mounted on it.

Ten minutes left to impact. Call it six thousand kilometers left to fall.

Our speed had been increasing over the past hour as Earth's gravity relentlessly accelerated us. We would max out at 11 kps—escape velocity—and the extra speed was carving away at our remaining time.

Bringing up one of the tug's arms, I extended a heating element and began working at the weld. It was a single spot, a rushed job, and I soon had the metal hot enough that I could pry the edge of the panel up. The locking mechanism appeared undamaged, at least, and after a few more anxious moments, the panel release appeared to be working.

"We confirm your parachute panel is operational," Garcia told me.

Good. Because I was running out of time. Seven minutes. Forty-two hundred kilometers at 10 kps.

With short, controlled bursts from my hydrazine thrusters, I drifted down to the back end of the beanpod, flipped, and reached out with all four arms. Garcia had pointed out four grapple-holds down there, evenly spaced around the hull. I grabbed hold, positioned the camera view directly on the beanpod's pointed end, and pulled.

My vid flickered, then went out as the end of the beanpod crushed my camera eye. The housing, though, would serve as a centering mount. Snugged in as tight as the mechanism could manage, I locked all four arms in place, took a deep breath, and said, "Right, everybody! Acceleration in three…two…one… go!"

I fired the main thrusters.

On-board the beanpod, we all felt the shudder as the meta-rocket's thrust took hold, followed by the abrupt, crushing sensation of weight…*lots* of weight.

In fact, it was just half-a-G for the test, but it felt like a lot more after almost an hour of free fall.

"SEA Control!" I called. "We have main engine burn! It feels like we're balanced okay!"

"Copy, Beanpod. We confirm your burn. Good luck!"

I glanced at a time read-out. Just six minutes until impact…3600 kilometers left to go. Over the past half hour, the globe of the Earth had been growing more and more rapidly, until now it filled almost half the sky. Quickly, I reconfigured the now-blank display to give me a schematic showing our falling pod and Earth's curving surface below. Alphanumerics gave me a constant check on our speed, G-force, remaining fuel in both kilograms and available delta-V, and the time to impact, all of the figures updating from second to second.

Gently, I throttled up, and the sensation of weight increased. One gravity.

Still okay…

And it increased some more. One point five gravities.

There was no sound—just the vibration transmitted through the hull from the tug beneath us.

And our speed decreased, slowing now by fifteen meters per second per second.

I throttled up yet again. *Two* gravities, twenty meters per second squared.

I glanced across the compartment at the other passengers. I was worried especially about the two older women. They'd been living on the Moon for some time, and their bones would be brittle. How much deceleration could they stand, and for how long?

And how did I balance their safety with the lives of everyone on-board the falling beanpod? With Lily's life…

Both of the elderly women were sagged back in the embrace of their seats. One of them, though, caught me looking at her. Somehow—I will never know how—she lifted her right arm, grimacing with the effort, and managed to shape her hand into a clawed but recognizable thumbs up.

I flashed the same gesture back, then returned my full attention to my screen.

At two gravities, I'd reached the limit of the Ranger tug's available thrust. There was a distinct, ongoing shudder now being transmitted through the deck.

Balanced atop a plume of hot helium-nitrogen plasma, we continued our descent.

Five minutes fifty seconds to impact.

Our fuel load was fast dwindling. That actually was helping us. Less fuel meant less mass, which meant better thrust efficiency. The question was whether it would help *enough.* I'd used up a lot of time fumbling with the rendezvous, and then, later, with the flubbed rocket test.

Eight kilometers per second.

Seven point five...

Seven...

Six...

I could feel the shudder through my seat increasing. That was probably the thrust of the rocket acting against our dwindling mass, and the subsequent increase in G-force. We were pushing 2.2Gs, now. I glanced again at the older women, then at the kids. No movement, no way to tell if they were okay...and nothing much I could do about it in any case. I throttled back slightly, dropping back to two gravities, juggling *way* too many factors in my head as I nudged the virtual controls this way and that.

Past the one thousand kilometer line, still falling at five kps. The revised time-to-impact was now three and a half minutes.

Five hundred kilometers and four kps. Two minutes.

Three hundred kilometers and three kps. One minute thirty.

Two hundred kilometers and two kps. Still one minute thirty...

One hundred twenty kilometers...and suddenly the shudder was much worse. We were beginning to plow through substantially thicker atmosphere now, thick enough that an ionization trail was forming above us.

Earth's atmosphere doesn't simply stop at some arbitrary point above the surface. It grows thinner and thinner with increasing altitude, but even 10,000 kilometers up there are still traces of gas present—a few handfuls of molecules per cubic centimeter, say.

Now we were punching straight down through the thermosphere, the upper reaches of Earth's atmosphere. This was the realm of LEO—Low Earth Orbit. For all intents and purposes it was still vacuum—satellites and space stations could orbit here for years before friction brought them down.

We would be through it and into the mesosphere in seconds.

We were approaching the Kármán line—the most official, if somewhat arbitrary, line marking the beginning of space—one hundred kilometers up.

The shuddering increased with the G-force. The atmosphere was thick enough now to add to our deceleration.

And that meant increasing heat.

This was where things got *really* dicey. We were down to dregs of fuel remaining in the tug—about five hundred kilos, half a ton. The tank insulation would keep the remaining meta inert for a while, but at some point very soon the insulation would fail, the insides of the tank would start to heat up, and then all of the remaining meta would blow. I had to juggle the numbers now to find the best balance: how much more thrust could I get from the engines, with what safety factor, before I had to jettison the remaining fuel?

One hundred kilometers. Point nine kps…and one minute forty-eight to impact.

Yes! I'd read that right! As we continued to slow, the time-to-impact readout was going *up*.

But were we slowing *enough*?

And how much longer could I keep the rocket engines going, because once I jettisoned the tanks, we would be in free fall once more, with the ground still a *long* way down.

Over the past several seconds, the sky visible through the pod's wall and deck displays had begun growing pink and hazy. When I glanced up now, they showed a solid wall of pink and orange light rapidly growing brighter as we reentered the atmosphere.

Someone yelled, shrill above the thundering roar of atmosphere across the hull. It was getting hotter…hotter…*hotter*, until I was convinced the outer hull was beginning to boil away. One panel of the internal display flickered, then went blank… followed by another. The external cameras that had been feeding us our panoramic view were beginning to fail.

External meta tank temperatures were reading nine hundred degrees or a bit higher. Internal tank temperature…*frag!* Almost eight degrees Kelvin.

Time to get rid of those ticking bombs.

I killed the thrust, and the crushing sensation of weight died away…though not entirely because the atmosphere was clawing at us, still slowing us, as well.

The meta tanks started to separate from the tug's framework, then were snatched away by the fiery rush of atmosphere, flashing to the side and up…and then we all felt the heavy *thud* as one of the tanks blew, knocking us to one side.

Another thud was transmitted through the shock wave, but more distant, muffled. Then we felt a savage, wrenching jolt and one of the businessmen screamed, clawing at his seatbelt.

"You stay put, fella!" Big Mike yelled.

I didn't pay them any attention, though, because now I was trying to use the tug's remaining reserves of hydrazine to add just a bit more deceleration. With a final, shrieking, shuddering, banging crash, the remnants of the Ranger tug tore free in a blazing rush of fragments and debris, and we saw huge, half-molten chunks flashing up past the remaining displays on the bulkheads.

We were in free fall now. My telemetry was gone. No more tug meant no more sensors giving me vector data, and the ionization outside was interfering with my radio link up to Midway. I no longer had any idea how fast we were falling…or how much time remained until impact.

Only two wall panels remained alive…and, miraculously, the view appeared to be clearing. The sky outside was a deep, intense and utterly brilliant and beautiful deep blue, and I could see clouds against the curve of Earth's horizon.

We began to tumble.

The rotation was slow and stately, but the Earth's horizon was swinging up and around with disconcerting finality.

Someone was praying out loud.

It was Cavallo.

The parachute *should* deploy automatically, if the panel was, indeed, functioning again. It was designed to fire at a programmed altitude in case a malfunction resulted in the beanpod falling off the elevator.

But the mechanism depended on a radar altimeter mounted somewhere inside the lower end of the beanpod, and the pod itself wasn't designed for high-velocity reentry. Its designers had intended the parachute as a safety mechanism to be deployed if the pod was knocked off the Beanstalk within the first couple of hundred kilometers up, before it had acquired much velocity.

Everything now depended on the emergency chute, and at this point my experience counted for nothing. I had no controls, no telemetry with Midway, no readouts, and no thrusters.

I looked at Lily. She had her monocam focused on me, and was continuing to mumble a low-voiced monologue, even in our dire situation. *Such a strong woman...* I bit back on the sentimental and carefully switched off the holographics and handed her back her PAD. "Thanks," I said.

My voice cracked. The inside of the beanpod was still stiflingly hot.

"Did we make it?" she asked.

"We'll know in a—"

The chute compartment opened with a sharp bang, and the drogue parachute deployed, streaming out behind the falling pod and bringing our tumble to a halt. A moment later, the main chute emerged, unfolding into an enormous, two-layered triangular ram-airfoil, bright orange in color and just visible on one of the wall displays, the one overhead, right beside the restroom.

The interior swung dizzily back and forth for a moment, then steadied, as the passengers erupted into a cacophony of cheers and shouts and laughter. The kids and the business people were unbuckled and dancing up and down on the sloping deck and there was nothing Big Mike or his friend could do about it.

A moment later, we punched through a cloud deck, and I could see land and water below—land parceled out in the neat and ordered geometries of the agroplexes, water gleaming in sunlight in some places, shadowed by clouds in others.

We descended…

Chapter Twenty-One

Day 9

I wasn't sure where we were coming down, but I knew it was well to the east of Cayambe and the Root, and it was going to take time to get a rescue craft to our location, get us pried out of the beanpod, and get us back to New Angeles. I was worried we would miss the press conference, the one Vaughn had called for 1600 this afternoon and which I'd been wanting to attend.

As it happened, though, we didn't miss a thing. The press conference never happened.

At 1315 we came down in *Lago de Secumbíos*.

Once, the entire stretch of low, rolling land east of the Andes across northeastern Ecuador, southern Colombia, northern Peru, and western Brazil had been rain forest—the vast and once-verdant *Amazonia*. Most of the forest is long gone now, save for a few struggling and pathetic reserves in Brazil. For the better part of a century, the agroplexes have been here, attempting to refertilize the poor soil and force-grow crops and gene-tailored animals to feed New Angeles. With the trees gone, erosion became a serious matter, especially along the banks of the larger tributaries of the Amazon—the Napo, the Caquetá, the Pastaza, and others. Eventually, the tributaries had been dammed to keep them from carrying away all of what was left of the topsoil, and the result was a series of large freshwater lakes and, in Brazil, the small, inland Amazon Sea.

Lago de Secumbíos is a fair-sized lake—twice the size of Lake Erie—now occupying eastern Ecuador and northern Peru, extending along the old valley of the Napo as far as the port of Iquitos. Dangling almost upright beneath its bright orange para-sail, our beanpod sailed out of a mostly sunny sky and in for a perfect splashdown in the northwestern corner of the lake.

The Ecuadorian lake patrol hoverfoil *Calicuchima* reached us first, but a big tilt-jet hover-lifter out of New Angeles and an escort of fliers arrived moments later. By the time they cut us out—the heat of reentry had warped and partially melted the doors to all three decks—it was past 1600 and all of us were seasick.

But we were alive.

A winch had hauled the entire pod out of the water and set it on the forward deck. With the side cut open, I stepped out, blinking in the sunlight with the others.

Lily was right behind me, capturing everything on camera and giving a steady, running commentary as she did so. She truly seemed to be in her element.

I moved through the crowd on the forward deck of the *Calicuchima*—the beanpod passengers exhausted but celebrating, the medics attending to injuries, the Ecuadorian sailors passing out blankets and water. All of us were soaked with sweat after the descent, and as our clothing dried we were all feeling chilly. The blankets helped.

There'd been thirty-two people on-board the beanpod, and ten had been hurt. Ms. Quintana, one of the women on my deck, had suffered a fractured femur during the high-G part of the ride down, and a teenager on Deck One had suffered a mild concussion when he chose a bad time to leave his seat. Those were the worst; the rest were bruises, contusions, and heat exhaustion.

All things considered, it could have been a *lot* worse.

I checked in on Ms. Quintana, and got another solid thumbs up from her. "A nice landing, Captain," she told me. "I didn't know the NAPD flew spaceships, too."

"Not all of us do," I admitted. "To tell you the truth, I wasn't really expecting to have to use that skill again."

It had been thirteen years ago and 160 million kilometers away when I'd last piloted a Striker.

I remembered the thud as the fuel tanks had detonated, and realized now just how very close we'd come to dying up there.

Wolf-boy hugged me. So did snake-girl. Others hugged me, or shook my hand, or just congratulated me on getting them all down in one piece. I smiled and accepted the good wishes, but kept pushing through the crowd, searching.

I spotted Big Mike and his friend, blankets over their shoulders, water bottles in their hands.

"Hey, the hero of the hour!" Mike Morales called.

"We're not quite done yet," I told him. I looked at his friend. "What's your name?"

"Steve Matloff."

"Okay, Steve. You and Big Mike here are now officially duly deputized officers of the law. Raise your hands and say 'I do.'"

"I do," they both said in unison, looking confused but playing along.

"Good. Come with me."

I found Federico Cavallo a few meters away. He saw me bearing down on him and just nodded. "Don't worry," he told me. "I'm not going anywhere."

"Steve? You stay with this guy. Don't let him out of your sight. Mike? You're with me."

I kept searching, Big Mike following behind. They were here. I knew they were here, somewhere.

And I found them at last, at the edge of the crowd—two

soggy, sweat-drowned rats: Coleman and Hodgkins. Hodgkins had a bloody swath of bandaging around his upper left arm and shoulder, where I'd shot him that morning. His face was white and drawn. They'd discarded their disguises as Wiggins and Callahan somewhere along the line, probably back at Midway.

"Ms. Coleman, Mr. Hodgkins," I said, "you are both under arrest for murder, for attempted murder, and for conspiracy to commit murder."

I'd first suspected that they just might be on-board this beanpod when I realized they'd gone down-Stalk from Challenger to Midway ahead of me. I hadn't been certain, though, until the bomb had gone off.

Oh, sure, I could flatter myself that the higher-ups in the conspiracy had been trying to kill *me* with that bomb, but until I'd actually arrived at Midway that morning, they couldn't have been certain as to which beanpod I was going to take. They might have assumed I was going to try to make it to Vaughn's press conference, but the hour or so that Lily and I were in the Freefall restaurant really wasn't enough time to get hold of a suitable quantity of high explosives, assemble a bomb, hack into SEA Control to hijack a work pod, and attach the explosives to the beanpod.

No, that bomb hadn't been meant for yours truly, much as that idea might tickle my ego. It had been intended to kill Coleman and Hodgkins, to make sure we didn't take them into custody and learn who was heading up this little conspiracy. They'd already been on-board by the time Lily and I got there; Cavallo had been watching for *them*, not me—watching to make sure they didn't get off the pod again, to be certain they were there—because chances were good that there wouldn't have been enough genetic material left at the end of the descent for a positive identification.

Hodgkins put a glower on his face and started to rise, but I pulled my pistol from inside my jacket and let him see it. I knew he wasn't armed—he'd gotten through the backscatter scan at Midway, after all—and he knew that I knew.

He hesitated, then sagged back, looking broken.

But Coleman laughed. "You're overlooking something, *gilún*," she said. "You're out of your jurisdiction."

"You think?"

"I *know*. You're a New Angeles cop. But right now we're in Ecuador. I checked with one of the sailors."

She had a point, actually. The city limits embraced the mountain of Cayambe, the eastern-most bit of New Angeles, but we'd come down at least a hundred kilometers east of there.

We weren't in the United States now. We were in the sovereign country of Ecuador.

I glanced around. The *Calicuchima*'s skipper—one Miguel Alvarado—was standing with a group of rescued survivors nearby. "*Capitán* Alvarado!" I called. "*Un momento de su tiempo, por favor.*"

"You're Captain Harrison," he said, beaming and coming to my side. His English was excellent. "The hero of the hour—"

"Thank you. I need your help."

"Anything."

I gestured with my pistol. "These two," I said, indicating Coleman and Hodgkins, "are wanted in New Angeles for murder, attempted murder, conspiracy, and probably quite a few other crimes once we get this sorted out. I intend to arrest them both and take them back with me."

Alvarado's smile vanished. "That could pose...problems, *señor.* This is Ecuador, not *Angeles Nuevo*..."

"Ah. So we would need to call in diplomats, contact the American Embassy in Quito, that sort of thing."

"I'm afraid so."

"There is a principle in law enforcement, Captain, called hot pursuit. I was in pursuit of these two coming down the Beanstalk."

He looked uncertain. In fact, there are provisions for hot pursuit enshrined both in international law and, specifically, in the Quito Accord. The Ecuadorian capital of Quito, for example, is in effect a suburb of New Angeles, with the international boarder running along the Dr. Manuel Cordova Galarza Highway for many kilometers—and in places zig-zagging through the *barrios* and even cutting through individual houses. There've been plenty of times when a New Angeles cop chased a perp into Quito without bothering to check in at the nearest border crossing. It happens.

"I don't understand, *señor*," Captain Alvarado said, "how you could have been pursuing these people when all of you were inside the same beanpod?"

I nudged Coleman. "What deck were you on?"

"One," she sneered.

"You see?" Alvarado said with an expressive Latino shrug. "She was following *you* down."

"Not when we started out."

"I am *most* sorry, *señor*." He looked genuinely miserable. His command and his rank in the Ecuadorian Navy were on the line, however. A diplomatic crisis could destroy both in short order. "But…I'm afraid that we need to refer this matter to the diplomats."

Which meant delays and appeals and, quite likely, freedom for these two.

Slowly, I holstered my pistol. "Well…if that's the way you want to play it," I said.

"You see?" Coleman said, laughing at me. "You've got *nothing*!"

Reaching out, I scooped her bodily up off the deck.

She screamed, and pounded at my head and shoulders. "What are you doing! *¡Malparido! ¡Hijo de puta!* Let me go!"

"Mike?" I said. "Get the other one. Bring him along."

"No! No!" Hodgkins said, throwing up his hands. "I'll come

with you!"

I strode across the deck with the furious, squirming, and kicking Coleman over my shoulder. My leg was hurting a lot now, but I used the pain to fuel my anger, my sense of purpose, and my determination to see this through. I reached the beanpod lying on the deck near the ship's bow, its once-bronze surface now charred and streaked with black. Three neat, square holes a meter on each side showed in the burned surface, one for each of the three decks.

I reached the opening into Deck One and unceremoniously shoved her inside.

She squealed again, then hit somewhere inside with a thump. Hodgkins followed her inside a moment later, urged on by Big Mike Morales.

I turned, hands on my hips, blocking the opening. "Captain Alvarado…I'm certain you haven't tried to claim this pod as salvage, since there were people on-board when you recovered it. So I am now declaring that this beanpod is, as a distressed New Angeles spacecraft, technically still American property and, therefore, American soil. I would like you to witness for me that these two American citizens are, in fact, on American soil and, as such, are subject to my jurisdiction."

A slow smile spread across Alvarado's face. "I don't think," he said, "I could possibly argue with you there."

"*Gracias.*"

I suppose Alvarado could have argued the fact of the beanpod being a spacecraft when it had no engines to call its own… but all he was looking for was a reasonable and face-saving way to get out of the way of a potential diplomatic clash between the U.S. and Ecuador.

I stood outside the pod, gun in hand, as the *Calicuchima* made her way northwest across the lake toward the port of San Rafael. After a lengthy radio exchange with the tilt-jet overhead, the *Calicuchima* came to a halt while cables were lowered from the aircraft and fastened on to grapple-holds in the pod's sides.

Mike, Steve, Cavallo, and I all clambered through the opening and into the pod. We strapped our prisoners in—awkwardly, since the seats were on their sides, now.

Lily climbed on-board with us.

"Where do you think you're going?" I asked her.

"With you, of course. I don't think you realize what a big deal this is. I'm the only representative of the news media for a hundred kilometers, and I'm following this story through to the end!"

As Alvarado had said, I couldn't possibly argue. A PAD call to the tilt-jet above us, and we were hoisted smoothly clear of the *Calicuchima*'s forward deck.

Thirty minutes later, we crossed the border into New Angeles.

"*Damn you*, Harrison!" Coleman growled. "You know we're *still* going to walk! You don't have proof of anything. It's just your word against ours! And Humanity Labor has the best lawyers in New Angeles!"

"Maybe," I told her. "But I think you're missing the point."

"And what's that?"

"Vaughn tried to *kill* both of you. Whoever put that bomb on the pod was doing so at his orders…and it was meant to silence the two of you. But you managed to get away—which means your boss is going to keep after you. He definitely can't afford to let you live now."

Her eyes got very wide at that.

"I suggest that you tell us everything you know…about Vaughn, about Martín, everything." I switched on my PAD. "And you can start by giving me the names of *everyone* connected with this…"

We touched down at the NAPD's private airstrip an hour later, lowered gently from the sky.

And Coleman, Hodgkins, and Cavallo were all still singing loud and long.

An hour later I was in the Commissioner's office.

"Nice job, Harrison," she said. Dawn didn't pass out compliments lightly, so the frank statement was the equivalent, for her, of a medal and an awards banquet.

"Thanks."

She offered me a cup of coffee and I accepted.

"Of course, our chances of getting Martín are just about zero," she added.

"Huh? Why?"

"Use your head. *All* we have is the word of Coleman and Hodgkins that he was running the deal. There's no proof. He'll disappear, his lawyers will fight a rearguard action, and eventually the case will be dropped for lack of evidence."

"Frag. What about Vaughn?"

She shook her head. "No physical proof linking him to the crime. Same thing."

"Come *on*, Commissioner!" I was on my feet. "What the hell was I out there for, then?"

"You got the triggerman, Harrison. And the trigger*woman*. And your timing couldn't have been better. Do you realize that you stopped what could have been a very nasty series of riots?"

"I figured Vaughn's press conference was going to blame androids for Dow's murder," I said. "That could have sparked something."

"Indeed it would have. Something widespread and very, very bad. Vaughn would have delivered his little speech, and then he had Dow's wife there with him to ask why we weren't doing anything about the murder. He even had ringers planted in the audience to make sure the right questions were asked, the right shouts of indignation, the right level of agitation. We think he had people throughout the city waiting to start leading mobs out hunting for clones. Bioroids, too, probably. It would have been bad."

"So what happened?"

She grinned. "*You* happened. Haven't you seen the newsrags yet?"

"I've been…busy."

She touched a key on her virtual keyboard, and turned in her chair. The wall behind her came on, filled with…my face.

It was footage from Lily's monocam, showing me hunched over the PAD on the beanpod, my hands moving back and forth through the holographic controls as I maneuvered the tug in for the rendezvous. Earth, blue and magnificent, drifted across a wall display in the background.

"*…no way to tell whether we're going to get out of this or not,*" Lily's voice was saying, "*but Captain Harrison is doing everything he can to bring us down safely. I can't interrupt him now, obviously, but he must be bringing to bear every gram of experience, training, and skill gained by his years as a fighter pilot during the War to see us safely down to Earth…*"

"You can't believe everything you see on the news," I said.

"No. But Lockwell uplinked her story live to Midway, and it went out over all three NBN channels and a dozen newsrag issues with maybe a five-minute delay for editing. Several hundred million people were watching you in New Angeles alone. When you lost signal coming through re-entry, the whole damned city held its breath. That hour became high drama for half the city. When Vaughn realized what was happening, he cancelled the news conference and disappeared."

"You tried to pick him up?"

"Of course. He's gone. Probably Shanghai, where he has business interests…and there are no extradition treaties."

"The rich generally find a way to get out when the getting's good."

"True. And you're going to have to watch your step. You've

made some powerful enemies today."

I shrugged. *That* went with the territory.

"You'll probably get a medal."

Another shrug. "Whatever. The important thing is that we have Coleman, Hodgkins, and Cavallo. I'd suggest some extra security for those three."

"Already taken care of. Assuming they *do* live long enough to come to trial, they'll be going away for a long time."

"You have enough evidence to make the charges stick?"

She chuckled. "*Oh,* yeah. Let's see...while you were playing Striker pilot this afternoon, we finally got a team up to Challenger. They just called down a few minutes ago. They picked up DNA traces of Cavallo, Hodgkins, and Coleman in the clean-sweep scan of the hotel room. You were right. All three were in there. We've found their DNA in Room Sixteen, as well. We've also positively IDed Cavallo as the man with the suitcase in the hotel lobby."

"Good."

"We found the suitcase in Cavallo's most recent room at the High Frontier. Two hotel towels inside—soaked with Dow's blood...and DNA for all three. Plus the cuffs that Dow used on the bioroid, a flogger, and some other S&M stuff they cleaned up to make it look...more normal. But, you know? We probably won't even have to bring any of that in as evidence. Oh, we *will*, of course, to make a tight, complete case...but it won't be necessary."

"Why not?"

"Thanks to you, Floyd, and Flint, we have a surprise witness."

"Who is that?"

She grinned again, and typed another entry into her computer. The wall display shifted to show Raymond Flint's grinning face.

"Hey, Commissioner," the recorded message said. "Flint, up

in Heinlein. Listen…I had a hunch and got into an electronic powwow with Dr. Cherchi and some of the double-domes over at Haas-Bioroid. It turns out that bioroid memory isn't quite the same as human memory. Stands to reason, I suppose. Bioroid memory is stored on silicon. We're still not sure how human beings do it.

"Anyway, they've been working on Eve, on the part of her digital memory that was blanked, and managed to find *this*."

Flint's face vanished…and was replaced by the face of Roger Dow at very close quarters. The face was huge and glowering, peering at us out of the wall with some dark and twisted inner fury.

It took me a moment to realize that I was looking at Dow through Eve 5VA3TC's eyes—that she was flat on her back, with him lying on top of her.

"You ugly little pile of spare parts!" he spat. "You synthetic piece of crap. You…"

A door announcer chimed.

"Who the hell is that?"

"Room service," a voice answered over the intercom. I recognized Coleman's voice. A voiceprint analysis would clinch it for the court.

"I didn't order room service!"

"This is very *special* room service, compliments of Mr. Fuchida—"

"Move, you," Dow growled, and the camera view tumbled as he pushed Eve out of the bed.

"Open!" Eve's voice said.

Eve was starting to get up as Coleman entered the room. "Thea!" Dow said from the tangled bed. "What the hell are—"

"Sorry, Roger. New business agenda."

Cavallo was right behind Coleman, already raising the taser pistol to aim at Eve. He fired—and Eve's vision blanked out in a burst of white static.

But the image cleared for a moment as she fell—still partially obscured by white noise but the picture was steady enough—to show Hodgkins coming through the door behind Cavallo with the mining laser.

Dow was still in bed, holding himself up with one arm against a wall as Coleman brought up the monoknife. "I see you found yourself a new girlfriend," she sneered, and her arm slashed down, viciously, repeatedly, and without mercy…

The screams went on and on as the vid faded once more into white static.

Dawn switched it off.

"Not often you can actually get a murder on vid this way."

"Eve let them in."

"She'd been ordered to, and she was just following her programming. According to Flint, they've recovered the complete list of operating commands."

"How the hell did they reprogram her? At Eliza's Toybox?"

"Nothing so complicated. We think they used the hotel's wireless network to access her surface programming—that's software that can be accessed by the clients using her for… shall we say…particular needs?"

"You mean if the client wants his sexbot to talk a certain way, or call him names or something."

"Exactly. Turns out you can download a list of simple commands from the Eliza's Toybox site on the Net. Anyone with any real programming skill at all could use that to slip in something extra…like a virus that has Eve order the door to open when she hears a particular voice."

I nodded. "I was thinking something like that when I was at the Toybox, actually. They could have used a wireless remote to infect her. Maybe when she walked past them in the hotel lobby. Or even from the hall outside Dow's room."

"That's what we think."

"I wouldn't like to see her disassembled because of that," I said. "Like you say, she was just following programming."

"It won't come to that. There's no proof that she was in on the conspiracy at all. She went where she was told, and did what she'd been told to do. Like any good bioroid. Haas-Bioroid will be going to bat for her if need be…but I don't anticipate any charges there."

"Mark Henry?"

"Same thing. They're bringing both of them down now. They'll be here sometime tomorrow for a thorough round of questioning, but I imagine we'll release them soon. Oh…by the way. Henry has positively identified a photo of Hodgkins as 'Mr. Green.' Flint showed it to him in Heinlein."

"So Vargas's murder was incidental. They were just getting Dow's bodyguard out of the way."

"Exactly. The bio-work-up on Eve turned up negative for any of Vargas's DNA. Vargas was sent away so Dow could play with her. We think Hodgkins put him out of the airlock, though it's possible they had some other toughs on their payroll. We're checking that. His arm was broken because of the osteoporosis, not because he was thrown out by a bioroid. Hodgkins was ex-military and had respirocytes, so he could have breathed vacuum for long enough to toss Vargas outside. Besides, Vargas had been at the Challenger complex for five years. Hodgkins was fresh up from Earth. Hodgkins could have twisted Vargas up like a pretzel. I'm wondering if Vargas was assigned to Dow deliberately, for just that reason." She sat back in her chair, hands flat on her desk. "In any case, it looks to me like this one is just about wrapped up and in the bag."

"But there must be something we can do about Vaughn and Martín! We can't just drop it!"

"We *can*, Harrison. And we will. It's *over*."

She looked angry…and just a little bit afraid…

Epilogue

Much later, I walked the streets of New Angeles.

Crowds of people jostled and pushed along Market Street as shopkeepers and pushcart venders shouted and hawked and wheedled in a dozen languages. Neon signs and building-sized holographs shifted in the murky air overhead. The sun had set, bringing darkness…but the darkness could never take hold of the New Angeles streets, not really.

A billion people crowded together, noisy, angry, scared, hopeful, lust-driven, happy, depressed, lonely, lost, found, giving up, catching hold, dying, living…

I like it in Heinlein. I like it on the Beanstalk. But Earthside New Angeles always feels like home when I return.

Not that I like it, mind you. I *hate* the city.

I hate the politics, the deals, and the corruption. I hated that Vaughn and Martín were going to walk on this one.

This one. They would be back, eventually.

And I'd still be here, waiting.

I was wondering about one thing…something Federico Cavallo had said up there in the beanpod as we fell from the sky.

"*Vaughn and someone on the Humanity Labor board were gonna get cabinet posts once the Feds took over the Beanstalk. And all of us stood to make a lot when that deal goes through…*"

People will do terrible things for money and power. Cliché, but true.

I remembered Dawn telling me that the Feds were waiting in the wings, waiting to step in if the mayor declared a state of emergency and seize the Beanstalk.

The Beanstalk meant trillions of dollars for whoever controlled it, for whoever controlled the flow of helium-3 down from Heinlein.

Riots in the city…martial law…and the Feds step in to save a priceless and irreplaceable resource—the Beanstalk.

And different people, different corporations, different power groups would be there to take the profits. With Vaughn as Secretary of Commerce, handing out choice plums to his cronies…

Yeah…what are a few bloody riots in the streets when you stand to gain control of that much raw wealth and power?

Was our own government, ultimately, behind the conspiracy?

Maybe. No wonder Commissioner Dawn had looked afraid.

Or maybe Cavallo had just been shooting off his mouth, trying to ingratiate himself. It happened. Lying sleazeballs happened more often than did massive conspiracies.

Who do you believe?

Some conspiracies are just *too* big to touch…too big to believe…

There was one thing I knew, though… Lily had told me she'd be waiting for me in the foyer of the Bradbury Towers, where I had my apartment up on the ninety-fifth floor.

I quickened my pace as it started to rain.

THE END

ABOUT THE AUTHOR

New York Times bestselling author William H. Keith began his career in the RPG industry almost 30 years ago, first as an artist and then as a writer; he returns to launch the first book in the *Android* universe. His work encompasses military science fiction, geopolitical technothrillers, young adult fiction, alternative military history, and now detective science fiction. As the author of over 150 titles, including games and game modules, short stories, non-fiction, and 90 novels, he occasionally lifts his nose from the grindstone long enough to attend SF cons and Mensa gatherings, hike in his beloved Laurel Mountains, and pet the cats.

You can keep up with what William H. Keith is up to by visiting his website at www.whkeith.com.

Bring the exciting events of Free Fall to Android!

Act now and claim an exclusive Event card for the *Android* board game. Players looking to incorporate *Free Fall* into their games of *Android* can shuffle this card into their Event deck in order to bring a pivotal event from the book to your tabletop. Simply send in this page, along with a check or money order for shipping and handling, to redeem your *Free Fall* Event card.

Make your check or money order out to:
Fantasy Flight Publishing, Inc.

Shipping and Handling

United States and Canada: $1.99
International: $2.99

To receive your card, fill out the form below and send this page with your check/money order to:

Free Fall Event Card Redemption
c/o Fantasy Flight Games
1975 W County Rd B2
Roseville, MN 55113

Allow 6-8 weeks for US delivery. (International orders may take longer.)

PLEASE LEGIBLY FILL OUT THE FOLLOWING INFORMATION*

Name: ____________________

Address: ____________________

City: ____________________

State: ____________________

Zip: ____________________

E-mail ____________________

*FFG is not responsible for address errors or illegible entries.